THE WILD, WILD WEST

THE WILD, WILD WEST

EDITED BY JOHN RICHARD STEPHENS

FALL RIVER PRESS

John Richard Stephens wishes to express his appreciation to Elaine Molina; Martha and Jim Goodwin; Scott Stephens; Marty Goeller; Terity, Natasha, and Debbie Burbach; Brandon, Alisha, and Kathy Hill; Jeff and Carol Whiteaker; Christopher, Doug, and Michelle Whiteaker; Pat Egner; Gabriel, Aurelia, Elijah, Nina Abeyta, and Justin Weinberger; Jayla, Anthony, Sin, and Bobby Gamboa; Anne and Jerry Buzzard; Krystyne Göhnert; Eric, Tim, and Debbie Cissna; Norene Hilden; Doug and Shirley Strong; Barbara and Stan Main; Joanne and Monte Goeller; Irma and Joe Rodriguez; Danny and Mary Schutt; Les Benedict; Dr. Rich Sutton; and to his agent, Charlotte Cecil Raymond.

Book design by Suraiya N. Hossain

Fall River Press
122 Fifth Avenue
New York, NY 10010

ISBN: 978-1-4351-2374-8

Printed and bound in the United States of America

1 3 5 7 9 10 8 6 4 2

This book is dedicated to

ANNE AND JERRY BUZZARD

CONTENTS

WILD WEST FICTIONS

THE WILD, WILD WEST

BY JOHN RICHARD STEPHENS

Deciding how exactly to refer to the early historical period of the American West is difficult, as all of the usual terms are faulty. We can't call it "Western History" since that refers to the history of Western Civilization—including both Europe and all of the Americas. While it may now seem like "the Old West" to us, looking back at it through the many years that have passed, it only appears that way because many of the surviving artifacts from the period are old and weather-beaten. To those who experienced it, it was really the New West. All of the buildings were brand new, having just been built, and newer ones were going up all the time as populations rapidly expanded. People brought a few old belongings with them, but they generally couldn't bring much because it was too expensive to transport it halfway across the continent. Just about everything was being made in the West or was being shipped from factories in from the East, but most of it was new.

Towns were rustic and primitive at first, but quickly brought in the finer things of life. For example, Tombstone, Arizona, at the time of the 1881 gunfight near the O.K. Corral, had a bowling alley, a gym, a swimming pool, a roller rink, baseball and football teams, a library, ice cream parlors, an oyster bar, and gourmet restaurants. A nationwide recession prompted an influx of a class of well-educated professionals, while the mines brought many wealthy businessmen. To entertain these people there were dances,

socials, costume balls, and even Shakespearean plays. About the only thing Tombstone didn't have was the elderly. It was a very new town. And so it was throughout the West—everything was new and fresh and open to possibilities.

Calling it "the Wild West" tends to give the wrong impression—largely from the fictions promoted by Westerns, both books and movies. The towns of the real West—including Dodge City—are usually presented as being much more violent than they actually were. From 1870 to 1885, the five main Kansas railheads and cowtowns— Abilene, Caldwell, Dodge City, Ellsworth, and Wichita—had a total of forty-five homicides, of which sixteen of these were committed by lawmen in the course of their duties. The highest amounts were five per year in two towns—Ellsworth in 1873 and

Dodge City in 1876. In its first fifteen years, Abilene had only seven homicides and all of them during a three-year period. Two of these were by Marshal Wild Bill Hickock.

Tombstone was and is often referred to as the town "that had a man for breakfast every morning," meaning a corpse would be found in the streets each sunrise. According to John Clum, Tombstone's fourth mayor who served from January 4, 1881 to January 3, 1882, "During the 365 days of my official administration as mayor of the City of Tombstone there were but three murders committed within the city limits. That is as near as we came to having 'a dead man for breakfast every morning.' It is my recollection that in each of the above instances the murderer was arrested by Deputy Marshal Wyatt Earp. The above total of violent deaths for the year does not include the three men killed in the street battle with the police [in the gunfight near the O.K. Corral]."

Wells, Fargo & Company records show that between 1870 and 1884 more than three hundred stages were robbed throughout the West, but that only four drivers and four passengers were killed.

Depredations by Native Americans have also been greatly exaggerated. Of course there were many horrible attacks and many people were killed, but many more Native Americans were killed by settlers and the Army than the other way around. There were evils on both sides, usually arising from ignorance, prejudice, and misunderstandings.

The popular notion that the battle for the West was fought between the cowboys and Indians is wrong. It was actually between the U.S. Army and the Native Americans. While there was a tremendous amount of violence, the vast majority of interactions between settlers and the natives were friendly. Of course, as it is today, it was the bad stuff that made the news . . . and that's also what is emphasized in fiction, because it's dramatic and exciting.

Of the various terms available, and in spite of its false connotations, overall I prefer "the Wild West" because it emphasizes the excitement and sense of danger people felt as they headed into the often unknown wildernesses. They were all hoping to better their lives. Essentially they were searching for the American Dream. They intended to move up in the world by getting a better job in a rapidly expanding economy, buying cheap land or starting a homestead, launching their own business, or discovering gold. It was also a place to escape from the restrictions of society. Of course, many wanted to take their society and religion with them, but not others. In the East, laws were made by politicians and judges, while initially in the West there were no laws except those created, often on the fly, by farmers, ranchers, and miners. And these laws often didn't restrict drinking, gambling, prostitution, or firing off one's guns in town. The landscape was pristine, natural, and wild—whether it was the flattened plains, rugged mountains, parched desert, or the remote Pacific coastline. The West was a place of hope, of new experiences, of vast potential, where just about anything seemed possible.

Most people in the East at that time had limited information about the West and they weren't sure what to expect. They heard many wild stories and rumors. Of course, from their perspective, the grass tended to look greener on the other side of the Mississippi. It turned out that for many, it actually was. For others it ended up being extremely harsh and deadly—from the blistering heat of the deserts where people died from heatstroke and dehydration, to the bitter cold of the snowy mountains where many froze to death.

It's almost hard to imagine that the remote site where the Donner Party became snowbound in the Sierra Nevadas, forcing some of its members to resort to cannibalism to survive, is now right next to a major freeway and a large ski resort. At the time it took four separate rescue parties two months to retrieve forty-eight members of the Donner Party. The other thirty-nine died.

The purpose of this book is not to dispel faulty notions of the West. It is to present the West as it appeared to many of the most famous literary figures of the time. While researching several other books on the West, I kept coming across interesting things written by these amazing authors—Charles Dickens, Washington Irving, or Jules Verne, for example—many of whom are not usually associated with West. So I decided to put this book together, gathering the best nonfiction accounts—many of them personal eyewitness experiences—along with the most interesting short fiction. I've divided the book into two sections, presenting the nonfiction narratives first, with the fictional stories and poems in the second section. To these classic authors, I've added stories by a few authors who became famous writing Westerns.

The Wild West is a fascinating period of history. These selections—set in beautiful, but harsh and demanding landscapes—feature the grandeur and wildness of the virgin grasslands, steep mountains, dense forests, and vast deserts, highlighted by the conflicts, struggles, cooperation, freedom, and heroics of the brave men and women who ventured into the Wild, Wild West to live, die, and make it their home.

TRUE TALES OF
THE WILD WEST

ACROSS WESTERN PLAINS and DESERTS

by
Robert Louis Stevenson

Scottish author Robert Louis Stevenson (1850–1894) was born into a family of Scottish lighthouse engineers. Because he suffered from severe lung ailments as a child, his education was somewhat neglected. However, he did study engineering and later became a lawyer—both to please his parents—but what he really wanted to do was write. He never practiced law, but rather worked at establishing himself in print. It took several years before his work was recognized. He went on to write the classics Treasure Island, Kidnapped, *"The Body Snatcher," and* The Strange Case of Dr. Jekyll and Mr. Hyde.

It's uncertain what caused Stevenson's illnesses. Some believe it was tuberculosis, others think it was bronchitis, bronchiectasis, or sarcoidosis. Whatever it was, his heath was fragile throughout his entire life and he often had to recover from severe bouts. On one occasion, while recuperating at an artists' colony in Grez-sur-Loing—a riverside village south-east of Paris, France—he met Californian artist Fanny Osbourne and her two kids. At the time, Osbourne was separated from her philandering husband and had moved to France, where she and Stevenson fell in love. He was twenty-five and she was thirty-six. Eventually Stevenson had to return to Britain and she reconciled with her husband, though she and Stevenson remained in contact. It was around this time that Stevenson's first book, An Inland Voyage, *was published. Osbourne's reconciliation failed and in 1879 she filed for divorce. She also fell very ill. On hearing this, Stevenson decided to head for California. The idea of Stevenson being involved with a married woman had alienated him from his parents, so he was penniless and in very poor health by the time he arrived in Monterey.*

Stevenson made his journey across America from New Jersey to Monterey by train. Already an extremely talented writer, he recorded some of his initial impressions of the country.

Our American sunrise had ushered in a noble summer's day. There was not a cloud; the sunshine was baking; yet in the woody river valleys among which we wound our way, the atmosphere preserved a sparkling freshness till late in the afternoon. It had an inland sweetness and variety to one newly from the sea; it smelt of woods, rivers, and the delved earth. These, though in so far a country, were airs from home.

I stood on the platform by the hour; and as I saw, one after another, pleasant villages, carts upon the highway and fishers by the stream, and heard cockcrows and cheery voices in the distance, and beheld the sun, no longer shining blankly on the plains of ocean, but striking among shapely hills and his light dispersed and coloured by a thousand accidents of form and surface, I began to exult with myself upon this rise in life like a man who had come into a rich estate. And when I had asked the name of a river from the brakesman, and heard that it was called the Susquehanna, the beauty of the name seemed to be part and parcel of the beauty of the land. As when Adam with divine fitness named the creatures, so this word Susquehanna was at once accepted by the fancy. That was the name, as no other could be, for that shining river and desirable valley.

None can care for literature in itself who do not take a special pleasure in the sound of names; and there is no part of the world where nomenclature is so rich, poetical, humorous, and picturesque as the United States of America. All times, races, and languages have brought their contribution. Pekin is in the same State with Euclid, with Bellefontaine, and with Sandusky. Chelsea, with its London associations of red brick, Sloane Square, and the King's Road, is own suburb to stately and primeval Memphis; there they have their seat, translated names of cities, where the Mississippi runs by Tennessee and Arkansas; and both, while I was crossing the continent, lay, watched by armed men, in the horror and isolation of a plague. Old, red Manhattan lies, like an Indian arrowhead under a steam factory, below anglified New York. The names of the States and Territories themselves form a chorus of sweet and most romantic vocables: Delaware, Ohio, Indiana, Florida, Dakota, Iowa, Wyoming, Minnesota, and the Carolinas; there are few poems with a nobler music for the ear: a songful, tuneful land; and if the new Homer shall arise from the Western continent, his verse will be enriched, his pages sing spontaneously, with the names of states and cities that would strike the fancy in a business circular.

In Chicago Stevenson was transferred to an emigrant train, which provided inexpensive transportation with minimal comfort.

THE EMIGRANT TRAIN

All this while I had been travelling by mixed trains, where I might meet with Dutch widows and little German gentry fresh from table. I had been but a latent emigrant; now I was to be branded once more, and put apart with my fellows. It was about two in the afternoon of Friday that I found myself in front of the Emigrant House, with more than a hundred others, to be sorted and boxed for the journey. A white-haired official, with a stick under one arm, and a list in the other hand, stood apart in front of us, and called name after name in the tone of a command. At each name you would see a family gather up its brats and bundles and run for the hindmost of the three cars that stood awaiting us, and I soon concluded that this was to be set apart for the women and children. The second or central car, it turned out, was devoted to men travelling alone, and the third to the Chinese. The official was easily moved to anger at the least delay; but the emigrants were both quick at answering their names, and speedy in getting themselves and their effects on board.

The families once housed, we men carried the second car without ceremony by simultaneous assault. I suppose the reader has some notion of an American railroad-car, that long, narrow wooden box, like a flat-roofed Noah's ark, with a stove and a convenience, one at either end, a passage down the middle, and transverse benches upon either hand. Those destined for emigrants on the Union Pacific are only remarkable for their extreme plainness, nothing but wood entering in any part into their constitution, and for the usual inefficacy of the lamps, which often went out and shed but a dying glimmer even while they burned. The benches are too short for anything but a young child. Where there is scarce elbow-room for two to sit, there will not be space enough for one to lie. Hence the company, or rather, as it appears from certain bills about the Transfer Station, the company's servants, have conceived a plan for the better accommodation of travellers. They prevail on every two to chum together. To each of the chums they sell a board and three square cushions stuffed with straw, and covered with thin cotton. The benches can be made to face each other in pairs, for the backs are reversible. On the approach of night the boards are laid from bench to bench, making a couch wide enough for two, and long enough for a man of the middle height;

and the chums lie down side by side upon the cushions with the head to the conductor's van and the feet to the engine. When the train is full, of course this plan is impossible, for there must not be more than one to every bench, neither can it be carried out unless the chums agree. It was to bring about this last condition that our white-haired official now bestirred himself. He made a most active master of ceremonies, introducing likely couples, and even guaranteeing the amiability and honesty of each. The greater the number of happy couples the better for his pocket, for it was he who sold the raw material of the beds. His price for one board and three straw cushions began with two dollars and a half; but before the train left, and, I am sorry to say, long after I had purchased mine, it had fallen to one dollar and a half.

The match-maker had a difficulty with me; perhaps, like some ladies, I showed myself too eager for union at any price; but certainly the first who was picked out to be my bedfellow, declined the honor without thanks. He was an old, heavy, slow-spoken man, I think from Yankeeland, looked me all over with great timidity, and then began to excuse himself in broken phrases. He didn't know the young man, he said. The young man might be very honest, but how was he to know that? There was another young man whom he had met already in the train; he guessed *he* was honest, and would prefer to chum with *him* upon the whole. All this without any sort of excuse, as though I had been inanimate or absent. I began to tremble lest every one should refuse my company, and I be left rejected. But the next in turn was a tall, strapping, long-limbed, small-headed, curly-haired Pennsylvania Dutchman, with a soldierly smartness in his manner. To be exact, he had acquired it in the navy. But that was all one; he had at least been trained to desperate resolves, so he accepted the match, and the white-haired swindler pronounced the connubial benediction, and pocketed his fees.

The rest of the afternoon was spent in making up the train. I am afraid to say how many baggage-wagons followed the engine, certainly a score; then came the Chinese, then we, then the families, and the rear was brought up by the conductor in what, if I have it rightly, is called his caboose. The class to which I belonged was of course far the largest, and we ran over, so to speak, to both sides; so that there were some Caucasians among the Chinamen, and some bachelors among the families. But our own car was pure from admixture, save for one little boy of eight or nine who had the whooping-cough. At last, about six, the long train crawled out of the Transfer Station and across the wide Missouri river to Omaha, westward bound.

As Stevenson's journey across America continued, he was particularly impressed by the terrain of the West, which to him was particularly alien.

THE PLAINS OF NEBRASKA

It [the train] had thundered on the Friday night, but the sun rose on Saturday without a cloud. We were at sea—there is no other adequate expression—on the plains of Nebraska. I made my observatory on the top of a fruit-waggon, and sat by the hour upon that perch to spy about me, and to spy in vain for something new. It was a world almost without a feature; an empty sky, an empty earth; front and back, the line of railway stretched from horizon to horizon, like a cue across a billiard-board; on either hand, the green plain ran till it touched the skirts of heaven. Along the track innumerable wild sunflowers, no bigger than a crown-piece, bloomed in a continuous flower-bed; grazing beasts were seen upon the prairie at all degrees of distance and diminution; and now and again we might perceive a few dots beside the railroad which grew more and more distinct as we drew nearer till they turned into wooden cabins, and then dwindled and dwindled in our wake until they melted into their surroundings, and we were once more alone upon the billiard-board. The train toiled over this infinity like a snail; and being the one thing moving, it was wonderful what huge proportions it began to assume in our regard. It seemed miles in length, and either end of it within but a step of the horizon. Even my own body or my own head seemed a great thing in that emptiness. I note the feeling the more readily as it is the contrary of what I have read of in the experience of others. Day and night, above the roar of the train, our ears were kept busy with the incessant chirp of grasshoppers—a noise like the winding up of

countless clocks and watches, which began after a while to seem proper to that land.

To one hurrying through by steam there was a certain exhilaration in this spacious vacancy, this greatness of the air, this discovery of the whole arch of heaven, this straight, unbroken, prison-line of the horizon. Yet one could not but reflect upon the weariness of those who passed by there in old days, at the foot's pace of oxen, painfully urging their teams, and with no landmark but that unattainable evening sun for which they steered, and which daily fled them by an equal stride. They had nothing, it would seem, to overtake; nothing by which to reckon their advance; no sight for repose or for encouragement; but stage after stage, only the dead green waste under foot, and the mocking, fugitive horizon. But the eye, as I have been told, found differences even here; and at the worst the emigrant came, by perseverance, to the end of his toil. It is the settlers, after all, at whom we have a right to marvel. Our consciousness, by which we live, is itself but the creature of variety. Upon what food does it subsist in such a land? What livelihood can repay a human creature for a life spent in this huge sameness? He is cut off from books, from news, from company, from all that can relieve existence but the prosecution of his affairs. A sky full of stars is the most varied spectacle that he can hope. He may walk five miles and see nothing; ten, and it is as though he had not moved; twenty, and still he is in the midst of the same great level, and has approached no nearer to the one object within view, the flat horizon which keeps pace with his advance. We are full at home of the question of agreeable wall-papers, and wise people are of opinion that the temper may be quieted by sedative surroundings. But what is to be said of the Nebraskan settler? His is a wall-paper with a vengeance—one quarter of the universe laid bare in all its gauntness.

His eye must embrace at every glance the whole seeming concave of the visible world; it quails before so vast an outlook, it is tortured by distance; yet there is no rest or shelter till the man runs into his cabin, and can repose his sight upon things near at hand. Hence, I am told, a sickness of the vision peculiar to these empty plains.

Yet perhaps with sunflowers and cicadae, summer and winter, cattle, wife and family, the settler may create a full and various existence. One person at least I saw upon the plains who seemed in every way superior to her lot. This was a woman who boarded us at a way station, selling milk. She was largely formed; her features were more than comely; she had that great rarity—a fine complexion which became her; and her eyes were kind, dark, and steady. She sold milk with patriarchal grace. There was not a line in her countenance, not a note in her soft and sleepy voice, but spoke of an entire contentment with her life. It would have been fatuous arrogance to pity such a woman. Yet the place where she lived was to me almost ghastly. Less than a dozen wooden houses, all of a shape and all nearly of a size, stood planted along the railway lines. Each stood apart in its own lot. Each opened direct off the billiard-board, as if it were a billiard-board indeed, and these only models that had been set down upon it ready made. Her own, into which I looked, was clean but very empty, and showed nothing homelike but the burning fire. This extreme newness, above all in so naked and flat a country, gives a strong impression of artificiality. With none of the litter and discoloration of human life; with the paths unworn, and the houses still sweating from the axe, such a settlement as this seems purely scenic. The mind is loth to accept it for a piece of reality; and it seems incredible that life can go on with so few properties, or the great child, man, find entertainment in so bare a playroom.

And truly it is as yet an incomplete society in some points; or at least it contained, as I passed through, one person incompletely civilised. At North Platte, where we supped that evening, one man asked another to pass the milk-jug. This other was well-dressed and of what we should call a respectable appearance; a darkish man, high spoken, eating as though he had some usage of society; but he turned upon the first speaker with extraordinary vehemence of tone—

"There's a waiter here!" he cried.

"I only asked you to pass the milk," explained the first.

Here is the retort verbatim—

"Pass! Hell! I'm not paid for that business; the waiter's paid for it. You should use civility at table, and, by God, I'll show you how!"

The other man very wisely made no answer, and the bully went on with his supper as though nothing had occurred. It pleases me to think that some day soon he will meet with one of his own kidney; and that perhaps both may fall.

THE DESERT OF WYOMING

To cross such a plain is to grow homesick for the mountains. I longed for the Black Hills of Wyoming, which I knew we were soon to enter, like an ice-bound whaler for the spring. Alas! and it was a worse country than the other. All Sunday and Monday we travelled through these sad mountains, or over the main ridge of the Rockies, which is a fair match to them for misery of aspect. Hour after hour it was the same unhomely and unkindly world about our onward path; tumbled boulders, cliffs that drearily imitate the shape of monuments and fortifications—how drearily, how tamely, none can tell who has not seen them; not a tree, not a patch of sward, not one shapely or commanding mountain form; sage-brush, eternal sage-brush; over all, the same weariful and gloomy coloring, grays warming into brown, grays darkening towards black; and for sole sign of life, here and there a few fleeing antelopes; here and there, but at incredible intervals, a creek running in a canon. The plains have a grandeur of their own; but here there is nothing but a contorted smallness. Except for the air, which was light and stimulating, there was not one good circumstance in that God-forsaken land.

I had been suffering in my health a good deal all the way; and at last, whether I was exhausted by my complaint or poisoned in some wayside eating-house, the evening we left Laramie, I fell sick outright. That was a night which I shall not readily forget. The lamps did not go out; each made a faint shining in its own neighborhood, and the shadows were confounded together in the long, hollow box of the car. The sleepers lay in uneasy attitudes; here two chums alongside, flat upon their backs like dead folk; there a man sprawling on the floor, with his face upon his arm; there another half seated with his head and shoulders on the bench. The most passive were continually and roughly shaken by the movement of the train; others stirred, turned, or stretched out their arms like children; it was surprising how many groaned and murmured in their sleep; and as I passed to and fro, stepping across the prostrate, and caught now a snore, now a gasp, now a half-formed word, it gave me a measure of the worthlessness of rest in that unresting vehicle. Although it was chill, I was obliged to open my window, for the degradation of the air soon became intolerable to one who was awake and using the full supply of life. Outside, in a glimmering night, I saw the black, amorphous hills shoot by unweariedly into our wake. They that long for morning have never longed for it more earnestly than I.

And yet when day came, it was to shine upon the same broken and unsightly quarter of the world. Mile upon mile, and not a tree, a bird, or a river. Only down the long, sterile canons, the train shot hooting and awoke the resting echo. That train was the one piece of life in all the deadly land; it was the one actor, the one spectacle fit to be observed in this paralysis of man and nature. And when I think how the railroad has been pushed through this unwatered wilderness and haunt of savage tribes, and now will bear an emigrant for some 12 pounds from the Atlantic to the Golden Gates; how at each stage of the construction, roaring, impromptu cities, full of gold and lust and death, sprang up and then died away again, and are now but wayside stations in the desert; how in these uncouth places pig-tailed Chinese pirates worked side by side with border ruffians and broken men from Europe, talking together in a mixed dialect, mostly oaths, gambling, drinking, quarrelling and murdering like wolves; how the plumed hereditary lord of all America heard, in this last fastness, the scream of the "bad medicine wagon" charioting his foes; and then when I go on to remember that all this epical turmoil was conducted by gentlemen in frock coats, and with a view to nothing more extraordinary than a fortune and a subsequent visit to Paris, it seems to me, I own, as if this railway were the one typical achievement of the age in which we live, as if it brought together into one plot all the ends of the world and all the degrees of social rank, and offered to some great writer the busiest, the most extended, and the most varied subject for an enduring literary work. If it be romance, if it be contrast, if it be heroism that we require, what was Troy town to this? But, alas! it is not these things that are necessary—it is only Homer.

Here also we are grateful to the train, as to some god who conducts us swiftly through these shades and by so many hidden perils. Thirst, hunger, the sleight and ferocity of Indians are all no more feared, so lightly do we skim these horrible lands; as the gull, who wings safely through the hurricane and past the shark. Yet we should not be forgetful of these hardships of the past; and to keep the balance true, since I have complained of the trifling discomforts of my journey, perhaps more than was enough, let me add an original document. It was not written by Homer, but by a boy of eleven, long since dead, and is dated only twenty years ago. I shall punctuate, to make things clearer, but not change the spelling.

"My dear Sister Mary,—I am afraid you will go nearly crazy when you read my letter. If Jerry" (the writer's eldest brother) "has not written to you before now, you will be surprised to heare that we are in California, and that poor Thomas" (another brother, of fifteen) "is dead. We started from—in July, with plenly of provisions and too yoke oxen. We went along very well till we got within six or seven hundred miles of California, when the Indians attacked us. We found places where they had killed the emigrants. We had one passenger with us, too guns, and one revolver; so we ran all the lead We had into bullets (and) hung the guns up in the wagon so that we could get at them in a minit. It was about two o'clock in the afternoon; droave the cattel a little way; when a prairie chicken alited a little way from the wagon.

"Jerry took out one of the guns to shoot it, and told Tom drive the oxen. Tom and I drove the oxen, and Jerry and the passenger went on. Then, after a little, I left Tom and caught up with Jerry and the other man. Jerry stopped Tom to come up; me and the man went on and sit down by a little stream. In a few minutes, we heard some noise; then three shots (they all struck poor Tom, I suppose); then they gave the war hoop, and as many as twenty of the redskins came down upon us. The three that shot Tom was hid by the side of the road in the bushes.

"I thought the Tom and Jerry were shot; so I told the other man that Tom and Jerry were dead, and that we had better try to escape, if possible. I had no shoes on; having a sore foot, I thought I would not put them on. The man and me run down the road, but We was soon stopped by an Indian on a pony. We then turend the other way, and run up the side of the Mountain, and hid behind some cedar trees, and stayed there till dark. The Indians hunted all over after us, and verry close to us, so close that we could here there tomyhawks Jingle. At dark the man and me started on, I stubing my toes against sticks and stones. We traveld on all night; and next morning, just as it was getting gray, we saw something in the shape of a man. It layed Down in the grass. We went up to it, and it was Jerry. He thought we ware Indians. You can imagine how glad he was to see me. He thought we was all dead but him, and we thought him and Tom was dead. He had the gun that he took out of the wagon to shoot the prairie Chicken; all he had was the load that was in it.

"We traveld on till about eight o'clock, We caught up with one wagon with too men with it. We had traveld with them before one day; we stopt and they Drove on; we knew that they was ahead of us, unless they had been killed to. My feet was so sore when we caught up with them that I had to ride; I could not step. We traveld on for too days, when the men that owned the cattle said they would (could) not drive them another inch. We unyoked the oxen; we had about seventy pounds of flour; we took it out and divided it into four packs. Each of the men took about 18 pounds apiece and a blanket. I carried a little bacon, dried meat, and little quilt; I had in all about twelve pounds. We had one pint of flour a day for our alloyance. Sometimes we made soup of it; sometimes we (made) pancakes; and sometimes mixed it up with cold water and eat it that way. We traveld twelve or fourteen days. The time came at last when we should have to reach some place or starve. We saw fresh horse and cattle tracks. The morning come, we scraped all the flour out of the sack, mixed it up, and baked it into bread, and made some soup, and eat everything we had. We traveld on all day without anything to eat, and that evening we Caught up with a sheep train of eight wagons. We traveld with them till we arrived at the settlements; and know I am safe in California, and got to good home, and going to school.

"Jerry is working in—. It is a good country. You can get from 50 to 60 and 75 Dollars for cooking. Tell me all about the affairs in the States, and how all the folks get along."

And so ends this artless narrative. The little man was at school again, God bless him, while his brother lay scalped upon the deserts.

NEVADA'S DEAD TOWNS

by
John Muir

Naturalist, conservationist, and author John Muir (1838–1914) is largely known for convincing President Teddy Roosevelt to protect Yosemite, Sequoia, Kings Canyon, the Grand Canyon, and Mt. Rainier as national parks. He co-founded the Sierra Club and was its president for twenty-two years. He also strongly influenced the modern environmental movement.

Early in his life Muir was an inventor, developing a thermometer that could sense a person's warmth from four feet away and creating an alarm clock he called an "early-rising machine" that would lift up his bed, dumping him onto the floor. He was fascinated by nature and geology, and even though he had almost no formal training, he was the first person to realize that Yosemite Valley was formed by glaciers, not earthquakes as scientists commonly believed at the time. In all, he wrote ten books and more than 300 articles.

Muir published the following article on Nevada's ghost towns in the San Francisco Evening Bulletin on January 15, 1879. Twenty years earlier, America's second great mining boom—following the Gold Rush ten years earlier—had begun when silver was discovered in Nevada. The Comstock Lode soon turned Virginia City into the West's most famous boomtown and for twenty years it was the world's most important mining camp. During the Civil War, the Comstock Lode produced more than $45 million—roughly $7.5 billion today—in silver and gold, enabling the U.S. Government to maintain its credit, which greatly contributed to the Union's victory. The Lode went on to produce $400 million, or around $66.6 billion today.

Nevada's silver mines were not like California's gold mines, where '49ers with a pick, shovel, gold pan, and sluice could separate gold from dirt and sand in streambeds. With silver mines, it was generally not the prospectors who struck it rich, but the speculators, developers, and middlemen. George Hearst, father of the media mogul William Randolph Hearst, was an exception to this. He got established in the beginning when the silver was near the surface. Initially gold was discovered, but then it was found that the blue-gray mud that stuck to their equipment was actually silver ore. Some of the heavy crusts were worth up to $27,000 a ton. Later the mines had to go extremely deep, while huge rock crushing mills and smelting furnaces were required to extract the *ore from stone. This required large teams of men and lots of expensive equipment. Of the thousands who joined the boom, hundreds became moderately wealthy, and only a few dozen made huge fortunes. The vast majority risked their lives down in the mines for low hourly wages. Just a few of the boomtowns struck pay dirt. Most were quickly abandoned, becoming ghost towns.*

N evada is one of the very youngest and wildest of the States; nevertheless it is already strewn with ruins that seem as gray and silent and time-worn as if the civilization to which they belonged had perished centuries ago. Yet, strange to say, all these ruins are results of mining efforts made within the last few years. Wander where you may throughout the length and breadth of this mountain-barred wilderness, you everywhere come upon these dead mining towns, with their tall chimney stacks, standing forlorn amid broken walls and furnaces, and machinery half buried in sand, the very names of many of them already forgotten amid the excitements of later discoveries, and now known only through tradition—tradition ten years old.

While exploring the mountain ranges of the State during a considerable portion of three summers, I think that I have seen at least five of these deserted towns and villages for every one in ordinary life. Some of them were probably only camps built by bands of prospectors, and inhabited for a few months or years, while some specially interesting canyon was being explored, and then carelessly abandoned for more promising fields. But many were real towns, regularly laid out and incorporated, containing well-built hotels, churches, schoolhouses, post offices, and jails, as well as the mills on which they all depended; and whose well-graded streets were filled with lawyers, doctors, brokers, hangmen, real estate agents, etc., the whole population numbering several thousand.

A few years ago the population of Hamilton is said to have been nearly eight thousand; that of Treasure Hill, six thousand; of Shermantown, seven thousand; of Swansea, three thousand. All of these were incorporated towns with mayors, councils, fire departments, and daily newspapers. Hamilton has now about one hundred inhabitants, most of whom are merely waiting in dreary inaction for something to turn up.

Treasure Hill has about half as many, Shermantown one family, and Swansea none, while on the other hand the graveyards are far too full.

In one canyon of the Toyabe range, near Austin, I found no less than five dead towns without a single inhabitant. The streets and blocks of "real estate" graded on the hillsides are rapidly falling back into the wilderness. Sagebrushes are growing up around the forges of the blacksmith shops, and lizards bask on the crumbling walls.

While traveling southward from Austin down Big Smoky Valley, I noticed a remarkably tall and imposing column, rising like a lone pine out of the sagebrush on the edge of a dry gulch. This proved to be a smokestack of solid masonry. It seemed strangely out of place in the desert, as if it had been transported entire from the heart of some noisy manufacturing town and left here by mistake. I learned afterwards that it belonged to a set of furnaces that were build by a New York company to smelt ore that never was found. The tools of the workmen are still lying in place beside the furnaces, as if dropped in some sudden Indian or earthquake panic and never afterwards handled. These imposing ruins, together with the desolate town, lying a quarter of a mile to the northward, present a most vivid picture of wasted effort. Coyotes now wander unmolested through the brushy streets, and of all the busy throng that so lavishly spent their time and money here only one man remains—a lone bachelor with one suspender.

Mining discoveries and progress, retrogression and decay, seem to have been crowded more closely against each other here than on any other portion of the globe. Some one of the band of adventurous prospectors who came from the exhausted placers of California would discover some rich ore—how much or little mattered not at first. These specimens fell among excited seekers after wealth like sparks in gunpowder, and in a few days the wilderness was disturbed with the noisy clang of miners and builders. A little town would then spring up, and before anything like a careful survey of any particular lode would be made, a company would be formed, and expensive mills built. Then, after all the machinery was ready for the ore, perhaps little, or none at all, was to be found. Meanwhile another discovery was reported, and the young town was abandoned as completely as a camp made for a single night; and so on, until some really valuable lode was found, such as those of Eureka, Austin, Virginia, etc., which

formed the substantial groundwork for a thousand other excitements.

Passing through the dead town of Schellbourne last month, I asked one of the few lingering inhabitants why the town was built.

"For the mines," he replied.

"And where are the mines?"

"On the mountains back here."

"And why were they abandoned?" I asked. "Are they exhausted?"

"Oh, no," he replied, "they are not exhausted; on the contrary, they have never been worked at all, for unfortunately, just as we were about ready to open them, the Cherry Creek mines were discovered across the valley in the Egan range, and everybody rushed off there, taking what they could with them—houses machinery, and all. But we are hoping that somebody with money and speculation will come and revive us yet."

The dead mining excitements of Nevada were far more intense and destructive in their action than those of California, because the prizes at stake were greater, while more skill was required to gain them. The long trains of gold-seekers making their way to California had ample time and means to recover from their first attacks of mining fever while crawling laboriously across the plains, and on their arrival on any portion of the Sierra gold belt, they at once began to make money. No matter in what gulch or canyon they worked, some measure of success was sure, however unskillful they might be. And though while making ten dollars a day they might be agitated by hopes of making twenty, or of striking their picks against hundred- or thousand-dollar nuggets, men of ordinary nerve could still work on with comparative steadiness, and remain rational.

But in the case of the Nevada miner, he too often spent himself in years of weary search without gaining a dollar, traveling hundreds of miles from mountain to mountain, burdened with wasting hopes of discovering some hidden vein worth millions, enduring hardships of the most destructive kind, driving innumerable tunnels into the hillsides, while his assayed specimens again and again proved worthless. Perhaps one in a hundred of these brave prospectors would "strike it rich," while ninety-nine died alone in the mountains or sank out of sight in the corners of saloons, in a haze of whiskey and tobacco smoke.

The healthful ministry of wealth is blessed; and surely it is a fine thing that so many are eager to find the gold and silver that lie hid in the veins of the mountains. But in the search the seekers too often become insane, and strike about blindly in the dark like raving madmen. Seven hundred and fifty tons of ore from the original Eberhardt mine on Treasure Hill yielded a million and a half dollars, the whole of this immense sum having been obtained within two hundred and fifty feet of the surface, the greater portion within one hundred and forty feet. Other ore masses were scarcely less marvelously rich, giving rise to one of the most violent excitements that ever occurred in the history of mining. All kinds of people—shoemakers, tailors, farmers, etc., as well as miners—left their own right work and fell in a perfect storm of energy upon the White Pine Hills, covering the ground like grasshoppers, and seeming determined by the very violence of their efforts to turn every stone to silver. But with few exceptions, these mining storms pass away about as suddenly as they rise, leaving only ruins to tell of the tremendous energy expended, as heaps of giant boulders in the valley tell of the spent power of the mountain floods.

In marked contrast with this destructive unrest is the orderly deliberation into which miners settle in developing a truly valuable mine. At Eureka we were kindly led through the treasure chambers of the Richmond and Eureka Consolidated, our guides leisurely leading the way from level to level, calling attention to the precious ore masses which the workmen were slowly breaking to pieces with their picks, like navvies [laborers] wearing away the day in a railroad cutting; while down at the smelting works the bars of bullion were handled with less eager haste than the farmer shows in gathering his sheaves.

The wealth Nevada has already given to the world is indeed wonderful, but the only grand marvel is the energy expended in its development. The amount of prospecting done in the face of so many dangers and sacrifices, the innumerable tunnels and shafts bored into the mountains, the mills that have been built—these would seem to require a race of giants. But, in full view of the substantial results achieved, the pure waste manifest in the ruins one meets never fails to produce a saddening effect.

The dim old ruins of Europe, so eagerly sought after by travelers, have something pleasing about them, whatever their historical associations; for they at least lend some beauty to the landscape. Their picturesque towers and arches seem to be kindly adopted by nature, and planted with wild flowers and wreathed with ivy; while their rugged angles are soothed and freshened and embossed with green mosses, fresh life and decay mingling in pleasing measures, and the whole vanishing softly like a ripe, tranquil day fading into night. So, also, among the older ruins of the East there is a fitness felt. They have served their time, and like the weather-beaten mountains are wasting harmoniously. The same is in some degree true of the dead mining towns of California.

But those lying to the eastward of the Sierra throughout the ranges of the Great Basin waste in the dry wilderness like the bones of cattle that have died of thirst. Many of them do not represent any good accomplishment, and have no right to be. They are monuments of fraud and ignorance—sins against science. The drifts and tunnels in the rocks may perhaps be regarded as the prayers of the prospector, offered for the wealth he so earnestly craves; but, like prayers of any kind not in harmony with nature, they are unanswered. But, after all, effort, however misapplied, is better than stagnation. Better toil blindly, beating every stone in turn for grains of gold, whether they contain any or not, than lie down in apathetic decay.

The fever period is fortunately passing away. The prospector is no longer the raving, wandering ghoul of ten years ago, rushing in random lawlessness among the hills, hungry and footsore; but cool and skillful, well supplied with every necessary, and clad in his right mind. Capitalists, too, and the public in general, have become wiser, and do not take fire so readily from mining sparks; while at the same time a vast amount of real work is being done, and the ratio between growth and decay is constantly becoming better.

LIFE IN A GHOST TOWN

by
Robert Louis Stevenson

On arriving in Monterey, Robert Louis Stevenson camped out until he became so sick that he was close to death and an old frontiersman took him in at a goat ranch until he recovered well enough. He stayed in the area for a time before moving on to San Francisco and Oakland, practically penniless and still suffering from his ailments, getting by "all alone on forty-five cents a day, and sometimes less, with quantities of hard work and many heavy thoughts." When his estranged parents heard of his dire straits, they wired him some money.

Fanny Osbourne finally received her divorce and she and Stevenson were married in May of 1880. For their honeymoon, they headed to Calistoga in the Napa Valley, about seventy miles north of San Francisco. They were accompanied by Fanny's son, Sam, and their dog, Chuchu—a spaniel-setter mix. They thought the drier climate would help Stevenson recover and, since their finances were meager, the idea of moving into an abandoned house and having no rent to pay, greatly appealed to them. Fanny was also recovering from an illness.

So off Osbourne and Stevenson went to live for two months in a ghost town on the side of a mountain, amongst the grizzly bears and mountain lions. While there he took many notes describing the enchanting scenery, some of which he used the following year when he wrote his classic novel, Treasure Island.

One thing in this new country very particularly strikes a stranger, and that is the number of antiquities. Already there have been many cycles of population succeeding each other, and passing away and leaving behind them relics. These, standing on into changed times, strike the imagination as forcibly as any pyramid or feudal tower. The towns, like the vineyards, are experimentally founded; they grow great and prosper by passing occasions; and when the lode comes to an end, and the miners move elsewhere, the town remains behind them, like Palmyra in the desert. I suppose there are in no country in the world so many deserted towns as here in California.

The whole neighborhood of Mount Saint Helena, now so quiet and rural, was once alive with mining camps and villages. Here there would be two thousand souls under canvas; there one thousand or fifteen hundred ensconced, as if forever, in a town of comfortable houses. But the luck had failed; the mines petered out; the army of miners had departed, and left this quarter of the world to the rattlesnakes and deer and grizzlies, and to the slower but steadier advance of husbandry.

It was with an eye on one of these deserted places, Pine Flat, on the geysers road, that we had come first to Calistoga. There is something singularly enticing in the idea of going, rent-free, into a ready-made house.

Since the mining boom in Napa was over, there were a number of abandoned ghost towns in the area. Initially they intended to find something in Pine Flat, but a storekeeper felt Silverado would be a more suitable place.

Silverado was just over 2,000 feet up the side of Mount St. Helena at the north end of Napa Valley, roughly seven miles north of Calistoga. Down below this abandoned silver mine was the Toll House—a lone stop on the stagecoach route through the mountains between Calistoga and Clear Lake.

The storekeeper recruited a local hunter named Rufe Hanson to deliver the Stevensons' belongings to them, along with hay for their bedding. Apparently the storekeeper and Hanson had some scheme of taking possession of the mine when the owner's term expired, by having the Stevensons occupy the property as squatters, who would then jump the claim. Stevenson didn't discover this until later.

By two [in the afternoon] we had been landed at the mine, the buggy was gone again, and we were left to our own reflections and the basket of cold provender until Hanson should arrive. Hot as it was by the sun, there was something chill in such a homecoming in that world of wreck and rust, splinter and rolling gravel, where for so many years no fire had smoked.

Silverado platform filled the whole width of the canyon. Above, as I have said, this was a wild, red, stony gully in the mountains; but below it was a wooded dingle. And through this, I was told, there had gone a path between the mine and the Toll House— our natural northwest passage to civilization.

I found and followed it, clearing my way as I went through fallen branches and dead trees. It went straight down that steep canyon, till it brought you out abruptly over the roofs of the hotel. There was nowhere any break in the descent. It almost seemed as if, were you to drop a stone down the old iron chute at our platform, it would never rest until it hopped upon the Toll House shingles.

Signs were not wanting of the ancient greatness of Silverado. The footpath was well marked and had been well trodden in the old days by thirsty miners. And far down, buried in foliage, deep out of sight of Silverado, I came on a last outpost of the mine—a mound of gravel, some wreck of wooden aqueduct, and the mouth of a tunnel, like a treasure grotto in a fairy story. A stream of water, fed by the invisible leakage from our shaft, and dyed red with cinnabar or iron, ran trippingly forth out of the bowels of the cave; and, looking far under the arch, I could see something like an iron lantern fastened on the rocky wall. It was a promising spot for the imagination. No boy could have left it unexplored.

The stream thenceforward stole along the bottom of the dingle, and made, for that dry land, a pleasant warbling in the leaves. Once, I suppose, it ran splashing down the whole length of the canyon, but now its head waters had been tapped by the shaft at Silverado, and for a great part of its course it wandered sunless among the joints of the mountain. No wonder that it should better its pace when it sees, far before it, daylight whitening in the arch, or that it should come trotting forth into the sunlight with a song.

The two stages had gone by when I got down and the Toll House stood dozing in sun and dust and silence, like a place enchanted. My mission was after hay for bedding, and that I was readily promised.

He didn't get it and was unable to find Rufe Hanson, so he headed back up the mountain.

The lower room [of our new home] had been the assayer's office. The floor was thick with debris part human, from the former occupants; part natural, sifted in by mountain winds. In a sea of red dust there swam or floated sticks, boards, hay, straw, stones, and paper; ancient newspapers, above all for the newspaper, especially when torn, soon becomes an antiquity and bills of the Silverado boarding-house, some dated Silverado, some Calistoga Mine. Here is one, verbatim; and if any one can calculate the scale of charges, he has my envious admiration.

Calistoga Mine, May 3rd, 1875.

John Stanley		
To S. Chapman, Dr.		
To board from April 1st to April 30		$25.75
" " May 1st, to 3rd	2.00	
		$27.75

Where is John Stanley mining now? Where is S. Chapman, within whose hospitable walls we were to lodge? The date was but five years old, but in that time the world had changed for Silverado[....]

As we were tumbling the mingled rubbish on the floor, kicking it with our feet and groping for these written evidences of the past, Sam, with a somewhat whitened face, produced a paper bag.

"What's this?" said he.

It contained a granulated powder, something the color of Gregory's Mixture, but rosier; and as there were several of the bags, and each more or less broken, the powder was spread widely on the floor.

Had any of us ever seen giant powder [dynamite]? No, nobody had; and instantly there grew up in my mind a shadowy belief, verging with every moment nearer to certitude, that I had somewhere heard somebody describe it as just such a powder as the one around us. I have learnt since that it is a substance not unlike tallow, and is made up in rolls for all the world like tallow candles.

Fanny, to add to our happiness, told us a story of a gentleman who had camped one night, like ourselves, by a deserted mine. He was a handy, thrifty fellow, and looked right and left for plunder, but all he could lay his hands on was a can of oil. After dark he had to see to the horses with a lantern; and not to miss an opportunity, filled up his lamp from the oil can. Thus equipped, he set forth into the forest. A little while after, his friends heard a loud explosion; the mountain echoes bellowed, and then all was still. On examination, the can proved to contain oil, with the trifling addition of nitro-glycerine; but no research disclosed a trace of either man or lantern.

It was a pretty sight, after this anecdote, to see us sweeping out the giant powder. It seemed never to be far enough away. And, after all, it was only some rock pounded for assay.

So much for the lower room. We scraped some of the rougher dirt off the floor, and left it. That was our sitting room and kitchen, though there was nothing to sit upon but the table, and no provision for a fire except a hole in the roof of the room above, which had once contained the chimney of a stove.

To that upper room we now proceeded. There were the eighteen bunks in a double tier, nine on either hand, where from eighteen to thirty-six miners had once snored together all night long, John Stanley, perhaps, snoring loudest. There was the roof, with a hole in it through which the sun now shot an arrow. There was the floor, in much the same state as the one below, though, perhaps, there was more hay, and certainly there was the added ingredient of broken glass, the man who stole the window-frames having apparently made a miscarriage with this one. Without a broom, without hay or bedding, we could but look about us with a beginning of despair.[…]

There was no stove, of course, and no hearth in our lodging, so we betook our-selves to the blacksmith's forge across the platform. If the platform be taken as a stage, and the out-curving margin of the dump to represent the line of the footlights, then our house would be the first wing on the actor's left, and this blacksmith's forge, although no match for it in size, the foremost on the right. It was a low, brown cottage, planted close against the hill, and overhung by the foliage and peeling boughs of a madrona thicket.

Within it was full of dead leaves and mountain dust, and rubbish from the mine. But we soon had a good fire brightly blazing, and sat close about it on impromptu seats.

Chuchu, the slave of sofa-cushions, whimpered for a softer bed; but the rest of us were greatly revived and comforted by that good creature fire, which gives us warmth and light and companionable sounds, and colors up the emptiest building with better than frescoes. For a while it was even pleasant in the forge, with the blaze in the midst and a look over our shoulders on the woods and mountains where the day was dying like a dolphin.

It was between seven and eight before Hanson arrived, with a wagonful of our effects and two of his wife's relatives to lend him a hand. The elder showed surprising strength. He would pick up a huge packing-case, full of books of all things, swing it on his shoulder, and away up the two crazy ladders and the breakneck spout of rolling mineral, familiarly termed a path, that led from the cart-track to our house. Even for a man unburdened, the ascent was toilsome and precarious; but Irvine scaled it with a light foot, carrying box after box, as the hero whisks the stage child up the practicable footway beside the waterfall of the fifth act. With so strong a helper, the business was speedily transacted.

Soon the assayer's office was thronged with our belongings, piled higgledy-piggledy, and upside down, about the floor. There were our boxes, indeed, but my wife had left her keys in Calistoga.

There was the stove, but, alas! our carriers had forgot the chimney, and lost one of the plates along the road. The Silverado problem was scarce solved.

Rufe himself was grave and good-natured over his share of blame; he even, if I remember right, expressed regret. But his crew, to my astonishment and anger, grinned from ear to ear and laughed aloud at our distress. They thought it "real funny" about the stovepipe they had forgotten; "real funny" that they should have lost a plate. As for hay, the whole party refused to bring us any till they should have supped.

See how late they were! Never had there been such a job as coming up that grade! Nor often, I suspect, such a game of poker as that before they started. But about nine, as a particular favor, we should have some hay.

So they took their departure, leaving me still staring, and we resigned ourselves to wait for their return. The fire in the forge had been suffered to go out, and we were one and all too weary to kindle another. We dined, or, not to take that word in vain, we ate after a fashion in the nightmare disorder of the assayer's office, perched among boxes. A single candle lighted us. It could scarce be called a house-warming; for there was, of course, no fire, and with the two open doors and the open window gaping on the night, like breaches in a fortress, it began to grow rapidly chill.

———————— •◦••◦• ————————

As to the success of Silverado in its time of being, two reports were current. According to the first, six hundred thousand dollars were taken out of that great upright seam, that still hung open above us on crazy wedges. Then the ledge pinched out, and there followed, in quest of the remainder, a great drifting and tunneling in all directions, and a great consequent effusion of dollars, until, all parties being sick of the expense, the mine was deserted and the town decamped.

According to the second version, told me with much secrecy of manner, the whole affair, mine, mill, and town, were parts of one majestic swindle. There had never come any silver out of any portion of the mine; there was no silver to come. At midnight trains of packhorses might have been observed winding by devious tracks about the shoulder of the mountain. They came from far away, from Amador or Placer, laden with silver in "old cigar boxes." They discharged their load at Silverado, in the hour of sleep; and before the morning they were gone again with their mysterious drivers to their unknown source. In this way, twenty thousand pounds' worth of silver was smuggled in under cover of night in these old cigar boxes; mixed with Silverado mineral; carted down to the mill; crushed, amalgamated, and refined, and dispatched to the city as the proper product of the mine. Stock-jobbing, if it can cover such expenses, must be a profitable business in San Francisco.

I give these two versions as I got them. But I place little reliance on either, my belief in history having been greatly shaken.[…]

[One evening] we were all out on the platform together, sitting there, under the tented heavens, with the same sense of privacy as if we had been cabined in a parlor, when the sound of brisk footsteps came mounting up the path. We pricked our ears at

this, for the tread seemed lighter and firmer than was usual with our country neighbors. And presently, sure enough, two town gentlemen with cigars and kid gloves, came debouching past the house. They looked in that place like a blasphemy.

"Good evening," they said. For none of us had stirred; we all sat stiff with wonder.

"Good evening," I returned; and then, to put them at their ease, "A stiff climb," I added.

"Yes," replied the leader; "but we have to thank you for this path."

I did not like the man's tone. None of us liked it. He did not seem embarrassed by the meeting, but threw us his remarks like favors and strode magisterially by us towards the shaft and tunnel.

Presently we heard his voice raised to his companion. "We drifted every sort of way, but couldn't strike the ledge." Then again: "It pinched out here." And once more: "Every miner that ever worked upon it says there's bound to be a ledge somewhere."

These were the snatches of his talk that reached us, and they had a damning significance. We, the lords of Silverado, had come face to face with our superior. It is the worst of all quaint and of all cheap ways of life that they bring us at last to the pinch of borne humiliation. I liked well enough to be a squatter when there was none but Hanson by; before Ronalds [the owner], I will own, I somewhat quailed. I hastened to do him fealty, said I gathered he was the Squattee, and apologized. He threatened me with ejection, in a manner grimly pleasant—more pleasant to him, I fancy, than to me; and then he passed off into praises of the former state of Silverado.

"It was the busiest little mining town you ever saw." A population of between a thousand and fifteen hundred souls, the engine in full blast, the mill newly erected; nothing going but champagne, and hope the order of the day. Ninety thousand dollars came out; a hundred and forty thousand were put in, making a net loss of fifty thousand.

The last days, I gathered—the days of John Stanley—were not so bright; the champagne had ceased to flow, the population was already moving elsewhere, and Silverado had begun to wither in the branch before it was cut at the root. The last shot that was fired knocked over the stove chimney and made that hole in the roof of our barrack, through which the sun was wont to visit slug-a-beds towards afternoon. A noisy last shot to inaugurate the days of silence.

Throughout this interview, my conscience was a good deal exercised; and I was moved to throw myself on my knees and own the intended treachery. But then I had Hanson to consider. I was in much the same position as Old Kowley, that royal humorist, whom "the rogue had taken into his confidence."

And again, here was Ronalds on the spot. He must know the day of the month as well as Hanson and I. If a broad hint were necessary, he had the broadest in the world. For a large board had been nailed by the crown prince [Sam] on the very front of our house, between the door and window, painted in cinnabar the pigment of the country with doggerel rhymes and contumelious pictures, and announcing, in terms unnecessarily figurative, that the trick was already played, the claim already jumped, and Master Sam the legitimate successor of Mr. Ronalds. But no, nothing could save that man; *quern deus vult perdere, prius dementat.* As he came so he went, and left his rights depending.

Late at night, by Silverado reckoning, and after we were all abed, Mrs. Hanson returned to give us the newest of her news. It was like a scene in a ship's steerage: all of us abed in our different tiers, the single candle struggling with the darkness, and this plump, handsome woman, seated on an upturned valise beside the bunks, talking and showing her fine teeth, and laughing till the rafters rang. Any ship, to be sure, with a hundredth part as many holes in it as our barrack, must long ago have gone to her last port.

Up to that time I had always imagined Mrs. Hanson's loquacity to be mere incontinence, that she said what was uppermost for the pleasure of speaking, and laughed and laughed again as a kind of musical accompaniment. But I now found there was an art in it. I found it less communicative than silence itself.

I wished to know why Ronalds had come; how he had found his way without Rufe; and why, being on the spot, he had not refreshed his title. She talked interminably on, but her replies were never answers. She fled under a cloud of words; and when I had made sure that she was purposely eluding me, I dropped the subject in my turn, and let her rattle where she would.

She had come to tell us that, instead of waiting for Tuesday, the claim was to be jumped on the morrow. How? If the time were not out, it was impossible. Why? If Ronalds had come and gone, and done nothing, there was the less cause for hurry. But again I could reach no satisfaction. The claim was to be jumped next morning, that was all that she would condescend upon.

And yet it was not jumped the next morning, nor yet the next, and a whole week had come and gone before we heard more of this exploit. That day week, however, a day of great heat, Hanson, with a little roll of paper in his hand, and the eternal pipe alight; Breedlove, his large, dull friend, to act, I suppose, as witness; Mrs. Hanson, in her Sunday best; and all the children, from the oldest to the youngest; arrived in a procession, tailing one behind another up the path.

Caliban was absent, but he had been chary of his friendly visits since the row; and with that exception, the whole family was gathered together as for a marriage or a christening. Strong was sitting at work in the shade of the dwarf madronas near the forge; and they planted themselves about him in a circle, one on a stone, another on the wagon rails, a third on a piece of plank.

Gradually the children stole away up the canyon to where there was another chute, somewhat smaller than the one across the dump; and down this chute, for the rest of the afternoon, they poured one avalanche of stones after another, waking the echoes of the glen. Meantime we elders sat together on the platform, Hanson and his friend smoking in silence like Indian sachems, Mrs. Hanson rattling on as usual with an adroit volubility, saying nothing, but keeping the party at their ease like a courtly hostess.

Not a word occurred about the business of the day. Once, twice, and thrice I tried to slide the subject in, but was discouraged by the stoic apathy of Rufe, and beaten down before the pouring verbiage of his wife. There is nothing of the Indian brave about me, and I began to grill with impatience.

At last, like a highway robber, I cornered Hanson and bade him stand and deliver his business. Thereupon he gravely rose, as though to hint that this was not a proper place, nor the subject one suitable for squaws, and I, following his example, led him up the plank into our barrack. There he bestowed himself on a box, and unrolled his papers with fastidious deliberation.

There were two sheets of note-paper, and an old mining notice, dated May 30th, 1879, part print, part manuscript, and the latter much obliterated by the rains. It was by this identical piece of paper that the mine had been held last year. For thirteen months it had endured the weather and the change of seasons on a cairn behind the shoulder of the canyon; and it was now my business, spreading it before me on the table, and sitting on a valise, to copy its terms, with some necessary changes, twice over on the two sheets of note-paper. One was then to be placed on the same cairn a "mound of rocks" the notice put it; and the other to be lodged for registration.

Rufe watched me, silently smoking, till I came to the place for the locator's name at the end of the first copy; and when I proposed that he should sign, I thought I saw a scare in his eye.

"I don't think that'll be necessary," he said slowly; "just you write it down."

Perhaps this mighty hunter, who was the most active member of the local school board, could not write. There would be nothing strange in that. The constable of Calistoga is, and has been for years, a bed-ridden man, and, if I remember rightly, blind. He had more need of the emoluments than another, it was explained; and it was easy for him to "depytize," with a strong accent on the last. So friendly and so free are popular institutions.

When I had done my scrivening, Hanson strolled out, and addressed Breedlove, "Will you step up here a bit?" and after they had disappeared a little while into the chaparral and madrona thicket, they came back again, minus a notice, and the deed was done. The claim was jumped; a tract of mountain-side, fifteen hundred feet long by six hundred wide, with all the earth's precious bowels, had passed from Ronalds to Hanson, and, in the passage, changed its name from the "Mammoth" to the "Calistoga."

I had tried to get Rufe to call it after his wife, after himself, and after Garfield, the Republican Presidential candidate of the hour, since then elected, and, alas! dead but all was in vain. The claim had once been called the Calistoga before and he seemed to feel safety in returning to that.

And so the history of that mine became once more plunged in darkness, lit only by some monster pyrotechnical displays of gossip. And perhaps the most curious feature of the whole matter is this: that we should have dwelt in this quiet corner of the mountains, with not a dozen neighbors, and yet struggled all the while, like desperate swimmers, in this sea of falsities and contradictions. Wherever a man is, there will be a lie.

Another of the areas where Hanson had not been quite honest with Stevenson concerned the safety of the land he was squatting on. Hanson had told Stevenson that the place was perfectly safe, but Stevenson and his family were fortunate they weren't killed.

The place abounded with rattlesnakes—the rattlesnake's nest, it might have been named. Wherever we brushed among the bushes, our passage woke their angry buzz. One dwelt habitually in the wood-pile, and sometimes, when we came for firewood, thrust up his small head between two logs and hissed at the intrusion. The rattle has a legendary credit; it is said to be awe-inspiring and, once heard, to stamp itself forever in the memory.

But the sound is not at all alarming; the hum of many insects and the buzz of the wasp convince the ear of danger quite as readily. As a matter of fact, we lived for weeks in Silverado, coming and going, with rattles sprung on every side, and it never occurred to us to be afraid. I used to take sun-baths and do calisthenics in a certain pleasant nook among azalea and calcanthus, the rattles whizzing on every side like spinning wheels, and the combined hiss or buzz rising louder and angrier at any sudden movement; but I was never in the least impressed, nor ever attacked.

It was only towards the end of our stay that a man down at Calistoga, who was expatiating on the terrifying nature of the sound, gave me at last a very good imitation; and it burst on me at once that we dwelt in the very metropolis of deadly snakes, and that the rattle was simply the commonest noise in Silverado.

Immediately on our return, we attacked the Hansons on the subject. They had formerly assured us that our canyon was favored, like Ireland, with an entire immunity from poisonous reptiles; but, with the perfect inconsequence of the natural man, they were no sooner found out than they went off at score in the contrary direction, and we were told that in no part of the world did rattlesnakes attain to such a monstrous bigness as among the warm, flower-dotted rocks of Silverado.

A DEADLY INSULT

by
Washington Irving

Washington Irving (1783–1859) is best known for his famous stories "Rip Van Winkle" and "The Legend of Sleepy Hollow," which appeared in a collection of miscellany titled The Sketch Book of Geoffrey Crayon, Gent.—*Geoffrey Crayon being one of his pseudonyms. This book played a major role in the development of the American short story. Besides being the first American writer to achieve fame both at home and abroad, Irving is also largely responsible for the way Christmas is celebrated in America today.*

Along with being friends with Charles Dickens, Henry Wadsworth Longfellow, and Sir Walter Scott, Irving was a close friend of John Jacob Astor—America's first multimillionaire and, according to Forbes' *rankings, the fourth wealthiest person in U.S. history. Adjusted for inflation, his estate in today's dollars would be worth approximately $120 billion. Astor came to America from Germany when he was twenty and soon established a fur trading empire that stretched from the Great Lakes to the Pacific. He then branched out into New York real estate and for a few years smuggled opium into China.*

Four years after Lewis and Clark returned from their expedition to the Pacific Coast, Astor sent two expeditions to establish a fur-trading outpost named Astoria at the mouth of the Columbia River in the British- and French-controlled Columbia, known to Americans as Oregon Country. One went by land and the other by sea. The seaborne expedition arrived there in March 1811, while those who went by land reached Astoria almost a year later.

Little was publicly known of the expeditions twenty years later when Astor suggested to Washington Irving that he write a book about them. Irving agreed and Astor gave him access to all of the papers, letters, journals, and reports connected to these expeditions. By this time Astor had exited the fur trade to focus on real estate.

Those who went by sea spent two months building Fort Astoria, after which Captain Jonathan Thorn and part of his crew sailed north to trade for furs. As a naval officer, six years earlier, Thorn fought against the Tripolitan pirates in what is now Libya during the Barbary Coast War. When the U.S. frigate Philadelphia *was captured in the harbor of Tripoli, Thorn was one of those who volunteered to sneak into the harbor with Lieutenant Stephen Decatur, Jr., and set the captured vessel on fire—a mission that British Admiral Horatio Nelson called "the most bold and daring act of the age."*

Thorn later returned—again serving under Decatur—with Commodore Edward Preble's squadron to attack Tripoli. It was these events that are referred to in the line, "To the shores of Tripoli," in the hymn of the U.S. Marine Corps.

Thorn was granted a two-year leave of absence from his position as the first commandant of the New York Navy Yard to lead this expedition. Unfortunately the inexperience, arrogance, and temper of the 32-year-old captain got the better of him and led to a horrible tragedy.

T he sailing of the *Tonquin*, and the departure of Mr. David Stuart and his detachment, had produced a striking effect on affairs at Astoria. The natives who had swarmed about the place began immediately to drop off, until at length not an Indian was to be seen. This, at first, was attributed to the want of peltries with which to trade; but in a little while the mystery was explained in a more alarming manner. A conspiracy was said to be on foot among the neighboring tribes to make a combined attack upon the white men, now that they were so reduced in number. For this purpose there had been a gathering of warriors in a neighboring bay, under pretext of fishing for sturgeon; and fleets of canoes were expected to join them from the north and south. Even Comcomly, the one-eyed chief, notwithstanding his professed friendship for Mr. M'Dougal, was strongly suspected of being concerned in this general combination.

Alarmed at rumors of this impending danger, the Astorians suspended their regular labor, and set to work, with all haste, to throw up temporary works for refuge and defense. In the course of a few days they surrounded their dwelling-house and magazines with a picket fence ninety feet square, flanked by two bastions, on which were mounted four four-pounders [i.e. cannons that fired four-pound balls]. Every day they exercised themselves in the use of their weapons, so as to qualify themselves for military duty, and at night ensconced themselves in their fortress and posted sentinels, to guard against surprise. In this way they hoped, even in case of attack, to be able to hold out until the arrival of the party to be conducted by Mr. Hunt across the Rocky Mountains, or until the return of the *Tonquin*. The latter dependence, however, was doomed soon to be destroyed.

Early in August, a wandering band of savages from the Strait of Juan de Fuca made their appearance at the mouth of the Columbia, where they came to fish for sturgeon. They brought disastrous accounts of the *Tonquin*, which were at first treated as fables, but which were too sadly confirmed by a different tribe that arrived a few days subsequently. We shall relate the circumstances of this melancholy affair as correctly as the casual discrepancies in the statements that have reached us will permit.

We have already stated that the *Tonquin* set sail from the mouth of the river on the fifth of June. The whole number of persons on board amounted to twenty-three. In one of the outer bays they picked up, from a fishing canoe, an Indian named Lamazee, who had already made two voyages along the coast and knew something of the language of the various tribes. He agreed to accompany them as interpreter.

Steering to the north, Captain Thorn arrived in a few days at Vancouver's Island, and anchored in the harbor of Neweetee, very much against the advice of his Indian interpreter, who warned him against the perfidious character of the natives of this part of the coast. Numbers of canoes soon came off, bringing sea-otter skins to sell. It was too late in the day to commence a traffic, but Mr. M'Kay, accompanied by a few of the men, went on shore to a large village to visit Wicananish, the chief of the surrounding territory, six of the natives remaining on board as hostages. He was received with great professions of friendship, entertained hospitably, and a couch of sea-otter skins prepared for him in the dwelling of the chieftain, where he was prevailed upon to pass the night.

In the morning, before Mr. M'Kay had returned to the ship, great numbers of the natives came off in their canoes to trade, headed by two sons of Wicananish. As they brought abundance of sea-otter skins, and there was every appearance of a brisk trade, Captain Thorn did not wait for the return of Mr. M'Kay, but spread his wares upon the deck, making a tempting display of blankets, cloths, knives, beads, and fish-hooks, expecting a prompt and profitable sale.

The Indians, however, were not so eager and simple as he had supposed, having learned the art of bargaining and the value of merchandise from the casual traders along the coast. They were guided, too, by a shrewd old chief named Nookamis, who had grown gray in traffic with New England skippers, and prided himself upon his acuteness. His opinion seemed to regulate the market. When Captain Thorn made what he considered a liberal offer for an otter-skin, the wily old Indian treated it with scorn, and asked more than double. His comrades all took their cue from him, and not an otter-skin was to be had at a reasonable rate.

The old fellow, however, overshot his mark, and mistook the character of the man he was treating with. Thorn was a plain, straightforward sailor, who never had two minds nor two prices in his dealings, was deficient in patience and pliancy, and totally wanting in the chicanery of traffic. He had a vast deal of stern but honest pride in his nature, and, moreover, held the whole savage race in sovereign contempt.

Abandoning all further attempts, therefore, to bargain with his shuffling customers, he thrust his hands into his pockets, and paced up and down the deck in sullen silence. The cunning old Indian followed him to and fro, holding out a sea-otter skin to him at every turn, and pestering him to trade. Finding other means unavailing, he suddenly changed his tone, and began to jeer and banter him upon the mean prices he offered.

This was too much for the patience of the captain, who was never remarkable for relishing a joke, especially when at his own expense. Turning suddenly upon his persecutor, he snatched the proffered otter-skin from his hands, rubbed it in his face, and dismissed him over the side of the ship with no very complimentary application to accelerate his exit. He then kicked the peltries to the right and left about the deck, and broke up the market in the most ignominious manner.

Old Nookamis made for shore in a furious passion, in which he was joined by Shewish, one of the sons of Wicananish, who went off breathing vengeance, and the ship was soon abandoned by the natives.

When Mr. M'Kay returned on board, the interpreter related what had passed, and begged him to prevail upon the captain to make sail, as from his knowledge of the temper and pride of the people of the place, he was sure they would resent the indignity offered to one of their chiefs. Mr. M'Kay, who himself possessed some experience of Indian character, went to the captain, who was still pacing the deck in moody humor,

represented the danger to which his hasty act had exposed the vessel, and urged him to weigh anchor.

The captain made light of his counsels, and pointed to his cannon and firearms as sufficient safeguard against naked savages. Further remonstrances only provoked taunting replies and sharp altercations. The day passed away without any signs of hostility, and at night the captain retired as usual to his cabin, taking no more than the usual precautions.

On the following morning, at daybreak, while the captain and Mr. M'Kay were yet asleep, a canoe came alongside in which were twenty Indians, commanded by young Shewish. They were unarmed, their aspect and demeanor friendly, and they held up otter-skins, and made signs indicative of a wish to trade. The caution enjoined by Mr. Astor, in respect to the admission of Indians on board of the ship, had been neglected for some time past, and the officer of the watch, perceiving those in the canoe to be without weapons, and having received no orders to the contrary, readily permitted them to mount the deck. Another canoe soon succeeded, the crew of which was likewise admitted. In a little while other canoes came off, and Indians were soon clambering into the vessel on all sides.

The officer of the watch now felt alarmed, and called to Captain Thorn and Mr. M'Kay. By the time they came on deck, it was thronged with Indians. The interpreter noticed to Mr. M'Kay that many of the natives wore short mantles of skins, and intimated a suspicion that they were secretly armed. Mr. M'Kay urged the captain to clear the ship and get under way. He again made light of the advice; but the augmented swarm of canoes about the ship, and the numbers still putting off from shore, at length awakened his distrust, and he ordered some of the crew to weigh anchor, while some were sent aloft to make sail.

The Indians now offered to trade with the captain on his own terms, prompted, apparently, by the approaching departure of the ship. Accordingly, a hurried trade was commenced. The main articles sought by the savages in barter were knives; as fast as some were supplied they moved off, and others succeeded. By degrees they were thus distributed about the deck, and all with weapons.

The anchor was now nearly up, the sails were loose, and the captain, in a loud and peremptory tone, ordered the ship to be cleared. In an instant, a signal yell was given; it was echoed on every side, knives and war-clubs were brandished in every direction, and the savages rushed upon their marked victims.

The first that fell was Mr. Lewis, the ship's clerk. He was leaning, with folded arms, over a bale of blankets, engaged in bargaining, when he received a deadly stab in the back, and fell down the companion-way.

Mr. M'Kay, who was seated on the taffrail, sprang on his feet, but was instantly knocked down with a war-club and flung backwards into the sea, where he was dispatched by the women in the canoes.

In the meantime Captain Thorn made desperate fight against fearful odds. He was a powerful as well as a resolute man, but he had come upon deck without weapons. Shewish, the young chief singled him out as his peculiar prey, and rushed upon him at the first outbreak. The captain had barely time to draw a clasp-knife with one blow of which he laid the young savage dead at his feet. Several of the stoutest followers of Shewish now set upon him. He defended himself vigorously, dealing crippling blows to right and left, and strewing the quarterdeck with the slain and wounded. His object was to fight his way to the cabin, where there were firearms; but he was hemmed in with foes, covered with wounds, and faint with loss of blood. For an instant he leaned upon the tiller wheel, when a blow from behind, with a war-club, felled him to the deck, where he was dispatched with knives and thrown overboard.

While this was transacting upon the quarterdeck, a chance-medley fight was going on throughout the ship. The crew fought desperately with knives, handspikes, and whatever weapon they could seize upon in the moment of surprise. They were soon, however, overpowered by numbers, and mercilessly butchered.

As to the seven who had been sent aloft to make sail, they contemplated with horror the carnage that was going on below. Being destitute of weapons, they let themselves down by the running rigging, in hopes of getting between decks. One fell in the attempt, and was instantly dispatched; another received a death-blow in the back as he was descending; a third, Stephen Weekes, the armorer, was mortally wounded as he was getting down the hatchway.

The remaining four made good their retreat into the cabin, where they found Mr. Lewis, still alive, though mortally wounded. Barricading the cabin door, they broke holes through the companion-way, and, with the muskets and ammunition which were at hand, opened a brisk fire that soon cleared the deck.

Thus far the Indian interpreter, from whom these particulars are derived, had been an eyewitness to the deadly conflict. He had taken no part in it, and had been spared by the natives as being of their race. In the confusion of the moment he took refuge with the rest, in the canoes. The survivors of the crew now sallied forth, and discharged some of the deck-guns, which did great execution among the canoes, and drove all the savages to shore.

For the remainder of the day no one ventured to put off to the ship, deterred by the effects of the firearms. The night passed away without any further attempts on the part of the natives. When the day dawned, the *Tonquin* still lay at anchor in the bay, her sails all loose and flapping in the wind, and no one apparently on board of her. After a time, some of the canoes ventured forth to reconnoiter, taking with them the interpreter.

They paddled about her, keeping cautiously at a distance, but growing more and more emboldened at seeing her quiet and lifeless. One man at length made his appearance on the deck, and was recognized by the interpreter as Mr. Lewis. He made friendly signs, and invited them on board. It was long before they ventured to comply. Those who mounted the deck met with no opposition; no one was to be seen on board; for Mr. Lewis, after inviting them, had disappeared.

Other canoes now pressed forward to board the prize; the decks were soon crowded, and the sides covered with clambering natives, all intent on plunder. In the midst of their eagerness and exultation, the ship blew up with a tremendous explosion. Arms, legs, and mutilated bodies were blown into the air, and dreadful havoc was made in the surrounding canoes.

The interpreter was in the main-chains at the time of the explosion, and was thrown unhurt into the water, where he succeeded in getting into one of the canoes. According to his statement, the bay presented an awful spectacle after the catastrophe.

The ship had disappeared, but the bay was covered with fragments of the wreck, with shattered canoes, and Indians swimming for their lives, or struggling in the agonies of death; while those who had escaped the danger remained aghast and stupefied, or made with frantic panic for the shore.

Upwards of a hundred natives were destroyed by the explosion, many more were shockingly mutilated, and for days afterwards the limbs and bodies of the slain were thrown upon the beach.

The inhabitants of Neweetee were overwhelmed with consternation at this astounding calamity, which had burst upon them in the very moment of triumph. The warriors sat mute and mournful, while the women filled the air with loud lamentations. Their weeping and walling, however, was suddenly changed into yells of fury at the sight of four unfortunate white men, brought captive into the village. They had been driven on shore in one of the ship's boats, and taken at some distance along the coast.

The interpreter was permitted to converse with them. They proved to be the four brave fellows who had made such desperate defense from the cabin. The interpreter gathered from them some of the particulars already related. They told him further, that after they had beaten off the enemy and cleared the ship, Lewis advised that they should slip the cable and endeavor to get to sea. They declined to take his advice, alleging that the wind set too strongly into the bay and would drive them on shore. They resolved, as soon as it was dark, to put off quietly in the ship's boat, which they would be able to do unperceived, and to coast along back to Astoria.

They put their resolution into effect; but Lewis refused to accompany them, being disabled by his wound, hopeless of escape, and determined on a terrible revenge. On the voyage out, he had repeatedly expressed a presentiment that he should die by his own hands; thinking it highly probable that he should be engaged in some contest with the natives, and being resolved, in case of extremity, to commit suicide rather than be made a prisoner. He now declared his intention to remain on board of the ship until daylight, to decoy as many of the natives on board as possible, then to set fire to the powder magazine, and terminate his life by a signal of vengeance.

How well he succeeded has been shown. His companions bade him a melancholy adieu, and set off on their precarious expedition. They strove with might and main to get out of the bay, but found it impossible to weather a point of land, and were at length compelled to take shelter in a small cove, where they hoped to remain concealed until the wind should be more favorable. Exhausted by fatigue and watching, they fell into a sound sleep, and in that state were surprised by the natives.

Better had it been for those unfortunate men had they remained with Lewis, and shared his heroic death: as it was, they perished in a more painful and protracted manner, being sacrificed by the natives to the manes of their friends with all the lingering tortures of savage cruelty. Sometime after their death, the interpreter, who had remained a kind of prisoner at large, effected his escape and brought the tragical tidings to Astoria.[…]

The loss of the *Tonquin* was a grievous blow to the infant establishment of Astoria, and one that threatened to bring after it a train of disasters. The intelligence of it did not reach Mr. Astor until many months afterwards. He felt it in all its force, and was aware that it must cripple, if not entirely defeat, the great scheme of his ambition. In his letters, written at the time, he speaks of it as "a calamity, the length of which he could not foresee." He indulged, however, in no weak and vain lamentation, but sought to devise a prompt and efficient remedy. The very same evening he appeared at the theatre with his usual serenity of countenance. A friend, who knew the disastrous intelligence he had received, expressed his astonishment that he could have calmness of spirit sufficient for such a scene of light amusement. "What would you have me do?" was his characteristic reply; "would you have me stay at home and weep for what I cannot help?"

The tidings of the loss of the *Tonquin*, and the massacre of her crew, struck dismay into the hearts of the Astorians. They found themselves a mere handful of men, on a savage coast, surrounded by hostile tribes, who would doubtless be incited and encouraged to deeds of violence by the late fearful catastrophe. In this juncture Mr. M'Dougal, we are told, had recourse to a stratagem by which to avail himself of the ignorance and credulity of the natives, and which certainly does credit to his ingenuity.

The natives of the coast, and, indeed, of all the regions west of the mountains, had an extreme dread of the small-pox; that terrific scourge having, a few years previously, appeared among them, and almost swept off entire tribes. Its origin and nature were wrapped in mystery, and they conceived it an evil inflicted upon them by the Great Spirit, or brought among them by the white men.

The last idea was seized upon by Mr. M'Dougal. He assembled several of the chieftains whom he believed to be in the conspiracy. When they were all seated around, he informed them that he had heard of the treachery of some of their northern brethren towards the *Tonquin*, and was determined on vengeance.

"The white men among you," said he, "are few in number, it is true, but they are mighty in medicine. See here," continued he, drawing forth a small bottle and holding it before their eyes, "in this bottle I hold the small-pox, safely corked up; I have but to draw the cork, and let loose the pestilence, to sweep man, woman, and child from the face of the earth."

The chiefs were struck with horror and alarm. They implored him not to uncork the bottle, since they and all their people were firm friends of the white men, and would always remain so; but, should the small-pox be once let out, it would run like wildfire throughout the country, sweeping off the good as well as the bad; and surely he would not be so unjust as to punish his friends for crimes committed by his enemies.

Mr. M'Dougal pretended to be convinced by their reasoning, and assured them that, so long as the white people should be unmolested, and the conduct of their Indian neighbors friendly and hospitable, the vial of wrath should remain sealed up; but, on the least hostility, the fatal cork should be drawn.

From this time, it is added, he was much dreaded by the natives, as one who held their fate in his hands, and was called, by way of preeminence, "the Great Small-pox Chief."

THE HUMAN HUNT

by
Washington Irving

The second expedition John Jacob Astor sent to the Pacific Coast went by land. Their mission was to find their way over the Rockies to the Astoria outpost, roughly following the footsteps of Lewis and Clark, who had traversed the region just five years earlier. It took them almost a year to reach their destination. Along the way they met some very interesting mountain men.

On the afternoon of the third day, January 17th, [1810,] the boats touched at Charette, one of the old villages founded by the original French colonists. Here they met with Daniel Boone, the renowned patriarch of Kentucky, who had kept in the advance of civilization, and on the borders of the wilderness, still leading a hunter's life, though now in his eighty-fifth year. He had but recently returned from a hunting and trapping expedition, and had brought nearly sixty beaver skins as trophies of his skill. The old man was still erect in form, strong in limb, and unflinching in spirit, and as he stood on the river bank, watching the departure of an expedition destined to traverse the wilderness to the very shores of the Pacific, very probably felt a throb of his old pioneer spirit, impelling him to shoulder his rifle and join the adventurous band. Boone flourished several years after this meeting, in a vigorous old age, the Nestor of hunters and backwoodsmen; and died, full of sylvan honor and renown, in 1818 in his ninety-second year.

The next morning early, as the party were yet encamped at the mouth of a small stream, they were visited by another of these heroes of the wilderness, one John Colter, who had accompanied Lewis and Clarke in their memorable expedition. He had recently made one of those vast internal voyages so characteristic of this fearless class of men, and of the immense regions over which they hold their lonely wanderings; having come from the head waters of the Missouri to St. Louis in a small canoe. This distance of three thousand miles he had accomplished in thirty days.

Colter kept with the party all the morning. He had many particulars to give them concerning the Blackfeet Indians, a restless and predatory tribe, who had conceived an implacable hostility to the white men, in consequence of one of their warriors having been killed by Captain Lewis, while attempting to steal horses. [Note: Apparently they were after guns, not horses. One teenage native was stabbed to death by one of Lewis's men, while Lewis shot another in the belly. The first one, Sidehill Calf, died wearing a peace medal Lewis had given him the day before. It's not known whether the second teenage warrior died. This incident soured relations with the Piegan Blackfeet for many years after.]

Through the country infested by these warriors the expedition would have to proceed, and Colter was urgent in reiterating the precautions that ought to be observed respecting them. He had himself experienced their vindictive cruelty, and his story deserves particular citation, as showing the hairbreadth adventures to which these solitary rovers of the wilderness are exposed.

Colter, with the hardihood of a regular trapper, had cast himself loose from the party of Lewis and Clarke in the very heart of the wilderness and had remained to trap beaver alone on the head waters of the Missouri. Here he fell in with another lonely trapper like himself, named Potts, and they agreed to keep together. They were in the very region of the terrible Blackfeet, at that time thirsting to revenge the death of their companion, and knew that they had to expect no mercy at their hands. They were obliged to keep concealed all day in the woody margins of the rivers, setting their traps after nightfall and taking them up before daybreak. It was running a fearful risk for the sake of a few beaver skins; but such is the life of the trapper.

They were on a branch of the Missouri called Jefferson Fork and had set their traps at night about six miles up a small river that emptied into the fork. Early in the morning they ascended the river in a canoe to examine the traps. The banks on each side were high and perpendicular, and cast a shade over the stream. As they were softly paddling along, they heard the trampling of many feet upon the banks.

Colter immediately gave the alarm of "Indians!" and was for instant retreat. Potts scoffed at him for being frightened by the trampling of a herd of buffaloes. Colter checked his uneasiness and paddled forward. They had not gone much further when frightful whoops and yells burst forth from each side of the river, and several hundred Indians appeared on either bank.

Signs were made to the unfortunate trappers to come on shore. They were obliged to comply. Before they could get out of their canoe, a savage seized the rifle belonging to Potts. Colter sprang on shore, wrestled the weapon from the hands of the Indian and restored it to his companion, who was still in the canoe, and immediately pushed into the stream. There was the sharp twang of a bow and Potts cried out that he was wounded. Colter urged him to come on shore and submit, as his only chance for life; but the other knew there was no prospect of mercy and determined to die game. Leveling his rifle, he shot one of the natives dead on the spot. The next moment he fell himself, pierced with innumerable arrows.

The vengeance of the savages now turned upon Colter. He was stripped naked, and, having some knowledge of the Blackfoot language, overheard a consultation as to the mode of dispatching him, so as to derive the greatest amusement from his death. Some were for setting him up as a mark, and having a trial of skill at his expense. The chief, however, was for nobler sport. He seized Colter by the shoulder, and demanded if he could run fast.

The unfortunate trapper was too well acquainted with Indian customs not to comprehend the drift of the question. He knew he was to run for his life, to furnish a kind of human hunt to his persecutors. Though in reality he was noted among his brother hunters for swiftness of foot, he assured the chief that he was a very bad runner.

His stratagem gained him some vantage ground. He was led by the chief into the prairie, about four hundred yards from the main body of natives, and then turned loose to save himself if he could. A tremendous yell let him know that the whole pack of bloodhounds were off in full cry.

Colter flew rather than ran; he was astonished at his own speed; but he had six miles of prairie to traverse before he should reach the Jefferson Fork of the Missouri; how could he hope to hold out such a distance with the fearful odds of several hundred to one against him! The plain, too, abounded with the prickly pear, which wounded his naked feet. Still he fled on, dreading each moment to hear the twang of a bow, and to feel an arrow quivering at his heart. He did not even dare to look round, lest he should lose an inch of that distance on which his life depended. He had run nearly half way across the plain when the sound of pursuit grew somewhat fainter and he ventured to turn his head.

The main body of his pursuers were a considerable distance behind; several of the fastest runners were scattered in the advance; while a swift-footed warrior, armed with a spear, was not more than a hundred yards behind him.

Inspired with new hope, Colter redoubled his exertions, but strained himself to such a degree that the blood gushed from his mouth and nostrils, and streamed down his breast. He arrived within a mile of the river. The sound of footsteps gathered upon him. A glance behind showed his pursuer within twenty yards and preparing to launch his spear. Stopping short he turned round and spread out his arms.

The warrior, confounded by this sudden action, attempted to stop and hurl his spear, but fell in the very act. His spear stuck in the ground, and the shaft broke in his hand.

Colter plucked up the pointed part, pinned the savage to the earth, and continued his flight.

The Indians, as they arrived at their slaughtered companion, stopped to howl over him. Colter made the most of this precious delay, gained the skirt of cottonwood bordering the river, dashed through it, and plunged into the stream. He swam to a neighboring islanvd, against the upper end of which the driftwood had lodged in such quantities as to form a natural raft; under this he dived, and swam below water until he succeeded in getting a breathing place between the floating trunks of trees, whose branches and bushes formed a covert several feet above the level of the water.

He had scarcely drawn breath after all his toils, when he heard his pursuers on the river bank, whooping and yelling like so many fiends. They plunged in the river, and swam to the raft. The heart of Colter almost died within him as he saw them, through the chinks of his concealment, passing and repassing, and seeking for him in all directions. They at length gave up the search, and he began to rejoice in his escape, when the idea presented itself that they might set the raft on fire. Here was a new source of horrible apprehension, in which he remained until nightfall. Fortunately the idea did not suggest itself to the Indians.

As soon as it was dark, finding by the silence around that his pursuers had departed, Colter dived again and came up beyond the raft. He then swam silently down the river for a considerable distance, when he landed, and kept on all night to get as far as possible from this dangerous neighborhood.

By daybreak he had gained sufficient distance to relieve him from the terrors of his savage foes; but now new sources of inquietude presented themselves. He was naked and alone, in the midst of an unbounded wilderness; his only chance was to reach a trading post of the Missouri Company, situated on a branch of the Yellowstone River.

Even should he elude his pursuers, days must elapse before he could reach this post, during which he must traverse immense prairies destitute of shade, his naked body exposed to the burning heat of the sun by day, and the dews and chills of the night season, and his feet lacerated by the thorns of the prickly pear.

Though he might see game in abundance around him, he had no means of killing any for his sustenance and must depend for food upon the roots of the earth. In defiance of these difficulties he pushed resolutely forward, guiding himself in his trackless course by those signs and indications known only to Indians and backwoodsmen; and after braving dangers and hardships enough to break down any spirit but that of a western pioneer, arrived safe at the solitary post in question.

Such is a sample of the rugged experience which Colter had to relate of savage life; yet, with all these perils and terrors fresh in his recollection, he could not see the present band on their way to those regions of danger and adventure, without feeling a vehement impulse to join them.

A western trapper is like a sailor; past hazards only stimulate him to further risks. The vast prairie is to the one what the ocean is to the other, a boundless field of enterprise and exploit. However he may have suffered in his last cruise, he is always ready to join a new expedition; and the more adventurous its nature, the more attractive is it to his vagrant spirit.

In the HEART of INDIAN COUNTRY

by
Washington Irving

While Washington Irving is best known for his writings about New York, he had a power-
ful fascination for the West, ultimately writing three books on the subject. One of these
was a travelogue of an expedition he joined in 1832 that took him into the plains of
what is now Texas and Oklahoma. Along the way he met Sam Houston and Black Hawk,
the Fox and Sac chief who had surrendered a few days earlier, ending the Black Hawk
War in what would later become Wisconsin.

Of course, the West was still the frontier at this time and was still in the process
of being explored. Thirty years earlier, Thomas Jefferson paid Napoleon for much of
the Midwest, but this had yet to be incorporated into the United States since the land
was still owned by the Native Americans. At the time of the expedition, the western-
most states were Louisiana, Missouri, and Illinois. Arkansas was still a territory, while
Wisconsin and part of Minnesota had not yet separated from the Michigan Territory.
Texas still belonged to the newly formed country of Mexico.

As Irving described it:

In the often vaunted regions of the Far West, several hundred miles beyond the Mississippi, extends a vast tract of uninhabited country, where there is neither to be seen the log house of the white man, nor the wigwam of the Indian. It consists of great grassy plains, interspersed with forests and groves, and clumps of trees, and watered by the Arkansas, the grand Canadian, the Red River, and their tributary streams. Over these fertile and verdant wastes still roam the elk, the buffalo, and the wild horse, in all their native freedom. These, in fact, are the hunting grounds of the various tribes of the Far West. Hither repair the Osage, the Creek, the Delaware and other tribes that have linked themselves with civilization, and live within the vicinity of the white settlements. Here resort also, the Pawnees, the Comanches, and other fierce, and as yet independent tribes, the nomads of the prairies, or the inhabitants of the skirts of the Rocky Mountains.[...]

It was early in October 1832 that I arrived at Fort Gibson, a frontier post of the Far West [in what is now eastern Oklahoma], situated on the Neosho, or Grand River, near its confluence with the Arkansas. I had been traveling for a month past with a small party from St. Louis up the banks of the Missouri, and along the frontier line of agencies and missions that extends from the Missouri to the Arkansas. Our party was headed by one of the Commissioners appointed by the government of the United States to superintend the settlement of the Indian tribes migrating from the east to the west of the Mississippi. [This forced resettlement became known as the Trail of Tears]. In the discharge of his duties, he was thus visiting the various outposts of civilization.[…]

On arriving at the fort, however, a new chance presented itself for a cruise on the prairies. We learnt that a company of mounted rangers, or riflemen, had departed but three days previous to make a wide exploring tour from the Arkansas to the Red River, including a part of the Pawnee hunting grounds where no party of white men had as yet penetrated. Here, then, was an opportunity of ranging over those dangerous and interesting regions under the safeguard of a powerful escort; for the Commissioner, in virtue of his office, could claim the service of this newly raised corps of riflemen, and the country they were to explore was destined for the settlement of some of the migrating tribes connected with his mission.

Ten days later they found themselves trudging through what is now central Oklahoma, having just struggled through the Cross Timbers—a sparse forest with heavy undergrowth that extends from today's southeast Kansas deep into northern Texas.

After a tedious ride of several miles, we came out upon an open tract of hill and dale, interspersed with woodland. Here we were roused by the cry of buffalo! buffalo! The effect was something like that of the cry of a sail! a sail! at sea. It was not a false alarm. Three or four of those enormous animals were visible to our sight grazing on the slope of a distant hill.

There was a general movement to set off in pursuit, and it was with some difficulty that the vivacity of the younger men of the troop could be restrained. Leaving orders that the line of march should be preserved, the Captain and two of his officers departed at quiet a pace, accompanied by [Pierre] Beatte [their hunter, guide, and interpreter, who was half French and half Osage], and by the ever-forward Tonish [a French creole named Antoine who served as groom, cook, tent man, and such]; for it was impossible any longer to keep the little Frenchman in check, being half crazy to prove his skill and prowess in hunting the buffalo.

The intervening hills soon hid from us both the game and the huntsmen. We kept on our course in quest of a camping place, which was difficult to be found; almost all the channels of the streams being dry, and the country being destitute of fountain heads.

After proceeding some distance, there was again a cry of buffalo, and two were pointed out on a hill to the left. The Captain being absent, it was no longer possible to restrain the ardor of the young hunters. Away several of them dashed, full speed, and soon disappeared among the ravines; the rest kept on, anxious to find a proper place for encampment.

Indeed we now began to experience the disadvantages of the season. The pasturage of the prairies was scanty and parched; the pea-vines which grew in the woody bottoms were withered, and most of the "branches" or streams were dried up. While wandering in this perplexity, we were overtaken by the Captain and all his party, except Tonish. They had pursued the buffalo for some distance without getting within shot, and had given up the chase, being fearful of fatiguing their horses, or being led off too far from camp. The little Frenchman, however, had galloped after them at headlong speed, and the last they saw of him, he was engaged, as it were, yard-arm and yard-arm, with a great buffalo bull, firing broadsides into him. "I tink dat little man crazy—somehow" observed Beatte, dryly.

We now came to a halt, and had to content ourselves with an indifferent encampment. It was in a grove of scrub-oaks, on the borders of a deep ravine, at the bottom of which were a few scanty pools of water. We were just at the foot of a gradually-sloping hill, covered with half-withered grass, that afforded meager pasturage. In the spot where we had encamped, the grass was high and parched. The view around us was circumscribed and much shut in by gently swelling hills.

Just as we were encamping, Tonish arrived, all glorious, from his hunting match; his white horse hung all round with buffalo meat. According to his own account, he had laid low two mighty bulls. As usual, we deducted one half from his boastings; but, now that he had something real to vaunt about, there was no restraining the valor of his tongue.

After having in some measure appeased his vanity by boasting of his exploit, he informed us that he had observed the fresh track of horses, which, from various circumstances, he suspected to have been made by some roving band of Pawnees. This caused some little uneasiness. The young men who had left the line of march in pursuit of the two buffaloes, had not yet rejoined us; apprehensions were expressed that they might be waylaid and attacked. Our veteran hunter, old Ryan, also, immediately on our halting to encamp, had gone off on foot, in company with a young disciple. "Dat old man will have his brains knocked out by de Pawnees yet," said Beatte. "He tink he know every ting, but he don't know Pawnees, anyhow."

Taking his rifle, the Captain repaired on foot to reconnoiter the country from the naked summit of one of the neighboring hills. In the meantime, the horses were hobbled and turned loose to graze; and wood was cut, and fires made, to prepare the evening's repast.

Suddenly there was an alarm of fire in the camp! The flame from one of the kindling fires had caught to the tall dry grass; a breeze was blowing; there was danger that the camp would soon be wrapped in a light blaze.

"Look to the horses!" cried one; "Drag away the baggage!" cried another. "Take care of the rifles and powder-horns!" cried a third. All was hurry-scurry and uproar. The horses dashed wildly about; some of the men snatched away rifles and powder-horns, others dragged off saddles and saddle-bags.

Meantime, no one thought of quelling the fire, nor indeed knew how to quell it. Beatte, however, and his comrades attacked it in the Indian mode, beating down the edges of the fire with blankets and horse-cloths, and endeavoring to prevent its spreading among the grass; the rangers followed their example, and in a little while the flames were happily quelled.

The fires were now properly kindled on places from which the dry grass had been cleared away. The horses were scattered about a small valley, and on the sloping hill-side, cropping the scanty herbage. Tonish was preparing a sumptuous evening's meal from his buffalo meat, promising us a rich soup and a prime piece of roast beef: but we were doomed to experience another and more serious alarm.

There was an indistinct cry from some rangers on the summit of the hill, of which we could only distinguish the words, "The horses! the horses! get in the horses!"

Immediately a clamor of voices arose; shouts, inquiries, replies, were all mingled together, so that nothing could be clearly understood, and everyone drew his own inference.

"The Captain has started buffaloes," cried one, "and wants horses for the chase." Immediately a number of rangers seized their rifles, and scampered for the hill-top. "The prairie is on fire beyond the hill," cried another; "I see the smoke—the Captain means we shall drive the horses beyond the brook."

By this time a ranger from the hill had reached the skirts of the camp. He was almost breathless, and could only say that the Captain had seen Indians at a distance.

"Pawnees! Pawnees!" was now the cry among our wild-headed youngsters. "Drive the horses into camp!" cried one. "Saddle the horses!" cried another. "Form the line!" cried a third. There was now a scene of clamor and confusion that baffles all description. The rangers were scampering about the adjacent field in pursuit of their horses. One might be seen tugging his steed along by a halter; another without a hat, riding bare-backed; another driving a hobbled horse before him, that made awkward leaps like a kangaroo.

The alarm increased. Word was brought from the lower end of the camp that there was a band of Pawnees in a neighboring valley. They had shot old Ryan through the head, and were chasing his companion! "No, it was not old Ryan that was killed—it was one of the hunters that had been after the two buffaloes." "There are three hundred Pawnees just beyond the hill," cried one voice. "More, more!" cried another.

Our situation, shut in among hills, prevented our seeing to any distance, and left us a prey to all these rumors. A cruel enemy was supposed to be at hand, and an immediate attack apprehended. The horses by this time were driven into the camp, and were dashing about among the fires, and trampling upon the baggage. Every one endeavored to prepare for action; but here was the perplexity. During the late alarm of fire, the saddles, bridles, rifles, powder-horns, and other equipments, had been snatched out of their places, and thrown helter-skelter among the trees.

"Where is my saddle?" cried one. "Has any one seen my rifle?" cried another. "Who will lend me a ball?" cried a third, who was loading his piece. "I have lost my bullet pouch." "For God's sake help me to girth this horse!" cried another; "he's so restive I can do nothing with him." In his hurry and worry, he had put on the saddle the hind part before!

Some affected to swagger and talk bold; others said nothing, but went on steadily, preparing their horses and weapons, and on these I felt the most reliance. Some were evidently excited and elated with the idea of an encounter with Indians; and none more so than my young Swiss fellow-traveler, who had a passion for wild adventure. [This was a Swiss count. Many of the West's first tourists were European aristocracy, who were escorted by the U.S. Army.] Our man, Beatte, led his horses in the rear of the camp, placed his rifle against a tree, then seated himself by the fire in perfect silence. On the other hand, little Tonish, who was busy cooking, stopped every moment from his work to play the fanfaron, singing, swearing, and affecting an unusual hilarity, which made me strongly suspect there was some little fright at bottom, to cause all this effervescence.

About a dozen of the rangers, as soon as they could saddle their horses, dashed off in the direction in which the Pawnees were said to have attacked the hunters. It was now determined, in case our camp should be assailed, to put our horses in the ravine in the rear, where they would be out of danger from arrow or rifle ball, and to take our stand within the edge of the ravine. This would serve as a trench, and the trees and thickets with which it was bordered, would be sufficient to turn aside any shaft of the enemy. The Pawnees, besides, are wary of attacking any covert of the kind; their warfare, as I have already observed, lies in the open prairie, where, mounted upon their fleet horses, they can swoop like hawks upon their enemy, or wheel about him and discharge their arrows. Still I could not but perceive, that, in case of being attacked by such a number of these well-mounted and war-like natives as were said to be at hand,

34-9-2.

we should be exposed to considerable risk from the inexperience and want of discipline of our newly raised rangers, and from the very courage of many of the younger ones who seemed bent on adventure and exploit.

By this time the Captain reached the camp, and everyone crowded round him for information. He informed us, that he had proceeded some distance on his reconnoitering expedition, and was slowly returning toward the camp, along the brow of a naked hill, when he saw something on the edge of a parallel hill, that looked like a man. He paused and watched it; but it remained so perfectly motionless, that he supposed it a bush, or the top of some tree beyond the hill. He resumed his course, when it likewise began to move in a parallel direction. Another form now rose beside it, of someone who had either been lying down, or had just ascended the other side of the hill. The Captain stopped and regarded them; they likewise stopped. He then lay down upon the grass, and they began to walk. On his rising, they again stopped, as if watching him.

Knowing that the Indians are apt to have their spies and sentinels thus posted on the summit of naked hills, commanding extensive prospects, his doubts were increased by the suspicious movements of these men. He now put his foraging cap on the end of his rifle, and waved it in the air. They took no notice of the signal. He then walked on, until he entered the edge of a wood, which concealed him from their view. Stopping out of sight for a moment, he again looked forth, when he saw the two men passing swiftly forward. As the hill on which they were walking made a curve toward that on which he stood, it seemed as if they were endeavoring to head him [off] before he should reach the camp. Doubting whether they might not belong to some large party of Indians, either in ambush or moving along the valley beyond the hill, the Captain hastened his steps homeward, and, descrying some rangers on an eminence between him and the camp, he called out to them to pass the word to have the horses driven in, as these are generally the first objects of Indian depredation.

Such was the origin of the alarm which had thrown the camp in commotion. Some of those who heard the Captain's narration, had no doubt that the men on the hill were Pawnee scouts, belonging to the band that had waylaid the hunters. Distant shots were heard at intervals, which were supposed to be fired by those who had sallied out to rescue their comrades. Several more rangers, having completed their equipments, now rode forth in the direction of the firing; others looked anxious and uneasy.

"If they are as numerous as they are said to be," said one, "and as well mounted as they generally are, we shall be a bad match for them with our jaded horses."

"Well," replied the Captain, "we have a strong encampment and can stand a siege."

"Ay, but they may set fire to the prairie in the night, and burn us out of our encampment."

"We will then set up a counter-fire!"

The word was now passed that a man on horseback approached the camp.

"It is one of the hunters! It is Clements! He brings buffalo meat!" was announced by several voices as the horseman drew near.

It was, in fact, one of the rangers who had set off in the morning in pursuit of the two buffaloes. He rode into the camp, with the spoils of the chase hanging round his horse, and followed by his companions, all sound and unharmed, and equally well laden. They proceeded to give an account of a grand gallop they had had after the two buffaloes, and how many shots it had cost them to bring one to the ground.

"Well, but the Pawnees—the Pawnees—where are the Pawnees?"

"What Pawnees?"

"The Pawnees that attacked you."

"No one attacked us."

"But have you seen no Indians on your way?"

"Oh yes, two of us got to the top of a hill to look out for the camp and saw a fellow on an opposite hill cutting queer antics, who seemed to be an Indian."

"Pshaw! that was I!" said the Captain.

Here the bubble burst. The whole alarm had risen from this mutual mistake of the Captain and the two rangers. As to the report of the three hundred Pawnees and their attack on the hunters, it proved to be a wanton fabrication, of which no further notice was taken; though the author deserved to have been sought out and severely punished.

There being no longer any prospect of fighting, every one now thought of eating; and here the stomachs throughout the camp were in unison. Tonish served up to us his promised regale of buffalo soup and buffalo beef. The soup was peppered most horribly, and the roast beef proved the bull to have been one of the patriarchs of the prairies; never did I have to deal with a tougher morsel. However, it was our first repast on buffalo meat, so we ate it with a lively faith; nor would our little Frenchman allow us any rest, until he had extorted from us an acknowledgment of the excellence of his cookery; though the pepper gave us the lie in our throats.

The night closed in without the return of old Ryan and his companion. We had become accustomed, however, to the aberrations of this old cock of the woods, and no further solicitude was expressed on his account.

After the fatigues and agitations of the day, the camp soon sunk into a profound sleep, excepting those on guard, who were more than usually on the alert; for the traces recently seen of Pawnees, and the certainty that we were in the midst of their hunting grounds, excited to constant vigilance. About half past ten o'clock we were all startled from sleep by a new alarm. A sentinel had fired off his rifle and run into camp, crying that there were Indians at hand.

Everyone was on his legs in an instant. Some seized their rifles; some were about to saddle their horses; some hastened to the Captain's lodge, but were ordered back to their respective fires. The sentinel was examined. He declared he had seen an Indian approach, crawling along the ground; whereupon he had fired upon him, and run into camp. The Captain gave it as his opinion, that the supposed Indian was a wolf; he reprimanded the sentinel for deserting his post, and obliged him to return to it.

Many seemed inclined to give credit to the story of the sentinel; for the events of the day had predisposed them to apprehend lurking foes and sudden assaults during the darkness of the night. For a long time they sat round their fires, with rifle in hand, carrying on low, murmuring conversations, and listening for some new alarm. Nothing further, however, occurred; the voices gradually died away; the gossipers nodded and dozed, and sunk to rest; and, by degrees, silence and sleep once more stole over the camp.

> In spite of all this, the expedition did meet several Native Americans on their journey. All of them were friendly, except for one incident where the natives no doubt thought the rangers came to their camp to steal their horses. Ten days before the episode of the fire and the imagined attack, the expedition camped next to an Osage village. Irving recorded in his journal, "After we retire to our tents the Indians lie by the fire before it and sing a nasal, low song in chorus, drumming on their breasts." In his book he later wrote:

In fact, the Indians that I have had an opportunity of seeing in real life are quite different from those described in poetry. They are by no means the stoics that they are represented, taciturn, unbending, without a tear or a smile. Taciturn they are, it is true, when in company with white men, whose goodwill they distrust, and whose language they do not understand; but the white man is equally taciturn under like circumstances. When the Indians are among themselves, however, there cannot be greater gossips. Half their time is taken up in talking over their adventures in war and hunting, and in telling whimsical stories.

They are great mimics and buffoons, also, and entertain themselves excessively at the expense of the whites with whom they have associated, and who have supposed them impressed with profound respect for their grandeur and dignity. They are curious observers, noting everything in silence, but with a keen and watchful eye; occasionally exchanging a glance or a grunt with each other, when anything particularly strikes them: but reserving all comments until they are alone. Then it is that they give full scope to criticism, satire, mimicry, and mirth.

In the course of my journey along the frontier, I have had repeated opportunities of noticing their excitability and boisterous merriment at their games; and have occasionally noticed a group of Osages sitting round a fire until a late hour of the night, engaged in the most animated and lively conversation; and at times making the woods resound with peals of laughter.

As to tears, they have them in abundance, both real and affected; at times they make a merit of them. No one weeps more bitterly or profusely at the death of a relative or friend: and they have stated times when they repair to howl and lament at their graves. I have heard doleful wailings at daybreak, in the neighboring Indian villages, made by some of the inhabitants, who go out at that hour into the fields, to mourn and weep for the dead: at such times, I am told, the tears will stream down their cheeks in torrents.

A PAWNEE
KNIFE CHIEF

by
James Fenimore Cooper

James Fenimore Cooper (1789–1851) achieved fame with his classic novel, The Last of the Mohicans. *This was one in the series of five novels featuring the character Natty Bumppo, better known as Hawkeye. Cooper's father was a judge, congressman, and founder of Cooperstown—now the home of the National Baseball Hall of Fame and Museum.*

At the age of 13, Cooper went to study at Yale, but was expelled from college after he set off an explosion in another student's room, setting it on fire. Previously he had pulled off other pranks, such as seating a donkey in one of his professors' chairs. Obviously he was too advanced for them, so took work as a sailor on a merchant ship, before joining the U.S. Navy a few years later. After that he tried farming, but bad investments and legal difficulties brought him to the brink of bankruptcy.

One night, the thirty-year-old Cooper threw down a novel he was reading, exclaiming to his wife that it was terrible and he could write better. His wife was skeptical, as she knew he didn't like even writing letters. To prove her wrong, he wrote his first novel. He became America's first professionally successful novelist and within seven years he was internationally famous. He went on to serve as U.S. Consul in Lyons, France. His friends included Washington Irving, Ralph Waldo Emerson, and Nathaniel Hawthorne.

The Last of the Mohicans *was one of the first novels to provide a sympathetic portrayal of Native Americans. In a letter to Sir Edward Waller from around 1827, Cooper described the Native Americans of that time and in particular one chief that he met.*

Most, if not all of the Indians who reside east of the Mississippi, live within the jurisdiction of some State or of some territory. In most cases they are left to the quiet enjoyment of the scanty rights which they retain; but the people of their vicinity commonly wish to get rid of neighbors that retard civilization, and who are so often troublesome. The policy of States is sometimes adverse to their continuance. Though there is no power, except that of the United States, which can effect their removal without their own consent, the State authorities can greatly embarrass the control of the general government. A question of policy, and, perhaps, of jurisdiction, lately arose on this subject between Georgia and the general government. In the course

⚹ **A PAWNEE KNIFE CHIEF** ⚹

of its disposal, the United States, in order to secure the rights of the Indians more effectually, and to prevent any future question of this sort, appear to have hit on the following plan.

West of the Mississippi they still hold large regions that belong to no State or territory. They propose to several tribes (Choctaws, Chickasaws, Cherokees, &c.) to sell their present possessions, improvements, houses, fences, stock, &c., and to receive, in return, acre for acre, with the same amount of stock, fences, and every other auxiliary of civilization they now possess. The inducements to make this exchange are as follow: Perpetuity to their establishments, since a pledge is given that no title shall ever be granted that may raise a pretext for another removal; an organization of a republican, or, as it is termed, a territorial government for them, such as now exist in Florida, Arkansas, and Michigan; protection, by the presence of troops; and a right to send delegates to Congress, similar to that now enjoyed by the other territories.

If the plan can be effected, there is reason to think that the constant diminution in the numbers of the Indians will be checked, and that a race, about whom there is so much that is poetic and fine in recollection, will be preserved.

———————————— ●●●● ————————————

The character of the American Indian has been too often faithfully described to need any repetition here. The majority of them, in or near the settlements, are an humbled and much degraded race. As you recede from the Mississippi, the finer traits of savage life become visible; and, although most of the natives of the Prairies, even there, are far from being the interesting and romantic heroes that poets love to paint, there are specimens of loftiness of spirit, of bearing, and of savage heroism, to be found among the chiefs, that might embarrass the fertility of the richest invention to equal. I met one of those heroes of the desert, and a finer physical and moral man, allowing for peculiarity of condition, it has rarely been my good fortune to encounter.

Peterlasharroo, or the young knife chief of the Pawnees, when I saw him, was a man of some six or seven-and-twenty years. He had already gained renown as a warrior, and he had won the confidence of his tribe by repeated exhibitions of wisdom and moderation. He had been signally useful in destroying a baneful superstition, which would have made a sacrifice of a female prisoner, whose life he saved by admirable energy, and a fearless exposure of his own. The reputation of even this remote and savage hero had spread beyond the narrow limits of his own country; and, when we met, I was prepared to yield him esteem and admiration. But the impression produced by his grave and haughty, though still courteous mien, the restless, but often steady, and bold glance of his dark, keen eye, and the quiet dignity of his air, are still present to my recollection.

With a view to propitiate so powerful a chief, I had prepared a present of peacock's feathers, which were so arranged as to produce as much effect as the fine plumage of that noble bird will allow. He received my offering with a quiet smile, and regarded the boon with a complacency that seemed to find more of its motive in a wish to be grateful, than in any selfish gratification. The gift was then laid aside, nor was it regarded again, during the whole of a long and interesting interview.

You may judge of my surprise, when I afterwards learned that this simple child of the plains considered my gift in some such light as a courtier would esteem a brilliant. The interpreter assured me that I had made him able to purchase thirty horses, a species of property that constitutes the chief wealth of his tribe. But, notwithstanding my unintentional liberality, no sign of pleasure, beyond that which I have related, was suffered to escape him, in the presence of a white man.

THE CARD of a
CHOCTAW CHIEF

by
Charles Dickens

When novelist and social reformer Charles Dickens (1812–1870) visited America in 1842 at the age of thirty, he was already famous. On arriving in Boston, he was mobbed everywhere he went.

The always-observant Dickens was acutely disgusted by the tremendous popularity of chewing tobacco in America, a habit that was even practiced in the U.S. Congress building. "Both Houses are handsomely carpeted," he observed, "but the state to which these carpets are reduced by the universal disregard of the spittoon with which every honorable member is accommodated, and the extraordinary improvements on the pattern which are squirted and dabbled upon it in every direction, do not admit of being described." And the situation was pretty much the same at the White House.

While taking a steamboat down the Ohio River from Cincinnati to St. Louis, Dickens met a Choctaw chief and had an interesting conversation with him.

Leaving Cincinnati at eleven o'clock in the forenoon, we embarked for Louisville in the [*Zebulon M.*] *Pike* steamboat, which, carrying the mails, was a packet of a much better class than that in which we had come from Pittsburg. As this passage does not occupy more than twelve or thirteen hours, we arranged, to go ashore that night: not coveting the distinction of sleeping in a state-room, when it was possible to sleep anywhere else.

There chanced to be on board this boat, in addition to the usual dreary crowd of passengers, one Pitchlynn, a chief of the Choctaw tribe of Indians, who sent in his card to me, and with whom I had the pleasure of a long conversation.

He spoke English perfectly well, though he had not begun to learn the language, he told me, until he was a young man grown. He had read many books; and Scott's poetry appeared to have left a strong impression on his mind: especially the opening of *The Lady of the Lake*, and the great battle scene in Marmion, in which, no doubt from the congeniality of the subjects to his own pursuits and tastes, he had great interest and delight. He appeared to understand correctly all he had read; and whatever fiction had enlisted his sympathy in its belief, had done so keenly and earnestly. I might almost say fiercely. He was dressed in our ordinary everyday costume, which hung about his fine figure loosely, and with indifferent grace. On my telling him that I regretted not to see him in his own attire, he threw up his right arm, for a moment, as though he were brandishing some heavy weapon, and answered, as he let it fall again, that his race were losing many things besides their dress; and would soon be seen upon the earth no more: but he wore it at home, he added proudly.

He told me that he had been away from his home, west of the Mississippi, seventeen months: and was now returning. He had been chiefly at Washington on some negotiations, pending between his Tribe and the Government: which were not settled yet (he said in a melancholy way), and he feared never would be: for what could a few poor Indians do, against such well-skilled men of business as the whitest? He had no love for Washington; tired of towns and cities very soon; and longed for the Forest and the Prairie.

I asked him what he thought of Congress? He answered, with a smile, that it wanted dignity, in an Indian's eyes.

He would very much like, he, said, to see England before he died; and spoke with much interest about the great things to be seen there. When I told, him of that chamber in the British Museum wherein are preserved household memorials of a race that ceased to be, thousands of years ago, he was very attentive, and it was not hard to see that he had a reference in his mind to the gradual fading away of his own people.

This led us to speak of Mr. [George] Catlin's gallery, which he praised highly: observing that his own portrait was among the collection, and that all the likenesses were "elegant." Mr. [James Fenimore] Cooper, he said, had painted the Red Man well; and so would I, he knew, if I would go home with him and hunt buffaloes, which he was quite anxious I should do. When I told him that supposing I went, I should not be very likely to damage the buffaloes much, he took it as a great joke and laughed, heartily.

He was a remarkably handsome man; some years past forty I should judge; with long black hair, an aquiline nose, broad check bones, a sunburnt complexion, and a very bright, keen, dark, and piercing eye. There were but twenty thousand of the Choctaws left, he said, and their number was decreasing every day. A few of his brother chiefs had been obliged to become civilized, and to make themselves acquainted with what the whites knew, for it was their only chance of existence. But they were not many; and the rest were as they always had been. He dwelt on this: and said several times that unless they tried to assimilate themselves to their conquerors, they must be swept away before the strides of civilized society.

When we shook hands at parting, I told him he must come to England, as he longed to see the land so much: that I should hope to see him there, one day: and that I could promise him he would be well received and kindly treated. He was evidently pleased by this assurance, though he rejoined with a good-humored smile and an arch shake of his head, that the English used to be very fond of the Red Men when they wanted their help, but had not cared much for them, since.

He took his leave; as stately and complete a gentleman of Nature's making, as ever I beheld; and moved among the people in the boat, another kind of being. He sent me a lithographed portrait of himself soon afterwards; very like, though scarcely handsome enough; which I have carefully preserved in memory of our brief acquaintance.

THE MOST BEAUTIFUL PART of AMERICA

by
Oscar Wilde

Oscar Wilde (1854–1900) was an Irish poet, novelist, and playwright. His fantastic novels like The Picture of Dorian Gray *and urbane social comedies like the classic play* The Importance of Being Earnest *would seem to mark him as a writer very far removed from the (then) proudly uncivilized American West.*

After spending more than a year and a half on a popular and controversial lecture tour of the United States, however, in 1883 Wilde gave a lecture on his travels to some university students back in England. Here, he talks about his impressions of the American West:

Perhaps the most beautiful part of America is the West; to reach which, however, involves a journey by rail of six days, racing along tied to an ugly tin-kettle of a steam engine. I found but poor consolation for this journey; in the fact, that the boys, who infest the cars and sell everything one can eat—or should not eat—were selling editions of my poems, vilely printed on a kind of grey blotting paper, for the low price of ten cents. Calling these boys on one side, I told them that, though poets like to be popular, they desire to be paid; and selling editions of my poems without giving me a profit is dealing a blow at literature, which must have a disastrous effect on poetical aspirants. The invariable reply that they made was that they themselves made a profit out of the transaction and that was all they cared about.

It is a popular superstition that in America a visitor is invariably addressed as "Stranger." I was never once addressed as "Stranger." When I went to Texas, I was called "Captain"; when I got to the centre of the country, I was addressed as "Colonel"; and on arriving at the borders of Mexico, as "General." On the whole, however, "Sir," the old English method of addressing people, is the most common.

It is, perhaps, worth while to note that what many people call Americanisms are really old English expressions; which have lingered in our colonies, while they have been lost in our own country. Many people imagine that the term "I guess," which is so common in America, is purely an American expression, but it was used by John Locke in his work on *The Understanding*; just as we now use "I think."

It is in the colonies, and not in the mother country, that the old life of the country really exists. If one wants to realize what English Puritanism is—not at its worst (when it is very bad), but at its best, and then it is not very good—I do not think one can find much of it in England, but much can be found about Boston and Massachusetts. We have got rid of it. America still preserves it, to be, I hope, a short-lived curiosity.

San Francisco is a really beautiful city. Chinatown, peopled by Chinese laborers, is the most artistic town I have ever come across. The people—strange, melancholy Orientals, whom many people would call common, and they are certainly very poor— have determined that they will have nothing about them that is not beautiful. In the Chinese restaurant, where these navvies [laborers] meet to have supper in the evening, I found them drinking tea out of china cups as delicate as the petals of a roseleaf, whereas at the gaudy hotels I was supplied with a delf cup an inch and a half thick. When the Chinese bill was presented it was made out on rice paper, the account being done in Indian ink as fantastically as if an artist had been etching little birds on a fan.

Salt Lake City contains only two buildings of note; the chief being the Tabernacle, which is in the shape of a soup-kettle. It is decorated by the only native artist, and he has treated religious subjects in the naive spirit of the early Florentine painters; representing people of our own day in the dress of the period side by side with people of Biblical history, who are clothed in some romantic costume.

The building next in importance is called the Amelia Palace, in honor of one of Brigham Young's wives. When he died, the present president of the Mormons stood up in the Tabernacle and said that it had been revealed to him, that he was to have the Amelia Palace, and that on this subject there were to be no more revelations of any kind!

From Salt Lake City one travels over great plains of Colorado and up the Rocky Mountains, on the top of which is Leadville, the richest city in the world. It has also got the reputation of being the roughest, and every man carries a revolver. I was told that if I went there they would be sure to shoot me or my traveling manager. I wrote and told them that nothing that they could do to my traveling manager would intimidate me.

They are miners—men working in metals, so I lectured them on the Ethics of Art. I read them passages from the autobiography of Benvenuto Cellini and they seemed much delighted. I was reproved by my hearers for not having brought him with me.

I explained that he had been dead for some little time which elicited the enquiry, "Who shot him?"

They afterwards took me to a dancing saloon where I saw the only rational method of art criticism I have ever come across. Over the piano was printed a notice:

Please do not shoot the pianist.
He is doing his best.

The mortality among pianists in that place is marvelous. Then they asked me to supper, and having accepted, I had to descend a mine in a rickety bucket in which it was impossible to be graceful. Having got into the heart of the mountain I had supper, the first course being whisky, the second whisky and the third whisky.

I went to the Theatre to lecture and I was informed that just before I went there two men had been seized for committing a murder, and in that theatre they had been brought on to the stage at eight o'clock in the evening, and then and there tried and executed before a crowded audience. But I found these miners very charming and not at all rough.

Among the more elderly inhabitants of the South I found a melancholy tendency to date every event of importance by the late war.

"How beautiful the moon is tonight," I once remarked to a gentleman who was standing next to me.

"Yes," was his reply, "but you should have seen it before the war."

So infinitesimal did I find the knowledge of Art, west of the Rocky Mountains, that an art patron—one who in his day had been a miner—actually sued the railroad company for damages because the plaster cast of Venus of Milo, which he had imported from Paris, had been delivered minus the arms. And, what is more surprising still, he gained his case and the damages.

Pennsylvania, with its rocky gorges and woodland scenery, reminded me of Switzerland. The prairie reminded me of a piece of blotting-paper.

The Spanish and French have left behind them memorials in the beauty of their names. All the cities that have beautiful names derive them from the Spanish or the French. The English people give intensely ugly names to places. One place had such an ugly name that I refused to lecture there. It was called Grigsville. Supposing I had founded a school of Art there—fancy "Early Grigsville." Imagine a School of Art teaching "Grigsville Renaissance."

As for slang, I did not hear much of it, though a young lady who had changed her clothes after an afternoon dance did say that "after the heel kick she had shifted her day goods."

***

It is well worth one's while to go to a country which can teach us the beauty of the word *Freedom* and the value of the thing *Liberty*.

THE ROWDIES
of the RIVERS

by
Ralph Waldo Emerson

While Ralph Waldo Emerson (1803–1882) is famous for his poetry, he is better known as a philosopher and founder of the Transcendentalist movement. A champion of individualism and a critic of the pressures of society, Emerson seemed oddly prejudiced against the West, even though it was a place where the individual reigned supreme.

The relative freedom on the Western frontier from society's moral restrictions tended to attract a lawless crowd. This was amplified with the discovery of gold, when prospectors were suddenly pulling fortunes from the ground. Unfortunately it was this desperate crew of claim jumpers, conmen, cardsharps, bandits, and murderers who flocked to the Wild West and drew Emerson's attention when he wrote of the Gold Rush. While he saw the West as a place where greatness could spring from self-interested lawlessness, he was ultimately unable to truly envision the sense of freedom, adventure, and tremendous potential that the West embodied.

I do not think very respectfully of the designs or the doings of the people who went to California, in 1849. It was a rush and a scramble of needy adventurers, and, in the western country, a general jail-delivery of all the rowdies of the rivers. Some of them went with honest purposes, some with very bad ones, and all of them with the very commonplace wish to find a short way to wealth. But Nature watches over all, and turns this malfeasance to good. California gets peopled and subdued—civilized in this immoral way—and, on this fiction, a real prosperity is rooted and grown. 'Tis a decoy-duck; 'tis tubs thrown to amuse the whale: but real ducks, and whales that yield oil, are caught. And, out of Sabine rapes, and out of robbers' forays, real Romes and their heroisms come in fullness of time.

In America, the geography is sublime, but the men are not: the inventions are excellent, but the inventors one is sometimes ashamed of. The agencies by which events so grand as the opening of California, of Texas, of Oregon, and the junction of the two oceans, are effected, are paltry,—coarse selfishness, fraud, and conspiracy: and most of the great results of history are brought about by discreditable means.

The benefaction derived in Illinois, and the great West, from railroads is inestimable, and vastly exceeding any intentional philanthropy on record.

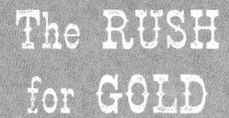

The RUSH
for GOLD

by
Henry David Thoreau

Regarding the Gold Rush, the opinions of transcendentalist and individualist Henry David Thoreau (1817–1862) were no doubt influenced by those of his friend and mentor, Ralph Waldo Emerson. The two became friends in the mid-1830s, and as Thoreau was very interested in living close to nature, Emerson allowed him to camp out for two years on his property at Walden Pond. There, Thoreau would write his landmark book, Walden, and essay "Civil Disobedience."

Thoreau's complete works comprise twenty volumes and include the journal he kept for much of his life. In it, on February 1, 1852, he wrote:

The recent rush to California and the attitude of the world, even of its philosophers and prophets, in relation to it appears to me to reflect the greatest disgrace on mankind. That so many are ready to get their living by the lottery of gold-digging without contributing any value to society, and that the great majority who stay at home justify them in this both by precept and example! It matches the infatuation of the Hindus who have cast themselves under the car of Juggernaut.

I know of no more startling development of the morality of trade and all the modes of getting a living than the rush to California affords. Of what significance the philosophy, or poetry, or religion of a world that will rush to the lottery of California gold-digging on the receipt of the first news, to live by luck, to get the means of commanding the labor of others less lucky—i.e. of slaveholding—without contributing any value to society? And that is called enterprise, and the devil is only a little more enterprising!

The philosophy and poetry and religion of such a mankind are not worth the dust of a puffball. The hog that *roots* his own living, and so makes manure, would be ashamed of such company. If I could command the wealth of all the worlds by lifting my finger, I would not pay such a price for it. It makes God to be a moneyed gentleman who scatters a handful of pennies in order to see mankind scramble for them.

Going to California. It is only three thousand miles nearer to hell. I will resign my life sooner than live by luck. The world's raffle. A subsistence in the domains of nature a thing to be raffled for! No wonder that they gamble there. I never heard that they did anything else there. What a comment, what a satire, on our institutions! The conclusion will be that mankind will hang itself upon a tree. And who would interfere to cut it down. And have all the precepts in all the bibles taught men only this? and is the last and most admirable invention of the Yankee race only an improved muck-rake? patented too!

If one came hither to sell lottery tickets, bringing satisfactory credentials, and the prizes were seats in heaven, this world would buy them with a rush.

Did God direct us so to get our living, digging where we never planted, and He would perchance reward us with lumps of gold? It is a text, oh! for the Jonahs of this generation, and yet the pulpits are as silent as immortal Greece, silent, some of them, because the preacher is gone to California himself.

The gold of California is a touchstone which has betrayed the rottenness, the baseness, of mankind. Satan, from one of his elevations, showed mankind the kingdom of California, and they entered into a compact with him at once.

While finding gold may have been something like a lottery in that a few won and most lost, many others did quite well establishing other types of businesses. And Thoreau was particularly wrong about one thing; the '49ers had to work like hell with long hours of back-breaking labor in order to scratch out a meager living. When the Gold Rush was over, most remained in the West. And they were joined by more pioneers who used ships, the Oregon Trail and other trails, and later on, the railroads, to establish their new lives in the West.

As for contributing to society, the gold and silver pulled out of the ground played a significant role enabling the Union to win the Civil War and then by financing the rapid growth of the United States as a world power.

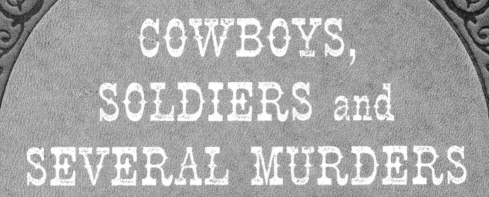

COWBOYS, SOLDIERS and SEVERAL MURDERS

by
Rudyard Kipling

Joseph Rudyard Kipling (1865–1936) was born in Bombay, India. When he was five years old, the son of a clergyman was sent to school in England, where he suffered six years of mental torture and beatings from his guardians before being rescued by his parents. He returned to India as a journalist, where he stayed for eight years before returning to England. Kipling wrote on many topics, but it was his stories and poems of India—from Kim and The Jungle Book to "The Man Who Would Be King"—that made him famous.

In 1888—when he was twenty-three years old—Kipling had seven books of fiction published in India, but at that time his fame was limited to that country. It wasn't until 1890 that he suddenly became famous in England and then the United States. Between those years, he was still working as the assistant editor of the Allahabad Pioneer in India, when he decided to travel to England, by way of Burma, Singapore, Hong Kong, Japan, and the United States.—traveling from San Francisco across to New York—writing a series of travel letters for the paper along the way. Kipling hoped to find publishers for his work in both America and Britain, but he had little luck in the States. (Though he did succeed in having a long conversation with Mark Twain.)

On arriving in America, Kipling described San Francisco as "a hopeless maze of small wooden houses, dust, street-refuse, and children who play with empty kerosene tins." This was at a time when the city was still reeling from the sudden influx of wealth from the Gold Rush. In the previous forty years its population had skyrocketed from roughly a thousand to almost 300,000. While San Francisco had become a major metropolitan city—the eighth largest in the United States—it still maintained its Wild West atmosphere.

Kipling eventually found his way to the Palace Hotel, where:

In a vast marble-paved hall under the glare of an electric light sat forty or fifty men; and for their use and amusement were provided spittoons of infinite capacity and generous gape. Most of the men wore frock-coats and top-hats—the things that we in India put on at a wedding breakfast if we possessed them—but they all spat. They spat on principle. The spittoons were on the staircases, in each bedroom—yea, and in

Palace Hotel, San Francisco

chambers even more sacred than these. They chased one into retirement, but they blossomed in chiefest splendor round the Bar, and they were all used, every reeking one of 'em.

Perhaps because he had just come from Asia, Kipling was particularly interested in exploring San Francisco's Chinatown.

MURDER IN CHINATOWN

It was a bad business throughout, and the only consolation is that it was all my fault. A man took me round the Chinese quarter of San Francisco, which is a ward of the city of Canton set down in the most eligible business-quarter of the place. The Chinese man with his usual skill has possessed himself of good brick fire-proof buildings and, following instinct, has packed each tenement with hundreds of souls, all living in filth and squalor not to be appreciated save by you in India.

That cursory investigation ought to have sufficed; but I wanted to know how deep in the earth the Pig-tail had taken root. Therefore I explored the Chinese quarter a second time and alone, which was foolishness. No one in the filthy streets (but for the blessed sea breezes San Francisco would enjoy cholera every season) interfered with my movements, though many asked for cumshaw [a handout].

I struck a house about four stories high full of celestial abominations, and began to burrow down; having heard that these tenements were constructed on the lines of icebergs—two-thirds below sight level. Downstairs I crawled past Chinese men in bunks, opium-smokers, brothels, and gambling hells, till I had reached the second cellar—was in fact, in the labyrinths of a warren. Great is the wisdom of the Chinese man. In time of trouble that house could be razed to the ground by the mob, and yet hide all its inhabitants in brick-walled and wooden-beamed subterranean galleries, strengthened with iron-framed doors and gates.

On the second underground floor a man asked for cumshaw and took me downstairs to yet another cellar, where the air was as thick as butter, and the lamps burned little holes in it not more than an inch square.

In this place a poker club had assembled and was in full swing. The Chinese man loves "pokel," and plays it with great skill, swearing like a cat when he loses. Most of the men round the table were in semi-European dress, their pig-tails curled up under billy-cock hats. One of the company looked like a Eurasian, whence I argued that he was a Mexican—a supposition that later inquiries confirmed. They were a picturesque set of fiends and polite, being too absorbed in their game to look at the stranger. We were all deep down under the earth, and save for the rustle of a blue gown sleeve and the ghostly whisper of the cards as they were shuffled and played, there was no sound.

The heat was almost unendurable. There was some dispute between the Mexican and the man on his left. The latter shifted his place to put the table between himself and his opponent, and stretched a lean yellow hand towards the Mexican's winnings.

Mark how purely man is a creature of instinct. Barely introduced to the pistol, I saw the Mexican half rise in his chair and at the same instant found myself full length on the floor. None had told me that this was the best attitude when bullets are abroad. I was there prone before I had time to think—dropping as the room was filled with an intolerable clamor like the discharge of a cannon. In those close quarters the pistol report had no room to spread any more than the smoke—then acrid in my nostrils. There was no second shot, but a great silence in which I rose slowly to my knees.

The Chinese man was gripping the table with both hands and staring in front of him at an empty chair. The Mexican had gone, and a little whirl of smoke was floating near the roof. Still gripping the table, the Chinese man said, "Ah!" in the tone that a man would use when, looking up from his work suddenly, he sees a well-known friend in the doorway. Then he coughed and fell over to his own right, and I saw that he had been shot in the stomach.

I became aware that, save for two men leaning over the stricken one, the room was empty; and all the tides of intense fear, hitherto held back by intenser curiosity, swept over my soul. I ardently desired the outside air. It was possible that the Chinese men would mistake me for the Mexican—everything horrible seemed possible just then—and it was more than possible that the stairways would be closed while they were hunting for the murderer.

The man on the floor coughed a sickening cough. I heard it as I fled, and one of his companions turned out the lamp. Those stairs seemed interminable, and to add to my dismay there was no sound of commotion in the house. No one hindered, no one even looked at me. There was no trace of the Mexican. I found the doorway and, my legs trembling under me, reached the protection of the clear cool night, the fog, and the rain.

I dared not run, and for the life of me I could not walk. I must have effected a compromise, for I remember the light of a street lamp showed the shadow of one half skipping—caracoling along the pavements in what seemed to be an ecstasy of suppressed happiness. But it was fear—deadly fear. Fear compounded of past knowledge of the Oriental—only other white man—available witness—three stories underground and the cough of the Chinese man now some forty feet under my clattering boot-heels.

It was good to see the shop-fronts and electric lights again. Not for anything would I have informed the police, because I firmly believed that the Mexican had been dealt with somewhere down there on the third floor long ere I had reached the air; and, moreover, once clear of the place, I could not for the life of me tell where it was.

My ill-considered flight brought me out somewhere a mile distant from the hotel; and the clank of the lift that bore me to a bed six stories above ground was music in my ears. Wherefore I would impress it upon you who follow after, do not knock about the Chinese quarters at night and alone. You may stumble across a picturesque piece of human nature that will unsteady your nerves for half a day.

Kipling journeyed north to Portland, Oregon, which—like most rapidly expanding Western towns—was still rather primitive. In the previous twenty years its population had shot from 8,300 to nearly 60,000, and it was still adjusting to the growth. This time Kipling missed another eruption of Wild West violence, but it gave him a chance to witness Western justice, though it left him completely mystified.

MURDER IN PORTLAND

Portland is so busy that it can't attend to its own sewage or paving, and the four-storey brick blocks front cobble-stones and plank sidewalks and other things much worse. I saw a foundation being dug out. The sewage of perhaps twenty years ago, had thoroughly soaked into the soil, and there was a familiar and Oriental look about the compost that flew up with each shovel-load. Yet the local papers, as was just and proper, swore there was no place like Portland, Oregon, U.S.A., chronicled the performances of Oregonians, "claimed" prominent citizens elsewhere as Oregonians, and fought tooth and nail for dock, rail, and wharfage projects. And you could find men who had thrown in their lives with the city, who were bound up in it, and worked their life out for what they conceived to be its material prosperity. Pity it is to record that in this strenuous, laboring town there had been, a week before, a shooting-case. One well-known man

had shot another on the street, and was now pleading self-defense because the other man had, or the murderer thought he had, a pistol about him. Not content with shooting him dead, he squibbed off his revolver into him as he lay. I read the pleadings, and they made me ill. So far as I could judge, if the dead man's body had been found with a pistol on it, the shooter would have gone free. Apart from the mere murder, cowardly enough in itself, there was a refinement of cowardice in the plea. Here in this civilized city the surviving brute was afraid he would be shot fancied he saw the other man make a motion to his hip-pocket, and so on. Eventually the jury disagreed. And the degrading thing was that the trial was reported by men who evidently understood all about the pistol, was tried before a jury who were versed in the etiquette of the hip-pocket, and was discussed on the streets by men equally initiate.

From Portland Kipling caught a steamboat and headed up the Columbia River to fish for Chinook salmon. Along the way he spied an interesting sight as they floated past.

On a rocky island we saw the white tomb of an old-time settler who had made his money in San Francisco, but had chosen to be buried in an Indian burying-ground. A decayed wooden "wickyup," where the bones of the Indian dead are laid, almost touched the tomb. The river ran into a canal of basaltic rock, painted in yellow, vermilion, and green by Indians and, by inferior brutes, adorned with advertisements of "bile beans."

Everywhere he went, Kipling was assailed by advertisements for Bile Beans, a patent medicine for headaches, biliousness, constipation, and other derangements of the digestive organs. Even on this remote island burial ground, civilization was quickly pouring into the West.

From Vancouver, Canada—which had burned to the ground in less than 45 minutes three years earlier, leaving very few buildings standing—Kipling set out for Yellowstone National Park in the Wyoming Territory.

Yellowstone became the world's first national park in 1872 after Jay Cooke, the director of the Northern Pacific Railroad, lobbied Congress into creating the park so he could sell train tickets and fill his hotel at Yellowstone. Kipling visited the park during the early days of tourism in the West, a time that also coincided with the rise of the Ghost Dance among rebelling Native American tribes and just seventeen months before the Sioux were massacred by the U.S. Army at Wounded Knee.

I went east—east to Montana, after another horrible night in Tacoma among the men who spat. Why does the Westerner spit? It can't amuse him, and it doesn't interest his neighbor.

But I am beginning to mistrust. Everything good as well as everything bad is supposed to come from the East. Is there a shooting-scrape between prominent citizens? Oh, you'll find nothing of that kind in the East. Is there a more than usually revolting lynching? They don't do that in the East. I shall find out when I get there whether this unnatural perfection be real.

Eastward then to Montana I took my way for the Yellowstone National Park, called in the guidebooks "Wonderland." But the real Wonderland began in the train. We were a merry crew. One gentleman announced his intention of paying no fare and grappled the conductor, who neatly cross-buttocked him through a double plate-glass window. His head was cut open in four or five places. A doctor on the train hastily stitched up the biggest gash, and he was dropped at a wayside station, spurting blood at every hair—a scarlet-headed and ghastly sight. The conductor guessed that he would die, and volunteered the information that there was no profit in monkeying with the North Pacific Railway.

Night was falling as we cleared the forests and sailed out upon a wilderness of sage brush. The desolation of Montgomery, the wilderness of Sind, the hummock-studded desert of Bikaneer, are joyous and homelike compared to the impoverished misery of the sage. It is blue, it is stunted, it is dusty. It wraps the rolling hills as a mildewed shroud wraps the body of a long-dead man. It makes you weep for sheer loneliness, and there is no getting away from it.

COWBOYS OF LIVINGSTONE

Livingstone is a town of two thousand people, and the junction for the little side-line that takes you to the Yellowstone National Park. It lies in a fold of the prairie, and behind it is the Yellowstone River and the gate of the mountains through which the river flows. There is one street in the town, where the cowboy's pony and the little foal of the brood-mare in the buggy rest contentedly in the blinding sunshine while the cowboy gets himself shaved at the only other barber's shop, and swaps lies at the bar. I exhausted the town, including the saloons, in ten minutes, and got away on the rolling grass downs where I threw myself to rest. Directly under the hill I was on, swept a drove of horses in charge of two mounted men. That was a picture I shall not soon

forget. A light haze of dust went up from the hoof-trodden green, scarcely veiling the unfettered deviltries of three hundred horses who very much wanted to stop and graze. "Yow! Yow! Yow!" yapped the mounted men in chorus like coyotes. The column moved forward at a trot, divided as it met a hillock and scattered into fan shape all among the suburbs of Livingstone. I heard the "snick" of a stock whip, half a dozen "Yow, yows," and the mob had come together again, and, with neighing and whickering and squealing and a great deal of kicking on the part of the youngsters, rolled like a wave of brown water toward the uplands.

I was within twenty feet of the leader, a gray stallion lord of many brood-mares all deeply concerned for the welfare of their fuzzy foals. A cream-colored beast I knew him at once for the bad character of the troop broke back, taking with him some frivolous fillies. I heard the snick of the whips somewhere in the dust, and the fillies came back at a canter, very shocked and indignant. On the heels of the last rode both the stockmen picturesque ruffians who wanted to know "what in hell" I was doing there, waved their hats, and sped down the slope after their charges.

When the noise of the troop had died there came a wonderful silence on all the prairie that silence, they say, which enters into the heart of the old-time hunter and trapper and marks him off from the rest of his race. The town disappeared in the darkness, and a very young moon showed herself over a bald-headed, snow-flecked peak. Then the Yellowstone, hidden by the water-willows, lifted up its voice and sang a little song to the mountains, and an old horse that had crept up in the dusk breathed inquiringly on the back of my neck.

When I reached the hotel I found all manner of preparation under way for the 4th of July, and a drunken man with a Winchester rifle over his shoulder patrolling the sidewalk. I do not think he wanted anyone. He carried the gun as other folk carry walking sticks. None the less I avoided the direct line of fire and listened to the blasphemies of miners and stockmen till far into the night.

Yellowstone itself was at that time, as Kipling put it, "guarded by soldiers who patrol it with loaded six-shooters, in order that the tourist may not bring up fence-rails and sink them in a pool, or chip the fretted tracery of the formations with a geological hammer, or, walking where the crust is too thin, foolishly cook himself." They were also there to catch poachers.

YELLOWSTONE

I was watching a solitary spring, when, far across the fields, stood up a plume of spun glass, iridescent and superb, against the sky.

"That," said the trooper, "is Old Faithful. He goes off every sixty-five minutes to the minute, plays for five minutes, and sends up a column of water a hundred and fifty feet high. By the time you have looked at all the other geysers he will be ready to play."

So we looked and we wondered at the Beehive, whose mouth is built up exactly like a hive; at the Turban (which is not in the least like a turban); and at many, many other geysers, hot holes, and springs. Some of them rumbled, some hissed, some went off spasmodically, and others lay still in sheets of sapphire and beryl.

Would you believe that even these terrible creatures have to be guarded by the troopers to prevent the irreverent American from chipping the cones to pieces, or worse still, making the geysers sick? If you take of soft-soap a small barrelful and drop it down a geyser's mouth, that geyser will presently be forced to lay all before you and for days afterwards will be of an irritated and inconsistent stomach. When they told me the tale I was filled with sympathy. Now I wish that I had stolen soap and tried the experiment on some lonely little beast of a geyser in the woods. It sounds so probable and so human.

Yet he would be a bold man who would administer emetics to the Giantess. She is flat-lipped, having no mouth, she looks like a pool, fifty feet long and thirty wide, and there is no ornamentation about her. At irregular intervals she speaks, and sends up a column of water over two hundred feet high to begin with; then she is angry for a day and a half sometimes for two days.

Owing to her peculiarity of going mad in the night not many people have seen the Giantess at her finest; but the clamor of her unrest, men say, shakes the wooden hotel, and echoes like thunder among the hills. When I saw her trouble was brewing. The pool bubbled seriously, and at five-minute intervals, sank a foot or two, then rose, washed over the rim, and huge steam bubbles broke on the top. Just before an eruption the water entirely disappears from view. Whenever you see the water die down in a geyser-mouth get away as fast as you can. I saw a tiny little geyser suck in its breath in this way, and instinct made me retire while it hooted after me.[…]

It was a sweltering hot day…and I left that raw pine-creaking caravanserai [the hotel] for the cool shade of a clump of pines between whose trunks glimmered tents. A batch of United States troopers came down the road and flung themselves across the country into their rough lines. The 'Melican cavalryman *can* ride, though he keeps his accoutrements pig-fashion and his horse cow-fashion. ["'Melican" being Kipling's Native American pronunciation of "American."]

I was free of that camp in five minutes—free to play with the heavy, lumpy carbines, have the saddles stripped, and punch the horses knowingly in the ribs. One of the men had been in the fight with "Wrap-Up-His-Tail," and he told me how that great chief, his horse's tail tied up in red calico, swaggered in front of the United States cavalry, challenging all to single combat. But he was slain, and a few of his tribe with him.

A couple of cowboys—real cowboys, not the Buffalo Bill article—jingled through the camp amid a shower of mild chaff. They were on their way to Cook City, I fancy, and I know that they never washed. But they were picturesque ruffians exceedingly, with long spurs, hooded stirrups, slouch hats, fur weather-cloth over their knees, and pistol-butts just easy to hand.

"The cowboy's goin' under before long," said my friend. "Soon as the country's settled up he'll have to go. But he's mighty useful now. What would we do without the cowboy?"

"As how?" said I, and the camp laughed.

"He has the money. We have the skill. He comes in winter to play poker at the military posts. *We* play poker—a few. When he's lost his money we make him drunk and let him go. Sometimes we get the wrong man."

And he told me a tale of an innocent cowboy who turned up, cleaned out, at an army post, and played poker for thirty-six hours. But it was the post that was cleaned out when that long-haired Caucasian Ah Sin removed himself, heavy with everybody's pay and declining the proffered liquor.

"Noaw," said the historian, "I don't play with no cowboy unless he's a little bit drunk first."

Ere I departed I gathered from more than one man the significant fact that *up to one hundred yards* he felt absolutely secure behind his revolver.

"In England, I understand," quoth the limber youth from the South, "in England a man isn't allowed to play with no firearms. He's got to be taught all that when he enlists. I didn't want much teaching how to shoot straight 'fore I served Uncle Sam. And that's just where it is. But you was talking about your Horse Guards now?"

I explained briefly some peculiarities of equipment connected with our crackest crack cavalry. I grieve to say the camp roared.

"Take 'em over swampy ground. Let 'em run around a bit an' work the starch out of 'em, an' then, Almighty, if we wouldn't plug 'em at ease I'd eat their horses!"[…]

There was a maiden—a very trim maiden—who had just stepped out of one of Mr. [Henry] James's novels. She owned a delightful mother and an equally delightful father—a heavy-eyed, slow-voiced man of finance. The parents thought that their daughter wanted change. She lived in New Hampshire. Accordingly, she had dragged them up to Alaska and to the Yosemite Valley, and was now returning leisurely via the Yellowstone, just in time for the tail-end of the summer season at Saratoga.

We had met once or twice before in the park, and I had been amazed and amused at her critical commendation of the wonders that she saw. From that very resolute little mouth I received a lecture on American literature, the nature and inwardness of Washington society, the precise value of [George Washington] Cable's works as compared with "Uncle Remus" [Joel Chandler] Harris, and a few other things that had nothing whatever to do with geysers, but were altogether pleasant.

Now, an English maiden who had stumbled on a dust-grimed, lime-washed, sun-peeled, collarless wanderer come from and going to goodness knows where, would, her mother inciting her and her father brandishing an umbrella, have regarded him as a dissolute adventurer—a person to be disregarded.

Not so those delightful people from New Hampshire. They were good enough to treat him—it sounds almost incredible—as a human being, possibly respectable, probably not in immediate need of financial assistance.

Papa talked pleasantly and to the point. The little maiden strove valiantly with the accent of her birth and that of her rearing, and mamma smiled benignly in the background.

Balance this with a story of a young English idiot I met mooning about inside his high collar, attended by a valet. He condescended to tell me that "you can't be too careful who you talk to in these parts," and stalked on, fearing, I suppose, every minute for his social chastity.

That man was a barbarian (I took occasion to tell him so), for he comported himself after the manner of the headhunters of Assam, who are at perpetual feud one with another.

You will understand that these foolish stories are introduced in order to cover the fact that this pen cannot describe the glories of the Upper Geyser Basin. The evening I spent under the lee of the Castle Geyser, sitting on a log with some troopers and watching a baronial keep forty feet high spouting hot water. If the Castle went off first, they said the Giantess would be quiet, and vice versa; and then they told tales till the moon got up and a party of campers in the woods gave us all something to eat.[…]

Then came soft, turfy forest that deadened the wheels, and two troopers—on detachment duty—stole noiselessly behind us. One was the Wrap-Up-His-Tail man, and they talked merrily while the half-broken horses bucked about among the trees till we got to a mighty hill strewn with moss agates, and everybody had to jump out and pant in that thin air. But how intoxicating it was! The old lady from Chicago ducked like an emancipated hen as she scuttled about the road, cramming pieces of rock into her reticule. She sent me fifty yards down to the hillside to pick up a piece of broken bottle which she insisted was moss agate.

"I've some o' that at home, an' they shine. Yes, you go get it, young feller."

As we climbed the long path the road grew viler and viler till it became, without disguise, the bed of a torrent; and just when things were at their rockiest we emerged into a little sapphire lake—but never sapphire was so blue—called Mary's Lake; and that between eight and nine thousand feet above the sea.

Then came grass downs, all on a vehement slope, so that the buggy, following the new-made road, ran on the two off-wheels mostly till we dipped head-first into a ford, climbed up a cliff, raced along down, dipped again, and pulled up disheveled at "Larry's" for lunch and an hour's rest.

[...] then we lay on the grass and laughed with sheer bliss of being alive. This have I known once in Japan, once on the banks of the Columbia, what time the salmon came in and "California" [a traveling companion on the Columbia steamboat] howled, and once again in the Yellowstone by the light of the eyes of the maiden from New Hampshire. Four little pools lay at my elbow, one was of black water (tepid), one clear water (cold), one clear water (hot), one red water (boiling). My newly washed handkerchief covered them all. We marveled as children marvel.

STAGECOACH TALES and SLADE'S UNTIMELY DEATH

by
Mark Twain

In spite of having virtually no formal education, Mark Twain (1835–1910)—whose real name was Samuel Clemens—went on to become one of America's greatest authors, labeled "the father of American literature" by no less than William Faulkner. He came to prominence during a period when America was still strongly divided into North and South, but Twain—as he showed in novels like The Adventures of Tom Sawyer—was a blend of the two, with a heavy dose of the West thrown in.

After the Civil War broke out, Twain formed a Confederate militia with some friends, but after two weeks they disbanded—or "resigned," as he called it—after which he headed for the Nevada Territory with his brother, who had just been appointed secretary to the territory's governor. They traveled by stagecoach for twenty days from St. Joseph, Missouri, to Carson City, the current capitol of Nevada. The fare was $150 per person, or about $3,700 today, and while it was a very unpleasant ride, the fare did include meals.

One traveler, Demas Barnes, described the experience as "fifteen inches of seat, with a fat man on one side, a poor widow on the other, a baby in your lap, a bandbox over your head, and three or more persons immediately in front, leaning against your knees, making the picture, as well as your sleeping place for the trip."

In the winter, metal footwarmers containing hot coals were provided for heat. During the summer, while crossing deserts the passengers had leather shades to block out the sun and dust. Meals of salted meat, boiled beans, and coffee were provided at "home stations," which were about six to eight hours apart, if there weren't any delays from storms, flooded roads, breakdowns, or Indian attacks. These meals had to be eaten rapidly, so the train could stay on schedule.

The brothers were passing through the Nebraska Territory when Twain saw a Pony Express rider streak by the stage. This service had begun on April 3, 1860. These hardy messengers rode around the clock, day and night. It usually took seven to ten days to complete the journey one way in summer and twelve to sixteen days during winter. They had messengers who transported the letters by train from both New York and Washington, D.C., to St. Joseph. Then about 500 top-rate horses and between ninety and 200 light-weight riders carried the letters through between 119 and 190 relay *stations along the two thousand-mile trail from St. Joseph to Sacramento, where the letters were taken by steamer to San Francisco. Parts of the route—both riders and stations—illegally trespassed on Native American land, which inevitably resulted in violent conflicts.*

Altogether, 308 runs were made each way, carrying 34,753 pieces of mail. That's equal to riding a horse twenty-four times around the earth. Although some credited the Pony Express with keeping California and its gold in the Union during the Civil War, it only lasted from April 1860 to October 1861, having been made obsolete by the completion of the transcontinental railroad. Financially, the Pony Express was a complete failure. It didn't really become a patriotic symbol of Western strength and heroism until the turn of the twentieth century—largely because Buffalo Bill included his tribute to the Pony Express in his Wild West Shows.

I n a little while all interest was taken up in stretching our necks and watching for the "pony-rider"—the fleet messenger who sped across the continent from St. Joe to Sacramento, carrying letters nineteen hundred miles in eight days! Think of that for perishable horse and human flesh and blood to do!

The pony-rider was usually a little bit of a man, brimful of spirit and endurance. No matter what time of the day or night his watch came on, and no matter whether it was winter or summer, raining, snowing, hailing, or sleeting, or whether his "beat" was a level straight road or a crazy trail over mountain crags and precipices, or whether it led through peaceful regions or regions that swarmed with hostile Indians, he must be always ready to leap into the saddle and be off like the wind!

There was no idling-time for a pony-rider on duty. He rode fifty miles without stopping, by daylight, moonlight, starlight, or through the blackness of darkness—just as it happened. He rode a splendid horse that was born for a racer and fed and lodged like a gentleman; kept him at his utmost speed for ten miles, and then, as he came crashing up to the station where stood two men holding fast a fresh, impatient steed, the transfer of rider and mail-bag was made in the twinkling of an eye, and away flew the eager pair and were out of sight before the spectator could get hardly the ghost of a look.

Both rider and horse went "flying light." The rider's dress was thin, and fitted close; he wore a "round-about," and a skull-cap, and tucked his pantaloons into his boot-tops like a race-rider. He carried no arms—he carried nothing that was not absolutely necessary, for even the postage on his literary freight was worth *five dollars a letter* [approximately $120 in today's dollars].

He got but little frivolous correspondence to carry—his bag had business letters in it, mostly. His horse was stripped of all unnecessary weight, too. He wore a little wafer of a racing-saddle, and no visible blanket. He wore light shoes, or none at all. The little flat mail-pockets strapped under the rider's thighs would each hold about the bulk of a child's primer. They held many and many an important business chapter and newspaper letter, but these were written on paper as airy and thin as gold-leaf, nearly, and thus bulk and weight were economized.

The stagecoach traveled about a hundred to a hundred and twenty-five miles a day (twenty-four hours), the pony-rider about two hundred and fifty. There were about eighty pony-riders in the saddle all the time, night and day, stretching in a long, scattering procession from Missouri to California, forty flying eastward, and forty toward the west, and among them making four hundred gallant horses earn a stirring livelihood and see a deal of scenery every single day in the year.

We had had a consuming desire, from the beginning, to see a pony-rider, but somehow or other all that passed us and all that met us managed to streak by in the night, and so we heard only a whiz and a hail, and the swift phantom of the desert was gone before we could get our heads out of the windows. But now we were expecting one along every moment, and would see him in broad daylight. Presently the driver exclaims, "Here he comes!"

Every neck is stretched further, and every eye strained wider. Away across the endless dead level of the prairie a black speck appears against the sky, and it is plain that it moves. Well, I should think so!

In a second or two it becomes a horse and rider, rising and falling, rising and falling—sweeping toward us nearer and nearer—growing more and more distinct, more and more sharply defined—nearer and still nearer, and the flutter of the hoofs

comes faintly to the ear—another instant a whoop and a hurrah from our upper deck, a wave of the rider's hand, but no reply, and man and horse burst past our excited faces, and go winging away like a belated fragment of a storm!

So sudden is it all, and so like a flash of unreal fancy, that but for the flake of white foam left quivering and perishing on a mail-sack after the vision had flashed by and disappeared, we might have doubted whether we had seen any actual horse and man at all, maybe.[…]

We breakfasted at Horseshoe Station [in what is now Wyoming], six hundred and seventy-six miles out from St. Joseph. We had now reached a hostile Indian country, and during the afternoon we passed Laparelle [or La Prele] Station, and enjoyed great discomfort all the time we were in the neighborhood, being aware that many of the trees we dashed by at arm's length concealed a lurking Indian or two.

During the preceding night an ambushed savage had sent a bullet through the pony-rider's jacket, but he had ridden on just the same because pony-riders were not allowed to stop and inquire into such things except when killed. As long as they had life enough left in them they had to stick to the horse and ride, even if the Indians had been waiting for them a week and were entirely out of patience.

About two hours and a half before we arrived at Laparelle Station, the keeper in charge of it had fired four times at an Indian, but he said with an injured air that the Indian had "skipped around so's to spile everything—and ammunition's blamed skurse, too."

The most natural inference conveyed by his manner of speaking was, that in "skipping around," the Indian had taken an unfair advantage.

The coach we were in had a neat hole through its front—a reminiscence of its last trip through this region. The bullet that made it wounded the driver slightly, but he did not mind it much. He said the place to keep a man "huffy" was down on the Southern Overland among the Apaches, before the company moved the stage line up on the northern route. He said the Apaches used to annoy him all the time down there, and that he came as near as anything to starving to death in the midst of abundance, because they kept him so leaky with bullet holes that he "couldn't hold his vittles."

This person's statements were not generally believed.

We shut the blinds down very tightly that first night in the hostile Indian country, and lay on our arms. We slept on them some, but most of the time we only lay on them. We did not talk much, but kept quiet and listened. It was an inky-black night, and occasionally rainy. We were among woods and rocks, hills and gorges—so shut in, in fact, that when we peeped through a chink in a curtain, we could discern nothing.

The driver and conductor on top were still, too, or only spoke at long intervals in low tones, as is the way of men in the midst of invisible dangers. We listened to rain-drops pattering on the roof; and the grinding of the wheels through the muddy gravel; and the low wailing of the wind; and all the time we had that absurd sense upon us, inseparable from travel at night in a close-curtained vehicle, the sense of remaining perfectly still in one place, notwithstanding the jolting and swaying of the vehicle, the trampling of the horses, and the grinding of the wheels.

We listened a long time, with intent faculties and bated breath; every time one of us would relax, and draw a long sigh of relief and start to say something, a comrade would be sure to utter a sudden "Hark!" and instantly the experimenter was rigid and listening again.

So the tiresome minutes and decades of minutes dragged away, until at last our tense forms filmed over with a dulled consciousness and we slept, if one might call such a condition by so strong a name—for it was a sleep set with a hair-trigger. It was a sleep seething and teeming with a weird and distressful confusion of shreds and fag-ends of dreams—a sleep that was a chaos.

Presently, dreams and sleep and the sullen hush of the night were startled by a ringing report, and cloven by *such* a long, wild, agonizing shriek! Then we heard—ten steps from the stage—

"Help! help! help!" (It was our driver's voice.)

"Kill him! Kill him like a dog!"

"I'm being murdered! Will no man lend me a pistol?"

"Look out! head him off! head him off!"

(Two pistol shots; a confusion of voices and the trampling of many feet, as if a crowd were closing and surging together around some object; several heavy, dull blows, as with a club; a voice that said appealingly, "Don't, gentlemen, please don't—I'm a dead man!" Then a fainter groan, and another blow, and away sped the stage into the darkness, and left the grisly mystery behind us.)

What a startle it was! Eight seconds would amply cover the time it occupied— maybe even five would do it. We only had time to plunge at a curtain and unbuckle and unbutton part of it in an awkward and hindering flurry, when our whip cracked sharply overhead, and we went rumbling and thundering away, down a mountain "grade."

We fed on that mystery the rest of the night—what was left of it, for it was waning fast. It had to remain a present mystery, for all we could get from the conductor in answer to our hails was something that sounded, through the clatter of the wheels, like, "Tell you in the morning!"

So we lit our pipes and opened the corner of a curtain for a chimney, and lay there in the dark, listening to each other's story of how he first felt and how many thousand Indians he first thought had hurled themselves upon us, and what his remembrance of the subsequent sounds was, and the order of their occurrence. And we theorized, too, but there was never a theory that would account for our driver's voice being out there, nor yet account for his Indian murderers talking such good English, if they *were* Indians.

So we chatted and smoked the rest of the night comfortably away, our boding anxiety being somehow marvelously dissipated by the real presence of something to be anxious *about*.

We never did get much satisfaction about that dark occurrence. All that we could make out of the odds and ends of the information we gathered in the morning, was that the disturbance occurred at a station; that we changed drivers there, and that the driver that got off there had [on a previous trip] been talking roughly about some of the outlaws that infested the region ("for there wasn't a man around there but had a price on his head and didn't dare show himself in the settlements," the conductor said); he had talked roughly about these characters, and ought to have "drove up there with his pistol cocked and ready on the seat alongside of him, and begun business himself, because any softy would know they would be laying for him."

That was all we could gather, and we could see that neither the conductor nor the new driver were much concerned about the matter. They plainly had little respect for a man who would deliver offensive opinions of people and then be so simple as to come into their presence unprepared to "back his judgment," as they pleasantly phrased the killing of any fellow-being who did not like said opinions. And likewise they plainly had a contempt for the man's poor discretion in venturing to rouse the wrath of such utterly reckless wild beasts as those outlaws—and the conductor added, "I tell you it's as much as Slade himself wants to do!"

This remark created an entire revolution in my curiosity. I cared nothing now about the Indians, and even lost interest in the murdered driver. There was such magic in that name, SLADE!

Day or night, now, I stood always ready to drop any subject in hand, to listen to something new about Slade and his ghastly exploits. Even before we got to Overland City, we had begun to hear about [Joseph "Jack"] Slade and his "division" (for he was a "division-agent") on the Overland; and from the hour we had left Overland City we had heard drivers and conductors talk about only three things—"Californy," the Nevada silver mines, and this desperado Slade. And a deal the most of the talk was about Slade.

We had gradually come to have a realizing sense of the fact that Slade was a man whose heart and hands and soul were steeped in the blood of offenders against his dignity; a man who awfully avenged all injuries, affront, insults or slights, of whatever kind—on the spot if he could, years afterward if lack of earlier opportunity compelled it; a man whose hate tortured him day and night till vengeance appeased it—and not an ordinary vengeance either, but his enemy's absolute death—nothing less; a man whose face would light up with a terrible joy when he surprised a foe and had him at a disadvantage.

A high and efficient servant of the Overland, an outlaw among outlaws and yet their relentless scourge, Slade was at once the most bloody, the most dangerous and the most valuable citizen that inhabited the savage fastnesses of the mountains.

Really and truly, two thirds of the talk of drivers and conductors had been about this man Slade, ever since the day before we reached Julesburg. In order that the eastern reader may have a clear conception of what a Rocky Mountain desperado is, in his highest state of development, I will reduce all this mass of overland gossip to one straightforward narrative, and present it in the following shape:

Slade was born in Illinois, of good parentage. At about twenty-six years of age he killed a man in a quarrel and fled the country. At St. Joseph, Missouri, he joined one of the early California-bound emigrant trains and was given the post of train-master. One day on the plains he had an angry dispute with one of his wagon-drivers and both drew their revolvers. But the driver was the quicker artist and had his weapon cocked first. So Slade said it was a pity to waste life on so small a matter and proposed that the pistols be thrown on the ground and the quarrel settled by a fist-fight. The unsuspecting driver agreed and threw down his pistol—whereupon Slade laughed at his simplicity and shot him dead!

He made his escape and lived a wild life for awhile, dividing his time between fighting Indians and avoiding an Illinois sheriff, who had been sent to arrest him for his first murder. It is said that in one Indian battle he killed three savages with his own hand, and afterward cut their ears off and sent them, with his compliments, to the chief of the tribe.

Slade soon gained a name for fearless resolution and this was sufficient merit to procure for him the important post of overland division-agent at Julesburg, in place of Mr. Jules [Beni or Reni], removed. For some time previously, the company's horses had been frequently stolen and the coaches delayed by gangs of outlaws, who were wont to laugh at the idea of any man's having the temerity to resent such outrages. Slade resented them promptly.

The outlaws soon found that the new agent was a man who did not fear anything that breathed the breath of life. He made short work of all offenders. The result was that delays ceased, the company's property was let alone, and no matter what happened or who suffered, Slade's coaches went through every time!

True, in order to bring about this wholesome change, Slade had to kill several men—some say three, others say four, and others six—but the world was the richer for their loss. The first prominent difficulty he had was with the ex-agent Jules, who bore the reputation of being a reckless and desperate man himself. Jules hated Slade for supplanting him and a good fair occasion for a fight was all he was waiting for. By and by Slade dared to employ a man whom Jules had once discharged. Next, Slade seized a team of stage-horses which he accused Jules of having driven off and hidden somewhere for his own use.

War was declared and for a day or two the two men walked warily about the streets, seeking each other, Jules armed with a double-barreled shot gun, and Slade with his history-creating revolver. Finally, as Slade stepped into a store, Jules poured the contents of his gun into him from behind the door. Slade was plucky and Jules got several bad pistol wounds in return.

Then both men fell and were carried to their respective lodgings, both swearing that better aim should do deadlier work next time. Both were bedridden a long time, but Jules got to his feet first, and gathering his possessions together, packed them on a couple of mules, and fled to the Rocky Mountains to gather strength in safety against the day of reckoning.

For many months he was not seen or heard of and was gradually dropped out of the remembrance of all save Slade himself. But Slade was not the man to forget him. On the contrary, common report said that Slade kept a reward standing for his capture, dead or alive!

After awhile, seeing that Slade's energetic administration had restored peace and order to one of the worst divisions of the road, the overland stage company transferred him to the Rocky Ridge division in the Rocky Mountains to see if he could perform a like miracle there.

It was the very paradise of outlaws and desperadoes. There was absolutely no semblance of law there. Violence was the rule. Force was the only recognized authority. The commonest misunderstandings were settled on the spot with the revolver or the knife. Murders were done in open day and with sparkling frequency, and nobody thought of inquiring into them.

It was considered that the parties who did the killing had their private reasons for it; for other people to meddle would have been looked upon as indelicate. After a murder, all that Rocky Mountain etiquette required of a spectator was that he should help the gentleman bury his game—otherwise his churlishness would surely be remembered against him the first time he killed a man himself and needed a neighborly turn in interring him.

Slade took up his residence sweetly and peacefully in the midst of this hive of horse-thieves and assassins, and the very first time one of them aired his insolent swaggerings in his presence he shot him dead!

He began a raid on the outlaws and in a singularly short space of time he had completely stopped their depredations on the stage stock, recovered a large number of stolen horses, killed several of the worst desperadoes of the district, and gained such a dread ascendancy over the rest that they respected him, admired him, feared him, obeyed him!

He wrought the same marvelous change in the ways of the community that had marked his administration at Overland City. He captured two men who had stolen overland stock and with his own hands, he hanged them. He was supreme judge in his district and he was jury and executioner likewise—and not only in the case of offences against his employers, but against passing emigrants as well. On one occasion some emigrants had their stock lost or stolen, and told Slade, who chanced to visit their camp. With a single companion he rode to a ranch, the owners of which he suspected, and opening the door, commenced firing, killing three, and wounding the fourth.

From a bloodthirstily interesting little Montana book.—*The Vigilantes of Montana*, by Prof. Thos. J. Dimsdale—I take this paragraph:

"While on the road, Slade held absolute sway. He would ride down to a station, get into a quarrel, turn the house out of windows, and maltreat the occupants most cruelly. The unfortunates had no means of redress, and were compelled to recuperate as best they could. On one of these occasions, it is said he killed the father of the fine little boy, Jemmy, whom he adopted and who lived with his widow after his execution. Stories of Slade's hanging men and of innumerable assaults, shootings, stabbings and beatings, in which he was a principal actor, form part of the legends of the stage line. As for minor quarrels and shootings, it is absolutely certain that a minute history of Slade's life would be one long record of such practices."

Slade was a matchless marksman with a navy revolver. The legends say that one morning at Rocky Ridge, when he was feeling comfortable, he saw a man approaching who had offended him some days before—observe the fine memory he had for matters like that—and, "Gentlemen," said Slade, drawing, "it is a good twenty-yard shot—I'll clip the third button on his coat!" Which he did. The bystanders all admired it. And they all attended the funeral, too.

On one occasion a man who kept a little whisky-shelf at the station did something which angered Slade—and went and made his will. A day or two afterward Slade came in and called for some brandy. The man reached under the counter (ostensibly to get a bottle—possibly to get something else), but Slade smiled upon him that peculiarly bland and satisfied smile of his which the neighbors had long ago learned to recognize as a death-warrant in disguise, and told him to "none of that!—pass out the high-priced article."

So the poor bar-keeper had to turn his back and get the high-priced brandy from the shelf; and when he faced around again he was looking into the muzzle of Slade's pistol.

"And the next instant," added my informant, impressively, "he was one of the deadest men that ever lived."

The stage-drivers and conductors told us that sometimes Slade would leave a hated enemy wholly unmolested, unnoticed and unmentioned, for weeks together—had done it once or twice at any rate. And some said they believed he did it in order to lull the victims into unwatchfulness, so that he could get the advantage of them, and others said they believed he saved up an enemy that way, just as a schoolboy saves up a cake, and made the pleasure go as far as it would by gloating over the anticipation.

One of these cases was that of a Frenchman who had offended Slade. To the surprise of everybody Slade did not kill him on the spot, but let him alone for a considerable time. Finally, however, he went to the Frenchman's house very late one night, knocked, and when his enemy opened the door, shot him dead—pushed the corpse inside the door with his foot, set the house on fire and burned up the dead man, his widow and three children!

I heard this story from several different people, and they evidently believed what they were saying. It may be true, and it may not. "Give a dog a bad name," etc.

Slade was captured, once, by a party of men who intended to lynch him. They disarmed him and shut him up in a strong log-house, and placed a guard over him. He prevailed on his captors to send for his wife [Maria Virginia Slade], so that he might have a last interview with her. She was a brave, loving, spirited woman. She jumped on a horse and rode for life and death. When she arrived they let her in without searching her, and before the door could be closed she whipped out a couple of revolvers and she and her lord marched forth defying the party. And then, under a brisk fire, they mounted double and galloped away unharmed!

In the fullness of time Slade's myrmidons captured his ancient enemy Jules, whom they found in a well-chosen hiding-place in the remote fastnesses of the mountains,

PONY EXPRESS!

CHANGE OF TIME!   REDUCED RATES!

10 Days to San Francisco!

LETTERS

WILL BE RECEIVED AT THE

OFFICE, 84 BROADWAY,

NEW YORK,

Up to **4** P. M. every TUESDAY,

AND

Up to **2½** P. M. every SATURDAY,

Which will be forwarded to connect with the PONY EXPRESS leaving
ST. JOSEPH, Missouri,

Every WEDNESDAY and SATURDAY at 11 P. M.

TELEGRAMS

Sent to Fort Kearney on the mornings of MONDAY and FRIDAY, will connect with **PONY** leaving St. Joseph, WEDNESDAYS and SATURDAYS.

EXPRESS CHARGES.

LETTERS weighing half ounce or under..............$1 00
For every additional half ounce or fraction of an ounce 1 00
In all cases to be enclosed in 10 cent Government Stamped Envelopes,
And all Express CHARGES Pre-paid.

☞ PONY EXPRESS ENVELOPES For Sale at our Office.

WELLS, FARGO & CO., Ag'ts.

New York, Ju'y 1, 1861.

SLOTE & JANES, STATIONERS AND PRINTERS, 82 FULTON STREET, NEW YORK gaining a precarious livelihood with his rifle. They brought him to Rocky Ridge, bound hand and foot, and deposited him in the middle of the cattle-yard with his back against a post.

It is said that the pleasure that lit Slade's face when he heard of it was something fearful to contemplate. He examined his enemy to see that he was securely tied, and then went to bed, content to wait till morning before enjoying the luxury of killing him. Jules spent the night in the cattle-yard, and it is a region where warm nights are never known.

In the morning Slade practiced on him with his revolver, nipping the flesh here and there, and occasionally clipping off a finger, while Jules begged him to kill him outright and put him out of his misery. Finally Slade reloaded, and walking up close to his victim, made some characteristic remarks and then dispatched him.

The body lay there half a day, nobody venturing to touch it without orders, and then Slade detailed a party and assisted at the burial himself. But he first cut off the dead man's ears and put them in his vest pocket where he carried them for some time with great satisfaction.

That is the story as I have frequently heard it told and seen it in print in California newspapers. It is doubtless correct in all essential particulars.

In due time we rattled up to a stage-station and sat down to breakfast with a half-savage, half-civilized company of armed and bearded mountaineers, ranchmen and station employees. The most gentlemanly appearing, quiet and affable officer we had yet found along the road in the Overland Company's service was the person who sat at the head of the table at my elbow. Never youth stared and shivered as I did when I heard them call him SLADE!

Here was romance, and I sitting face to face with it!—looking upon it—touching it—hobnobbing with it, as it were!

Here, right by my side, was the actual ogre who, in fights and brawls and various ways, *had taken the lives of twenty-six human beings,* or all men lied about him!

I suppose I was the proudest stripling that ever traveled to see strange lands and wonderful people.

He was so friendly and so gentle-spoken that I warmed to him in spite of his awful history. It was hardly possible to realize that this pleasant person was the pitiless scourge of the outlaws, the raw-head-and-bloody-bones the nursing mothers of the mountains terrified their children with. And to this day I can remember nothing remarkable about Slade except that his face was rather broad across the cheek bones, and that the cheek bones were low and the lips peculiarly thin and straight. But that was enough to leave something of an effect upon me, for since then I seldom see a face possessing those characteristics without fancying that the owner of it is a dangerous man.

The coffee ran out. At least it was reduced to one tin-cupful and Slade was about to take it when he saw that my cup was empty.

He politely offered to fill it, but although I wanted it, I politely declined. I was afraid he had not killed anybody that morning and might be needing diversion. But still with firm politeness he insisted on filling my cup, and said I had traveled all night and better deserved it than he—and while he talked he placidly poured the fluid to the last drop.

I thanked him and drank it, but it gave me no comfort, for I could not feel sure that he would not be sorry, presently, that he had given it away and proceed to kill me to distract his thoughts from the loss.

But nothing of the kind occurred. We left him with only twenty-six dead people to account for, and I felt a tranquil satisfaction in the thought that in so judiciously taking care of No. 1 at that breakfast-table I had pleasantly escaped being No. 27.

Slade came out to the coach and saw us off, first ordering certain rearrangements of the mail-bags for our comfort, and then we took leave of him, satisfied that we should hear of him again, some day, and wondering in what connection.

And sure enough, two or three years afterward, we did hear him again. News came to the Pacific coast that the Vigilance Committee in Montana (whither Slade had removed from Rocky Ridge) had hanged him.

I find an account of the affair in the thrilling little book I quoted a paragraph from in the last chapter—*The Vigilantes of Montana; being a Reliable Account of the Capture, Trial and Execution of Henry Plummer's Notorious Road Agent Band*: By Prof. Thos. J. Dimsdale, Virginia City, M.T. [Montana Territory].

Mr. Dimsdale's chapter is well worth reading as a specimen of how the people of the frontier deal with criminals when the courts of law prove inefficient. Mr. Dimsdale makes two remarks about Slade, both of which are accurately descriptive and one of which is exceedingly picturesque: "Those who saw him in his natural state only, would pronounce him to be a kind husband, a most hospitable host and a courteous gentleman; on the contrary, those who met him when maddened with liquor and surrounded by a gang of armed roughs, would pronounce him a fiend incarnate."

And this: "From Fort Kearney, west, he was feared *a great deal more than the Almighty.*"

For compactness, simplicity and vigor of expression, I will "back" that sentence against anything in literature.

Mr. Dimsdale's narrative is as follows. In all places where italics occur, they are mine:

After the execution of the five men on the 14th of January, the Vigilantes considered that their work was nearly ended. They had freed the country of highwaymen and murderers to a great extent, and they determined that in the absence of the regular civil authority they would establish a People's Court where all offenders should be tried by judge and jury.

This was the nearest approach to social order that the circumstances permitted, and, though strict legal authority was wanting, yet the people were firmly determined to maintain its efficiency and to enforce its decrees. It may here be mentioned that the overt act which was the last round on the fatal ladder leading to the scaffold on which Slade perished, *was the tearing in pieces and stamping upon a writ of this court, followed by his arrest of the Judge Alex. Davis, by authority of a presented Derringer, and with his own hands.*

J. A. Slade was himself, we have been informed, a Vigilante; he openly boasted of it, and said he knew all that they knew. He was never accused, or even suspected, of either murder or robbery committed in this Territory (the latter crime was never laid to his charge, in any place); but that he had killed several men in other localities was notorious, and his bad reputation in this respect was a most powerful argument in determining his fate when he was finally arrested for the offence above mentioned.

On returning from Milk River he became more and more addicted to drinking, until at last it was a common feat for him and his friends to "take the town." He and a couple of his dependents might often be seen on one horse, galloping through the streets, shouting and yelling, firing revolvers, etc. On many occasions he would ride his horse into stores, break up bars, toss the scales out of doors and use most insulting language to parties present.

Just previous to the day of his arrest, he had given a fearful beating to one of his followers; but such was his influence over them that the man wept bitterly at the gallows and begged for his life with all his power.

It had become quite common, when Slade was on a spree, for the shopkeepers and citizens to close the stores and put out all the lights; being fearful of some outrage at his hands. For his wanton destruction of goods and furniture, he was always ready to pay, when sober, if he had money; but there were not a few who regarded payment as small satisfaction for the outrage, and these men were his personal enemies.

From time to time Slade received warnings from men that he well knew would not deceive him, of the certain end of his conduct. There was not a moment, for weeks previous to his arrest, in which the public did not expect to hear of some bloody outrage. The dread of his very name and the presence of the armed band of hangers-on who followed him, alone prevented a resistance which must certainly have ended in the instant murder or mutilation of the opposing party.

Slade was frequently arrested by order of the court whose organization we have described, and had treated it with respect by paying one or two fines and promising to pay the rest when he had money; but in the transaction that occurred at this crisis, he forgot even this caution, and goaded by passion and the hatred of restraint, he sprang into the embrace of death.

Slade had been drunk and "cutting up" all night. He and his companions had made the town a perfect hell. In the morning, J. M. Fox, the sheriff, met him, arrested him, took him into court and commenced reading a warrant that he had for his arrest, by way of arraignment. He became uncontrollably furious, *and seizing the writ, he tore it up, threw it on the ground and stamped upon it.*

The clicking of the locks of his companions' revolvers was instantly heard and a crisis was expected. The sheriff did not attempt his retention; but being at least as prudent as he was valiant, he succumbed, leaving Slade the *master of the situation and the conqueror and ruler of the courts, law and lawmakers.*

This was a declaration of war, and was so accepted. The Vigilance Committee now felt that the question of social order and the preponderance of the law-abiding citizens had then and there to be decided. They knew the character of Slade, and they were well aware that they must submit to his rule without murmur, or else that he must be dealt with in such fashion as would prevent his being able to wreak his vengeance on the committee, who could never have hoped to live in the Territory secure from outrage or death, and who could never leave it without encountering his friend, whom his victory would have emboldened and stimulated to a pitch that would have rendered them reckless of consequences.

The day previous he had ridden into Dorris's store, and on being requested to leave, he drew his revolver and threatened to kill the gentleman who spoke to him. Another saloon he had led his horse into, and buying a bottle of wine, he tried to make the animal drink it. This was not considered an uncommon performance, as he had often entered saloons and commenced firing at the lamps, causing a wild stampede.

A leading member of the committee met Slade and informed him in the quiet, earnest manner of one who feels the importance of what he is saying: "Slade, get your horse at once and go home, or there will be hell to pay."

Slade started and took a long look with his dark and piercing eyes at the gentleman.

"What do you mean?" said he.

"You have no right to ask me what I mean," was the quiet reply, "get your horse at once and remember what I tell you."

After a short pause he promised to do so, and actually got into the saddle; but, being still intoxicated, he began calling aloud to one after another of his friends, and at last seemed to have forgotten the warning he had received and became again uproarious, shouting the name of a well-known courtesan in company with those of two men whom he considered heads of the committee, as a sort of challenge; perhaps, however, as a simple act of bravado.

It seems probable that the intimation of personal danger he had received had not been forgotten entirely; though fatally for him, he took a foolish way of showing his remembrance of it. He sought out Alexander Davis, the Judge of the Court, and drawing a cocked Derringer, he presented it at his head and told him that he should hold him as a hostage for his own safety. As the judge stood perfectly quiet and offered no resistance to his captor, no further outrage followed on this score.

Previous to this, on account of the critical state of affairs, the committee had met, and at last resolved to arrest him. His execution had not been agreed upon, and, at that time, would have been negatived, most assuredly.

A messenger rode down to Nevada ffiCampffl to inform the leading men of what was on hand, as it was desirable to show that there was a feeling of unanimity on the subject, all along the gulch.

The miners turned out almost en masse, leaving their work and forming in solid column about six hundred strong, armed to the teeth, they marched up to Virginia ffiCityffl. The leader of the body well knew the temper of his men on the subject. He spurred on ahead of them and hastily calling a meeting of the executive, he told them plainly that the miners meant "business," and that, if they came up, they would not stand in the street to be shot down by Slade's friends; but that they would take him and hang him.

The meeting was small, as the Virginia men were loath to act at all. This momentous announcement of the feeling of the Lower Town was made to a cluster of men, who were deliberating behind a wagon at the rear of a store on Main street.

The committee were most unwilling to proceed to extremities. All the duty they had ever performed seemed as nothing to the task before them; but they had to decide, and that quickly. It was finally agreed that if the whole body of the miners were of the opinion that he should be hanged, that the committee left it in their hands to deal with him. Off, at hot speed, rode the leader of the Nevada men to join his command.

Slade had found out what was intended, and the news sobered him instantly. He went into P. S. Pfouts' store, where Davis was, and apologized for his conduct, saying that he would take it all back.

The head of the column now wheeled into Wallace street and marched up at quick time. Halting in front of the store, the executive officer of the committee stepped forward and arrested Slade, who was at once informed of his doom, and inquiry was made as to whether he had any business to settle.

Several parties spoke to him on the subject; but to all such inquiries he turned a deaf ear, being entirely absorbed in the terrifying reflections on his own awful position. He never ceased his entreaties for life, and to see his dear wife. The unfortunate lady referred to, between whom and Slade there existed a warm affection, was at this time living at their ranch on the Madison. She was possessed of considerable personal attractions; tall, well-formed, of graceful carriage, pleasing manners, and was, withal, an accomplished horsewoman.

A messenger from Slade rode at full speed to inform her of her husband's arrest. In an instant she was in the saddle and with all the energy that love and despair could lend to an ardent temperament and a strong physique, she urged her fleet charger over the twelve miles of rough and rocky ground that intervened between her and the object of her passionate devotion.

Meanwhile a party of volunteers had made the necessary preparations for the execution, in the valley traversed by the branch. Beneath the site of Pfouts and Russell's stone building there was a corral, the gateposts of which were strong and high. Across the top was laid a beam to which the rope was fastened, and a dry-goods box served for the platform.

To this place Slade was marched, surrounded by a guard, composing the best armed and most numerous force that has ever appeared in Montana Territory.

The doomed man had so exhausted himself by tears, prayers and lamentations, that he had scarcely strength left to stand under the fatal beam. He repeatedly exclaimed, "My God! my God! must I die? Oh, my dear wife!"

On the return of the fatigue party, they encountered some friends of Slade, staunch and reliable citizens and members of the committee, but who were personally attached to the condemned. On hearing of his sentence, one of them—a stout-hearted man—pulled out his handkerchief and walked away, weeping like a child.

Slade still begged to see his wife, most piteously, and it seemed hard to deny his request; but the bloody consequences that were sure to follow the inevitable attempt at a rescue that her presence and entreaties would have certainly incited, forbade the granting of his request.

Several gentlemen were sent for to see him in his last moments, one of whom Judge Davis made a short address to the people, but in such low tones as to be inaudible, save to a few in his immediate vicinity.

One of his friends, after exhausting his powers of entreaty, threw off his coat and declared that the prisoner could not be hanged until he himself was killed. A hundred guns were instantly leveled at him; whereupon he turned and fled; but, being brought back, he was compelled to resume his coat and to give a promise of future peaceable demeanor.

Scarcely a leading man in Virginia could be found, though numbers of the citizens joined the ranks of the guard when the arrest was made. All lamented the stern necessity which dictated the execution.

Everything being ready, the command was given, "Men, do your duty," and the box being instantly slipped from beneath his feet, he died almost instantaneously.

The body was cut down and carried to the Virginia Hotel, where, in a darkened room, it was scarcely laid out when the unfortunate and bereaved companion of the deceased arrived at headlong speed to find that all was over and that she was a widow. Her grief and heart-piercing cries were terrible evidences of the depth of her attachment for her lost husband, and a considerable period elapsed before she could regain the command of her excited feelings.

There is something about the desperado-nature that is wholly unaccountable—at least it looks unaccountable. It is this. The true desperado is gifted with splendid courage, and yet he will take the most infamous advantage of his enemy; armed and free, he will stand up before a host and fight until he is shot all to pieces, and yet when he is under the gallows and helpless he will cry and plead like a child.

Words are cheap and it is easy to call Slade a coward (all executed men who do not "die game" are promptly called cowards by unreflecting people), and when we read of Slade that he "had so exhausted himself by tears, prayers and lamentations, that he had scarcely strength left to stand under the fatal beam," the disgraceful word suggests itself in a moment—yet in frequently defying and inviting the vengeance of banded Rocky Mountain cut-throats by shooting down their comrades and leaders, and never offering to hide or fly, Slade showed that he was a man of peerless bravery. No coward would dare that.

Many a notorious coward, many a chicken-livered poltroon, coarse, brutal, degraded, has made his dying speech without a quaver in his voice and been swung into eternity with what looked liked the calmest fortitude, and so we are justified in believing—from the low intellect of such a creature—that it was not *moral* courage that enabled him to do it.

Then, if moral courage is not the requisite quality, what could it have been that this stout-hearted Slade lacked?—this bloody, desperate, kindly-mannered, urbane gentleman, who never hesitated to warn his most ruffianly enemies that he would kill them whenever or wherever he came across them next! I think it is a conundrum worth investigating.

Much of what Twain wrote is fact, some is fiction, and some exaggeration. Legends paint Jack Slade as a mad killer, which might overstate the reality, though it is known that he killed at least two people. One of Slade's victims, Jules Beni, was a stage line district superintendent and also part of a gang of outlaws who robbed those stages. It's thought Slade was unarmed when Beni shot him with a shotgun. Beni left him for dead, but Slade recovered and later took his revenge. It's not known whether Slade tortured Beni before killing him, but he did keep Beni's ears on his watch chain. It's also likely that Slade presided over the lynchings of some stage robbers and horse thieves.

Slade's father had been a congressman and U.S. Marshal for Illinois. Those who knew Slade describe him as generous and considerate, and he was a competent manager for the Overland Stage Line, but he was very aggressive and dangerous when drunk. Eventually he was fired after a drunken spree. Moving on to Virginia City, Montana, he was soon arrested for shooting up a saloon and tearing up his arrest warrant. Even though he was a member of the Committee on Vigilance, the vigilantes made Slade dance the "Strangulation Jig" on March 10, 1864.

There is more to the story than can be presented here, but like many Wild West figures, Slade may have been a deadly desperado to some people, while a hero to others.

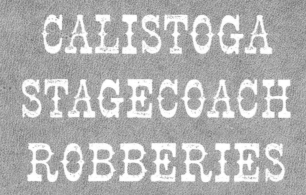

CALISTOGA STAGECOACH ROBBERIES

by
Robert Louis Stevenson

Calistoga, California is about seventy miles north of San Francisco at the northern end of the Napa Valley. It is near the base of Mount St. Helena and about five miles from the ghost town where Robert Louis Stevenson and his wife honeymooned in 1880. Settlers began arriving in that area by 1831; at first because of the volcanic geysers and hot springs—later because of the mines and wineries.

I t is difficult for a European to imagine Calistoga; the whole place is so new, and of such an occidental pattern; the very name, I hear, was invented at a supper-party by the man who found the springs.

The railroad and the highway come up the valley about parallel to one another. The street of Calistoga joins them, perpendicular to both—a wide street, with bright, clean, low houses, here and there a veranda over the sidewalk, here and there a horse-post, here and there lounging townsfolk. Other streets are marked out, and most likely named; for these towns in the New World begin with a firm resolve to grow larger, Washington and Broadway, and then First and Second, and so forth, being boldly plotted out as soon as the community indulges in a plan. But, in the meanwhile, all the life and most of the houses of Calistoga are concentrated upon that street between the railway-station and the road. I never heard it called by any name, but I will hazard a guess that it is either Washington or Broadway. Here are the blacksmith's, the chemist's, the general merchant's, and Kong Sam Kee, the Chinese laundryman's; here, probably, is the office of the local paper (for the place has a paper—they all have papers); and here certainly is one of the hotels, Cheeseborough's, whence the daring Foss, a man dear to legend, starts his horses for the geysers.

It must be remembered that we are here in a land of stage-drivers and highway-men—a land, in that sense, like England a hundred years ago. The highway robber—road-agent, he is quaintly called—is still busy in these parts. The fame of Vasquez is still young. Only a few years ago the Lakeport stage was robbed a mile or two from Calistoga. In 1879, the dentist of Mendocino City, fifty miles away up on the coast, suddenly threw off the garments of his trade, like Grindoff in "The Miller and his Men," and flamed forth in his second dress as a captain of banditti.

A great robbery was followed by a long chase, a chase of days if not of weeks, among the intricate hill-country; and the chase was followed by much desultory fighting, in which several—and the dentist, I believe, among the number—bit the dust. The grass was springing for the first time, nourished upon their blood, when I arrived in Calistoga. I am reminded of another highwayman of that same year. "He had been unwell," so ran his humorous defense, "and the doctor told him to take something, so he took the express-box."

The cultus of the stage-coachman always flourishes highest where there are thieves on the road, and where the guard travels armed, and the stage is not only a link between country and city, and the vehicle of news, but has a faint war-faring aroma, like a man who should be brother to a soldier.

California boasts her famous stage-drivers, and among the famous, Foss is not forgotten. Along the unfenced, abominable mountain roads, he launches his team with small regard to human life or the doctrine of probabilities. Flinching travellers, who behold themselves coasting eternity at every corner, look with natural admiration at their driver's huge, impassive, fleshy countenance. He has the very face for the driver in Sam Weller's anecdote, who upset the election party at the required point. Wonderful tales are current of his readiness and skill. One in particular, of how one of his horses fell at a ticklish passage of the road, and how Foss let slip the reins, and, driving over the fallen animal, arrived at the next stage with only three.

This I relate as I heard it, without guarantee.[…]

I only saw Foss once, though, strange as it may sound, I have twice talked with him. He lives out of Calistoga, at a ranch called Fossville. One evening, after he was long gone home, I dropped into Cheeseborough's, and was asked if I should like to speak with Mr. Foss.

Supposing that the interview was impossible, and that I was merely called upon to subscribe the general sentiment, I boldly answered "Yes." Next moment, I had one instrument at my ear, another at my mouth, and found myself, with nothing in the world to say, conversing with a man several miles off among desolate hills. Foss rapidly and somewhat plaintively brought the conversation to an end; and he returned to his night's grog at Fossville, while I strolled forth again on Calistoga high street. But it was an odd thing that here, on what we are accustomed to consider the very skirts of civilization, I should have used the telephone for the first time in my civilized career. So it goes in these young countries ; telephones, and telegraphs, and newspapers, and advertisements running far ahead among the Indians and the grizzly bears.

A POET'S WESTERN JOURNEY

by
Walt Whitman

In 1879, American poet Walt Whitman (1819–1892) took a three- to four-month journey into the American West. This was only three years after Wild Bill Hickok was murdered in Deadwood and Custer was killed at Little Bighorn.

Whitman traveled primarily by train along the route of the Kansas Pacific Railroad from Kansas City, Missouri, to the Pacific, which was just part of the first true coast-to-coast railway network in the United States, since—at the time of its completion just nine years earlier—travelers on the First Transcontinental Railroad to the north still had to cross the Mississippi by boat.

During his journey, Whitman recorded his impressions of the stunning landscapes of West, infused with his own unique poetical style.

NEW SENSES—NEW JOYS

We follow the stream of amber and bronze brawling along its bed, with its frequent cascades and snow-white foam. Through the canyon we fly—mountains not only each side, but seemingly, till we get near, right in front of us—every rood a new view flashing, and each flash defying description—on the almost perpendicular sides, clinging pines, cedars, spruces, crimson sumach bushes, spots of wild grass—but dominating all, those towering rocks, rocks, rocks, bathed in delicate vari-colors, with the clear sky of autumn overhead. New senses, new joys, seem develop'd. Talk as you like, a typical Rocky Mountain canyon, or a limitless sea-like stretch of the great Kansas or Colorado plains, under favoring circumstances, tallies, perhaps expresses, certainly awakes, those grandest and subtlest element-emotions in the human soul, that all the marble temples and sculptures from Phidias to Thorwaldsen—all paintings, poems, reminiscences, or even music, probably never can.

STEAM-POWER, TELEGRAPHS, ETC.

I get out on a ten minutes' stoppage at Deer creek, to enjoy the unequal'd combination of hill, stone and wood. As we speed again, the yellow granite in the sunshine, with natural spires, minarets, castellated perches far aloft—then long stretches of straight-

upright palisades, rhinoceros color—then gamboge and tinted chromos. Ever the best of my pleasures the cool-fresh Colorado atmosphere, yet sufficiently warm. Signs of man's restless advent and pioneerage, hard as Nature's face is—deserted dug-outs by dozens in the side-hills—the scantling-hut, the telegraph-pole, the smoke of some impromptu chimney or outdoor fire—at intervals little settlements of log-houses, or parties of surveyors or telegraph builders, with their comfortable tents. Once, a canvas office where you could send a message by electricity anywhere around the world! Yes, pronounc'd signs of the man of latest dates, dauntlessly grappling with these grisliest shows of the old kosmos. At several places steam saw-mills, with their piles of logs and boards, and the pipes puffing.

Occasionally Platte canyon expanding into a grassy flat of a few acres. At one such place, toward the end, where we stop, and I get out to stretch my legs, as I look skyward, or rather mountain-topward, a huge hawk or eagle (a rare sight here) is idly soaring, balancing along the ether, now sinking low and coming quite near, and then up again in stately-languid circles—then higher, higher, slanting to the north, and gradually out of sight.[…]

But perhaps as I gaze around me the rarest sight of all is in atmospheric hues. The prairies—as I cross'd them in my journey hither—and these mountains and parks, seem to me to afford new lights and shades. Everywhere the aerial gradations and sky-effects inimitable; nowhere else such perspectives, such transparent lilacs and grays. I can conceive of some superior landscape painter, some fine colorist, after sketching awhile out here, discarding all his previous work, delightful to stock exhibition amateurs, as muddy, raw and artificial. Near one's eye ranges an infinite variety; high up, the bare whitey-brown, above timber line; in certain spots afar patches of snow any time of year; (no trees, no flowers, no birds, at those chilling altitudes.) As I write I see the Snowy Range through the blue mist, beautiful and far off, I plainly see the patches of snow.

DENVER IMPRESSIONS

Through the long-lingering half-light of the most superb of evenings we return'd to Denver, where I staid several days leisurely exploring, receiving impressions, with which I may as well taper off this memorandum, itemizing what I saw there. The best was the men, three-fourths of them large, able, calm, alert, American. And cash! why they create it here [at the Denver mint]. Out in the smelting works—the biggest and most improv'd ones for the precious metals in the world—I saw long rows of vats, pans, cover'd by bubbling-boiling water, and fill'd with pure silver, four or five inches thick, many thousand dollars' worth in a pan.

The foreman who was showing me shovel'd it carelessly up with a little wooden shovel, as one might toss beans. Then large silver bricks, worth $2,000 a brick, dozens of piles, twenty in a pile. In one place in the mountains, at a mining camp, I had a few days before seen rough bullion on the ground in the open air, like the confectioner's pyramids at some swell dinner in New York. (Such a sweet morsel to roll over with a poor author's pen and ink—and appropriate to slip in here—that the silver product of Colorado and Utah, with the gold product of California, New Mexico, Nevada and Dakota, foots up an addition to the world's coin of considerably over a hundred millions every year.)

A city, this Denver, well-laid out—Laramie street, and 15th and 16th and Champa streets, with others, particularly fine—some with tall storehouses of stone or iron, and windows of plate-glass—all the streets with little canals of mountain water running along the sides—plenty of people, "business," modernness—yet not without a certain racy wild smack, all its own. A place of fast horses, (many mares with their colts,) and I saw lots of big greyhounds for antelope hunting. Now and then groups of miners, some just come in, some starting out, very picturesque.

One of the papers here interview'd me, and reported me as saying off-hand: "I have lived in or visited all the great cities on the Atlantic third of the republic— Boston, Brooklyn with its hills, New Orleans, Baltimore, stately Washington, broad Philadelphia, teeming Cincinnati and Chicago, and for thirty years in that wonder, wash'd by hurried and glittering tides, my own New York, not only the New World's but the world's city—but, newcomer to Denver as I am, and threading its streets, breathing its air, warm'd by its sunshine, and having what there is of its human as well as aerial ozone flash'd upon me now for only three or four days, I am very much like a man feels sometimes toward certain people he meets with, and warms to, and hardly knows why. I, too, can hardly tell why, but as I enter'd the city in the slight haze of a late September afternoon, and have breath'd its air, and slept well o' nights, and have roam'd or rode leisurely, and watch'd the comers and goers at the hotels, and absorb'd the climatic magnetism of this curiously attractive region, there has steadily grown upon me a feeling of affection for the spot, which, sudden as it is, has become so definite and strong that I must put it on record."

So much for my feeling toward the Queen city of the plains and peaks, where she sits in her delicious rare atmosphere, over 5000 feet above sea-level, irrigated by mountain streams, one way looking east over the prairies for a thousand miles, and having the other, westward, in constant view by day, draped in their violet haze, mountain tops innumerable. Yes, I fell in love with Denver, and even felt a wish to spend my declining and dying days there.[…]

THE PRAIRIES AND GREAT PLAINS IN POETRY

(*After traveling Illinois, Missouri, Kansas, and Colorado.*)

Grand as is the thought that doubtless the child is already born who will see a hundred millions of people, the most prosperous and advanc'd of the world, inhabiting these Prairies, the great Plains, and the valley of the Mississippi, I could not help thinking it would be grander still to see all those inimitable American areas fused in the alembic of a perfect poem, or other esthetic work, entirely western, fresh and limitless—altogether our own, without a trace or taste of Europe's soil, reminiscence, technical letter or spirit.

My days and nights, as I travel here—what an exhilaration!—not the air alone, and the sense of vastness, but every local sight and feature. Everywhere something characteristic—the cactuses, pinks, buffalo grass, wild sage—the receding perspective, and the far circle-line of the horizon all times of day, especially forenoon—the clear, pure, cool, rarefied nutriment for the lungs, previously quite unknown—the black patches and streaks left by surface-conflagrations—the deep-plough'd furrow of the "fire-guard"—the slanting snow-racks built all along to shield the railroad from winter drifts—the prairie-dogs and the herds of antelope—the curious "dry rivers"—occasionally a "dug-out" or corral—Fort Riley and Fort Wallace—those towns of the northern plains, (like ships on the sea,) Eagle-Tail, Coyote, Cheyenne, Agate, Monotony, Kit Carson—with ever the ant-hill and the buffalo-wallow—ever the herds of cattle and the cow-boys ("cow-punchers") to me a strangely interesting class, bright-eyed as hawks, with their swarthy complexions and their broad-brimm'd hats—apparently always on horseback, with loose arms slightly raised and swinging as they ride.

THE SPANISH PEAKS—EVENING ON THE PLAINS

Between Pueblo and Bent's fort, southward, in a clear afternoon sun-spell I catch exceptionally good glimpses of the Spanish peaks. We are in southeastern Colorado— pass immense herds of cattle as our first-class locomotive rushes us along—two or three times crossing the Arkansas, which we follow many miles, and of which river I get fine views, sometimes for quite a distance, its stony, upright, not very high, palisade banks, and then its muddy flats.

We pass Fort Lyon—lots of adobe houses—limitless pasturage, appropriately fleck'd with those herds of cattle—in due time the declining sun in the west—a sky of limpid pearl over all—and so evening on the great plains. A calm, pensive, boundless land-scape—the perpendicular rocks of the north Arkansas, hued in twilight—a thin line of violet on the southwestern horizon—the palpable coolness and slight aroma—a belated cow-boy with some unruly member of his herd—an emigrant wagon toiling yet a little further, the horses slow and tired—two men, apparently father and son, jogging along on foot—and around all the indescribable chiaroscuro and sentiment, (profounder than anything at sea,) athwart these endless wilds.

WILD WEST
FICTIONS

ALL GOLD CANYON

by
Jack London

The author of White Fang *and* Call of the Wild, *Jack London (1876–1916) was born in San Francisco, the illegitimate son of a traveling astrologer. As a child, poverty forced him to work ten-hour days in a canning factory for ten cents an hour. At the age of fourteen he borrowed money to buy a small boat and joined in raids on privately owned oyster fields, before switching to the other side, working for law enforcement. When London was seventeen he signed on for a ship bound for Japan. On his return he became a hobo, traveling throughout the United States, spending ninety days in prison for vagrancy.*

In 1897 London left for the Klondike to take part in the gold rush there. On returning to San Francisco, he tried to make a living by writing, but had little luck until his adventure stories set in the Yukon began to be published. These were a tremendous success. An active socialist, he claimed he only wrote for money, saying, "if I could have my choice about it, I never would put pen to paper—except to write a socialist essay to tell the bourgeois world how much I despise it." But this didn't slow him down, for he wrote close to fifty books in seventeen years. His stories remain tremendously popular, largely for capturing the American ideal of rugged individualism.

This piece, set in a remote canyon, explores some of the hazards of greed and the lust for gold.

It was the green heart of the canyon, where the walls swerved back from the rigid plan and relieved their harshness of line by making a little sheltered nook and filling it to the brim with sweetness and roundness and softness. Here all things rested. Even the narrow stream ceased its turbulent down-rush long enough to form a quiet pool. Knee-deep in the water, with drooping head and half-shut eyes, drowsed a red-coated, many-antlered buck.

On one side, beginning at the very lip of the pool, was a tiny meadow, a cool, resilient surface of green that extended to the base of the frowning wall. Beyond the pool a gentle slope of earth ran up and up to meet the opposing wall. Fine grass covered the slope—grass that was spangled with flowers, with here and there patches of color, orange and purple and golden. Below, the canyon was shut in. There was no view. The walls leaned together abruptly and the canyon ended in a chaos of rocks, moss-covered and hidden by a green screen of vines and creepers and boughs of trees. Up the canyon rose far hills and peaks, the big foothills, pine-covered and remote. And far beyond, like clouds upon the border of the sky, towered minarets of white, where the Sierra's eternal snows flashed austerely the blazes of the sun.

There was no dust in the canyon. The leaves and flowers were clean and virginal. The grass was young velvet. Over the pool three cottonwoods sent their snowy fluffs fluttering down the quiet air. On the slope the blossoms of the wine-wooded manzanita filled the air with springtime odors, while the leaves, wise with experience, were already beginning their vertical twist against the coming aridity of summer. In the open spaces on the slope, beyond the farthest shadow-reach of the manzanita, poised the mariposa lilies, like so many flights of jewelled moths suddenly arrested and on the verge of trembling into flight again. Here and there that woods harlequin, the madrone, permitting itself to be caught in the act of changing its pea-green trunk to madder-red, breathed its fragrance into the air from great clusters of waxen bells. Creamy white were these bells, shaped like lilies-of-the-valley, with the sweetness of perfume that is of the springtime.

There was not a sigh of wind. The air was drowsy with its weight of perfume. It was a sweetness that would have been cloying had the air been heavy and humid. But the air was sharp and thin. It was as starlight transmuted into atmosphere, shot through and warmed by sunshine, and flower-drenched with sweetness.

An occasional butterfly drifted in and out through the patches of light and shade. And from all about rose the low and sleepy hum of mountain bees—feasting Sybarites that jostled one another good-naturedly at the board, nor found time for rough discourtesy. So quietly did the little stream drip and ripple its way through the canyon that it spoke only in faint and occasional gurgles. The voice of the stream was as a drowsy whisper, ever interrupted by dozings and silences, ever lifted again in the awakenings.

The motion of all things was a drifting in the heart of the canyon. Sunshine and butterflies drifted in and out among the trees. The hum of the bees and the whisper of the stream were a drifting of sound. And the drifting sound and drifting color seemed to weave together in the making of a delicate and intangible fabric which was the spirit of the place. It was a spirit of peace that was not of death, but of smooth-pulsing life, of quietude that was not silence, of movement that was not action, of repose that was quick with existence without being violent with struggle and travail. The spirit of the place was the spirit of the peace of the living, somnolent with the easement and content of prosperity, and undisturbed by rumors of far wars.

The red-coated, many-antlered buck acknowledged the lordship of the spirit of the place and dozed knee-deep in the cool, shaded pool. There seemed no flies to vex him and he was languid with rest. Sometimes his ears moved when the stream awoke and whispered; but they moved lazily, with foreknowledge that it was merely the stream grown garrulous at discovery that it had slept.

But there came a time when the buck's ears lifted and tensed with swift eagerness for sound. His head was turned down the canyon. His sensitive, quivering nostrils scented the air. His eyes could not pierce the green screen through which the stream rippled away, but to his ears came the voice of a man. It was a steady, monotonous, singsong voice. Once the buck heard the harsh clash of metal upon rock. At the sound he snorted with a sudden start that jerked him through the air from water to meadow, and his feet sank into the young velvet, while he pricked his ears and again scented the air. Then he stole across the tiny meadow, pausing once and again to listen, and faded away out of the canyon like a wraith, soft-footed and without sound.

The clash of steel-shod soles against the rocks began to be heard, and the man's voice grew louder. It was raised in a sort of chant and became distinct with nearness, so that the words could be heard:

> "Tu'n around an' tu'n yo' face
> Untoe them sweet hills of grace
> (D' pow'rs of sin yo' am scornin'!).
> Look about an' look aroun'
> Fling yo' sin-pack on d' groun'
> (Yo' will meet wid d' Lord in d' mornin'!)."

A sound of scrambling accompanied the song, and the spirit of the place fled away on the heels of the red-coated buck. The green screen was burst asunder, and a man peered out at the meadow and the pool and the sloping side-hill. He was a deliberate sort of man. He took in the scene with one embracing glance, then ran his eyes over the details to verify the general impression. Then, and not until then, did he open his mouth in vivid and solemn approval:

"Smoke of life an' snakes of purgatory! Will you just look at that! Wood an' water an' grass an' a side-hill! A pocket-hunter's delight an' a cayuse's paradise! Cool green for tired eyes! Pink pills for pale people ain't in it. A secret pasture for prospectors and a resting-place for tired burros. It's just booful!"

He was a sandy-complexioned man in whose face geniality and humor seemed the salient characteristics. It was a mobile face, quick-changing to inward mood and thought. Thinking was in him a visible process. Ideas chased across his face like wind-flaws across the surface of a lake. His hair, sparse and unkempt of growth, was as indeterminate and colorless as his complexion. It would seem that all the color of his frame had gone into his eyes, for they were startlingly blue. Also, they were laughing and merry eyes, within them much of the naiveté and wonder of the child; and yet, in an unassertive way, they contained much of calm self-reliance and strength of purpose founded upon self-experience and experience of the world.

From out the screen of vines and creepers he flung ahead of him a miner's pick and shovel and gold-pan. Then he crawled out himself into the open. He was clad in faded overalls and black cotton shirt, with hobnailed brogans on his feet, and on his head a hat whose shapelessness and stains advertised the rough usage of wind and rain and sun and camp-smoke. He stood erect, seeing wide-eyed the secrecy of the scene and sensuously inhaling the warm, sweet breath of the canyon-garden through nostrils that dilated and quivered with delight. His eyes narrowed to laughing slits of blue, his face wreathed itself in joy, and his mouth curled in a smile as he cried aloud:

"Jumping dandelions and happy hollyhocks, but that smells good to me! Talk about your attar o' roses an' cologne factories! They ain't in it!"

He had the habit of soliloquy. His quick-changing facial expressions might tell every thought and mood, but the tongue, perforce, ran hard after, repeating, like a second Boswell.

The man lay down on the lip of the pool and drank long and deep of its water. "Tastes good to me," he murmured, lifting his head and gazing across the pool at the side-hill, while he wiped his mouth with the back of his hand. The side-hill attracted his attention. Still lying on his stomach, he studied the hill formation long and carefully. It was a practised eye that traveled up the slope to the crumbling canyon-wall and back and down again to the edge of the pool. He scrambled to his feet and favored the side-hill with a second survey.

"Looks good to me," he concluded, picking up his pick and shovel and gold-pan.

He crossed the stream below the pool, stepping agilely from stone to stone. Where the side-hill touched the water he dug up a shovelful of dirt and put it into the gold-pan. He squatted down, holding the pan in his two hands, and partly immersing it in the stream. Then he imparted to the pan a deft circular motion that sent the water sluicing in and out through the dirt and gravel. The larger and the lighter particles worked to the surface, and these, by a skilful dipping movement of the pan, he spilled out and over the edge. Occasionally, to expedite matters, he rested the pan and with his fingers raked out the large pebbles and pieces of rock.

The contents of the pan diminished rapidly until only fine dirt and the smallest bits of gravel remained. At this stage he began to work very deliberately and carefully. It was fine washing, and he washed fine and finer, with a keen scrutiny and delicate and fastidious touch. At last the pan seemed empty of everything but water; but with a quick semi-circular flirt that sent the water flying over the shallow rim into the stream, he disclosed a layer of black sand on the bottom of the pan. So thin was this layer that it was like a streak of paint. He examined it closely. In the midst of it was a tiny golden speck. He dribbled a little water in over the depressed edge of the pan. With a quick flirt he sent the water sluicing across the bottom, turning the grains of black sand over and over. A second tiny golden speck rewarded his effort.

The washing had now become very fine—fine beyond all need of ordinary placer-mining. He worked the black sand, a small portion at a time, up the shallow rim of the pan. Each small portion he examined sharply, so that his eyes saw every grain of it before he allowed it to slide over the edge and away. Jealously, bit by bit, he let the black sand slip away. A golden speck, no larger than a pin-point, appeared on the rim, and by his manipulation of the water it returned to the bottom of the pan. And in such fashion another speck was disclosed, and another. Great was his care of them. Like a shepherd he herded his flock of golden specks so that not one should be lost. At last, of the pan of dirt nothing remained but his golden herd. He counted it, and then, after all his labor, sent it flying out of the pan with one final swirl of water.

But his blue eyes were shining with desire as he rose to his feet. "Seven," he muttered aloud, asserting the sum of the specks for which he had toiled so hard and which he had so wantonly thrown away. "Seven," he repeated, with the emphasis of one trying to impress a number on his memory.

He stood still a long while, surveying the hillside. In his eyes was a curiosity, new-aroused and burning. There was an exultance about his bearing and a keenness like that of a hunting animal catching the fresh scent of game.

He moved down the stream a few steps and took a second panful of dirt.

Again came the careful washing, the jealous herding of the golden specks, and the wantonness with which he sent them flying into the stream.

"Five," he muttered, and repeated, "five."

He could not forbear another survey of the hill before filling the pan farther down the stream. His golden herds diminished. "Four, three, two, two, one," were his memory tabulations as he moved down the stream. When but one speck of gold rewarded his washing, he stopped and built a fire of dry twigs. Into this he thrust the gold-pan and burned it till it was blue-black. He held up the pan and examined it critically. Then he nodded approbation. Against such a color-background he could defy the tiniest yellow speck to elude him.

Still moving down the stream, he panned again. A single speck was his reward. A third pan contained no gold at all. Not satisfied with this, he panned three times again, taking his shovels of dirt within a foot of one another. Each pan proved empty of gold, and the fact, instead of discouraging him, seemed to give him satisfaction. His elation increased with each barren washing, until he arose, exclaiming jubilantly:

"If it ain't the real thing, may God knock off my head with sour apples!"

Returning to where he had started operations, he began to pan up the stream. At first his golden herds increased—increased prodigiously. "Fourteen, eighteen, twenty-one, twenty-six," ran his memory tabulations. Just above the pool he struck his richest pan—thirty-five colors.

"Almost enough to save," he remarked regretfully as he allowed the water to sweep them away.

The sun climbed to the top of the sky. The man worked on. Pan by pan, he went up the stream, the tally of results steadily decreasing.

"It's just booful, the way it peters out," he exulted when a shovelful of dirt contained no more than a single speck of gold. And when no specks at all were found in several pans, he straightened up and favored the hillside with a confident glance.

"Ah, ha! Mr. Pocket!" he cried out, as though to an auditor hidden somewhere above him beneath the surface of the slope. "Ah, ha! Mr. Pocket! I'm a-comin,' I'm a-comin,' an' I'm shorely gwine to get yer! You heah me, Mr. Pocket? I'm gwine to get yer as shore as punkins ain't cauliflowers!"

He turned and flung a measuring glance at the sun poised above him in the azure of the cloudless sky. Then he went down the canyon, following the line of shovel-holes he had made in filling the pans. He crossed the stream below the pool and disappeared through the green screen. There was little opportunity for the spirit of the place to return with its quietude and repose, for the man's voice, raised in ragtime song, still dominated the canyon with possession.

After a time, with a greater clashing of steel-shod feet on rock, he returned. The green screen was tremendously agitated. It surged back and forth in the throes of a struggle. There was a loud grating and clanging of metal. The man's voice leaped to a higher pitch and was sharp with imperativeness. A large body plunged and panted. There was a snapping and ripping and rending, and amid a shower of falling leaves a horse burst through the screen. On its back was a pack, and from this trailed broken vines and torn creepers. The animal gazed with astonished eyes at the scene into which it had been precipitated, then dropped its head to the grass and began contentedly to graze. A second horse scrambled into view, slipping once on the mossy rocks and regaining equilibrium when its hoofs sank into the yielding surface of the meadow. It was riderless, though on its back was a high-horned Mexican saddle, scarred and discolored by long usage.

The man brought up the rear. He threw off pack and saddle, with an eye to camp location, and gave the animals their freedom to graze. He unpacked his food and got out frying-pan and coffee-pot. He gathered an armful of dry wood, and with a few stones made a place for his fire.

"My!" he said, "but I've got an appetite. I could scoff iron-filings an' horseshoe nails an' thank you kindly, ma'am, for a second helpin.'"

He straightened up, and, while he reached for matches in the pocket of his overalls, his eyes traveled across the pool to the side-hill. His fingers had clutched the match-box, but they relaxed their hold and the hand came out empty. The man wavered perceptibly. He looked at his preparations for cooking and he looked at the hill.

"Guess I'll take another whack at her," he concluded, starting to cross the stream.

"They ain't no sense in it, I know," he mumbled apologetically. "But keepin' grub back an hour ain't goin' to hurt none, I reckon."

A few feet back from his first line of test-pans he started a second line. The sun dropped down the western sky, the shadows lengthened, but the man worked on. He began a third line of test-pans. He was cross-cutting the hillside, line by line, as he ascended. The center of each line produced the richest pans, while the ends came where no colors showed in the pan. And as he ascended the hillside the lines grew perceptibly shorter. The regularity with which their length diminished served to indicate that somewhere up the slope the last line would be so short as to have scarcely length at all, and that beyond could come only a point. The design was growing into an inverted "V." The converging sides of this "V" marked the boundaries of the gold-bearing dirt.

The apex of the "V" was evidently the man's goal. Often he ran his eye along the converging sides and on up the hill, trying to divine the apex, the point where the gold-bearing dirt must cease. Here resided "Mr. Pocket"—for so the man familiarly addressed the imaginary point above him on the slope, crying out:

"Come down out o' that, Mr. Pocket! Be right smart an' agreeable, an' come down!"

"All right," he would add later, in a voice resigned to determination. "All right, Mr. Pocket. It's plain to me I got to come right up an' snatch you out bald-headed. An' I'll do it! I'll do it!" he would threaten still later.

Each pan he carried down to the water to wash, and as he went higher up the hill the pans grew richer, until he began to save the gold in an empty baking powder can which he carried carelessly in his hip-pocket. So engrossed was he in his toil that he did not notice the long twilight of oncoming night. It was not until he tried vainly to see the gold colors in the bottom of the pan that he realized the passage of time. He straightened up abruptly. An expression of whimsical wonderment and awe overspread his face as he drawled:

"Gosh darn my buttons! if I didn't plumb forget dinner!"

He stumbled across the stream in the darkness and lighted his long-delayed fire. Flapjacks and bacon and warmed-over beans constituted his supper. Then he smoked a pipe by the smouldering coals, listening to the night noises and watching the moonlight stream through the canyon. After that he unrolled his bed, took off his heavy shoes, and pulled the blankets up to his chin. His face showed white in the moonlight, like the face of a corpse. But it was a corpse that knew its resurrection, for the man rose suddenly on one elbow and gazed across at his hillside.

"Good night, Mr. Pocket," he called sleepily. "Goodnight."

He slept through the early gray of morning until the direct rays of the sun smote his closed eyelids, when he awoke with a start and looked about him until he had established the continuity of his existence and identified his present self with the days previously lived.

To dress, he had merely to buckle on his shoes. He glanced at his fireplace and at his hillside, wavered, but fought down the temptation and started the fire.

"Keep yer shirt on, Bill; keep yer shirt on," he admonished himself. "What's the good of rushin'? No use in gettin' all het up an' sweaty. Mr. Pocket'll wait for you. He ain't a-runnin' away before you can get your breakfast. Now, what you want, Bill, is something fresh in yer bill o' fare. So it's up to you to go an' get it."

He cut a short pole at the water's edge and drew from one of his pockets a bit of line and a draggled fly that had once been a royal coachman.

"Mebbe they'll bite in the early morning," he muttered, as he made his first cast into the pool. And a moment later he was gleefully crying: "What'd I tell you, eh? What'd I tell you?"

He had no reel, nor any inclination to waste time, and by main strength, and swiftly, he drew out of the water a flashing ten-inch trout. Three more, caught in rapid succession, furnished his breakfast. When he came to the stepping-stones on his way to his hillside, he was struck by a sudden thought, and paused.

"I'd just better take a hike down-stream a ways," he said. "There's no tellin' who may be snoopin' around."

But he crossed over on the stones, and with a "I really oughter take that hike," the need of the precaution passed out of his mind and he fell to work.

At nightfall he straightened up. The small of his back was stiff from stooping toil, and as he put his hand behind him to soothe the protesting muscles, he said:

"Now what d'ye think of that? I clean forgot my dinner again! If I don't watch out, I'll sure be degeneratin' into a two-meal-a-day crank."

"Pockets is the hangedest things I ever see for makin' a man absent-minded," he communed that night, as he crawled into his blankets. Nor did he forget to call up the hillside, "Good night, Mr. Pocket! Good night!"

Rising with the sun, and snatching a hasty breakfast, he was early at work. A fever seemed to be growing in him, nor did the increasing richness of the test-pans allay this fever. There was a flush in his cheek other than that made by the heat of the sun, and he was oblivious to fatigue and the passage of time. When he filled a pan with dirt, he ran down the hill to wash it; nor could he forbear running up the hill again, panting and stumbling profanely, to refill the pan.

He was now a hundred yards from the water, and the inverted "V" was assuming definite proportions. The width of the pay-dirt steadily decreased, and the man extended in his mind's eye the sides of the "V" to their meeting place far up the hill. This was his goal, the apex of the "V," and he panned many times to locate it.

"Just about two yards above that manzanita bush an' a yard to the right," he finally concluded.

Then the temptation seized him. "As plain as the nose on your face," he said, as he abandoned his laborious cross-cutting and climbed to the indicated apex. He filled a pan and carried it down the hill to wash. It contained no trace of gold. He dug deep, and he dug shallow, filling and washing a dozen pans, and was unrewarded even by the tiniest golden speck. He was enraged at having yielded to the temptation, and berated himself blasphemously and pridelessly. Then he went down the hill and took up the cross-cutting.

"Slow an' certain, Bill; slow an' certain," he crooned. "Short-cuts to fortune ain't in your line, an' it's about time you know it. Get wise, Bill; get wise. Slow an' certain's the only hand you can play; so go to it, an' keep to it, too."

As the cross-cuts decreased, showing that the sides of the "V" were converging, the depth of the "V" increased. The gold-trace was dipping into the hill. It was only at thirty inches beneath the surface that he could get colors in his pan. The dirt he found at twenty-five inches from the surface, and at thirty-five inches yielded barren pans. At the base of the "V," by the water's edge, he had found the gold colors at the grass roots. The higher he went up the hill, the deeper the gold dipped. To dig a hole three feet deep in order to get one test-pan was a task of no mean magnitude; while between the man and the apex intervened an untold number of such holes to be dug.

"An' there's no tellin' how much deeper it'll pitch," he sighed, in a moment's pause, while his fingers soothed his aching back.

Feverish with desire, with aching back and stiffening muscles, with pick and shovel gouging and mauling the soft brown earth, the man toiled up the hill. Before him was the smooth slope, spangled with flowers and made sweet with their breath. Behind him was devastation. It looked like some terrible eruption breaking out on the smooth skin of the hill. His slow progress was like that of a slug, befouling beauty with a monstrous trail.

Though the dipping gold-trace increased the man's work, he found consolation in the increasing richness of the pans. Twenty cents, thirty cents, fifty cents, sixty cents, were the values of the gold found in the pans, and at nightfall he washed his banner pan, which gave him a dollar's worth of gold-dust from a shovelful of dirt.

"I'll just bet it's my luck to have some inquisitive one come buttin' in here on my pasture," he mumbled sleepily that night as he pulled the blankets up to his chin.

Suddenly he sat upright. "Bill!" he called sharply. "Now, listen to me, Bill; d'ye hear! It's up to you, to-morrow mornin,' to mosey round an' see what you can see. Understand? To-morrow morning, an' don't you forget it!"

He yawned and glanced across at his side-hill. "Good night, Mr. Pocket," he called.

In the morning he stole a march on the sun, for he had finished breakfast when its first rays caught him, and he was climbing the wall of the canyon where it crumbled away and gave footing. From the outlook at the top he found himself in the midst of loneliness. As far as he could see, chain after chain of mountains heaved themselves into his vision. To the east his eyes, leaping the miles between range and range and between many ranges, brought up at last against the white-peaked Sierras—the main crest, where the backbone of the Western world reared itself against the sky. To the north and south he could see more distinctly the cross-systems that broke through the main trend of the sea of mountains. To the west the ranges fell away, one behind the other, diminishing and fading into the gentle foothills that, in turn, descended into the great valley which he could not see.

And in all that mighty sweep of earth he saw no sign of man nor of the handiwork of man—save only the torn bosom of the hillside at his feet. The man looked long and carefully. Once, far down his own canyon, he thought he saw in the air a faint hint of smoke. He looked again and decided that it was the purple haze of the hills made dark by a convolution of the canyon wall at its back.

"Hey, you, Mr. Pocket!" he called down into the canyon. "Stand out from under! I'm a-comin,' Mr. Pocket! I'm a-comin'!"

The heavy brogans on the man's feet made him appear clumsy-footed, but he swung down from the giddy height as lightly and airily as a mountain goat. A rock, turning under his foot on the edge of the precipice, did not disconcert him. He seemed to know the precise time required for the turn to culminate in disaster, and in the meantime he utilized the false footing itself for the momentary earth-contact necessary to carry him on into safety. Where the earth sloped so steeply that it was impossible to stand for a second upright, the man did not hesitate. His foot pressed the impossible surface for but a fraction of the fatal second and gave him the bound that carried him onward. Again, where even the fraction of a second's footing was out of the question, he would swing his body past by a moment's hand-grip on a jutting knob of rock, a crevice, or a precariously rooted shrub. At last, with a wild leap and yell, he exchanged the face of the wall for an earth-slide and finished the descent in the midst of several tons of sliding earth and gravel.

His first pan of the morning washed out over two dollars in coarse gold. It was from the centre of the "V." To either side the diminution in the values of the pans was swift. His lines of cross-cutting holes were growing very short. The converging sides of the inverted "V" were only a few yards apart. Their meeting-point was only a few yards above him. But the pay-streak was dipping deeper and deeper into the earth. By early afternoon he was sinking the test-holes five feet before the pans could show the gold-trace.

For that matter, the gold-trace had become something more than a trace; it was a placer mine in itself, and the man resolved to come back after he had found the pocket and work over the ground. But the increasing richness of the pans began to worry him. By late afternoon the worth of the pans had grown to three and four dollars. The man scratched his head perplexedly and looked a few feet up the hill at the manzanita bush that marked approximately the apex of the "V." He nodded his head and said oracularly:

"It's one o' two things, Bill: one o' two things. Either Mr. Pocket's spilled himself all out an' down the hill, or else Mr. Pocket's so rich you maybe won't be able to carry him all away with you. And that'd be an awful shame, wouldn't it, now?" He chuckled at contemplation of so pleasant a dilemma.

Nightfall found him by the edge of the stream, his eyes wrestling with the gathering darkness over the washing of a five-dollar pan.

"Wisht I had an electric light to go on working," he said.

He found sleep difficult that night. Many times he composed himself and closed his eyes for slumber to overtake him; but his blood pounded with too strong desire, and as many times his eyes opened and he murmured wearily, "Wisht it was sun-up."

Sleep came to him in the end, but his eyes were open with the first paling of the stars, and the gray of dawn caught him with breakfast finished and climbing the hillside in the direction of the secret abiding-place of Mr. Pocket.

The first cross-cut the man made, there was space for only three holes, so narrow had become the pay-streak and so close was he to the fountainhead of the golden stream he had been following for four days.

"Be ca'm, Bill; be ca'm," he admonished himself, as he broke ground for the final hole where the sides of the "V" had at last come together in a point.

"I've got the almighty cinch on you, Mr. Pocket, an' you can't lose me," he said many times as he sank the hole deeper and deeper.

Four feet, five feet, six feet, he dug his way down into the earth. The digging grew harder. His pick grated on broken rock. He examined the rock. "Rotten quartz," was his conclusion as, with the shovel, he cleared the bottom of the hole of loose dirt. He attacked the crumbling quartz with the pick, bursting the disintegrating rock asunder with every stroke.

He thrust his shovel into the loose mass. His eye caught a gleam of yellow. He dropped the shovel and squatted suddenly on his heels. As a farmer rubs the clinging earth from fresh-dug potatoes, so the man, a piece of rotten quartz held in both hands, rubbed the dirt away.

"Sufferin' Sardanopolis!" he cried. "Lumps an' chunks of it! Lumps an' chunks of it!"

It was only half rock he held in his hand. The other half was virgin gold. He dropped it into his pan and examined another piece. Little yellow was to be seen, but with his strong fingers he crumbled the rotten quartz away till both hands were filled with glowing yellow. He rubbed the dirt away from fragment after fragment, tossing them into the gold-pan. It was a treasure-hole. So much had the quartz rotted away that there was less of it than there was of gold. Now and again he found a piece to which no rock clung—a piece that was all gold. A chunk, where the pick had laid open the heart of the gold, glittered like a handful of yellow jewels, and he cocked his head at it and slowly turned it around and over to observe the rich play of the light upon it.

"Talk about yer Too Much Gold diggin's!" the man snorted contemptuously. "Why, this diggin' 'd make it look like thirty cents. This diggin' is All Gold. An' right here an' now I name this yere canyon 'All Gold Canyon,' b' gosh!"

Still squatting on his heels, he continued examining the fragments and tossing them into the pan. Suddenly there came to him a premonition of danger. It seemed a shadow had fallen upon him. But there was no shadow. His heart had given a great jump up into his throat and was choking him. Then his blood slowly chilled and he felt the sweat of his shirt cold against his flesh.

He did not spring up nor look around. He did not move. He was considering the nature of the premonition he had received, trying to locate the source of the mysterious force that had warned him, striving to sense the imperative presence of the unseen thing that threatened him. There is an aura of things hostile, made manifest by messengers too refined for the senses to know; and this aura he felt, but knew not how he felt it. His was the feeling as when a cloud passes over the sun. It seemed that between him and life had passed something dark and smothering and menacing; a gloom, as it were, that swallowed up life and made for death—his death.

Every force of his being impelled him to spring up and confront the unseen danger, but his soul dominated the panic, and he remained squatting on his heels, in his hands a chunk of gold. He did not dare to look around, but he knew by now that there was something behind him and above him. He made believe to be interested in the gold in his hand. He examined it critically, turned it over and over, and rubbed the dirt from it. And all the time he knew that something behind him was looking at the gold over his shoulder.

Still feigning interest in the chunk of gold in his hand, he listened intently and he heard the breathing of the thing behind him. His eyes searched the ground in front of him for a weapon, but they saw only the uprooted gold, worthless to him now in his extremity. There was his pick, a handy weapon on occasion; but this was not such an occasion. The man realized his predicament. He was in a narrow hole that was seven feet deep. His head did not come to the surface of the ground. He was in a trap.

He remained squatting on his heels. He was quite cool and collected; but his mind, considering every factor, showed him only his helplessness. He continued rubbing the dirt from the quartz fragments and throwing the gold into the pan. There was nothing else for him to do. Yet he knew that he would have to rise up, sooner or later, and face the danger that breathed at his back. The minutes passed, and with the passage of each minute he knew that by so much he was nearer the time when he must stand up, or else—and his wet shirt went cold against his flesh again at the thought—or else he might receive death as he stooped there over his treasure.

Still he squatted on his heels, rubbing dirt from gold and debating in just what manner he should rise up. He might rise up with a rush and claw his way out of the hole to meet whatever threatened on the even footing above ground. Or he might rise up slowly and carelessly, and feign casually to discover the thing that breathed at his back. His instinct and every fighting fibre of his body favored the mad, clawing rush to the surface. His intellect, and the craft thereof, favored the slow and cautious meeting with the thing that menaced and which he could not see. And while he debated, a loud, crashing noise burst on his ear. At the same instant he received a stunning blow on the left side of the back, and from the point of impact felt a rush of flame through his flesh. He sprang up in the air, but halfway to his feet collapsed. His body crumpled in like a leaf withered in sudden heat, and he came down, his chest across his pan of gold, his face in the dirt and rock, his legs tangled and twisted because of the restricted space at the bottom of the hole. His legs twitched convulsively several times. His body was shaken as with a mighty ague. There was a slow expansion of the lungs, accompanied by a deep sigh. Then the air was slowly, very slowly, exhaled, and his body as slowly flattened itself down into inertness.

Above, revolver in hand, a man was peering down over the edge of the hole. He peered for a long time at the prone and motionless body beneath him. After a while the stranger sat down on the edge of the hole so that he could see into it, and rested the revolver on his knee. Reaching his hand into a pocket, he drew out a wisp of brown paper. Into this he dropped a few crumbs of tobacco. The combination became a cigarette, brown and squat, with the ends turned in. Not once did he take his eyes from the body at the bottom of the hole. He lighted the cigarette and drew its smoke into his lungs with a caressing intake of the breath. He smoked slowly. Once the cigarette went out and he relighted it. And all the while he studied the body beneath him.

In the end he tossed the cigarette stub away and rose to his feet. He moved to the edge of the hole. Spanning it, a hand resting on each edge, and with the revolver still in the right hand, he muscled his body down into the hole. While his feet were yet a yard from the bottom he released his hands and dropped down.

At the instant his feet struck bottom he saw the pocket-miner's arm leap out, and his own legs knew a swift, jerking grip that overthrew him. In the nature of the jump his revolver hand was above his head. Swiftly as the grip had flashed about his legs, just as swiftly he brought the revolver down. He was still in the air, his fall in process of completion, when he pulled the trigger. The explosion was deafening in the confined space. The smoke filled the hole so that he could see nothing. He struck the bottom on his back, and like a cat's the pocket-miner's body was on top of him. Even as the miner's body passed on top, the stranger crooked in his right arm to fire; and even in that instant the miner, with a quick thrust of elbow, struck his wrist. The muzzle was thrown up and the bullet thudded into the dirt of the side of the hole.

The next instant the stranger felt the miner's hand grip his wrist. The struggle was now for the revolver. Each man strove to turn it against the other's body. The smoke in the hole was clearing. The stranger, lying on his back, was beginning to see dimly. But suddenly he was blinded by a handful of dirt deliberately flung into his eyes by his antagonist. In that moment of shock his grip on the revolver was broken. In the next moment he felt a smashing darkness descend upon his brain, and in the midst of the darkness even the darkness ceased.

But the pocket-miner fired again and again, until the revolver was empty. Then he tossed it from him and, breathing heavily, sat down on the dead man's legs.

The miner was sobbing and struggling for breath. "Measly skunk!" he panted; "a-campin' on my trail an' lettin' me do the work, an' then shootin' me in the back!"

He was half crying from anger and exhaustion. He peered at the face of the dead man. It was sprinkled with loose dirt and gravel, and it was difficult to distinguish the features.

"Never laid eyes on him before," the miner concluded his scrutiny. "Just a common an' ordinary thief, hang him! An' he shot me in the back! He shot me in the back!"

He opened his shirt and felt himself, front and back, on his left side.

"Went clean through, and no harm done!" he cried jubilantly. "I'll bet he aimed all right all right; but he drew the gun over when he pulled the trigger—the cur! But I fixed 'm! Oh, I fixed 'm!"

His fingers were investigating the bullet-hole in his side, and a shade of regret passed over his face. "It's goin' to be stiffer'n hell," he said. "An' it's up to me to get mended an' get out o'here."

He crawled out of the hole and went down the hill to his camp. Half an hour later he returned, leading his pack-horse. His open shirt disclosed the rude bandages with which he had dressed his wound. He was slow and awkward with his left-hand movements, but that did not prevent his using the arm.

The bight of the pack-rope under the dead man's shoulders enabled him to heave the body out of the hole. Then he set to work gathering up his gold. He worked steadily for several hours, pausing often to rest his stiffening shoulder and to exclaim:

"He shot me in the back, the measly skunk! He shot me in the back!"

When his treasure was quite cleaned up and wrapped securely into a number of blanket-covered parcels, he made an estimate of its value.

"Four hundred pounds, or I'm a Hottentot," he concluded. "Say two hundred in quartz an' dirt—that leaves two hundred pounds of gold. Bill! Wake up! Two hundred pounds of gold! Forty thousand dollars! An' it's yourn—all yourn!"

He scratched his head delightedly and his fingers blundered into an unfamiliar groove. They quested along it for several inches. It was a crease through his scalp where the second bullet had ploughed.

He walked angrily over to the dead man.

"You would, would you!" he bullied. "You would, eh? Well, I fixed you good an' plenty, an' I'll give you decent burial, too. That's more'n you'd have done for me."

He dragged the body to the edge of the hole and toppled it in. It struck the bottom with a dull crash, on its side, the face twisted up to the light. The miner peered down at it.

"An' you shot me in the back!" he said accusingly.

With pick and shovel he filled the hole. Then he loaded the gold on his horse. It was too great a load for the animal, and when he had gained his camp he transferred part of it to his saddle-horse. Even so, he was compelled to abandon a portion of his outfit—pick and shovel and gold-pan, extra food and cooking utensils, and divers odds and ends.

The sun was at the zenith when the man forced the horses at the screen of vines and creepers. To climb the huge boulders the animals were compelled to uprear and struggle blindly through the tangled mass of vegetation. Once the saddle-horse fell heavily and the man removed the pack to get the animal on its feet. After it started on its way again the man thrust his head out from among the leaves and peered up at the hillside.

"The measly skunk!" he said, and disappeared.

There was a ripping and tearing of vines and boughs. The trees surged back and forth, marking the passage of the animals through the midst of them. There was a clashing of steel-shod hoofs on stone, and now and again a sharp cry of command. Then the voice of the man was raised in song:—

"Tu'n around an' tu'n yo' face
Untoe them sweet hills of grace
(D' pow'rs of sin yo' am scornin'!).
Look about an' look aroun'
Fling yo' sin-pack on d' groun'
(Yo' will meet wid d' Lord in d' mornin'!)."

The song grew faint and fainter, and through the silence crept back the spirit of the place. The stream once more drowsed and whispered; the hum of the mountain bees rose sleepily. Down through the perfume-weighted air fluttered the snowy fluffs of the cottonwoods. The butterflies drifted in and out among the trees, and over all blazed the quiet sunshine. Only remained the hoof-marks in the meadow and the torn hillside to mark the boisterous trail of the life that had broken the peace of the place and passed on.

TWELVE O'CLOCK

by
Stephen Crane

While Stephen Crane (1871–1900) is primarily remembered for his realistic war novel, The Red Badge of Courage, *he wrote many other excellent tales during his short career. Originally from the New Jersey-New York area, and the son of a Methodist minister, he taught himself to read at the age of four and began writing poetry when he was eight.*

After the deaths of his parents, Crane struggled to support himself as a freelance journalist and novelist. He achieved instant international fame at the age of twenty-three with his second novel, The Red Badge of Courage.

In 1897, while awaiting in Jacksonville, Florida, to set sail on a doomed cargo ship carrying ammunition and machetes for the rebels during Jose Marti's Cuban revolution, he fell in love with brothel madam Cora Taylor. After the ship sank off the coast of Florida and he spent a day and a half adrift in a lifeboat, he almost drowned swimming ashore. Taylor immediately came to his aid and the couple soon moved to England. They never married, but they lived together for the remainder of his life—except when he was on assignment—and she changed her name to Cora Crane.

Crane produced his Wild West stories while living in England with Taylor, but his inspiration sprang from a tour he made of the West immediately after the publication of The Red Badge of Courage.

"Where were you at twelve o'clock, noon, on the 9th of June, 1875?"
—*Question on intelligent cross-examination.*

"Excuse *me*," said Ben Roddle with graphic gestures to a group of citizens in Nantucket's store. "Excuse *me*. When them fellers in leather pants an' six-shooters ride in, I go home an' set in th' cellar. That's what I do. When you see me pirooting through the streets at th' same time an' occasion as them punchers, you kin put me down fer bein' crazy. Excuse *me*."

"Why, Ben," drawled old Nantucket, "you ain't never really seen 'em turned loose. Why, I kin remember—in th' old days—when—"

"Oh, damn yer old days!" retorted Roddle. Fixing Nantucket with the eye of scorn and contempt, he said, "I suppose you'll be sayin' in a minute that in th' old days you used to kill Injuns, won't you?"

There was some laughter, and Roddle was left free to expand his ideas on the periodic visits of cowboys to the town. "Mason Rickets, he had ten big punkins a-sittin' in front of his store, an' them fellers from the Upsided-Down-F Ranch shot 'em up— shot 'em all up—an' Rickets lyin' on his belly in th' store a-callin' fer 'em to quit it. An' what did they do! Why, they *laughed* at 'im!—just *laughed* at 'im! That don't do a town no good. Now, how would an eastern capiterlist"—(it was the town's humor to be always gassing of phantom investors who were likely to come any moment and pay a thousand prices for everything)—"how would an eastern capiterlist like that? Why, you couldn't see 'im fer th' dust on his trail. Then he'd tell all his friends that 'their town may be all right, but ther's too much loose-handed shootin' fer my money.' An' he'd be right, too. Them rich fellers, they don't make no bad breaks with their money. They watch it all th' time b'cause they know blame well there ain't hardly room fer their feet fer th' pikers an' tin-horns an' thimble-riggers what are layin' fer 'em. I tell you, one puncher racin' his cow-pony hell-bent-fer-election down Main Street an' yellin' an' shootin' an' nothin' at all done about it, would scare away a whole herd of capiterlists. An' it ain't right. It oughter be stopped."

A pessimistic voice asked: "How you goin' to stop it, Ben?"

"Organise," replied Roddle pompously. "Organise: that's the only way to make these fellers lay down. I—"

From the street sounded a quick scudding of pony hoofs, and a party of cowboys swept past the door. One man, however, was seen to draw rein and dismount. He came clanking into the store. "Mornin,' gentlemen," he said, civilly.

"Mornin,'" they answered in subdued voices.

He stepped to the counter and said, "Give me a paper of fine cut, please." The group of citizens contemplated him in silence. He certainly did not look threatening. He appeared to be a young man of twenty-five years, with a tan from wind and sun, with a remarkably clear eye from perhaps a period of enforced temperance, a quiet young man

✳ **TWELVE O'CLOCK** ✳

who wanted to buy some tobacco. A six-shooter swung low on his hip, but at the moment it looked more decorative than warlike; it seemed merely a part of his odd gala dress—his sombrero with its band of rattlesnake skin, his great flaming neckerchief, his belt of embroidered Mexican leather, his high-heeled boots, his huge spurs. And, above all, his hair had been watered and brushed until it lay as close to his head as the fur lays to a wet cat. Paying for his tobacco, he withdrew.

Ben Roddle resumed his harangue. "Well, there you are! Looks like a calm man now, but in less'n half an hour he'll be as drunk as three bucks an' a squaw, an' then... excuse *me*!"

On this day the men of two outfits had come into town, but Ben Roddle's ominous words were not justified at once. The punchers spent most of the morning in an attack on whiskey which was too earnest to be noisy.

At five minutes of eleven, a tall, lank, brick-colored cowboy strode over to Placer's Hotel. Placer's Hotel was a notable place. It was the best hotel within two hundred miles. Its office was filled with arm-chairs and brown papier-maché receptacles. At one end of the room was a wooden counter painted a bright pink, and on this morning a man was behind the counter writing in a ledger. He was the proprietor of the hotel, but his customary humor was so sullen that all strangers immediately wondered why in life he had chosen to play the part of mine host. Near his left hand, double doors opened into the dining-room, which in warm weather was always kept darkened in order to discourage the flies, which was not compassed at all.

Placer, writing in his ledger, did not look up when the tall cowboy entered.

"Mornin,' mister," said the latter. "I've come to see if you kin grub-stake th' hull crowd of us fer dinner t'day."

Placer did not then raise his eyes, but with a certain churlishness, as if it annoyed him that his hotel was patronized, he asked: "How many?"

"Oh, about thirty," replied the cowboy. "An' we want th' best dinner you kin raise an' scrape. Everything th' best. We don't care what it costs s'long as we git a good square meal. We'll pay a dollar a head: by God, we will! We won't kick on nothin' in the bill if you do it up fine. If you ain't got it in th' house russle th' hull town fer it. That's our gait. So you just tear loose, an' we'll—"

At this moment the machinery of a cuckoo-clock on the wall began to whirr, little doors flew open and a wooden bird appeared and cried, "Cuckoo!" And this was repeated until eleven o'clock had been announced, while the cowboy, stupefied, glassy-eyed, stood with his red throat gulping. At the end he wheeled upon Placer and demanded: *"What in hell is that?"*

Placer revealed by his manner that he had been asked this question too many times. "It's a clock," he answered shortly.

"I know it's a clock," gasped the cowboy; "but what *kind* of a clock?"

"A cuckoo-clock. Can't you see?"

The cowboy, recovering his self-possession by a violent effort, suddenly went shouting into the street. "Boys! Say, boys! Come' 'ere a minute!"

His comrades, comfortably inhabiting a near-by saloon, heard his stentorian calls, but they merely said to one another: "What's th' matter with Jake?—he's off his nut again."

But Jake burst in upon them with violence. "Boys," he yelled, "come over to th' hotel! They got a clock with a bird inside it, an' when it's eleven o'clock or anything like that, th' bird comes out an' says, '*toot*-toot, *toot*-toot!' that way, as many times as what-ever time of day it is. It's immense! Come on over!"

The roars of laughter which greeted his proclamation were of two qualities; some men laughing because they knew all about cuckoo-clocks, and other men laughing because they had concluded that the eccentric Jake had been victimized by some wise child of civilization.

Old Man Crumford, a venerable ruffian who probably had been born in a corral, was particularly offensive with his loud guffaws of contempt. "Bird a-comin' out of a clock an' a-tellin' ye th' time! Haw-haw-haw!" He swallowed his whiskey. "A bird! a-tellin' ye th' time! Haw-haw! Jake, you ben up agin some new drink. You ben drinkin' lonely an' got up agin some snake-medicine licker. A bird a-tellin' ye th' time! Haw-haw!"

The shrill voice of one of the younger cowboys piped from the background. "Brace up, Jake. Don't let 'em laugh at ye. Bring 'em that salt cod-fish of yourn what kin pick out th' ace."

"Oh, he's only kiddin' us. Don't pay no 'tention to 'im. He thinks he's smart."

A cowboy whose mother had a cuckoo-clock in her house in Philadelphia spoke with solemnity. "Jake's a liar. There's no such clock in the world. What? a bird inside a clock to tell the time? Change your drink, Jake."

Jake was furious, but his fury took a very icy form. He bent a withering glance upon the last speaker. "I don't mean a *live* bird," he said, with terrible dignity. "It's a wooden bird, an'—"

"A wooden bird!" shouted Old Man Crumford. "Wooden bird a-tellin' ye th' time! Haw-haw!"

But Jake still paid his frigid attention to the Philadelphian. "An' if yer sober enough to walk, it ain't such a blame long ways from here to th' hotel, an' I'll bet my pile agin yours if you only got two bits."

"I don't want your money, Jake," said the Philadelphian. "Somebody's been stringin' you—that's all. I wouldn't take your money." He cleverly appeared to pity the other's innocence.

"You couldn't *git* my money," cried Jake, in sudden hot anger. "You couldn't git it. Now—since yer so fresh—let's see how much you got." He clattered some large gold pieces noisily upon the bar.

The Philadelphian shrugged his shoulders and walked away. Jake was triumphant. "Any more bluffers 'round here?" he demanded. "Any more? Any more bluffers? Where's all these here hot sports? Let 'em step up. Here's my money—come an' git it."

But they had ended by being afraid. To some of them his tale was absurd, but still one must be circumspect when a man throws forty-five dollars in gold upon the bar and bids the world come and win it. The general feeling was expressed by Old Man Crumford, when with deference he asked: "Well, this here bird, Jake—what kinder lookin' bird is it?"

"It's a little brown thing," said Jake briefly. Apparently he almost disdained to answer.

"Well—how does it work?" asked the old man meekly.

"Why in blazes don't you go an' look at it?" yelled Jake. "Want me to paint it in iles fer you? Go an' look!"

Placer was writing in his ledger. He heard a great trample of feet and clink of spurs on the porch, and there entered quietly the band of cowboys, some of them swaying a trifle, and these last being the most painfully decorous of all. Jake was in advance. He waved his hand toward the clock. "There she is," he said laconically. The cowboys drew up and stared. There was some giggling, but a serious voice said half-audibly, "I don't see no bird."

Jake politely addressed the landlord. "Mister, I've fetched these here friends of mine in here to see yer clock—"

Placer looked up suddenly. "Well, they can see it, can't they?" he asked in sarcasm. Jake, abashed, retreated to his fellows.

There was a period of silence. From time to time the men shifted their feet. Finally, Old Man Crumford leaned towards Jake, and in a penetrating whisper demanded, "Where's th' bird?" Some frolicsome spirits on the outskirts began to call "Bird! Bird!" as men at a political meeting call for a particular speaker.

Jake removed his big hat and nervously mopped his brow.

The young cowboy with the shrill voice again spoke from the skirts of the crowd. "Jake, is ther' sure-'nough a bird in that thing?"

"Yes. Didn't I tell you once?"

"Then," said the shrill-voiced man, in a tone of conviction, "it ain't a clock at all. It's a birdcage."

"I tell you it's a clock," cried the maddened Jake, but his retort could hardly be heard above the howls of glee and derision which greeted the words of him of the shrill voice.

Old Man Crumford was again rampant. "Wooden bird a-tellin' ye th' time! Haw-haw!"

Amid the confusion Jake went again to Placer. He spoke almost in supplication. "Say, mister, what time does this here thing go off again?"

Placer lifted his head, looked at the clock, and said, "Noon."

There was a stir near the door, and Big Watson of the Square-X outfit, and at this time very drunk indeed, came shouldering his way through the crowd and cursing everybody. The men gave him much room, for he was notorious as a quarrelsome person when drunk. He paused in front of Jake, and spoke as through a wet blanket. "What's all this—monkeyin' about?"

Jake was already wild at being made a butt for everybody, and he did not give backward. "None a' your damn business, Watson."

"Huh?" growled Watson, with the surprise of a challenged bull.

"I said," repeated Jake distinctly, "it's none a' your damn business."

Watson whipped his revolver half out of its holster. "I'll make it m' business, then, you—"

But Jake had backed a step away, and was holding his left-hand palm outward toward Watson, while in his right he held his six-shooter, its muzzle pointing at the floor. He was shouting in a frenzy, "No—don't you try it, Watson! Don't you dare try it, or, by Gawd, I'll kill you, sure—*sure*!"

He was aware of a torment of cries about him from fearful men; from men who protested, from men who cried out because they cried out. But he kept his eyes on Watson, and those two glared murder at each other, neither seeming to breathe, fixed like statues.

A loud new voice suddenly rang out, "Hol' on a minute!" All spectators who had not stampeded turned quickly, and saw Placer standing behind his bright pink counter, with an aimed revolver in each hand.

"Cheese it!" he said. "I won't have no fightin' here. If you want to fight, git out in the street."

Big Watson laughed, and, speeding up his six-shooter like a flash of blue light, he shot Placer through the throat—shot the man as he stood behind his absurd pink counter with his two aimed revolvers in his incompetent hands. With a yell of rage and despair, Jake smote Watson on the pate with his heavy weapon, and knocked him sprawling and bloody. Somewhere a woman shrieked like windy, midnight death. Placer fell behind the counter, and down upon him came his ledger and his inkstand, so that one could not have told blood from ink.

The cowboys did not seem to hear, see, or feel, until they saw numbers of citizens with Winchesters running wildly upon them. Old Man Crumford threw high a passionate hand. "Don't shoot! We'll not fight ye for 'im."

Nevertheless two or three shots rang, and a cowboy who had been about to gallop off suddenly slumped over on his pony's neck, where he held for a moment like an old sack, and then slid to the ground, while his pony, with flapping rein, fled to the prairie.

"In God's name, don't shoot!" trumpeted Old Man Crumford. "We'll not fight ye fer 'im!"

"It's murder," bawled Ben Roddle.

In the chaotic street it seemed for a moment as if everybody would kill everybody. "Where's the man what done it?" These hot cries seemed to declare a war which would result in an absolute annihilation of one side. But the cowboys were singing out against it. They would fight for nothing—yes—they often fought for nothing—but they would not fight for this dark something.

At last, when a flimsy truce had been made between the inflamed men, all parties went to the hotel. Placer, in some dying whim, had made his way out from behind the pink counter, and, leaving a horrible trail, had traveled to the centre of the room, where he had pitched headlong over the body of Big Watson.

The men lifted the corpse and laid it at the side.

"Who done it?" asked a white, stern man.

A cowboy pointed at Big Watson. "That's him," he said huskily.

There was a curious grim silence, and then suddenly, in the death-chamber, there sounded the loud whirring of the clock's works, little doors flew open, a tiny wooden bird appeared and cried "Cuckoo"—twelve times.

THE
CABALLERO'S
WAY

by
O. Henry

Master American short story writer O. Henry's (1862–1910) real name was William Sidney Porter. Initially he was a licensed pharmacist in North Carolina, but because of a persistent cough he moved to Texas in 1882 to work as a ranch hand and shepherd on a sheep ranch. Here O. Henry began writing and became a journalist at the Houston Post. *He also held several other jobs and was a bank teller, but in 1896 he was arrested for embezzling. He denied the charges, but the day before his court appearance he fled to Honduras, where he coined the term "banana republic."*

After several months O. Henry learned his wife was dying from tuberculosis and would be unable to join him, so he returned to the United States and spent three years in prison. Using various pseudonyms, he continued writing—getting fourteen stories published while in prison. He went on to write more than 600 short stories. Despite being world famous, he was virtually penniless when he passed away. The prestigious short story prize—the O. Henry Award—was, of course, named in his honor.

This story marks the first appearance of the Cisco Kid. Today he is a heroic, chivalrous Mexican caballero, while in O. Henry's original incarnation he is a cruel, but savvy, Texas outlaw who has a lot of people gunning for him.

The Cisco Kid had killed six men in more or less fair scrimmages, had murdered twice as many (mostly Mexicans), and had winged a larger number whom he modestly forbore to count. Therefore a woman loved him.

The Kid was twenty-five, looked twenty; and a careful insurance company would have estimated the probable time of his demise at, say, twenty-six. His habitat was anywhere between the Frio and the Rio Grande. He killed for the love of it—because he was quick-tempered—to avoid arrest—for his own amusement—any reason that came to his mind would suffice. He had escaped capture because he could shoot five-sixths of a second sooner than any sheriff or ranger in the service, and because he rode a speckled roan horse that knew every cow-path in the mesquite and pear thickets from San Antonio to Matamoras.

Tonia Perez, the girl who loved the Cisco Kid, was half Carmen, half Madonna, and the rest—oh, yes, a woman who is half Carmen and half Madonna can always be something more—the rest, let us say, was humming-bird. She lived in a grass-roofed jacal near a little Mexican settlement at the Lone Wolf Crossing of the Frio. With her lived a father or grandfather, a lineal Aztec, somewhat less than a thousand years old, who herded a hundred goats and lived in a continuous drunken dream from drinking mescal. Back of the jacal a tremendous forest of bristling pear, twenty feet high at its worst, crowded almost to its door. It was along the bewildering maze of this spinous thicket that the speckled roan would bring the Kid to see his girl. And once, clinging like a lizard to the ridge-pole, high up under the peaked grass roof, he had heard Tonia, with her Madonna face and Carmen beauty and humming-bird soul, parley with the sheriff's posse, denying knowledge of her man in her soft mélange of Spanish and English.

One day the adjutant-general of the State, who is, *ex offico*, commander of the ranger forces, wrote some sarcastic lines to Captain Duval of Company X, stationed at Laredo, relative to the serene and undisturbed existence led by murderers and desperadoes in the said captain's territory.

The captain turned the color of brick dust under his tan, and forwarded the letter, after adding a few comments, per ranger Private Bill Adamson, to ranger Lieutenant Sandridge, camped at a water hole on the Nueces with a squad of five men in preservation of law and order.

Lieutenant Sandridge turned a beautiful couleur de rose through his ordinary strawberry complexion, tucked the letter in his hip pocket, and chewed off the ends of his gamboge moustache.

The next morning he saddled his horse and rode alone to the Mexican settlement at the Lone Wolf Crossing of the Frio, twenty miles away.

Six feet two, blond as a Viking, quiet as a deacon, dangerous as a machine gun, Sandridge moved among the Jacales, patiently seeking news of the Cisco Kid.

Far more than the law, the Mexicans dreaded the cold and certain vengeance of the lone rider that the ranger sought. It had been one of the Kid's pastimes to shoot Mexicans "to see them kick": if he demanded from them moribund Terpsichorean feats, simply that he might be entertained, what terrible and extreme penalties would be certain to follow should they anger him! One and all they lounged with upturned palms and shrugging shoulders, filling the air with "quien sabes" and denials of the Kid's acquaintance.

But there was a man named Fink who kept a store at the Crossing—a man of many nationalities, tongues, interests, and ways of thinking.

"No use to ask them Mexicans," he said to Sandridge. "They're afraid to tell. This hombre they call the Kid—Goodall is his name, ain't it?—he's been in my store once or twice. I have an idea you might run across him at—but I guess I don't keer to say, myself. I'm two seconds later in pulling a gun than I used to be, and the difference is worth thinking about. But this Kid's got a half-Mexican girl at the Crossing that he comes to see. She lives in that jacal a hundred yards down the arroyo at the edge of the pear. Maybe she—no, I don't suppose she would, but that jacal would be a good place to watch, anyway."

Sandridge rode down to the jacal of Perez. The sun was low, and the broad shade of the great pear thicket already covered the grass-thatched hut. The goats were enclosed for the night in a brush corral near by. A few kids walked the top of it, nibbling the chaparral leaves. The old Mexican lay upon a blanket on the grass, already in a stupor from his mescal, and dreaming, perhaps, of the nights when he and Pizarro touched glasses to their New World fortunes—so old his wrinkled face seemed to proclaim him to be. And in the door of the jacal stood Tonia. And Lieutenant Sandridge sat in his saddle staring at her like a gannet agape at a sailorman.

The Cisco Kid was a vain person, as all eminent and successful assassins are, and his bosom would have been ruffled had he known that at a simple exchange of glances two persons, in whose minds he had been looming large, suddenly abandoned (at least for the time) all thought of him.

Never before had Tonia seen such a man as this. He seemed to be made of sun-shine and blood-red tissue and clear weather. He seemed to illuminate the shadow of the pear when he smiled, as though the sun were rising again. The men she had known had been small and dark. Even the Kid, in spite of his achievements, was a stripling no larger than herself, with black, straight hair and a cold, marble face that chilled the noonday.

As for Tonia, though she sends description to the poorhouse, let her make a millionaire of your fancy. Her blue-black hair, smoothly divided in the middle and bound close to her head, and her large eyes full of the Latin melancholy, gave her the Madonna touch. Her motions and air spoke of the concealed fire and the desire to charm that she had inherited from the gitanas of the Basque province. As for the hummingbird part of her, that dwelt in her heart; you could not perceive it unless her bright red skirt and dark blue blouse gave you a symbolic hint of the vagarious bird.

The newly lighted sun-god asked for a drink of water. Tonia brought it from the red jar hanging under the brush shelter. Sandridge considered it necessary to dismount so as to lessen the trouble of her ministrations.

I play no spy; nor do I assume to master the thoughts of any human heart; but I assert, by the chronicler's right, that before a quarter of an hour had sped, Sandridge was teaching her how to plaint a six-strand rawhide stake-rope, and Tonia had explained to him that were it not for her little English book that the peripatetic padre had given her and the little crippled chivo, that she fed from a bottle, she would be very, very lonely indeed.

Which leads to a suspicion that the Kid's fences needed repairing, and that the adjutant-general's sarcasm had fallen upon unproductive soil.

In his camp by the water hole Lieutenant Sandridge announced and reiterated his intention of either causing the Cisco Kid to nibble the black loam of the Frio country prairies or of haling him before a judge and jury. That sounded business-like. Twice a week he rode over to the Lone Wolf Crossing of the Frio, and directed Tonia's slim, slightly lemon-tinted fingers among the intricacies of the slowly growing lariata. A six-strand plait is hard to learn and easy to teach.

The ranger knew that he might find the Kid there at any visit. He kept his armament ready, and had a frequent eye for the pear thicket at the rear of the jacal. Thus he might bring down the kite and the hummingbird with one stone.

While the sunny-haired ornithologist was pursuing his studies the Cisco Kid was also attending to his professional duties. He moodily shot up a saloon in a small cow village on Quintana Creek, killed the town marshal (plugging him neatly in the centre of his tin badge), and then rode away, morose and unsatisfied. No true artist is uplifted by shooting an aged man carrying an old-style .38 bulldog.

On his way the Kid suddenly experienced the yearning that all men feel when wrong-doing loses its keen edge of delight. He yearned for the woman he loved to reassure him that she was his in spite of it. He wanted her to call his bloodthirstiness bravery and his cruelty devotion. He wanted Tonia to bring him water from the red jar under the brush shelter, and tell him how the chivo was thriving on the bottle.

The Kid turned the speckled roan's head up the ten-mile pear flat that stretches along the Arroyo Hondo until it ends at the Lone Wolf Crossing of the Frio. The roan whickered; for he had a sense of locality and direction equal to that of a belt-line streetcar horse; and he knew he would soon be nibbling the rich mesquite grass at the end of a forty-foot stake-rope while Ulysses rested his head in Circe's straw-roofed hut.

More weird and lonesome than the journey of an Amazonian explorer is the ride of one through a Texas pear flat. With dismal monotony and startling variety the uncanny and multiform shapes of the cacti lift their twisted trunks, and fat, bristly hands to encumber the way. The demon plant, appearing to live without soil or rain, seems to taunt the parched traveler with its lush grey greenness. It warps itself a thousand times about what look to be open and inviting paths, only to lure the rider into blind and impassable spine-defended "bottoms of the bag," leaving him to retreat, if he can, with the points of the compass whirling in his head.

To be lost in the pear is to die almost the death of the thief on the cross, pierced by nails and with grotesque shapes of all the fiends hovering about.

But it was not so with the Kid and his mount. Winding, twisting, circling, tracing the most fantastic and bewildering trail ever picked out, the good roan lessened the distance to the Lone Wolf Crossing with every coil and turn that he made.

While they fared the Kid sang. He knew but one tune and sang it, as he knew but one code and lived it, and but one girl and loved her. He was a single-minded man of conventional ideas. He had a voice like a coyote with bronchitis, but whenever he chose to sing his song he sang it. It was a conventional song of the camps and trail, running at its beginning as near as may be to these words:

and so on. The roan was inured to it, and did not mind.

But even the poorest singer will, after a certain time, gain his own consent to refrain from contributing to the world's noises. So the Kid, by the time he was within a mile or two of Tonia's jacal, had reluctantly allowed his song to die away—not because his vocal performance had become less charming to his own ears, but because his laryngeal muscles were aweary.

As though he were in a circus ring the speckled roan wheeled and danced through the labyrinth of pear until at length his rider knew by certain landmarks that the Lone Wolf Crossing was close at hand. Then, where the pear was thinner, he caught sight of the grass roof of the jacal and the hackberry tree on the edge of the arroyo. A few yards farther the Kid stopped the roan and gazed intently through the prickly openings. Then he dismounted, dropped the roan's reins, and proceeded on foot, stooping and silent, like an Indian. The roan, knowing his part, stood still, making no sound.

The Kid crept noiselessly to the very edge of the pear thicket and reconnoitered between the leaves of a clump of cactus.

Ten yards from his hiding-place, in the shade of the jacal, sat his Tonia calmly plaiting a rawhide lariat. So far she might surely escape condemnation; women have been known, from time to time, to engage in more mischievous occupations. But if all must be told, there is to be added that her head reposed against the broad and comfortable chest of a tall red-and-yellow man, and that his arm was about her, guiding her nimble fingers that required so many lessons at the intricate six-strand plait.

Sandridge glanced quickly at the dark mass of pear when he heard a slight squeaking sound that was not altogether unfamiliar. A gun-scabbard will make that sound when one grasps the handle of a six-shooter suddenly. But the sound was not repeated; and Tonia's fingers needed close attention.

And then, in the shadow of death, they began to talk of their love; and in the still July afternoon every word they uttered reached the ears of the Kid.

"Remember, then," said Tonia, "you must not come again until I send for you. Soon he will be here. A vaquero at the tienda said today he saw him on the Guadalupe three days ago. When he is that near he always comes. If he comes and finds you here he will kill you. So, for my sake, you must come no more until I send you the word."

"All right," said the stranger. "And then what?"

"And then," said the girl, "you must bring your men here and kill him. If not, he will kill you."

"He ain't a man to surrender, that's sure," said Sandridge. "It's kill or be killed for the officer that goes up against Mr. Cisco Kid."

"He must die," said the girl. "Otherwise there will not be any peace in the world for thee and me. He has killed many. Let him so die. Bring your men, and give him no chance to escape."

"You used to think right much of him," said Sandridge.

Tonia dropped the lariat, twisted herself around, and curved a lemon-tinted arm over the ranger's shoulder.

"But then," she murmured in liquid Spanish, "I had not beheld thee, thou great, red mountain of a man! And thou art kind and good, as well as strong. Could one choose him, knowing thee? Let him die; for then I will not be filled with fear by day and night lest he hurt thee or me."

"How can I know when he comes?" asked Sandridge.

"When he comes," said Tonia, "he remains two days, sometimes three. Gregorio, the small son of old Luisa, the lavendera, has a swift pony. I will write a letter to thee and send it by him, saying how it will be best to come upon him. By Gregorio will the letter come. And bring many men with thee, and have much care, oh, dear red one, for the rattlesnake is not quicker to strike than is 'El Chivato,' as they call him, to send a ball from his pistola."

"The Kid's handy with his gun, sure enough," admitted Sandridge, "but when I come for him I shall come alone. I'll get him by myself or not at all. The Cap wrote one or two things to me that make me want to do the trick without any help. You let me know when Mr. Kid arrives, and I'll do the rest."

"I will send you the message by the boy Gregorio," said the girl. "I knew you were braver than that small slayer of men who never smiles. How could I ever have thought I cared for him?"

It was time for the ranger to ride back to his camp on the water hole. Before he mounted his horse he raised the slight form of Tonia with one arm high from the earth for a parting salute. The drowsy stillness of the torpid summer air still lay thick upon the dreaming afternoon. The smoke from the fire in the jacal, where the frijoles blubbered in the iron pot, rose straight as a plumb-line above the clay-daubed chimney. No sound or movement disturbed the serenity of the dense pear thicket ten yards away.

When the form of Sandridge had disappeared, loping his big dun down the steep banks of the Frio crossing, the Kid crept back to his own horse, mounted him, and rode back along the tortuous trail he had come.

But not far. He stopped and waited in the silent depths of the pear until half an hour had passed. And then Tonia heard the high, untrue notes of his unmusical singing coming nearer and nearer; and she ran to the edge of the pear to meet him.

The Kid seldom smiled; but he smiled and waved his hat when he saw her. He dismounted, and his girl sprang into his arms. The Kid looked at her fondly. His thick, black hair clung to his head like a wrinkled mat. The meeting brought a slight ripple of some undercurrent of feeling to his smooth, dark face that was usually as motionless as a clay mask.

"How's my girl?" he asked, holding her close.

"Sick of waiting so long for you, dear one," she answered. "My eyes are dim with always gazing into that devil's pincushion through which you come. And I can see into it such a little way, too. But you are here, beloved one, and I will not scold. Que mal muchacho! not to come to see your alma more often. Go in and rest, and let me water your horse and stake him with the long rope. There is cool water in the jar for you."

The Kid kissed her affectionately.

"Not if the court knows itself do I let a lady stake my horse for me," said he. "But if you'll run in, chica, and throw a pot of coffee together while I attend to the caballo, I'll be a good deal obliged."

Besides his marksmanship the Kid had another attribute for which he admired himself greatly. He was muy caballero, as the Mexicans express it, where the ladies were concerned. For them he had always gentle words and consideration. He could not have spoken a harsh word to a woman. He might ruthlessly slay their husbands and brothers, but he could not have laid the weight of a finger in anger upon a woman. Wherefore many of that interesting division of humanity who had come under the spell of his politeness declared their disbelief in the stories circulated about Mr. Kid. One shouldn't believe everything one heard, they said. When confronted by their indignant men folk with proof of the caballero's deeds of infamy, they said maybe he had been driven to it, and that he knew how to treat a lady, anyhow.

Considering this extremely courteous idiosyncrasy of the Kid and the pride he took in it, one can perceive that the solution of the problem that was presented to him by what he saw and heard from his hiding-place in the pear that afternoon (at least as to one of the actors) must have been obscured by difficulties. And yet one could not think of the Kid overlooking little matters of that kind.

At the end of the short twilight they gathered around a supper of frijoles, goat steaks, canned peaches, and coffee, by the light of a lantern in the jacal. Afterward, the ancestor, his flock corralled, smoked a cigarette and became a mummy in a grey blanket. Tonia washed the few dishes while the Kid dried them with the flour-sacking towel. Her eyes shone; she chatted volubly of the inconsequent happenings of her small world since the Kid's last visit; it was as all his other homecomings had been.

Then outside Tonia swung in a grass hammock with her guitar and sang sad canciones de amor.

"Do you love me just the same, old girl?" asked the Kid, hunting for his cigarette papers.

"Always the same, little one," said Tonia, her dark eyes lingering upon him.

"I must go over to Fink's," said the Kid, rising, "for some tobacco. I thought I had another sack in my coat. I'll be back in a quarter of an hour."

"Hasten," said Tonia, "and tell me—how long shall I call you my own this time? Will you be gone again to-morrow, leaving me to grieve, or will you be longer with your Tonia?"

"Oh, I might stay two or three days this trip," said the Kid, yawning. "I've been on the dodge for a month, and I'd like to rest up."

He was gone half an hour for his tobacco. When he returned Tonia was still lying in the hammock.

"It's funny," said the Kid, "how I feel. I feel like there was somebody lying behind every bush and tree waiting to shoot me. I never had mullygrubs like them before. Maybe it's one of them presumptions. I've got half a notion to light out in the morning before day. The Guadalupe country is burning up about that old Dutchman I plugged down there."

"You are not afraid—no one could make my brave little one fear."

"Well, I haven't been usually regarded as a jack-rabbit when it comes to scrapping;

but I don't want a posse smoking me out when I'm in your jacal. Somebody might get hurt that oughtn't to."

"Remain with your Tonia; no one will find you here."

The Kid looked keenly into the shadows up and down the arroyo and toward the dim lights of the Mexican village.

"I'll see how it looks later on," was his decision.

At midnight a horseman rode into the rangers' camp, blazing his way by noisy "halloes" to indicate a pacific mission. Sandridge and one or two others turned out to investigate the row. The rider announced himself to be Domingo Sales, from the Lone Wolf Crossing. he bore a letter for Senor Sandridge. Old Luisa, the lavendera, had persuaded him to bring it, he said, her son Gregorio being too ill of a fever to ride.

Sandridge lighted the camp lantern and read the letter. These were its words:

Dear One:

He has come. Hardly had you ridden away when he came out of the pear. When he first talked he said he would stay three days or more. Then as it grew later he was like a wolf or a fox, and walked about without rest, looking and listening. Soon he said he must leave before daylight when it is dark and stillest. And then he seemed to suspect that I be not true to him. He looked at me so strange that I am frightened. I swear to him that I love him, his own Tonia. Last of all he said I must prove to him I am true. He thinks that even now men are waiting to kill him as he rides from my house. To escape he says he will dress in my clothes, my red skirt and the blue waist I wear and the brown mantilla over the head, and thus ride away. But before that he says that I must put on his clothes, his pantalones and camisa and hat, and ride away on his horse from the jacal as far as the big road beyond the crossing and back again. This before he goes, so he can tell if I am true and if men are hidden to shoot him. It is a terrible thing. An hour before daybreak this is to be. Come, my dear one, and kill this man and take me for your Tonia. Do not try to take hold of him alive, but kill him quickly. Knowing all, you should do that. You must come long before the

time and hide yourself in the little shed near the jacal where the wagon and saddles
are kept. It is dark in there. He will wear my red skirt and blue waist and brown man-
tilla. I send you a hundred kisses. Come surely and shoot quickly and straight.

Thine Own

Tonia.

Sandridge quickly explained to his men the official part of the missive. The rangers protested against his going alone.

"I'll get him easy enough," said the lieutenant. "The girl's got him trapped. And don't even think he'll get the drop on me."

Sandridge saddled his horse and rode to the Lone Wolf Crossing. He tied his big dun in a clump of brush on the arroyo, took his Winchester from its scabbard, and carefully approached the Perez jacal. There was only the half of a high moon drifted over by ragged, milk-white gulf clouds.

The wagon-shed was an excellent place for ambush; and the ranger got inside it safely. In the black shadow of the brush shelter in front of the jacal he could see a horse tied and hear him impatiently pawing the hard-trodden earth.

He waited almost an hour before two figures came out of the jacal. One, in man's clothes, quickly mounted the horse and galloped past the wagon-shed toward the crossing and village. And then the other figure, in skirt, waist, and mantilla over its head, stepped out into the faint moonlight, gazing after the rider. Sandridge thought he would take his chance then before Tonia rode back. He fancied she might not care to see it.

"Throw up your hands," he ordered loudly, stepping out of the wagon-shed with his Winchester at his shoulder.

There was a quick turn of the figure, but no movement to obey, so the ranger pumped in the bullets—one—two—three—and then twice more; for you never could be too sure of bringing down the Cisco Kid. There was no danger of missing at ten paces, even in that half moonlight.

The old ancestor, asleep on his blanket, was awakened by the shots. Listening further, he heard a great cry from some man in mortal distress or anguish, and rose up grumbling at the disturbing ways of moderns.

The tall, red ghost of a man burst into the jacal, reaching one hand, shaking like a tule reed, for the lantern hanging on its nail. The other spread a letter on the table.

"Look at this letter, Perez," cried the man. "Who wrote it?"

"Ah, Dios! it is Señor Sandridge," mumbled the old man, approaching. "Pues, señor, that letter was written by 'El Chivato,' as he is called—by the man of Tonia. They say he is a bad man; I do not know. While Tonia slept he wrote the letter and sent it by this old hand of mine to Domingo Sales to be brought to you. Is there anything wrong in the letter? I am very old; and I did not know. Valgame Dios! it is a very foolish world; and there is nothing in the house to drink—nothing to drink."

Just then all that Sandridge could think of to do was to go outside and throw himself face downward in the dust by the side of his humming-bird, of whom not a feather fluttered. He was not a caballero by instinct, and he could not understand the niceties of revenge.

A mile away the rider who had ridden past the wagon-shed struck up a harsh, untuneful song, the words of which began:

Don't you monkey with my Lulu girl
Or I'll tell you what I'll do—

PHANTOMS
of
PEACE

by
Zane Grey

Although with novels like Riders of the Purple Sage, *Zane Grey (1872–1938) would become nearly synonymous with the Western genre, at first he was deluged with rejections from publishers, causing him to write, "I cannot decide what to write next. That which I desire to write does not seem to be what the editors want...,". Grey kept at it, becoming one of the first American authors whose writing made him a millionaire. In all, he published more than ninety books, sixty of which were Westerns, which played a major role in shaping the myths of the Wild West.*

In this story of two prospectors, Grey accurately captures the desolation and magic of the desert.

Dwire judged him to be another of those strange desert prospectors in whom there was some relentless driving power besides the lust for gold. He saw a stalwart man from whose lined face deep luminous eyes looked out with yearning gaze, as if drawn by something far beyond the ranges.

The man had approached Dwire back in the Nevada mining-camp, and had followed him down the trail leading into the Mohave. He spoke few words, but his actions indicated that he answered to some subtle influence in seeking to accompany the other.

When Dwire hinted that he did not go down into the desert for gold alone, the only reply he got was a singular flashing of the luminous eyes. Then he explained, more from a sense of duty than from hope of turning the man back, that in the years of his wandering he had met no one who could stand equally with him the blasting heat, the blinding storms, the wilderness of sand and rock and lava and cactus, the terrible silence and desolation of the desert.

"Back there they told me you were Dwire," replied the man. "I'd heard of you; and if you don't mind, I'd like to go with you."

"Stranger, you're welcome," replied Dwire. "I'm going inside"—he waved a hand toward the wide, shimmering, shadowy descent of plain and range—"and I don't know where. I may cross the Mohave into the Colorado Desert. I may go down into Death Valley."

The prospector swept his far-reaching gaze over the colored gulf of rock and sand. For moments he seemed to forget himself. Then, with gentle slaps, he drove his burro into the trail behind Dwire's, and said, "My name's Hartwell."

They began a slow, silent march down into the desert. At sundown they camped near Red Seeps. Dwire observed that his companion had acquired the habit of silence so characteristic of the lone wanderer in the wilds—a habit not easily broken when two of these men are thrown together.

Next sunset they made camp at Coyote Tanks; the next at Indian Well; the following night at a nameless water-hole. For five more days they plodded down with exchange of few words. When they got deep into the desert, with endless stretches of drifting sand and rugged rock between them and the outside world, there came a breaking of reserve, noticeable in Dwire, almost imperceptibly gradual in his companion. At night, round their meager mesquite campfire, Dwire would remove his black pipe to talk a little. The other man would listen, and would sometimes unlock his lips to speak a word.

And so, as Dwire responded to the influence of his surroundings, he began to notice his companion, and found him different from any man he had encountered in the desert. Hartwell did not grumble at the heat, the glare, the driving sand, the sour water, the scant fare. During the daylight hours he was seldom idle; at night he sat dreaming before the fire, or paced to and fro in the gloom. If he ever slept, it must have been long after Dwire had rolled in his blanket and dropped to rest. He was tireless and patient.

Dwire's awakened interest in Hartwell brought home to him the realization that for years he had shunned companionship. In those years only three men had wandered into the desert with him, and they had found what he believed they had sought there—graves in the shifting sands. He had not cared to know their secrets; but the more he watched this latest comrade, the more he began to suspect that he might have missed something in these other men.

In his own driving passion to take his secret into the limitless abode of silence and desolation, where he could be alone with it, he had forgotten that life dealt shocks to other men. Somehow this silent comrade reminded him.

Two weeks of steady marching saw the prospectors merging into the Mohave. It was naked, rock-ribbed, sand-sheeted desert. They lost all trails but those of the coyote and wildcat, and these they followed to the water-holes.

At length they got into desert that appeared new to Dwire. He could not recognize landmarks near at hand. Behind them, on the horizon line, stood out a blue peak that marked the plateau from which they had descended. Before them loomed a jagged range of mountains, which were in line with Death Valley.

The prospectors traveled on, halting now and then to dig at the base of a mesa or pick into a ledge. As they progressed over ridges and across plains and through canyons, the general trend was toward the jagged range, and every sunset found them at a lower level. The heat waxed stronger every day, and the water-holes were harder to find.

One afternoon, late, after they had toiled up a white, winding wash of sand and gravel, they came upon a dry water-hole. Dwire dug deep into the sand, but without avail. He was turning to retrace the weary steps to the last water when his comrade asked him to wait.

Dwire watched Hartwell search in his pack and bring forth what appeared to be a small forked branch of a peach-tree. He firmly grasped the prongs of the fork, and held them before him, with the end standing straight out. Then he began to walk along the dry stream-bed.

At first amused, then amazed, then pityingly, and at last curiously, Dwire kept pace with Hartwell. He saw a strong tension of his comrade's wrists, as if he was holding hard against a considerable force. The end of the peach branch began to quiver and turn downward. Dwire reached out a hand to touch it, and was astounded at feeling a powerful vibrant force pulling the branch down. He felt it as a quivering magnetic shock. The branch kept turning, and at length pointed to the ground.

"Dig here," said Hartwell.

"What?" ejaculated Dwire.

He stood by while Hartwell dug in the sand. Three feet he dug—four—five. The sand grew dark, then moist. At six feet water began to seep through.

"Get the little basket in my pack," said Hartwell.

Dwire complied, though he scarcely comprehended what was happening. He saw Hartwell drop the basket into the deep hole and carefully pat it down, so that it kept the sides from caving in and allowed the water to seep through. While Dwire watched, the basket filled.

Of all the strange incidents of his desert career, this was the strangest. Curiously, he picked up the peach branch, and held it as he had seen Hartwell hold it. However, the thing was dead in his hands.

"I see you haven't got it," remarked Hartwell. "Few men have."

"Got what?" demanded Dwire.

"A power to find water that way. I can't explain it. Back in Illinois an old German showed me I had it."

"What a gift for a man in the desert!" Dwire accepted things there that elsewhere he would have regarded as unbelievable.

Hartwell smiled—the first time in all those days that his face had changed. The light of it struck Dwire.

They entered a region where mineral abounded, and their march became slower. Generally they took the course of a wash, one on each side, and let the burros travel leisurely along, nipping at the bleached blades of scant grass, or at sage or cactus, while the prospectors searched in the canyons and under the ledges for signs of gold.

Descending among the splintered rocks, clambering over boulders, climbing up weathered slopes, always picking, always digging—theirs was toilsome labor that wore more and more on them each day. When they found any rock that hinted of gold, they picked off a piece and gave it a chemical test. The search was fascinating.

They interspersed the work with long restful moments when they looked afar, down the vast reaches and smoky shingles, to the line of dim mountains. Some impelling desire, not all the lure of gold, took them to the top of mesas and escarpments; and here, when they dug and picked, they rested and gazed out at the wide prospect.

Then, as the sun lost its heat and sank, lowering, to dent its red disk behind far distant spurs, they halted in a shady canyon, or some likely spot in a dry wash, and tried for water. When they found it, they unpacked, gave drink to the tired burros, and turned them loose. Dead greasewood served for the campfire. They made bread and coffee and cooked bacon, and when each simple meal ended they were still hungry. They were chary of their supplies. They even limited themselves to one pipe of tobacco.

While the strange twilight deepened into weird night, they sat propped against stones, with eyes on the embers of the fire, and soon they lay on the sand with the light of great white stars on their dark faces.

Each succeeding day and night Dwire felt himself more and more drawn to Hartwell. He found that after hours of burning toil he had insensibly grown nearer to his comrade. The fact bothered him. It was curious, perplexing. And finally, in wonder, he divined that he cared for Hartwell.

He reflected that after a few weeks in the desert he had always become a different man. In civilization, in the rough mining camps, he had been a prey to unrest and gloom; but once down on the great heave and bulge and sweep of this lonely world, he could look into his unquiet soul without bitterness. Always he began to see and to think and to feel. Did not the desert magnify men?

Dwire believed that wild men in wild places, fighting cold, heat, starvation, thirst, barrenness, facing the elements in all their primal ferocity, usually retrograded, descended to the savage, lost all heart and soul, and became mere brutes. Likewise he believed that men wandering or lost in the wilderness often reversed that brutal order of life, and became noble, wonderful, superhuman.

He had the proof in the serene wisdom of his soul when for a time the desert had been his teacher. And so now he did not marvel at a slow stir, stealing warmer and warmer along his veins, and at the premonition that he and Hartwell, alone on the desert, driven there by life's mysterious and remorseless motive, were to see each other through God's eyes.

Hartwell was a man who thought of himself last. It humiliated Dwire that in spite of growing keenness he could not hinder his companion from doing more than his share of the day's work. It spoke eloquently of what Hartwell might be capable of on the burdened return journey.

The man was mild, gentle, quiet, mostly silent, yet under all his softness he seemed to be made of the fiber of steel. Dwire could not thwart him.

Moreover, he appeared to want to find gold for Dwire, not for himself. If he struck his pick into a ledge that gave forth a promising glint, instantly he called to his companion. Dwire's hands always trembled at the turning of rock that promised gold. He had enough of the prospector's passion for fortune to thrill at the chance of a strike; but Hartwell never showed the least trace of excitement.

And his kindness to the burros was something that Dwire had never seen equaled. Hartwell always found the water and dug for it, ministered to the weary burros, and then led them off to the best patch of desert growth. Last of all he bethought himself to eat a little.

One night they were encamped at the head of a canyon. The day had been exceedingly hot, and long after sundown the radiation of heat from the rocks persisted. A desert bird whistled a wild, melancholy note from a dark cliff, and a distant coyote wailed mournfully. The stars shone white until the huge moon rose to burn out all their whiteness.

Many times, since they started their wanderings, Dwire had seen Hartwell draw something from his pocket and peer long at it. On this night Dwire watched him again, and yielded to an interest which he had not heretofore voiced.

"Hartwell, what drives you into the desert?"

"Comrade, do I seem to be a driven man?" asked Hartwell.

"No. But I feel it. Do you come to forget?"

"I come to remember."

"Ah!" softly exclaimed Dwire.

Always he seemed to have known that.

He said no more. He watched Hartwell rise and begin his nightly pace to and fro, up and down.

With slow, soft tread, forward and back, tirelessly and ceaselessly, the man paced his beat. He did not look up at the stars or follow the radiant track of the moon along the canyon ramparts. He hung his head. He was lost in another world. It was a world which the lonely desert made real. He looked a dark, sad, plodding figure, and somehow impressed Dwire with the helplessness of men.

"He is my brother," muttered Dwire.

He grew acutely conscious of the pang in his own breast, of the fire in his heart, the strife and torment of his own passion-driven soul. Dwire had come into the desert to forget a woman. She appeared to him then as she had looked when first she entered his life—a golden-haired girl, blue-eyed, white-skinned, red-lipped, tall and slender and beautiful. He saw her as she had become after he had ruined her—a wild and passionate woman, mad to be loved, false and lost, and still cursed with unforgettable allurements. He had never forgotten, and an old, sickening remorse knocked at his heart.

Rising, Dwire climbed out of the canyon to the top of a mesa, where he paced to and fro. He looked down into the weird and mystic shadows, like the darkness of his passion, and farther on down the moon-track and the glittering stretches that vanished in the cold, blue horizon.

The moon soared radiant and calm, the white stars shone serene. The vault of heaven seemed illimitable and divine. The desert surrounded him, silver-streaked and black-mantled, a chaos of rock and sand, a dead thing, silent, austere, ancient, waiting, majestic. It spoke to Dwire. It was a naked corpse, but it had a soul.

In that wild solitude, the white stars looked down upon him pitilessly and pityingly. They had shone upon a desert that had once been alive and was now dead, and that would again throb to life, only to die. It was a terrible ordeal for Dwire to stand there alone and realize that he was only a man facing eternity; but that was what gave him strength to endure. Somehow he was a part of it all, some atom in that vastness, somehow necessary to an inscrutable purpose, something indestructible in that desolate world of ruin and death and decay, something perishable and changeable and growing under all the fixity of heaven. In that endless, silent hall of desert there was a spirit; and Dwire felt hovering near him phantoms of peace.

He returned to camp and sought his comrade.

"Hartwell, I reckon we're two of a kind. It was a woman who drove me into the desert. But I come to forget. The desert's the only place I can do that."

"Was she your wife?" asked the other.

"No."

A long silence ensued. A cool wind blew up the canyon, sifting the sand through the dry sage, driving away the last of the lingering heat. The campfire wore down to a ruddy ashen heap.

"I had a daughter," said Hartwell, speaking as if impelled. "She lost her mother at birth. And I—I didn't know how to bring up a girl. She was pretty and gay. She went to the bad. I tried to forget her and failed. Then I tried to find her. She had disappeared. Since then I haven't been able to stay in one place, or to work or sleep or rest."

Hartwell's words were peculiarly significant to Dwire. They distressed him. He had been wrapped up in his remorse for wronging a woman. If ever in the past he had thought of anyone connected with her, he had long forgotten it; but the consequences of such wrong were far-reaching. They struck at the roots of a home. And here, in the desert, he was confronted by the spectacle of a splendid man—the father of a wronged girl—wasting his life because he could not forget—because there was nothing left to live for.

Suddenly Dwire felt an inward constriction, a cold, shivering clamp of pain, at the thought that perhaps he had blasted the life of a father. He shared his companion's grief. He knew why the desert drew him. Since Hartwell must remember, he could do so best in this solitude, where the truth of the earth lay naked, where the truth of life lay stripped bare. In the face of the tragedy of the universe, as revealed in the desert, what were the error of one frail girl, or the sorrow of one unfortunate man?

"Hartwell, it's bad enough to be driven by sorrow for someone you've loved, but to suffer sleepless and eternal remorse for the *ruin* of one you've loved—that is worse. Listen! In my younger days—it seems long ago now, yet it's only ten years—I was a wild fellow. I didn't mean to do wrong. I was just a savage. I gambled and drank. I got into scrapes. I made love to girls, and one, the sweetest and loveliest girl who ever breathed, I—I ruined. I disgraced her. Not knowing, I left her to bear the brunt of that disgrace alone. Then I fell into terrible moods. I changed. I discovered that I really and earnestly loved that girl. I went back to her, to make amends—but it was too late!"

Hartwell leaned forward a little in the waning campfire glow, and looked strangely into Dwire's face, as if searching it for the repentance and remorse that alone would absolve him from scorn and contempt; but he said nothing.

The prospectors remained in that camp for another day, held by some rust-stained ledges that contained mineral.

Late in the afternoon Dwire returned to camp, to find Hartwell absent. His pick, however, was leaning against a stone, and his coat lying over one of the packs. Hartwell was probably out driving the burros up to water.

Gathering a bundle of greasewood. Dwire kindled a fire. Then into his gold-pan he measured out flour and water. Presently it was necessary for him to get into one of the packs, and in so doing he knocked down Hartwell's coat. From a pocket fell a small plush case, badly soiled and worn.

Dwire knew that this case held the picture at which Hartwell looked so often, and as he bent to pick it up he saw the face shining in the light. He experienced a shuddering ripple through all his being. The face resembled the one that was burned forever into his memory. How strange and fatal it was that every crag, every cloud, everything which attracted his eye, took on the likeness of the girl he loved!

He gazed down upon the thing in his hand. It was not curiosity; only a desire to dispel his illusion.

Suddenly, when he actually recognized the face of Nell Warren, he seemed to feel that he was paralyzed. He stared and gasped. The blood thrummed in his ears.

This picture was Nell when she was a mere girl. It was youthful, soft, pure, infinitely sweet. A tide of emotion rushed irresistibly over him.

The hard hoofs of the burros, cracking the stones, broke the spell that held Dwire, and he saw Hartwell approaching.

"Nell was *his* daughter!" whispered Dwire.

Trembling and dazed, he returned the picture to the pocket from which it had fallen, and with bent head and clumsy hands he busied himself about the campfire. Strange and bewildering thoughts raced through his mind. He ate little; it seemed that he could scarcely wait to be off; and when the meal was ended, and work done, he hurried away.

As thought and feeling multiplied, he was overwhelmed. It was beyond belief that out of the millions of men in the world two who had never seen each other could have been driven into the desert by memory of the same woman. It brought the past so close. It showed Dwire how inevitably all his spiritual life was governed by what had happened long ago.

That which made life significant to him was a wandering in silent places where no eye could see him with his secret. He was mad, blinded, lost.

Some fateful chance had thrown him with the father of the girl he had wrecked. It was incomprehensible; it was terrible. It was the one thing of all possible happenings in the world of chance that both father and lover would have declared unendurable. It would be the scoring of unhealed wounds. In the thoughtful brow, the sad, piercing eye, the plodding, unquiet mood of the other, each man would see his own ruin.

Dwire's pain reached to despair when he felt this insupportable relation between Hartwell and himself.

Something within him cried out and commanded him to reveal his identity. Hartwell would kill him, probably, but it was not fear of death that put Dwire on the rack. He had faced death too often to be afraid. It was the thought of adding torture to this long-suffering man whom he had come to love.

All at once Dwire swore that he would not augment Hartwell's trouble, or let him stain his hands with blood, however just that act might be. He would reveal himself, but he would so twist the truth of Nell's sad story that the father would lose his agony and hate, his driving passion to wander over this desolate desert.

This made Dwire think of Nell as a living, breathing woman. She was somewhere beyond the dim horizon line. She would be thirty years old—that time of a woman's life when she was most beautiful and wonderful. She would be in the glare and glitter, sought and loved by men, in some great and splendid city. At that very moment she would be standing somewhere, white-gowned, white-faced, with her crown of golden

hair, with the same old haunting light in her eyes—lost, and bitterly indifferent to her doom.

Dwire gazed out over the blood-red, darkening desert, and suddenly, strangely, unconsciously, the strife in his soul ceased. The moment that followed was one of incalculable realization of change, in which his eyes seemed to pierce the vastness of cloud and range and the mystery of gloom and shadow—to see with strong vision the illimitable space of sand and rock. He felt the grandeur of the desert, its simplicity, its truth, and he learned at last the lesson it taught.

No longer strange or unaccountable was his meeting with Hartwell. Each had marched in the steps of destiny, and as the lines of their fates had been inextricably tangled in the years that were gone, so now their steps had crossed and turned them toward one common goal.

For years they had been two men marching alone, answering to an inward and driving search, and the desert had brought them together. For years they had wandered alone, in silence and solitude, where the sun burned white all day and the stars burned white all night, blindly following the whisper of a spirit. But now Dwire knew that he was no longer blind. Truth had been revealed—wisdom had spoken—unselfish love had come—and in this flash of revelation Dwire felt that it had been given him to relieve Hartwell of his burden.

Dwire returned to camp. As always, at that long hour when the afterglow of sunset lingered in the west, Hartwell was plodding to and fro in the gloom.

"I'm wondering if Hartwell is your right name," said Dwire.

"It's not," replied the other.

"Well, out here men seem to lose old names, old identities. Dwire's not my real name."

Hartwell slowly turned. It seemed that there might have been a suspension, a blank, between his usual quiet, courteous interest and some vivifying, electrifying mood to come.

"Was your real name Warren?" asked Dwire.

Hartwell moved with sudden start.

"Yes," he replied.

"I've got something to tell you," Dwire went on. "A while back I knocked your coat down, and a picture fell out of your pocket. I looked at it. I recognized it. I knew your daughter Nell."

"You!"

The man grasped Dwire and leaned close, his eyes shining out of the gloom.

"Don't drag at me like that! Listen. I was Nell's lover. I ruined her. I am Gail Hamlin!"

Hartwell became as a man struck by lightning, still standing before he fell.

"Yes, I'm Hamlin," repeated Dwire.

With a convulsive spring Hartwell appeared to rise and tower over Dwire. Then he plunged down upon him, and clutched at his throat with terrible, stifling hands. Dwire fought desperately, not to save his life, but for breath to speak a few words that would pierce Hartwell's maddened mind.

"Warren, kill me, if you want," gasped Dwire; "but wait! It's for your own sake. Give me a little time! If you don't, you'll never know. *Nell didn't go to the bad!*"

Dwire felt the shock that vibrated through Hartwell at those last words. He repeated them again and again.

As if wrenched by some resistless force, Hartwell released Dwire, staggered back, and stood with uplifted, shaking hands. The horrible darkness of his face showed his lust to kill. The awful gleam of hope in his luminous eyes revealed what had checked his fury.

"Comrade," panted Dwire, "it's no stranger that you should kill me than that we should meet out here. But give me a little time. Listen! I want to tell you. I'm Hamlin— I'm the man who broke Nell's heart. Only she never went to the bad. You thought wrong—you heard wrong. When she left Peoria, and I learned my true feelings, I hunted her. I traced her to St. Louis. She worked there, and on Sundays sang in a church. She was more beautiful than ever. The men lost their heads about her. I pleaded and pleaded with her to forgive me—to marry me—to let me make it all up to her. She forgave, but she would not marry me. I would not give up, and so I stayed on there. I was wild and persistent; but Nell had ceased to care for me. Nor did she care for any of the men who courted her. Her trouble had made her a good and noble woman. She was like a nun. She came to be loved by women and children—by everyone who knew her.

"Then some woman who had known Nell in Peoria came to St. Louis. She had a poison tongue. She talked. No one believed her; but when the gossip got to Nell's ears, she faded—she gave up. It drove her from St. Louis. I traced her—found her again. Again I was too late. The disgrace and shock, coming so near a critical time for her, broke her down, and—she died. You see you were mistaken. As for me—well, I drifted West, and now for a long time I've been taking to the desert. It's the only place where I can live with my remorse. It's the only place where I can forget she is dead!"

"Dead! Dead all these years!" murmured Hartwell, brokenly. "All these years that I've thought of her as—"

"You've thought wrong," interrupted Dwire. "Nell was good, as good as she was lovable and beautiful. I was the one who was evil, who failed, who turned my back on the noblest chance life offers to a man. I was young, selfish, savage. What did I know? But when I got away from the world and grew old in thought and pain I learned much. Nell was a good woman."

"Oh, thank God! Thank God!" cried Hartwell, and he fell on his knees.

Dwire stole away into the darkness, with that broken cry quivering in his heart.

How long he absented himself from camp, or what he did, he had no idea. When he returned, Hartwell was sitting before the fire, and once more he appeared composed. He spoke, and his voice had a deeper note, but otherwise he seemed as usual. The younger man understood, then, how Hartwell's wrath had softened.

Dwire experienced a singular exaltation in the effect of his falsehood. He had lightened his comrade's burden. Wonderfully it came to him that he had also lightened his own. From that moment he never again suffered a pang in his thought of Nell. Subtly and unconsciously his falsehood became truth to him, and he remembered her as he had described her to her father.

He saw that he had uplifted Hartwell, and the knowledge gave him happiness. He had rolled away a comrade's heavy, somber grief; and, walking with him in the serene, luminous light of the stars, again he began to feel the haunting presence of his phantoms of peace.

In the moan of the cool wind, in the silken seep of sifting sand, in the distant rumble of a slipping ledge, in the faint rush of a shooting star, he heard these phantoms of peace coming, with whispers of the long pain of men at the last made endurable. Even in the white noonday, under the burning sun, these phantoms came to be real to him. And in the dead silence, the insupportable silence of the midnight hours, he heard them breathing nearer on the desert wind—whispers of God's peace in the solitude.

Dwire and Hartwell meandered on down into the desert. There came a morning when the sun shone angry and red through a dull, smoky haze.

"We're in for sandstorms," said Dwire. "We'd better turn back. I don't know where we are, but I think we're in Death Valley. We'd better get back to the last water."

But they had scarcely covered a mile on their back trail when a desert-wide, moaning, yellow wall of flying sand swooped down upon them. Seeking shelter in the lee of a rock, they waited, hoping that the storm was only a squall, such as frequently whipped across the open places.

The moan increased to a roar, the dull red slowly dimmed, to disappear in the yellow pall, and the air grew thick and dark. Dwire slipped the packs from the burros. He feared the sandstorms had arrived some weeks ahead of their usual season.

The men covered their heads and patiently waited. The long hours dragged, and the storm increased in fury. Dwire and Hartwell wet scarfs with water from the canteens, bound them round their faces, and then covered their heads.

The steady, hollow bellow of flying sand went on. It flew so thickly that enough sifted down under the shelving rock to weight the blankets and almost bury the men. They were frequently compelled to shake off the sand to keep from being borne to the ground. And it was necessary to keep digging out the packs, for the floor of their shelter rose higher and higher.

They tried to eat, and seemed to be grinding only sand between their teeth. They lost the count of time. They dared not sleep, for that would have meant being buried alive. They could only crouch close to the leaning rock, shake off the sand, blindly dig out their packs, and every moment gasp and cough and choke to fight suffocation.

The storm finally blew itself out. It left the prospectors heavy and stupid for want of sleep. Their burros had wandered away, or had been buried in the sand.

Far as eye could reach, the desert had marvelously changed; it was now a rippling sea of sand-dunes. Away to the north rose the peak that was their only guiding mark. They headed toward it, carrying a shovel and part of their packs.

At noon the peak vanished in the shimmering glare of the desert. Dwire and Hartwell pushed on, guided by the sun. In every wash they tried for water. With the forked branch in his magnetic hands, Hartwell always succeeded in locating water, and always they dug and dug; but the water lay too deep.

Toward sunset, in a pocket under a canyon wall, they dug in the sand and found water; but as fast as they shoveled the sand out, the sides of the hole caved in, and darkness compelled them to give up. Spent and sore, they fell, and slept where they lay through that night and part of the next day. Then they succeeded in getting water, quenched their thirst, filled the canteens, and cooked a meal.

Here, abandoning all their outfit except the shovel, the basket with a scant store of food, and the canteens, they set out, both silent and grim in the understanding of what lay before them. They traveled by the sun, and after dark, by the north star. At dawn they crawled into a shady wash and slept till afternoon. Hours were wasted in vain search for water. Hartwell located it, but it lay too deep.

That night, deceived by a hazy sky, they toiled on, to find at dawn that they had turned back into Death Valley. Again the lonely desert peak beckoned to them, and again they wearily faced toward it, only to lose it in the glare of the noonday heat.

The burning day found them in an interminably wide plain, where there was no shelter from the fierce sun. They were exceedingly careful with their water, though there was absolute necessity of drinking a little every hour.

Late in the afternoon they came to a canyon which they believed to be the lower end of the one in which they had last found water. For hours they traveled toward its head. After night had set in, they found what they sought. Yielding to exhaustion, they slept, and next day were loath to leave the water-hole. Cool night spurred them on with canteens full and renewed strength.

The day opened for them in a red inferno of ragged, wind-worn stone. Like a flame the sun glanced up from the rock, to scorch and peel their faces. Hartwell went blind from the glare, and Dwire had to lead him.

Once they rested in the shade of a ledge. Dwire, from long habit, picked up a piece of rock and dreamily examined it. Its weight lent him sudden interest. It had a peculiar black color. He scraped through the black rust to find that he held a piece of gold.

Around him lay scattered heaps of black pebbles, bits of black, weathered rock, and pieces of broken ledge. All contained gold.

"Hartwell! See it! Feel it! Gold! Gold everywhere!"

But Hartwell had never cared, and now he was too blind to see.

Dwire was true to such instinct for hunting gold as he possessed. He built up stone monuments to mark his strike. Then he filled his pockets with the black pebbles.

As he was about to turn away, he came suddenly upon a rusty pick. Some prospector had been there before him. Dwire took hold of the pick handle, to feel it crumble in his hand. He searched for further evidence of a prior discoverer of the ledge of gold, but was unsuccessful.

Then Dwire and Hartwell dragged themselves on, resting often, wearing out, and at night they dropped. In the morning, as they pressed on, Dwire caught sight of the bleached bones of a man, half hidden in hard-packed sand. He did not speak of his gruesome find to Hartwell; but after a little he went back and erected a monument of stones near the skeleton. It was not the first pile of white bones that he had found in Death Valley. Then he went forward to catch up with his comrade.

That day Hartwell's sight cleared, but he began to fail, to show his age. Dwire saw it, and gave both aid and encouragement.

The blue peak once more appeared to haunt them. It loomed high and apparently close. The ascent toward it was heartbreaking, not in steepness, but in its league after league of long, monotonous rise.

Dwire knew now that there was but one hope—to make the water hold out, and never stop to rest; but Hartwell was growing weaker, and had to rest often.

The burning white day passed, and likewise the white night, with its stars shining so pitilessly cold and bright. Dwire measured the water in his canteen by the feel of its weight. Evaporation by heat consumed as much as he drank.

He found opportunity in one of the rests, when he had wetted his parched mouth and throat, to pour a little water from his canteen into Hartwell's.

When dawn came, the bare peak glistened in the rosy sunlight. Its bare ribs stood out, and its dark lines of canyons. It seemed so close; but in that wonderfully clear atmosphere, before the dust and sand began to blow, Dwire could not be deceived as to distance—and the peak was a hundred miles away!

Muttering low, Dwire shook his head, and again found opportunity to pour a little water from his canteen into Hartwell's.

The zone of bare, sand-polished rock appeared never to have an end. The rising heat waved up like black steam. It burned through the men's boots, driving them to seek relief in every bit of shade, and here a drowsiness made Hartwell sleep standing. Dwire ever kept watch over his comrade.

Their marches from place to place became shorter. A belt of cactus blocked their passage. Its hooks and spikes, like poisoned iron fangs, tore grimly at them.

At infrequent intervals, when chance afforded, Dwire continued to pour a little water from his canteen into Hartwell's.

At first Dwire had curbed his restless activity to accommodate the pace of his elder comrade; but now he felt that he was losing something of his instinctive and passionate zeal to get out of the desert. The thought of water came to occupy his mind. Mirages appeared on all sides. He saw beautiful clear springs and heard the murmur and tinkle of running water.

He looked for water in every hole and crack and canyon; but all were glaring red and white, hot and dry—as dry as if there had been no moisture on that desert since the origin of the world. The white sun, like the surface of a pot of boiling iron, poured down its terrific heat. The men tottered into corners of shade, and rose to move blindly on.

It had become habitual with Dwire to judge his quantity of water by its weight, and by the faint splash it made as his canteen rocked on his shoulder. He began to imagine that his last little store of liquid did not appreciably diminish. He knew he was not quite right in his mind regarding water; nevertheless he felt this to be more of fact than fancy, and he began to ponder.

When next they rested, he pretended to be in a kind of stupor, but he covertly watched Hartwell. The man appeared far gone, yet he had cunning. He cautiously took up Dwire's canteen, and poured water into it from his own.

Dwire reflected that he had been unwise not to expect this very thing from Hartwell. Then, as his comrade dropped into weary rest, the younger man lifted both canteens. If there were any water in Hartwell's, it was only very little. Both men had been enduring the terrible desert thirst, concealing it, each giving his water to the other, and the sacrifice had been all for naught. Instead of ministering to either man's parched throat, the water had evaporated.

When Dwire made sure of this, he took one more drink, the last. Then, pouring the little water left into Hartwell's canteen, he threw his own away.

Hartwell discovered the loss.

"Where's your canteen?" he asked.

"The heat was getting my water, so I drank what was left and threw the can away."

"My son!" said Hartwell gently.

Then he silently compelled Dwire to drink half his water, and drank the other half himself.

They did not speak again. In another hour speaking was impossible. Their lips dried out; their tongues swelled to coarse ropes. Hartwell sagged lower and lower, despite Dwire's support.

All that night Dwire labored on under a double burden. In the white glare of the succeeding day Hartwell staggered into a strip of shade, where he fell, wearily lengthened out, and seemed to compose himself to rest.

It was still in Dwire to fight sleep—that last sleep. He had the strength and the will in him to go on a little farther; but now that the moment had come, he found that he could not leave his comrade.

While sitting there, Dwire's racking pain appeared to pass out in restful ease. He watched the white sun burn to gold, and then to red, and sink behind bold mountains in the west.

Twilight came suddenly. It lingered, slowly turning to gloom. The vast vault of blue-black lightened to the blinking of stars; and then fell the serene, silent, luminous desert night.

Dwire kept his vigil. As the long hours wore on, he felt stealing over him the comforting sense that he need not forever fight sleep.

A wan glow flared behind the dark, uneven horizon, and a melancholy, misshapen moon rose to make the white night one of shadows. Absolute silence claimed the desert. It was mute. But something breathed to Dwire, telling him when he was alone. He covered the dark, still face of his comrade from the light of the stars.

That action was the severing of his hold on realities. They fell away from him in final separation. Vaguely, sweetly, dreamily, he seemed to behold his soul.

Then up out of the vast void of the desert, from the silence and illimitableness, trooped his phantoms of peace. Majestically they formed about him, marshaling and mustering in ceremonious state, and moved to lay upon him their passionless serenity.

FROM FAR DAKOTA'S CANYONS

by
Walt Whitman

The title of this poem is a play on words by Whitman, using publishing terms meaning "pages of little value." His Leaves of Grass *was initially surrounded by controversy for its sumptuous physicality and homosexual references. While many critics labeled the book obscene, as with many such books, today it's considered a work of great value. "From Far Dakota's Canyons" was included in later editions of this book.*

It was during the 1876 Centennial celebration of the birth of the United States that reports of Lieutenant Colonel George Custer's defeat at the Battle of Little Bighorn began filtering in. When the shocking story hit the newspapers, most people had been led to believe the "Indian problem" was under control and were busy celebrating the opening of the West and the hopeful beginning of the nation's second century. To the horrified public, this was the 9/11 of that day. While the military initially blamed Custer, the public responded by embracing the myth of Custer's Last Stand and that's been the dominant theme up to today.

Whitman expressed these general feelings in this poem honoring Custer's death and that of his men. Whitman biographer Jerome Loving noted, "The poem and its sentiment were something of a contradiction for the poet who had since his newspaper days stood up for the victims of capitalism." Here Whitman paints Custer as a heroic victim—an image that was very popular at the time, though not very accurate, especially considering it was Custer who launched a poorly planned surprise attack on the unsuspecting villages that prompted the devastating retaliation. While Custer's Sioux scouts prepared for their deaths, Custer's outsized ego and his passion for glory got the better of his judgment, insisting, "The largest Indian camp on the North America continent is ahead and I am going to attack it!"

June 25, 1876

From far Dakota's cañons,
Lands of the wild ravine, the dusky Sioux, the lonesome stretch, the silence,
Haply to-day a mournful wail, haply a trumpet-note for heroes.
The battle-bulletin,

The Indian ambuscade, the craft, the fatal environment,

The cavalry companies fighting to the last in sternest heroism,

In the midst of their little circle, with their slaughter'd horses for breastworks,

The fall of Custer and all his officers and men.

Continues yet the old, old legend of our race,

The loftiest of life upheld by death,

The ancient banner perfectly maintain'd,

O lesson opportune, O how I welcome thee!

As sitting in dark days,

Lone, sulky, through the time's thick murk looking in vain for light, for hope,

From unsuspected parts a fierce and momentary proof,

(The sun there at the centre though conceal'd,

Electric life forever at the centre,)

Breaks forth a lightning flash.

Thou of the tawny flowing hair in battle,

I erewhile saw, with erect head, pressing ever in front, bearing a bright sword
     in thy hand,

Now ending well in death the splendid fever of thy deeds,

(I bring no dirge for it or thee, I bring a glad triumphal sonnet,)

Desperate and glorious, aye in defeat most desperate, most glorious,

After thy many battles in which never yielding up a gun or a color

Leaving behind thee a memory sweet to soldiers,

Thou yieldest up thyself.

THE REVENGE
of RAIN-in-the-FACE

by
Henry Wadsworth Longfellow

The works of Henry Wadsworth Longfellow (1807–1882) were popular enough that he became world famous during his lifetime—a rarity for a poet. Some say he was the most famous American of his day. His masterpieces include "Paul Revere's Ride," "Evangeline," and The Song of Hiawatha. *Some of his lines have become part of our culture, such as "Ships that pass in the night" and "Footprints on the sands of time." His theme of individuals overcoming adversity strongly appealed to general public. That theme is evident in this poem, which emphasizes the Native American point-of-view of the Battle of Little Bighorn.*

After the battle, a story began to circulate that Hunkpapa Sioux Chief Rain-in-the-Face had killed Captain Thomas Custer—George's brother—because Thomas had arrested him a couple of years earlier for murder. This tale is what inspired Longfellow's poem, but Chief Rain-in-the-Face said, "Many lies have been told of me. Some say that I killed the Chief [George Custer], and others that I cut out the heart of his brother [Tom Custer], because he had caused me to be imprisoned. Why, in that fight the excitement was so great that we scarcely recognized our nearest friends! Everything was done like lightning."

Like many Western myths, it makes a good story.

In that desolate land and lone,
Where the Big Horn and Yellowstone
    Roar down their mountain path,
By their fires the Sioux Chiefs
Muttered their woes and griefs
    And the menace of their wrath.

"Revenge!" cried Rain-in-the-Face,
"Revenge upon all the race
    Of the White Chief with yellow hair!"
And the mountains dark and high

From their crags re-echoed the cry
      Of his anger and despair.
In the meadow, spreading wide
By woodland and river-side
      The Indian village stood;
All was silent as a dream,
Save the rushing of the stream
      And the blue-jay in the wood.

In his war paint and his beads,
Like a bison among the reeds,
      In ambush the Sitting Bull
Lay with three thousand braves
Crouched in the clefts and caves,
      Savage, unmerciful!

Into the fatal snare
The White Chief with yellow hair
      And his three hundred men
Dashed headlong, sword in hand;
But of that gallant band
      Not one returned again.

The sudden darkness of death
Overwhelmed them like the breath
      And smoke of a furnace fire:
By the river's bank, and between
The rocks of the ravine,
      They lay in their bloody attire.

But the foemen fled in the night,
And Rain-in-the-Face, in his flight,
    Uplifted high in air
As a ghastly trophy, bore
The brave heart, that beat no more,
    Of the White Chief with yellow hair.

Whose was the right and the wrong?
Sing it, O funeral song,
    With a voice that is full of tears,
And say that our broken faith
Wrought all this ruin and scathe,
    In the Year of a Hundred Years.

TWO ALIKE
and a LADY

by
Jules Verne

French author Jules Verne (1828–1905) was the first modern science fiction writer. He was fascinated by adventure, travel, and exploration. At the age of twelve he tried to stowaway aboard a ship bound for India, but he was caught and severely thrashed by his father. Later, when Verne was at college ostensibly to study law, his father discovered he was writing instead of studying and cut off his financial support. He was forced to become a stockbroker to support himself.

I discovered this long-forgotten tale almost by accident. Originally serialized in, of all places, The Delphos Daily Herald *of Delphos, Ohio, beginning on July 30, 1895, the piece ran with the simple byline "written by Jules Verne." While it's likely to have appeared elsewhere, this is the only instance I've located so far during the past hundred-plus years.*

Verne is known to have written thirty-six short stories. "Two Alike and a Lady" could be the thirty-seventh. It has yet to be examined by Verne scholars, meaning that it may have been written by some unknown imitator. (At least three other stories are now attributed to his son, Michel.) Still, this tale does contain many of the elements of Verne's stories. Also, the description of the Native American ceremony appears to indicate it was written by someone who had never been to the West and was unfamiliar with Native Americans. This ceremony is, of course, pure fantasy, bordering on pulp fiction, but that aside, this is a masterful tale wrought with danger and suspense.

The tar on the roof of the railway station at Sierra Blanca was molten in a July sun at noonday. It had been a mistake to swab the surface with stuff that would melt at a temperature of 100 unshaded. Alternation of liquefaction and congealment had let the layer of pebbles alternately slip and stop, slip and stop, until half of them had slid off the steep eaves into the tin gutter, which had also caught the drippings of tar until it was full of the mixture. Not much is done in this lazy town on the Mexican border of the United States, and what is done once is hardly ever done over again, even by the railroad folks, who are all activity as contrasted with the local stagnation. So the roof had become bare boards near the ridgepole, and a black muck toward the lower edges. It suggested a volcanic peak, from which lava had lately run down, and the still hot output, overflowing the eave-troughs, dribbled thence to the ground, making a black streak where it soaked slowly into the gravel. Along that mark an occasional drop of the resinous jet was falling.

An indolent group of American adventurers sat or half reclined under the portico. Their wide-brimmed hats were scattered on the floor, their red, blue or gray shirts were opened low at the necks, and several had pulled off their long boots. These fellows had thus made easy efforts to be cool. Not so the several Mexicans, Indians and mixed-bloods who stood in a half circle around the others, for they were too lazy to uncover their heads—too lazy, seemingly, to even sit down. All were watching the stripe of tar on the ground. One bearded man, in the semi-uniform of a railway employee, lay on his breast, with his head uplifted like a half-torpid boa, and there was something like the snake's dull glitter in his eyes—as they moved warily along a six-foot section of the black line. That piece was marked at each end by a stone, and in the same way at the center. On the edge of the low platform, beside this man, lay silver coins of various small values. Not a word was spoken by anybody. Inert sleepiness prevailed, and some of the eyes that were fixed on the money and the tar were half shut.

After something like ten speechless minutes, all the eyelids were suddenly raised, and the company stirred in an animate manner. A globule of tar had fallen from the eave and struck, with a little spatter, between the two stones at the left of the prostrate man.

"Left it is, and left wins," he said.

Then he duplicated every exposed coin by laying on it one of a like denomination; and, after a rearrangement of the silver by its owners, another interval of expectant waiting ensued. Again there was a drop of tar within the limits, but this time it was at the right of the dividing stone.

"Right it is, and right loses," said the operator of this slow and singular game of chance, and he gathered in all the risked cash.

The distant whistle of a locomotive stopped the gambling, and drove the men to their feet. At the same time a ramshackle wagon was drawn up to the station. The vehicle held, besides a driver, two men marvelously alike. They were bearded and stalwart, in years about thirty apiece, and in countenance handsomely intelligent. Their costumes were similar, although not exactly duplicates, and consisted of garments of civilization only a little affected by the unconventionality of the far Southwest. They alighted from the wagon with an activity which proved that they had not lived long in the lazy region of Sierra Blanca, and quickly, but very carefully, lifted out a large box. This was made smoothly and substantially of new boards. There were handles at the ends, but in one respect it differed strongly from any ordinary traveling trunk. There was no sign of a lid to open. Lines of screwheads ran along all the edges, but no hinge or lock was to be seen. It was clear that the contents, whatever they were, had been securely enclosed for a long journey, and were not meant to be disturbed on the way. The two men carried the box to the platform, set it down as though it was something at once heavy and fragile, and one remained with it, while the other entered the station to purchase tickets for New York.

"Seems as if you two oughter travel on one ticket," the agent remarked, glancing at the purchaser and then at the other outside the doorway; "you're so jest alike."

"Wish we could," was the meditative response, as the speaker returned to his wallet the small remainder of his money, after paying for the costly tickets for the railway trip across the continent.

"Twins?" the agent asked.

"Yes, twins," was the reply, with a touch of weariness, for how many thousands of times had he been compelled to answer that question? Then he forestalled the pleasantry, which he had come to regard as almost inevitable, by adding: "Yes—brothers, too—twins and brothers. We are Daniel and Donald Warren. I am Dan, and he is Don. O, yes; all the incidents that could suggest, in the way of confused identity, have happened to us," and he rejoined his brother at the box.

A second and nearer whistle of the locomotive was heard, and half a minute later a train arrived; but it came on the tracks of the San Antonio line, which ends at Sierra Blanca, and it waited there for a connection with a through train on the Texas and Pacific main route. A hundred passengers emerged from the cars, and the place had a spell of enlivenment through their presence, who huddled in the shade of the station, or reported to the makeshift restaurants and groggeries close by, during the hour that the coming train was belated. They were such a singularly mixed assemblage as can only be found near the southwestern border region of the Rio Grande. Three-fourths of them were men, and the women were either Indians, Mexicans or vicious specimens of eastern civilization—with one marked exception. This was a lady, whose gentility, like her beauty, was to be seen at a glance. She was twenty years old, but worry aged her to twenty-five, and jollity would soon have rejuvenated her to a similar extent. It was not the ordinary fret and fear of travel without male escort that gave anxiety to the fair passenger. She was in manifestly serious trouble. Looking about her for succor, and at first seeing repellant faces only, she at length went to the brothers Warren, who sat on their box.

"Will you pardon me, gentlemen," she said, in a politely modulated but agitated voice, "and advise me? I have come from Fort Davis. I am on my way to Kansas City—or I was, but how to *get there* I do not know. I purchased a ticket to Sierra Blanca only, because none for the main line could be had there. I had money enough to pay my way from here, but it has been stolen from me in the car. I have not a dollar left."

Her eyes were full of tears, her cheeks were scarlet, and her lips quivered. She was in a plight out of which her diffidence and inexperience pointed no escape, save that of piteous appeal to the two strangers who, of all the assemblage, looked likely to befriend her considerately.

With an inquiring look at each other, and an assenting nod, Dan and Don were agreed that she was truthful.

"We will buy you a ticket to Fort Davis," said Don.

"I am grateful," sobbed the lady, "but that would not help me. It is a most important matter—a question of life or death, sir, literally life or death—that requires me to be in Kansas City the very day that this next train will arrive there;" and she wrung her small hands piteously, with the twitching symptoms of hysteria. "And there is only one train daily from here."

"I will speak to the ticket agent," said Don, "and maybe he will trust you for a ticket until you arrive in Kansas City."

"I have already begged him to do so, and he refuses. The most he will do is to telegraph to my friends there, and let them pay the money at that end of the route; but that would make me miss this train, you see."

Don went to the agent, and pleaded in vain. That unimpressionable official's judgment was that the lady was a professional pretender, but he expressed it less considerately than that whereupon Don and he parted angrily. Then Don and Dan alternately guarded their box and canvassed the company for contributions toward the requisite forty-two dollars, first putting in the sixteen which comprised all the money left after their own expenditure for passage. Women pretty and good were so scarce in that bad part of the country that the men would not believe in this one, and their responses to the appeal were prompt denials, coupled in several instances with remarks so uncharitable that the Warrens could hardly restrain an impulse to whip the offenders.

The whistle of the expected train was followed by the rumble of its wheels, and then it slowed and stopped at the station. It had more and better cars than the other, for it was on a transcontinental route, and carried a more presentable assortment of travelers. It would be off in four minutes. Should it leave the lady behind?

"Dan, we did it once," said Don, suggestively.

"When we both got our meals and bed at a San Francisco hotel for a week, and paid for only one," Dan responded.

"That was in a financial emergency."

"Well, so is this."

"Shall we try?"

"Yes."

During the dialogue the twin brothers were getting their box so placed in the baggage car, that it would not be subjected to rough usage, and the lady stood by herself on the platform, pale now with alarm at what seemed to her a certainty of being delayed for a day.

"We will try to take you along—" Dan said to her.

"Because we feel sure that you are not deceiving us," Don interposed.

The bell rang, the conductor cried, "All aboard!" and there was no time for explanation. The Warrens and the lady entered a car, and found two empty seats adjoining. Each of the brothers took one, and Don placed their companion beside himself, next to the window.

"Take this ticket," he said to her, "and show it when the conductor comes along. Don't pay any attention to what my brother and I do. We will attempt a dishonest trick because we believe you are honest."

Then he and Dan conversed in a low tone, not in secrecy from her, but so as not to be overheard by anybody else. They stopped on hearing the call, "Tickets, please." The conductor had entered the car by the rear door, according to usage, scrutinizing and punching the tickets right and left of the aisle as he proceeded. Dan had one of the two tickets in his party of three persons, and Don had none. The conductor took a long strip of sectionally printed cardboard from Dan, and clipped a hole through the portion representing the journey as far as Fort Worth, about five hundred miles away. Then he turned to the passenger directly across the aisle, and after dealing with him in the same manner, crossed back to the seat in which Don sat with the lady. At that instant Don was settling down into his place, as though he had just moved there from the seat next rearward, while the only part of Dan's head visible was the back, for he was very intently looking out at the window.

It is a practice of American conductors, especially on long routes, to gaze directly into the face of every passenger upon the first inspection of the ticket, in order to memorize the visage, so that there may be no need of asking for another sight of the ticket until a junction with another road brings an influx of new passengers, with a necessity of a general punching. By this system he can, with remarkable facility, distinguish the comparatively few additional faces gained at the small way stations, from those which he has seen in his previous rounds of the cars. Only of the recruits does he demand a showing of tickets at these times.

When Don sank into the seat that he had already occupied, with the deceptive motion of having moved forward from the other, the conductor was for an instant confused; but it seemed clear enough, when he looked into the Warren twin face, that he had just attended to this passenger. Any lingering, careless doubt was displaced when Don, with a smile, extended the ticket that Dan had surreptitiously passed to him behind the official's back, showing the hole that the punch had made. The conductor reached over to deal with the lady's ticket, and then passed unsuspectingly along.

"We're good for a few hundred miles anyhow," said Don to the lady, "if my brother and I are careful not to let the conductor see both of our faces close together."

"So I'll go back to the rear car," said Dan, "to put a safe distance between us," and he quietly departed.

"It is a shame in me to let you gentlemen do this," the lady said to Don; "and I wouldn't allow it, only that I am in a great strait. Forgive me if I do not fully explain the vital importance to me and mine, of my arriving in Kansas City on this train: but this message will indicate how urgent the matter is." She drew from her pocketbook a telegram, which Don read.

"Mrs. Henry Carter, Fort Davis. Tex; If you are not here with me at Kansas City by noon of July 17 you will be too late. For God's sake, do not fail. Henry."

"Henry is Lient. Henry Carter, of the regular army," she went on, "and I am his wife. We have been living a year at the military post at Fort Davis, but now he is in Kansas City, and it will be a calamity if I do not get to him in time to—" and she stopped without completing the sentence.

The time to Fort Worth was a few minutes more than twenty-four hours, and the distance was 524 miles. The train left Sierra Blanca at 1 o'clock P.M. There was no incident of consequence during the remainder of the afternoon. Donald Warren and Mrs. Carter conversed about the objects which they saw along the route, and their fraudulent method of transportation. The lady proved keenly intelligent, and her gratitude was charming. Don left her alone several times to go to his brother, being careful to hold these meetings at the greatest separation from the conductor possible. At the station, one or the other went to the baggage car to see if anything had happened to the box. There was no re-examination of tickets to dread, and the fear was slight that the conductor, seeing a Warren face twice in his walk through the train, would discover the repetition. Danger was foreseen for the night, however, for how could the problem of quarters in a sleeping car be solved? If the three travelers should remain in seats all night, that fact would direct attention to them, because they did not look like persons who would save a few dollars by earning them so arduously. The difficulty had to be encountered, however, and Daniel engaged a section in a sleeping car. There were the usual upper and lower berths, thus giving a lower one for the comfort of Mrs. Carter and an upper one that would hold the brothers well enough, but how about the paucity of tickets? The practice is common to all United States railways, in the matter of slumberers, to see to it once for the night that every one of them has a transit ticket. After that is done, the lodgers are not disturbed, and it does not matter how many occupants there are in a section. The problem for the Warrens, then, was to occupy their berth without letting the conductor, or the porter, ever alert for fees, suspect that they were not one and the same person.

At this season darkness did not fall until 8 o'clock, and it was about an hour later that the feat was undertaken, Don had thus far led in the deception, and he now relinquished the leadership to Dan, but they were such perfect counterparts in appearance that Mrs. Carter was hardly aware which he was who escorted her to the sleeping car. Their manners and speech were as alike as their faces and figures. Dan directed the negro porter to make up the beds. When that was done, Mrs. Carter retired behind her own curtain and bestowed herself for the night snugly and safely, with a ticket under her pillow ready to produce upon demand. Dan quickly climbed into the berth above. Don entered the car fifteen minutes later, choosing a moment when the porter was not close by, and made his way to the section. As two pairs of masculine boots, standing alongside the daintier gaiters of Mrs. Carter, would clearly indicate three sets of feet, he was guilty of the impropriety of going to bed with his boots on. No mishap in getting into the berth was anticipated, and none occurred. Even if the porter had seen the Warrens, if not together, he would not have imagined there were two of them. The crisis would come when the sleeping car conductor, making his special round, might discover—as it was his duty to do—that two men were there with only one ticket.

The device for safety was ingenious but very simple. Dan lay with feet in the direction that the train was moving, in accordance with the common usage. Don reversed this posture, and stretched out instead to ride head foremost. The practical operation of this plan was not long delayed. As soon as all the passengers in the car had gone to bed, the conductor went through, calling out for tickets, and, after that warning, pulling each curtain gently aside at the head of the shelf-like couch, to see how many were inside. Mrs. Carter trembled with apprehension as her turn came, knowing that the success or failure of the fraud would immediately follow; but the twin brothers were cool and careful. Dan raised himself a little, so as to be sure that the blanket would not disclose outlines of Don's feet and legs behind him, and Don was further hidden by a handbag and several garments, heaped in careless disorder. The quick eyes of the conductor, however, saw a possibility of some thing wrong. He said nothing as he scrutinized the ticket, however, and then he dropped the curtain. Don had pinned the drapery tightly at his end of the berth, and now he was alarmed to hear the conductor pulling it loose. His head and shoulders were crowded as small and close as possible at the back corner of the berth, and were covered by the blanket. He realized, however, that exposure was now certain. Acting upon impulse, and yet adroitly, he threw the coverings off, and with the same movement covered Dan, while snatching the ticket from his hand.

"I'm fussy about sleeping in a car," he said, as the conductor looked in; and at that instant he seemed to be changing end for end in the berth; "I suppose I'm the only traveler on earth who likes to go head first, eh?"

It was the same face that had appeared at the other edge of the curtain. Its owner was floundering in the only space that could hold a second lodger. The ticket with its new hole just punched, was in his hand. The conductor went along.

Mrs. Carter prayed that heaven would bless her benefactors, and forgive their lies.

Worry and excitement had prepared Mrs. Carter to sleep soundly from nervous exhaustion, and the sun was up high enough to throw a gleam of light through an interstice of the window shade into her pretty, peaceful face while she still slumbered. But the Warrens were astir earlier, and anxious to get safely out. They tapped softly on the woodwork close to their charge's head, and in momentary bewilderment at awakening in a strange place, she gave a small exclamation of alarm.

"It is time for us to scatter," Don whispered, "but you need be in no hurry. Stay abed as late as you like."

"Thank you," she responded, "but I've slept quite long enough."

"We will leave the section to you, then, and you may remain. One of us will drop in to see you in a little while. At Fort Worth there will be a change of cars, but our train isn't due there until after noon, and in the meantime make your mind easy."

"You are very, very good to me," she sincerely responded.

The brothers completed their garb by putting on the few garments that they had taken off. Then one slipped out to the lavatory, bathed his face, brushed his hair and retreated to a rear car. The other awaited a favorable opportunity to duplicate that process, but first gave a fee to the porter, and told him to serve the lady in any way indicated by her.

It was 8 o'clock when the train stopped at Abilene, a place which is to be a crossing of the Texas and Pacific Railway by the Austin and Northwestern, and where work on this uncompleted line was going on. Meal cars were not yet in use on the former route, and Abilene was the stopping point for breakfast, which was served in a hasty, catchy manner in a shed-like structure. It was Don who took Mrs. Carter in, while Dan went alone to the remotest corner, to lessen the risk of the twinship being observed by anybody. Thereafter the forenoon passed uneventfully, and at a few minutes past 1 o'clock the train rolled into Fort Worth, the busy intersection of three railways. It was here that our travelers were to transfer to the Missouri Pacific line, over which lay the route prescribed by their two tickets. It was the place for dinner, too, and 2 o'clock struck before the wheels once more rumbled under them. They knew that a change of conductors, and a fresh punching of tickets, were now to imperil their journey. The trick of the previous day was to be tried again. Instead of being reassured by a first success, the brothers awaited the repetition with lessened confidence, and at the juncture requiring the nicest address they were palpably nervous. Professional tricksters would have had no such qualms of conscience, nor such fright at the disgrace of exposure, as these honorable gentlemen felt. But the conductor was fooled, exactly as his predecessor had been, except that there was aroused in his mind a vague idea of something irregular. This did not amount at the time to a suspicion of imposture, but it did prepare him for an alertness which brought the party to disaster soon afterward.

The next stoppage was at Denison, where a branch of the Missouri Pacific joins the main railway, which at this point crosses the Red river from Texas into Indian territory—or, in more descriptive words, from a State of considerable civilization directly into a territory of the wildest savagery. To the northward the railroad runs for nearly three hundred miles through the region allotted by the Government to the Choctaw Indians, and by them still kept a wilderness for their aboriginal possession. A distance of no more than ten miles had been traveled before the conductor made his demand for tickets from the score or so of passengers who had boarded the train at Denison. The Warrens were separated by three car lengths. Don sat with Mrs. Carter, and they had the two tickets. To their surprise the official asked to see the credentials, and when be had inspected them his eyes were lifted to Don's face with an ominously piercing gaze. Five minutes later he came to Dan, and astonished him by saying, peremptorily:

"Ticket, please."

"Why, you don't punch 'em again now, do you?" Dan replied, with as much composure as he could command.

"Show your ticket, please," was the obdurate rejoinder.

Of course Don had none to show. He dallied, he fumbled in his pockets, and he even pretended to be angrily annoyed, but subterfuges were of no use, and then he resorted to contrite confession. He went with the conductor to Don, and the predicament of Mrs. Carter was explained; but the officer disbelieved the lady, and was possibly proud of having defeated a scheme which had been successful on the other train.

"Very well," Dan said; "I will get off at the next station, and my brother and the lady can use the two tickets for the rest of the way to Kansas City. You're an obstinate ass, but you can't eject more than one of us."

If there had been any chance of a compromise, this epithet destroyed it.

"I can't, eh?" the conductor exclaimed. "We'll see about that. You've used these tickets," and he retained them in his hand, "to defraud the railroad company. They're forfeited, as I look at it, and I shall put you off—all three of you."

He pulled the bell cord, and the train came to a standstill. Brakesmen came to the support of the conductor. The brothers' appeal to passengers was overbalanced by a state-ment of the clear case of cheat. The three travelers, ashamed and humiliated, were led out of the car. The box was taken from among the baggage and set down beside the track.

"Surely, you're not heartless enough to abandon a lady in this place." said Don, seeing that no sign of habitation was visible. "At least take her along."

"O, I'm not heartless," was the conductor's reply. "I knew there was a handcar lying yonder," and he pointed to one that stood near the road. That's why I pulled up just here. It is in good running order. Some repairers left it only a week ago. You can take it and work your way back to Denison. The track will be clear for two hours, so there's no danger, and you'll have the satisfaction of earning your passage. Good day. All aboard."

The final call was to those passengers who had got off the train. They re-embarked, most of them laughing, and all convinced that only justice was being done. Then the train rolled on out of sight and hearing.

The ejected three stood for a minute mutely gazing toward the distance into which the cars had disappeared. They saw a single pair of rails stretch closer and closer together until they reached the vanishing point, and this roadway was the only disturbance of rugged nature. There was no other sign of humanity. The brothers turned their eyes upon each other quizzically.

"Honesty is the best policy, Don."

"Never abandon a lady in distress, Dan."

Mrs. Carter sank down on the box and wept hysterically. "I am so ashamed and sorry to have got you into this dreadful situation," she said, between sobs. "But I had an excuse—indeed, I had. My husband is the paymaster of his regiment. He is in trouble—awful trouble. Tempted by what seemed to be a chance to double the money in a week, by means of a speculation in Oklahoma lands, he used the funds which he had received for the payment of the soldiers. It looked certain that there was no risk—that by only delaying the disbursement for a week he would be a gainer by about twenty thousand dollars, and nobody a loser. Well, the scheme failed, or appeared to, and exposure seemed inevitable. He went to Kansas City, on a pretended errand, to gain a little time. But word of the defalcation has reached Washington, and an agent has been sent with an order of arrest, to be served in case my husband does not show a receipted pay-roll. After he had gone, a saving was made of most of the money, and, borrowing all I could from several friends, I made up the remainder, so that the regiment was paid off yesterday. With the pay-roll all signed I started with it to save my husband. If I had not been robbed, I should reach him to-morrow afternoon, three hours before the agent from Washington could get there. But now—he and I will be disgraced—ruined—it would kill me."

The agony of the woman was pitiful. What could be done? A return in the handcar to Denison would involve only two or three hours of work at the crank, so far as inconvenience to the Warrens was concerned, and there they could resume their journey by the next train. But the delay would be very consequential to Mrs. Carter.

"Don't mind me," she weepingly said. I am very selfish, I fear. It is of myself that I am thinking mostly. I will conceal nothing from you, who have befriended me at such a cost. My husband is not a good husband. He no longer loves me, and I think I have never loved him—or, if I did, a knowledge of his true character has destroyed my affection. But his public dishonor would be mine—it would kill me—I couldn't live."

Once more the brothers looked inquiringly at each other, and Don said; "Why not make the experiment now, with the handcar?"

"Why not?" Dan echoed. "Let us do it."

They at once set about opening the box. Each had one of those knives of Yankee manufacture, in which a single handle holds a number of miniature but excellent tools —including a small screw driver. They soon had the mysterious receptacle taken apart.

"It is barely possible," said Dan to the wondering Mrs. Carter, as they worked, "that we may complete our journey in spite of our mishap. But we must enjoin secrecy upon you as to the method, whether we fail or succeed."

The case was soon removed, and Mrs. Carter saw that the enclosure consisted of a large, irregular stone, mass of ore, or other substance to which was attached some machinery.

"My brother and I," Don explained, while they carefully lifted this thing out on the ground and inspected its parts, "have been for three months on a mission to a monastery at Lag de Patos, across the Rio Grande in Mexico. It wasn't a religious mission, however. We had been told by a friend that an old monk possessed a meteorite—this hunk of blackened stuff that you see here—which had fallen very many years ago in that region. The holy man placed it on a high, exposed rock, and made a sort of shrine of it. Something in its composition attracted lightning strongly, and it drew down thunderbolts, in violent electrical storms, until the good man has no idea how many hundreds of times it has been hit. It became magnetized to a marvelous degree—a magnet of enormous power. It was regarded with superstitious awe by the ignorant Mexicans of the neighborhood, and the frequent sight of a lightning flash, zig-zagging from the heavens down to it, impressed them mightily. The priest was something of a scientist, though, and he knew that there wasn't anything supernatural about his meteorite, however wonderful it might be. Brother Dan and I went to Lag de Patos and teased and tempted the priest until he sold it to us."

The story of the meteorite had accompanied the removal of it and its attached mechanism completely from the box.

"And what do you mean to do with it?" Mrs. Carter asked.

"Our plan was to turn it into money," was Dan's reply, "by making it run a machine with its magnetic power. That would be a great curiosity, if nothing more. So strong is its attraction toward the north pole that, were it to be dropped from a height of a thousand feet it would strike the earth as much as a hundred feet to the northward of the spot where a perpendicular descent would have landed it Well, this toggery utilizes our stupendous magnet's northerly inclination, by alternately applying the force to a balance wheel and disconnecting it. By operating this small button, with a light touch of a forefinger, we can keep the wheel in motion."

A railroad train came into view from the direction in which the other had gone. This was the daily, south-bound express. It thundered past.

"That clears our track for the next twenty-four hours, pretty nearly," Dan said.

"And now for the handcar," Don added.

They found the vehicle to be simply one of those low, small and light platform cars, with two cranks geared to an axletree, in such a manner that two men may propel it. Such conveyances are used by track layers and repairers, and muscular hands at the cranks can force it to a fair speed. After setting this car on the rails, the meteorite and its apparatus were placed in it.

"We shall try whether we can turn our toy into a practical motor," Don said to the now wide-eyed lady.

"In constructing it," Dan added, "we were both convinced that, while the power of our stationary machine was no more than barely sufficient to keep a wheel revolving, it might be expected to have increased force if at each effort it moved toward the north pole. Of course, that wouldn't constitute a very valuable motor, because it would be too much like tobogganing—you would have to haul your vehicle back southward for each ride you took northward."

"But northward is the way we wish to go." Don interposed, with rising enthusiasm.

"And why shouldn't we make this light car go with our magno-meteor-motor?" Dan exclaimed, quite excitedly extemporizing a name for the contrivance.

The crank power of the handcar conveyed to the axletree by means of an elastic steel band, encircling a weighty, evenly poised balance wheel. The Warrens first fastened the magno-meteor-motor firmly to the bottom of the car, using for that purpose the boards and screw of the box. Then they made a band to connect the two balance wheels. A sharp knife, cutting a leather handbag into a ribbon, provided one strong enough for the purpose. Two hours of rapid, skillful labor completed the job, and the experiment was ready to be made.

A trial trip of a few rods did not terminate the uncertainty of the enterprise. Dan slowly worked a crank, and Don cautiously operated the bottom of the more unusual machine. The car moved readily, but how much it was helped by the meteorite was not evident. There was no great encouragement, and the brothers' faces clouded a little, as the quick eyes of Mrs. Carter saw.

"All aboard, passenger!" cried Dan.

Don more politely assisted Mrs. Carter to a place on the car. A broad seat was at the back of the skeleton of a vehicle, and thereon she placed herself, obediently but with a show of natural nervousness. Once more the two men took their posts. Dan laid hold of one of the cranks, and Don at the same time slowly set the magno-meteor-motor going. As before, the car moved so nearly in its usual manner that, if there was any assistance from the meteorite, it was not appreciable. But a dozen rods had not been traversed before the polar magnetism, as ingeniously utilized, accelerated the speed. Don manipulated the button faster by cautious degrees, and simultaneously Dan ceased his efforts at the crank, of which he soon had to let go altogether, so rapidly did it revolve.

For a positive fact, the strange motor was propelling the car!

Swifter and swifter until the breath of the travelers was caught away from them, and they felt as though facing a gale of wind, their vehicle flew over the rails, making the iron sing out with low, metallic music as the wheels touched them lightly in passing, like the fingers of a player on the strings of a harp.

The three peculiar travelers, astounded by their car's swiftness, bewildered by their unexampled experience, felt at first exultation and exhilaration only. No sense of danger came to them for a little while. Ten miles had been made in twice as many minutes, or at a rate equal to that of the express train from which they had been expelled, before Don realized the recklessness of what they were doing, and ceased to finger the button by which the vibrations of the magno-meteor-motor were controlled. The car had no brake, and it ran fully half a mile by its own momentum before it slowed enough that Dan could stop it by holding back on a crank. The brothers hastened to inspect the machine. As it had been rather crudely constructed, and not for the purpose to which it was now being applied, they feared that it had not borne the strain of such a test; but it was found to have worked, without breakage or any other injury.

"Will it be a safe trip to undertake?" Dan said, addressing Don. "What do you think?"

"It would be safe enough, I imagine, if we were to go slowly," was the thoughtful reply; "but if we are to try to reach Kansas City in time—well, I don't know."

"We needn't make the whole distance with this car, remember. Indian territory is only 200 miles wide, and the railroad doesn't go fifty miles further than that in crossing it. The desolation ceases at the Kansas border. At Oswego, no more than ten or twelve miles beyond, there is an intersecting railroad, as well as additional trains on the main line. The stations become numerous, too, and we would be sure to dash into a disaster of some sort."

"But as you say, we needn't stick to our own private car after we are where we can board a train. We have money enough to pay our fares between Oswego and Kansas City."

"Oswego is our goal, then. Shall we make for it, or return to Denison, as we can do by using the cranks?"

The question was directed to Mrs. Carter. "It is not fair to make me decide," she replied. "I will not ask you gentlemen, who are already involved so seriously on my account, to incur the perils of the two hundred miles to the northward. If I must say yes or no, I say no."

"You are not alarmed for yourself?"

"I would take any risk."

"We are now in the land of the Choctaws, most of whom are utterly untouched by civilization, and whose savagery is notorious. An accident disabling our motor would leave us only the cranks as a means of propulsion, and we might be at the mercy of the Indians, who sometimes even attack the regular trains. Have you the courage for such an adventure?"

"Yes."

"Then we will go ahead—eh, Dan?"

"Certainly we will, Don. All aboard!"

Again Mrs. Carter was bestowed on the rear seat, and Dan started the car by use of the cranks, while Don operated the motor. At before, the power of the meteorite was not sufficient to move the car from a standstill, but with a track almost straight and perfectly level, and the light vehicle once under way, the strange machine soon sent the car along at a rate which, while it would have been commonplace to occupants of an enclosed car, was exciting to these exposed persons. A novice's ride on a locomotive is a test of the nerves, notwithstanding his confidence in the engine and its engineer; but these adventurers had no reason for faith in their machine or their management of it. They could only estimate uncertainly the rate they were going. They were unacquainted with the landmarks, and their only basis of judgment was to endeavor as calmly as possible to see whether the landscape was left behind more or less rapidly than they had observed it to be when in an express train. As nearly as the Warrens could determine, the car was soon going at least twenty-five miles an hour. The land was a rolling prairie, wild with grass and low bushes, but with only here and there a clump of trees, and not often with unevenness sufficient to obscure the track for a mile ahead. The brothers kept a sharp lookout for obstacles. Two hours after the second start they came to where a rude shed was labeled "Fort McCullough," but the fort was a military post several miles away, and not a person was visible. The passage of one passenger train and one freight train each way daily did not require the constant presence of a custodian, it seemed. The car was slowed, but not stopped, and very quickly it was again under rapid headway. After that the travelers' shadows which raced along with them, lengthened further and further out on the ground to their right, and finally disappeared, for it was sundown.

"Is there an early moon to-night?" Dan yelled, for the wheels rattled and resounded loudly on the tracks, and there was only a thin boarding between this racket and the ears of the riders.

"I don't remember," Don returned in a shout.

Mrs. Carter leaned over to Don and said. "If I am not mistaken, there'll be no moon until midnight," and in getting close, so as to be heard, she chanced to be lurched a little by a motion of the car. Her lips, still open with the utterance, still emitting the breath of her words, were brought into contact with the listener's cheek. The modest woman blushed for the mishap, which to the man was a delightful accident, however decorously she deplored it by look, gesture and exclamation. Had he ever encountered so lovable a lady? Surely none so charming had touched her lips to his cheek.

But the more practical question was whether they could hope to travel through the night. The brothers discussed it, in short sentences, and at the top of their voices, while daylight dimmed and twilight fell; and then it was decided for awhile by the approach of a train! The whistle of a locomotive was heard, and a little later the rumble of wheels, so much more heavily laden than those of the handcar that the distant noise was not entirely deadened by the one underneath.

Nothing was visible forward or back. Then, just as the direction of the sound defined itself to be off laterally to the westward, the car dashed past an intersecting track, and the red lanterns of a man at a switch glimmered briefly. The place was Atoka, with one small shelter in the wilderness to mark a station. The branch railway extended to a coal mine twelve miles away, where the Missouri Pacific Company digs out a partial supply of fuel for its locomotives. It chanced that no less a potential official than Jay Gould, controlling owner of the railway, was on a tour of inspection, as it was his private train that the switchman was to transfer at this point to the main line. He was ready to shift the switch when the approach of the Warrens' car delayed and puzzled him, and he was so bewildered by the sight of it dashing past that, if the Gould train had not been cautiously slowed at the junction he would not have had the rails placed aright.

"What's chasing us?" Dan cried.

"Must be a special of some sort," Don answered.

"Then we've got to go."

"Yes, we've got to go."

Jay Gould is not content with the schedule speed of twenty-five miles an hour for his own travel over his railroad. His train thundered onward from Atoka at a rate at least a third faster. The engineer could not see the small vehicle ahead, for it was unlighted in the darkness, nor could he hear it, for its sound was drowned by that of the heavy locomotive. It was like a lion raging through a jungle, unconscious of the rabbit fleeing in his path. The rabbit bounded away, with no time to get out of the track of its pursuer, and only a forlorn hope of escape by keeping straight on. Dan abandoned his outlook ahead—for a collision with some obstacle would be no more dreadful thing than to be run down—and stood beside Don, whose hand was already fatigued with operating the motor.

"Let me relieve you," he said.

Don permitted this, and devoted himself to watching the headlight of the locomotive, scanning the now accelerated motor, and advising of any apparent loss or gain in the flight from Jay Gould's special. Mrs. Carter was terrified, but not the less alert. Her only sign of cowardice was when Don placed his hand on her shoulder, by way of encouragement, for the noise had become too loud to permit conversation. She clung to his hand, but let go again almost instantly and clutched the seat instead. The jolting and swaying threatened to throw the frail vehicle from the rails. The motor seemed sure to break into fragments. But there was nothing else to do than force the unique engine, if possible, to a continuance of speed equal to that of the locomotive, which was unconsciously chasing at a distance of no more than a quarter of a mile, with its demoniac headlight relentlessly in sight.

From Atoka to McAllister is fifty-three miles. The distance was covered in an hour and a half. The figures were afterward ascertained. But at the time the adventurers only knew that, after speeding the magno-meteor-motor to its utmost, and at length discerning unmistakable premonitions of breakage, they saw the special stop. There are coal mines at McAllister, and Jay Gould was to remain there for an inspection. Ignorant of that, the Warrens kept on, but with considerably slackened speed, in order to make the distance safe. Very soon they crossed a wide stream, the Canadian river, and four miles beyond came to a branch called North Fork. These are tributaries of the Arkansas river, and the region of their own junction is a primeval forest. The gloom of the trees was black, in the absence of a moon, for even starlight was shut out by a clouded sky. Suddenly, on slowly rounding from a curve to a straight section of the railway, a bright light was seen ahead.

"A locomotive!" Dan cried, and stopped the slow action of the motor.

"No—a fire!" responded Don, springing to the cranks, nevertheless, to use them in lieu of a brake.

The car stopped within a hundred feet of a heap of blazing wood, around which Indians were dancing grotesquely. The flames fitfully illumined them, showing that they were half naked, or rather that their legs, arms and bodies were covered only by bright red and yellow paints. On their heads were feathers, standing in an upright row from the middle of the forehead over to the nape of the neck, and trailing thence down the back. Their necks, shoulders and hips were encircled by gaudily woven beads, feathers and cloths. The men were all middle-aged or older. They were Choctaws who had resisted the influences of civilization, except to take their rations of Government food, and to swap for smuggled whisky some of the proceeds of their traps and guns. This tribe retains, especially among its older members, much of the superstitious savagery which characterized it when, before the forced removal to Indian territory, it had an extensive domain along the Gulf of Mexico. On this night these untamed Choctaw braves had assembled for an annual rite of religion, or voudou worship, and they were weirdly at it when the travelers came upon them. They seemed amazed by the intrusion. With vicious yells they broke the circle of the dance and started pell-mell towards the car. The motor was somehow disarranged by the stoppage, and refused to work.

"Roll under the seat, Dan—quick—before they see there are two men of us," Don said, and so peremptorily that his brother obeyed. "And lie close."

Don hastily but quietly seated himself beside Mrs. Carter, and the presence of Dan was not suspected by the Indians, who gathered menacingly around, and gibbered in their native tongue.

"Does any one of you speak English?" Don asked.

A purely Choctaw hubbub afforded a negative reply.

"They mean mischief," said Don, satisfied that they could not understand his words. "Now, an Indian agent told us only the other day—don't you remember it, Dan?—that the sight of us twins—so exactly alike—would mystify and frighten a Choctaw."

The Indians were now pressing closely around the car, gesticulating violently, and making outcries.

"They kill one of every pair of twins at birth," Don rapidly went on; "so they don't know of such likenesses as we present, and they'd take us for 'Musamontah,' or a man who can multiply himself by the devil's help."

At this juncture two Indians laid hold of Don, and dragged him roughly from the car, while two others, with a gentleness the ominousness of which she did not comprehend, removed Mrs. Carter. The captives were conducted to the fire; and while that was being done Dan crawled away unseen into the woods. The evident leader of the band directed the tying of Don to the trunk of a tree, and it was done mercilessly; but Mrs. Carter was seated on the ground with a ceremoniousness almost polite.

A voudouish ceremony had evidently been going on. Green saplings, bent and spliced into a hoop about thirty feet in diameter, encircled the fire, with enclosed space sufficient for the dancers. Fastened to the ring in alternation, and at intervals of about a foot, were snakes and squirrels. The serpents were tied at their middles, with their loose heads and tails darting and wriggling. The scared squirrels had leash enough to permit them to dodge one of the aggressive reptiles at a time, but in doing so the timid creatures often leaped within reach of poisonous fangs at the other side. Thus there was a horrible circlet of madly enlivened snakes and squirrels, with the shifting glow of the fire illumining it. The torture had a sacrificial significance, clearly, and what might not the human captives expect to suffer at the hands of these fiendish zealots?

The Indians began to remove a section of the snake-entwined saplings, on which some of the squirrels were in the agonies of death by poison. The intention was evident. Donald Warren was to be subjected to the serpents' fangs. Suddenly Daniel Warren stalked into view. His assumed air was one of very solemn dignity. The Indians gazed at him in amazement. Cries of "Musamontah!" were intermingled with the yelping exclamations. Dan strode slowly to his brother and cut the wythes that bound him. The Choctaws stood awestruck and bewildered at what was to them a most appalling phenomenon. A "musamontah" was before them. The exactness of the likeness between the Warrens left no ground for incredulity. According to their traditional belief, each double was able to double himself again, and so on until there might be a thousand multitudes. The Warrens wasted no time, and yet acted with impressive deliberation. As slow and grave as ghosts in *Hamlet*, they took Mrs. Carter between them, and composedly walked to the car. Once aboard, they seized the cranks and were safely away before the dumfounded savages regained their activity.

⚹ **TWO ALIKE AND A LADY** ⚹

There was for awhile no thought in the party save that of exultation over the escape from the Choctaws. The men were nearly exhausted by their violent handpower propulsion of the car, and soon let the wheels revolve leisurely. The lady was weak and weary, and her words of gratitude were low, but very fervent. Then they spoke jocosely of the twinship which had made the journey remarkable.

"No wonder the conductors and the Indians were deceived," Dan said.

"And what a pity that the last conductor took a materialistic view of the resemblance," Don said, "instead of passing us superstitiously along, as the Indians did."

"The likeness is exact," Mrs. Carter dreamily remarked, "and yet I could easily distinguish you, Mr. Donald Warren, from you. Mr. Daniel."

"How?" Dan asked.

"Oh, I don't know."

Don did not know, either; but he noticed that it was he in when she found something distinctive from his brother, and he mused whether that quality was an agreeable one.

The car went trundling slowly alone. It was too dark at first to examine the disabled motor, but when at length the moon shone, and the sky cleared, it was seen that the injury could not be mended without screws, cord and a suitable piece of wood. The brothers knew that they had by this time passed into the land of the Cherokees, the most civilized of the tribes, and that by daylight they might easily reach Gibson, an important military post, and only a few miles from Tahiequah, the center of so much enlightenment as the white men have contrived to impart to the reds. The decision was to get to Gibson, take breakfast there, repair the machine, and resume the journey. The dawn and the car reached the station together. The keeper was aroused, and was misled to believe that the Warrens were inspectors, with authority to pass over the line in any manner they pleased. He was a mixed-blood with no intelligence to spare from his regular duties for an indulgence in skepticism. He provided a plain but wholesome breakfast, and *the* simple requisites for repairing the motor. He could also tell that the track would be clear to Oswego, where at 10 o'clock in the forenoon a local train would start for Kansas City. The distance between Gibson and Oswego was 100 miles. It was 6 o'clock when all was ready, and the meteorite's polar magnetism was again available.

"Twenty-seven miles an hour will take us to Oswego on time," said Dan to Mrs. Carter, "and you shall be in Kansas City before the Government agent arrives there."

Don showed no enthusiasm at this probability of seeing the dishonest officer, until the lady said: "And we may avert my disgrace yet;" whereupon he recalled her previous declaration that she could not live under the odium of a husband's obloquy, and accordingly he viewed the matter as one vitally concerning herself.

The first occurrence that made the transit different from that of the previous day was a sudden and dense clouding of the sky. It was then 9 o'clock, and three-quarters of the way to Oswego had been run. They had traversed a valley between low mountains, seeing once in a while a specimen of the semi-civilized Cherokee, dressed absurdly in mixtures of native and foreign garments, and passing only two shed-like stations, in which were no signs of life. A flash of lightning and a peal of thunder were followed by a dash of rain.

"Shall we stop?" Dan asked of Don.

"There is danger in keeping on," was the reply.

"But the rain can't hurt us," Mrs. Carter urged.

No, but a stroke of lightning might kill them. The Warrens knew how apt the clouds were to bestow electricity upon the meteorite. Should the risk be taken? If not, the disaster which Mrs. Carter dreaded more than death would come to her. The brothers removed the lady as far from the now dangerous thing as the limits of the small car would permit. Then it was a question which of the men should take the peril of operating the motor. One proposed "ten minutes apiece," and the other assented. The rain poured down, the lightning became vivid and the thunder sounded like a cannonade. The car sped on through nearly an hour of the storm and was within less than a quarter of a mile of Oswego.

Then there was a blinding flash, and the travelers did not hear the burst of thunder after it, for they were smitten insensible. The lightning struck the meteorite. That conglomerate mass burst into fragments. Very likely it was already surcharged with electricity when this hundredth additional injection, or thousandth exceeded its receptive capacity. The momentum of the car carried it to within a few rods of the station,

with its occupants lying like corpses in the wreck of the machine. They were conveyed into the building and placed on the floor. Dan and Mrs. Carter revived quickly. They had only been stunned. But Don had been at the motor when the lightning struck. He was slower to regain consciousness. When he awoke his head was in Mrs. Carter's lap, and her hands were gently stroking his forehead, while Dan and others were using less charming restoratives.

"Have we missed the train?" he drowsily inquired.

"No, it's an hour behind time, and I've got three tickets for Kansas City," Dan replied.

Into Don's dazed head came a vague jealousy of the husband to whom this ministering woman, with her pretty face so close, and her hands so caressing, was consigned.

"You feel better?" she murmured, solicitously.

Her palms were cool upon his heated brows, her eyes gazed into his for signs of returning vitality, her mouth smiled encouragingly with her utterance, and the man could only reply, incoherently, that he was entirely comfortable.

Don next heard a harsher voice. It was that of a telegraph operator, who was also the ticket agent, addressing a lounger. "A dispatch has just gone through to Fort Davis," he said. "It was from St. Louis and had to be repeated here. It said that Lieut. Carter—and there he stopped.

Don felt the hands of Mrs. Carter lie limp and still on his forehead, and her knees tremble under him, as she listened.

"I don't know as I ought to give away a private message," the man continued, "but it'll all come out in the papers, anyhow. Lieut. Carter eloped from Kansas City with a rich girl. It seems, and I guess there was some money trouble, too—from the wording of the message. Well, the lieutenant was in a bad mess, anyhow, and in St. Louis he blew his brains out—"

The lady's hands slid from Don's forehead, and her face fell on his, for she had fainted.

The awaited train arrived and departed without taking on Mrs. Carter. She was too prostrated to continue the journey, the original purpose of which no longer existed. She was not now endangered by the possible exposure of a husband's dishonesty, and grief could not be acute when the news of his suicide also brought that of his marital infidelity. Was it a wonder that one of her regrets was that she had not been wedded instead to a man like Donald Warren? Yet she reproved herself for such a thought. About the same time Don was wondering whether he might not win this widow for a wife. Time will tell.

A DRIFT
from
REDWOOD CAMP

by
Bret Harte

Rudyard Kipling was a big fan of Bret Harte (1836–1902), to say the least, having been largely drawn to California because of his love for Harte's tales. "But I am sorry for Bret Harte," Kipling wrote shortly after arriving in San Francisco. "It happened this way. A reporter asked me what I thought of the city and I made answer suavely that it was hallowed ground to me because of Bret Harte. That was true. 'Well,' said the reporter, 'Bret Harte claims California, but California don't claim Bret Harte. He's been so long in England that he's quite English. Have you seen our cracker-factories and the new offices of the Examiner?' He could not understand that to the outside world the city was worth a great deal less than the man."

Harte is known for his many excellent stories of the wild days of California, particularly "The Luck of Roaring Camp" and "The Outcasts of Poker Flat." He began his writing career with controversy. He was living in the small coastal town of Union (now Arcata), in Northern California near the Oregon border, when he wrote an strong editorial condemning the massacre of between eighty and two hundred Wiyots during a three-day religious ceremony, saying, "a more shocking and revolting spectacle never was exhibited to the eyes of a Christian and civilized people. Old women wrinkled and decrepit lay weltering in blood, their brains dashed out and dabbled with their long grey hair. Infants scarcely a span along, with their faces cloven with hatchets and their bodies ghastly with wounds."

Harte soon had to flee town after receiving death threats. Despite there being evidence that the premeditated massacre was carried out by specific individuals, no one ever went to trial. Harte ended up in San Francisco.

Harte was close friends with both Ambrose Bierce and Mark Twain, having met the latter in the early days before Twain was famous. In fact he said he was the one who encouraged Twain to write down "The Celebrated Jumping Frog of Calaveras County"— the story that initially launched Twain onto the international stage. They went on to write a play, Ah Sin, together.

At the time Twain told him the jumping frog story, Harte was working as a clerk and superintendent of the U.S. Mint in San Francisco. It was also at this time that Harte became friends with Ambrose Bierce, who had worked at the Mint several years *earlier and would work there again later on. Around this time, all three were writing and working on and off as newspaper and magazine editors.*

Harte had grown up in Albany and Brooklyn, living there until he'd left for California at the age of 18. Since Harte's stories of the West were very popular in the East, he headed back to New York and soon landed work at The Atlantic Monthly. *Eventually he was appointed as a U.S. Consul in Germany, and then in Scotland. He finally moved to England, where he remained until his death from throat cancer.*

Traveling out of San Francisco, Kipling wrote, "At six in the morning the heat was distinctly unpleasant, but seeing with the eye of the flesh that I was in Bret Harte's own country, I rejoiced. There were the pines and madrone-clad hills his miners lived and fought among; there was the heated red earth that showed whence the gold had been washed; the dry gulch, the red, dusty road where Hamblin was used to stop the stage in the intervals of his elegant leisure and superior card-play; there was the timber felled and sweating resin in the sunshine; and, above all, there was the quivering pungent heat that Bret Harte drives into your dull brain with the magic of his pen."

The following ironic tale is set on the coast of Northern California.

They had all known him as a shiftless, worthless creature. From the time he first entered Redwood Camp, carrying his entire effects in a red handkerchief on the end of a long-handled shovel, until he lazily drifted out of it on a plank in the terrible inundation of '56, they never expected anything better of him.

In a community of strong men with sullen virtues and charmingly fascinating vices, he was tolerated as possessing neither—not even rising by any dominant human weakness or ludicrous quality to the importance of a butt. In the dramatis personae of Redwood Camp he was a simple "super"—who had only passive, speechless roles in those fierce dramas that were sometimes unrolled beneath its green-curtained pines.

Nameless and penniless, he was overlooked by the census and ignored by the tax collector, while in a hotly-contested election for sheriff, when even the headboards of the scant cemetery were consulted to fill the poll-lists, it was discovered that neither candidate had thought fit to avail himself of his actual vote.

He was debarred the rude heraldry of a nickname of achievement, and in a camp made up of "Euchre Bills," "Poker Dicks," "Profane Pete," and "Snap-shot Harry," was known vaguely as "him," "Skeesicks," or "that coot."

It was remembered long after, with a feeling of superstition, that he had never even met with the dignity of an accident, nor received the fleeting honor of a chance shot meant for somebody else in any of the liberal and broadly comprehensive encounters which distinguished the camp. And the inundation that finally carried him out of it was partly anticipated by his passive incompetency, for while the others escaped—or were drowned in escaping—he calmly floated off on his plank without an opposing effort.

For all that, Elijah Martin—which was his real name—was far from being unamiable or repellent. That he was cowardly, untruthful, selfish, and lazy, was undoubtedly the fact; perhaps it was his peculiar misfortune that, just then, courage, frankness, generosity, and activity were the dominant factors in the life of Redwood Camp. His submissive gentleness, his unquestioned modesty, his half refinement, and his amiable exterior consequently availed him nothing against the fact that he was missed during a raid of the Digger Indians, and lied to account for it; or that he lost his right to a gold discovery by failing to make it good against a bully, and selfishly kept this discovery from the knowledge of the camp. Yet this weakness awakened no animosity in his companions, and it is probable that the indifference of the camp to his fate in this final catastrophe came purely from a simple forgetfulness of one who at that supreme moment was weakly incapable.

Such was the reputation and such the antecedents of the man who, on the 15th of March, 1856, found himself adrift in a swollen tributary of the Minyo. A spring freshet of unusual volume had flooded the adjacent river until, bursting its bounds, it escaped through the narrow, wedge-shaped valley that held Redwood Camp. For a day and night the surcharged river poured half its waters through the straggling camp. At the end of that time every vestige of the little settlement was swept away; all that was left was scattered far and wide in the country, caught in the hanging branches of water-side willows and alders, embayed in sluggish pools, dragged over submerged meadows, and one fragment—bearing up Elijah Martin—pursuing the devious courses of an unknown tributary fifty miles away. Had he been a rash, impatient man, he would have been speedily drowned in some earlier desperate attempt to reach the shore; had he been an ordinary bold man, he would have succeeded in transferring himself to the branches of some obstructing tree; but he was neither, and he clung to his broken raft-like berth with an endurance that was half the paralysis of terror and half the patience of habitual misfortune. Eventually he was caught in a side current, swept to the bank, and cast ashore on an unexplored wilderness.

His first consciousness was one of hunger that usurped any sentiment of gratitude for his escape from drowning. As soon as his cramped limbs permitted, he crawled out of the bushes in search of food. He did not know where he was; there was no sign of habitation—or even occupation—anywhere. He had been too terrified to notice the direction in which he had drifted—even if he had possessed the ordinary knowledge of a backwoodsman, which he did not. He was helpless. In his bewildered state, seeing a squirrel cracking a nut on the branch of a hollow tree near him, he made a half-frenzied dart at the frightened animal, which ran away. But the same association of ideas in his torpid and confused brain impelled him to search for the squirrel's hoard in the hollow of the tree. He ate the few hazel-nuts he found there, ravenously. The purely animal instinct satisfied, he seemed to have borrowed from it a certain strength and intuition. He limped through the thicket not unlike some awkward, shy quadrumane, stopping here and there to peer out through the openings over the marshes that lay beyond. His sight, hearing, and even the sense of smell had become preternaturally acute. It was the latter which suddenly arrested his steps with the odor of dried fish. It had a significance beyond the mere instincts of hunger—it indicated the contiguity of some Indian encampment. And as such—it meant danger, torture, and death.

He stopped, trembled violently, and tried to collect his scattered senses. Redwood Camp had embroiled itself needlessly and brutally with the surrounding Indians, and only held its own against them by reckless courage and unerring marksmanship. The frequent use of a casual wandering Indian as a target for the practicing rifles of its members had kept up an undying hatred in the heart of the aborigines and stimulated them to terrible and isolated reprisals. The scalped and skinned dead body of Jack Trainer, tied on his horse and held hideously upright by a cross of wood behind his saddle, had passed, one night, a slow and ghastly apparition, into camp; the corpse of Dick Ryner had been found anchored on the riverbed, disemboweled and filled with stone and gravel. The solitary and unprotected member of Redwood Camp who fell into the enemy's hands was doomed.

Elijah Martin remembered this, but his fears gradually began to subside in a certain apathy of the imagination, which, perhaps, dulled his apprehensions and allowed the instinct of hunger to become again uppermost. He knew that the low bark tents, or wigwams, of the Indians were hung with strips of dried salmon, and his whole being was new centered upon an attempt to stealthily procure a delicious morsel.

As yet he had distinguished no other sign of life or habitation; a few moments later, however, and grown bolder with an animal-like trustfulness in his momentary security, he crept out of the thicket and found himself near a long, low mound or burrow-like structure of mud and bark on the riverbank. A single narrow opening, not unlike the entrance of an Eskimo hut, gave upon the river.

Martin had no difficulty in recognizing the character of the building. It was a "sweathouse," an institution common to nearly all the aboriginal tribes of California. Half a religious temple, it was also half a sanitary asylum, was used as a Russian bath or superheated vault, from which the braves, sweltering and stifling all night, by smothered fires, at early dawn plunged, perspiring, into the ice-cold river. The heat and smoke were further utilized to dry and cure the long strips of fish hanging from the roof, and it was through the narrow aperture that served as a chimney that the odor escaped which Martin had detected. He knew that as the bathers only occupied the house from midnight to early morn, it was now probably empty. He advanced confidently toward it.

He was a little surprised to find that the small open space between it and the river was occupied by a rude scaffolding, like that on which certain tribes exposed their dead, but in this instance it only contained the feathered leggings, fringed blanket, and eagle-plumed head-dress of some brave. He did not, however, linger in this plainly visible area, but quickly dropped on all fours and crept into the interior of the house. Here he completed his feast with the fish, and warmed his chilled limbs on the embers of the still smoldering fires. It was while drying his tattered clothes and shoeless feet that he thought of the dead brave's useless leggings and moccasins, and it occurred to him that he would be less likely to attract the Indians' attention from a distance and provoke a ready arrow, if he were disguised as one of them.

Crawling out again, he quickly secured, not only the leggings, but the blanket and headdress, and putting them on, cast his own clothes into the stream. A bolder, more energetic, or more provident man would have followed the act by quickly making his way back to the thicket to reconnoiter, taking with him a supply of fish for future needs. But Elijah Martin succumbed again to the recklessness of inertia; he yielded once more to the animal instinct of momentary security. He returned to the interior of the hut, curled himself again on the ashes, and weakly resolving to sleep until moonrise, and as weakly hesitating, ended by falling into uneasy but helpless stupor.

When he awoke, the rising sun, almost level with the low entrance to the sweathouse, was darting its direct rays into the interior, as if searching it with fiery spears. He had slept ten hours. He rose tremblingly to his knees. Everything was quiet without; he might yet escape. He crawled to the opening. The open space before it was empty, but the scaffolding was gone. The clear, keen air revived him.

As he sprang out, erect, a shout that nearly stunned him seemed to rise from the earth on all sides. He glanced around him in a helpless agony of fear. A dozen concentric circles of squatting Indians, whose heads were visible above the reeds, encompassed the banks around the sunken base of the sweat-house with successive dusky rings. Every avenue of escape seemed closed. Perhaps for that reason the attitude of his surrounding captors was passive rather than aggressive, and the shrewd, half-Hebraic profiles nearest him expressed only stoical waiting. There was a strange similarity of expression in his own immovable apathy of despair.

His only sense of averting his fate was a confused idea of explaining his intrusion. His desperate memory yielded a few common Indian words. He pointed automatically to himself and the stream. His white lips moved.

"I come—from—the river!"

A guttural cry, as if the whole assembly were clearing their throats, went round the different circles. The nearest rocked themselves to and fro and bent their feathered heads toward him. A hollow-cheeked, decrepit old man arose and said, simply:

"It is he! The great chief has come!"

He was saved. More than that, he was re-created. For, by signs and intimations he was quickly made aware that since the death of their late chief, their medicine-men had prophesied that his perfect successor should appear miraculously before them, borne noiselessly on the river *from the sea*, in the plumes and insignia of his predecessor.

This mere coincidence of appearance and costume might not have been convincing to the braves had not Elijah Martin's actual deficiencies contributed to their unquestioned faith in him. Not only his inert possession of the sweat-house and his apathetic attitude in their presence, but his utter and complete unlikeness to the white frontiersmen of their knowledge and tradition—creatures of fire and sword and malevolent activity—as well as his manifest dissimilarity to themselves, settled their conviction of his supernatural origin. His gentle, submissive voice, his yielding will, his lazy helplessness, the absence of strange weapons and fierce explosives in his possession, his unwonted sobriety—all proved him an exception to his apparent race that was in itself miraculous. For it must be confessed that, in spite of the cherished theories of most romances and all statesmen and commanders, that *fear* is the great civilizer of the savage barbarian, and that he is supposed to regard the prowess of the white man and his mysterious death-dealing weapons as evidence of his supernatural origin and superior creation, the facts have generally pointed to the reverse.

Elijah Martin was not long in discovering that when the Minyo hunter, with his obsolete bow, dropped dead by a bullet from a viewless and apparently noiseless space, it was *not* considered the lightnings of an avenging Deity, but was traced directly to the ambushed rifle of Kansas Joe, swayed by a viciousness quite as human as their own; the spectacle of Blizzard Dick, verging on delirium tremens, and riding "amuck" into an Indian village with a revolver in each hand, did *not* impress them as a supernatural act, nor excite their respectful awe as much as the less harmful frenzy of one of their own medicine-men; they were *not* influenced by implacable white gods, who relaxed only to drive hard bargains and exchange mildewed flour and shoddy blankets for their fish and furs.

I am afraid they regarded these raids of Christian civilization as they looked upon grasshopper plagues, famines, inundations, and epidemics; while an utterly impassive God washed his hands of the means he had employed, and even encouraged the faithful to resist and overcome his emissaries—the white devils!

Had Elijah Martin been a student of theology, he would have been struck with the singular resemblance of these theories—although the application thereof was reversed—to the Christian faith. But Elijah Martin had neither the imagination of a theologian nor the insight of a politician. He only saw that he, hitherto ignored and despised in a community of half-barbaric men, now translated to a community of men wholly savage, was respected and worshipped!

It might have turned a stronger head than Elijah's. He was at first frightened, fearful lest his reception concealed some hidden irony, or that, like the flower-crowned victim of ancient sacrifice, he was exalted and sustained to give importance and majesty to some impending martyrdom.

Then he began to dread that his innocent deceit—if deceit it was—should be discovered; at last, partly from meekness and partly from the animal contentment of present security, he accepted the situation. Fortunately for him it was purely passive. The Great Chief of the Minyo tribe was simply an expressionless idol of flesh and blood. The previous incumbent of that office had been an old man, impotent and senseless of late years through age and disease. The chieftains and braves had consulted in council before him, and perfunctorily submitted their decisions, like offerings, to his unresponsive shrine. In the same way, all material events—expeditions, trophies, industries—were supposed to pass before the dull, impassive eyes of the great chief, for direct acceptance.

On the second day of Elijah's accession, two of the braves brought a bleeding human scalp before him. Elijah turned pale, trembled, and averted his head, and then, remembering the danger of giving way to his weakness, grew still more ghastly. The warriors watched him with impassioned faces. A grunt—but whether of astonishment, dissent, or approval, he would not tell—went round the circle. But the scalp was taken away and never again appeared in his presence.

An incident still more alarming quickly followed. Two captives, white men, securely bound, were one day brought before him on their way to the stake, followed by a crowd of old and young squaws and children. The unhappy Elijah recognized in the prisoners two packers from a distant settlement who sometimes passed through Redwood Camp.

An agony of terror, shame, and remorse shook the pseudo chief to his crest of high feathers, and blanched his face beneath its paint and yellow ochre. To interfere to save them from the torture they were evidently to receive at the hands of those squaws and children, according to custom, would be exposure and death to him as well as themselves; while to assist by his passive presence at the horrible sacrifice of his countrymen was too much for even his weak selfishness. Scarcely knowing what he did as the lugubrious procession passed before him, he hurriedly hid his face in his blanket and turned his back upon the scene.

There was a dead silence. The warriors were evidently unprepared for this extraordinary conduct of their chief. What might have been their action it was impossible to conjecture, for at that moment a little squaw, perhaps impatient for the sport and partly emboldened by the fact that she had been selected, only a few days before, as the betrothed of the new chief, approached him slyly from the other side.

The horrified eyes of Elijah, momentarily raised from his blanket, saw and recognized her. The feebleness of a weak nature, that dared not measure itself directly with the real cause, vented its rage on a secondary object. He darted a quick glance of indignation and hatred at the young girl. She ran back in startled terror to her companions, a hurried consultation followed, and in another moment the whole bevy of girls, old women, and children were on the wing, shrieking and crying, to their wigwams.

"You see," said one of the prisoners coolly to the other, in English, "I was right. They never intended to do anything to us. It was only a bluff. These Minyos are a

different sort from the other tribes. They never kill anybody if they can help it."

"You're wrong," said the other, excitedly. "It was that big chief there, with his head in a blanket, that sent those dogs to the right about. Hell! did you see them run at just a look from him? He's a high and mighty feller, you bet. Look at his dignity!"

"That's so—he ain't no slouch," said the other, gazing at Elijah's muffled head, critically. "Damned if he ain't a born king."

The sudden conflict and utter revulsion of emotion that those simple words caused in Elijah's breast was almost incredible. He had been at first astounded by the revelation of the peaceful reputation of the unknown tribe he had been called upon to govern; but even this comforting assurance was as nothing compared to the greater revelations implied in the speaker's praise of himself.

He, Elijah Martin! the despised, the rejected, the worthless outcast of Redwood Camp, recognized as a "born king," a leader; his power felt by the very men who had scorned him! And he had done nothing—stop! had he actually done *nothing*? Was it not possible that he was *really* what they thought him?

His brain reeled under the strong, unaccustomed wine of praise; acting upon his weak selfishness, it exalted him for a moment to their measure of his strength, even as their former belief in his inefficiency had kept him down. Courage is too often only the memory of past success. This was his first effort; he forgot he had not earned it, even as he now ignored the danger of earning it. The few words of unconscious praise had fallen like the blade of knighthood on his cowering shoulders; he had risen ennobled from the contact. Though his face was still muffled in his blanket, he stood erect and seemed to have gained in stature.

The braves had remained standing irresolute, and yet watchful, a few paces from their captives. Suddenly, Elijah, still keeping his back to the prisoners, turned upon the braves, with blazing eyes, violently throwing out his hands with the gesture of breaking bonds. Like all sudden demonstrations of undemonstrative men, it was extravagant, weird, and theatrical. But it was more potent than speech—the speech that, even if effective, would still have betrayed him to his countrymen.

The braves hurriedly cut the thongs of the prisoners; another impulsive gesture from Elijah, and they, too, fled. When he lifted his eyes cautiously from his blanket, captors and captives had dispersed in opposite directions, and he was alone—and triumphant!

From that moment Elijah Martin was another man. He went to bed that night in an intoxicating dream of power; he arose a man of will, of strength. He read it in the eyes of the braves, albeit at times averted in wonder. He understood, now, that although peace had been their habit and custom, they had nevertheless sought to test his theories of administration with the offering of the scalps and the captives, and in this detection of their common weakness he forgot his own.

Most heroes require the contrast of the unheroic to set them off; and Elijah actually found himself devising means for strengthening the defensive and offensive character of the tribe, and was himself strengthened by it. Meanwhile the escaped packers did not fail to heighten the importance of their adventure by elevating the character and achievements of their deliverer; and it was presently announced throughout the frontier settlements that the hitherto insignificant and peaceful tribe of Minyos, who inhabited a large territory bordering on the Pacific Ocean, had developed into a powerful nation, only kept from the warpath by a more powerful but mysterious chief. The Government sent an Indian agent to treat with them, in its usual half-paternal, half-aggressive, and wholly inconsistent policy.

Elijah, who still retained the imitative sense and adaptability to surroundings which belong to most lazy, impressible natures, and in striped yellow and vermilion features looked the chief he personated, met the agent with silent and becoming gravity. The council was carried on by signs. Never before had an Indian treaty been entered into with such perfect knowledge of the intentions and designs of the whites by the Indians, and such profound ignorance of the qualities of the Indians by the whites.

It need scarcely be said that the treaty was an unquestionable Indian success. They did not give up their arable lands; what they did sell to the agent they refused to exchange for extravagant-priced shoddy blankets, worthless guns, damp powder, and moldy meal. They took pay in dollars, and were thus enabled to open more profitable commerce with the traders at the settlements for better goods and better bargains; they simply declined beads, whiskey, and Bibles at any price.

The result was that the traders found it profitable to protect them from their coun-trymen, and the chances of wantonly shooting down a possible valuable customer stopped the old indiscriminate rifle-practice. The Indians were allowed to cultivate their fields in peace. Elijah purchased for them a few agricultural implements. The catching, curing, and smoking of salmon became an important branch of trade. They waxed prosperous and rich; they lost their nomadic habits—a centralized settlement bearing the external signs of an Indian village took the place of their old temporary encamp-ments, but the huts were internally an improvement on the old wigwams. The dried fish were banished from the tent-poles to long sheds especially constructed for that purpose. The sweat-house was no longer utilized for worldly purposes. The wise and mighty Elijah did not attempt to reform their religion, but to preserve it in its integrity.

That these improvements and changes were due to the influence of one man was undoubtedly true, but that he was necessarily a superior man did not follow. Elijah's success was due partly to the fact that he had been enabled to impress certain negative virtues, which were part of his own nature, upon a community equally constituted to receive them. Each was strengthened by the recognition in each other of the unexpected value of those qualities; each acquired a confidence begotten of their success. "He-hides-his-face," as Elijah Martin was known to the tribe after the episode of the released captives, was really not so much of an autocrat as many constitutional rulers.

Two years of tranquil prosperity passed. Elijah Martin, foundling, outcast, without civilized ties or relationship of any kind, forgotten by his countrymen, and lifted into alien power, wealth, security, and respect, became—homesick!

It was near the close of a summer afternoon. He was sitting at the door of his lodge, which overlooked, on one side, the far-shining levels of the Pacific and, on the other, the slow descent to the cultivated meadows and banks of the Minyo River, that debouched through a waste of salt-marsh, beach-grass, sand-dunes, and foamy estuary into the ocean. The headland, or promontory—the only eminence of the Minyo territory—had been reserved by him for his lodge, partly on account of its isolation from the village at its base, and partly for the view it commanded of his territory.

Yet his wearying and discontented eyes were more often found on the ocean, as a possible highway of escape from his irksome position, than on the plain and the distant range of mountains, so closely connected with the nearer past and his former detractors. In his vague longing he had no desire to return to them, even in triumph in his present security there still lingered a doubt of his ability to cope with the old conditions. It was more like his easy, indolent nature—which revived in his prosperity—to trust to this least practical and remote solution of his trouble. His homesickness was as vague as his plan for escape from it; he did not know exactly what he regretted, but it was probably some life he had not enjoyed, some pleasure that had escaped his former incompetency and poverty.

He had sat thus a hundred times, as aimlessly blinking at the vast possibilities of the shining sea beyond, turning his back upon the nearer and more practicable mountains, lulled by the far-off beating of monotonous rollers, the lonely cry of the curlew and plover, the drowsy changes of alternate breaths of cool, fragrant reeds and warm, spicy sands that blew across his eyelids, and succumbed to sleep, as he had done a hundred times before.

The narrow strips of colored cloth, insignia of his dignity, flapped lazily from his tent-poles, and at last seemed to slumber with him; the shadows of the leaf-tracery thrown by the bay-tree, on the ground at his feet, scarcely changed its pattern. Nothing moved but the round, restless, berry-like eyes of Wachita, his child-wife, the former heroine of the incident with the captive packers, who sat near her lord, armed with a willow wand, watchful of intruding wasps, sand-flies, and even the more ostentatious advances of a rotund and clerical-looking humble-bee, with his monotonous homily.

Content, dumb, submissive, vacant, at such times, Wachita, debarred her husband's confidences through the native customs and his own indifferent taciturnity, satisfied herself by gazing at him with the wondering but ineffectual sympathy of a faithful dog. Unfortunately for Elijah her purely mechanical ministration could not prevent a more dangerous intrusion upon his security.

He awoke with a light start, and eyes that gradually fixed upon the woman a look of returning consciousness. Wachita pointed timidly to the village below.

"The Messenger of the Great White Father has come today, with his wagons and horses; he would see the chief of the Minyos, but I would not disturb my lord."

Elijah's brow contracted. Relieved of its characteristic metaphor, he knew that this meant that the new Indian agent had made his usual official visit, and had exhibited the usual anxiety to see the famous chieftain.

"Good!" he said. "White Rabbit [his lieutenant] will see the Messenger and exchange gifts. It is enough."

"The white messenger has brought his wangee [white] woman with him. They would look upon the face of him who hides it," continued Wachita, dubiously. "They would that Wachita should bring them nearer to where my lord is, that they might see him when he knew it not."

Elijah glanced moodily at his wife, with the half suspicion with which he still regarded her alien character. "Then let Wachita go back to the squaws and old women, and let her hide herself with them until the wangee strangers are gone," he said curtly. "I have spoken. Go!"

Accustomed to these abrupt dismissals, which did not necessarily indicate displeasure, Wachita disappeared without a word. Elijah, who had risen, remained for a few moments leaning against the tent-poles, gazing abstractedly toward the sea. The bees droned uninterruptedly in his ears, the far-off roll of the breakers came to him distinctly; but suddenly, with greater distinctness, came the murmur of a woman's voice.

"He don't look savage a bit! Why, he's real handsome."

"Hush! you—" said a second voice, in a frightened whisper.

"But if he *did* hear he couldn't understand," returned the first voice. A suppressed giggle followed.

Luckily, Elijah's natural and acquired habits of repression suited the emergency. He did not move, although he felt the quick blood fly to his face, and the voice of the first speaker had suffused him with a strange and delicious anticipation. He restrained himself, though the words she had naively dropped were filling him with new and tremulous suggestion. He was motionless, even while he felt that the vague longing and yearning which had possessed him hitherto was now mysteriously taking some unknown form and action.

The murmuring ceased. The humble-bees' drone again became ascendant—a sudden fear seized him. She was *going*; he should never see her! While he had stood there a dolt and sluggard, she had satisfied her curiosity and stolen away.

With a sudden yielding to impulse, he darted quickly in the direction where he had heard her voice. The thicket moved, parted, crackled, and rustled, and then undulated thirty feet before him in a long wave, as if from the passage of some lithe, invisible figure. But at the same moment a little cry, half of alarm, half of laughter, broke from his very feet, and a bent Manzanita-bush, relaxed by frightened fingers, flew back against his breast. Thrusting it hurriedly aside, his stooping, eager face came almost in contact with the pink, flushed cheeks and tangled curls of a woman's head. He was so near, her moist and laughing eyes almost drowned his eager glance; her parted lips and white teeth were so close to his that her quick breath took away his own.

She had dropped on one knee, as her companion fled, expecting he would overlook her as he passed, but his direct onset had extracted the feminine outcry. Yet even then she did not seem greatly frightened.

"It's only a joke, sir," she said, coolly lifting herself to her feet by grasping his arm. "I'm Mrs. Dall, the Indian agent's wife. They said you wouldn't let anybody see you— and I determined I would. That's all!"

She stopped, threw back her tangled curls behind her ears, shook the briers and thorns from her skirt, and added, "Well, I reckon you aren't afraid of a woman, are you? So no harm's done. Goodbye!"

She drew slightly back as if to retreat, but the elasticity of the Manzanita against which she was leaning threw her forward once more. He again inhaled the perfume of her hair; he saw even the tiny freckles that darkened her upper lip and brought out the moist, red curve below. A sudden recollection of a playmate of his vagabond childhood flashed across his mind; a wild inspiration of lawlessness, begotten of his past experi- ence, his solitude, his dictatorial power, and the beauty of the woman before him, mounted to his brain. He threw his arms passionately around her, pressed his lips to hers, and with a half-hysterical laugh drew back and disappeared in the thicket.

Mrs. Dall remained for an instant dazed and stupefied. Then she lifted her arm mechanically, and with her sleeve wiped her bruised mouth and the ochre-stain that his paint had left, like blood, upon her cheek. Her laughing face had become instantly grave, but not from fear; her dark eyes had clouded, but not entirely with indignation. She suddenly brought down her hand sharply against her side with a gesture of discovery.

"That's no Injun!" she said, with prompt decision. The next minute she plunged back into the trail again, and the dense foliage once more closed around her. But as she did so the broad, vacant face and the mutely wondering eyes of Wachita rose, like a placid moon, between the branches of a tree where they had been hidden, and shone serenely and impassively after her.

A month elapsed. But it was a month filled with more experience to Elijah than his past two years of exaltation. In the first few days following his meeting with Mrs. Dall, he was possessed by terror, mingled with flashes of desperation, at the remembrance of his rash imprudence. His recollection of extravagant frontier chivalry to womankind, and the swift retribution of the insulted husband or guardian, alternately filled him with abject fear or extravagant recklessness. At times prepared for flight, even to the desperate abandonment of himself in a canoe to the waters of the Pacific: at times he was on the point of inciting his braves to attack the Indian agency and precipitate the war that he felt would be inevitable.

As the days passed, and there seemed to be no interruption to his friendly relations with the agency, with that relief a new, subtle joy crept into Elijah's heart. The image of the agent's wife framed in the leafy screen behind his lodge, the perfume of her hair and breath mingled with the spicing of the bay, the brief thrill and tantalization of the stolen kiss still haunted him. Through his long, shy abstention from society, and his two years of solitary exile, the fresh beauty of this young Western wife, in whom the frank artlessness of girlhood still lingered, appeared to him like a superior creation. He forgot his vague longings in the inception of a more tangible but equally unpractical passion. He remembered her unconscious and spontaneous admiration of him; he dared to connect it with her forgiving silence. If she had withheld her confidences from her husband, he could hope—he knew not exactly what!

One afternoon Wachita put into his hand a folded note. With an instinctive presentiment of its contents, Elijah turned red and embarrassed in receiving it from the woman who was recognized as his wife. But the impassive, submissive manner of this household drudge, instead of touching his conscience, seemed to him a vulgar and brutal acceptance of the situation that dulled whatever compunction he might have had. He opened the note and read hurriedly as follows:

"You took a great freedom with me the other day, and I am justified in taking one with you now. I believe you understand English as well as I do. If you want to explain that and your conduct to me, I will be at the same place this afternoon. My friend will accompany me, but she need not hear what you have to say."

Elijah read the letter, which might have been written by an ordinary schoolgirl, as if it had conveyed the veiled rendezvous of a princess. The reserve, caution, and shyness which had been the safeguard of his weak nature were swamped in a flow of immature passion. He flew to the interview with the eagerness and inexperience of first love. He was completely at her mercy. So utterly was he subjugated by her presence that she did not even run the risk of his passion. Whatever sentiment might have mingled with her curiosity, she was never conscious of a necessity to guard herself against it.

At this second meeting she was in full possession of his secret. He had told her everything; she had promised nothing in return—she had not even accepted anything. Even her actual after-relations to the denouement of his passion are still shrouded in mystery.

Nevertheless, Elijah lived two weeks on the unsubstantial memory of this meeting. What might have followed could not be known, for at the end of that time an outrage— so atrocious that even the peaceful Minyos were thrilled with savage indignation—was committed on the outskirts of the village.

An old chief, who had been specially selected to deal with the Indian agent, and who kept a small trading outpost, had been killed and his goods despoiled by a reck-less Redwood packer. The murderer had coolly said that he was only "serving out" the tool of a fraudulent imposture on the Government, and that he dared the arch-impostor himself, the so-called Minyo chief, to help himself.

A wave of ungovernable fury surged up to the very tent-poles of Elijah's lodge and demanded vengeance. Elijah trembled and hesitated. In the thraldom of his selfish passion for Mrs. Dall, he dared not contemplate a collision with her countrymen. He would have again sought refuge in his passive, non-committal attitude, but he knew the impersonal character of Indian retribution and compensation—a sacrifice of equal value, without reference to the culpability of the victim—and he dreaded some sponta-neous outbreak.

To prevent the enforced expiation of the crime by some innocent brother packer, he was obliged to give orders for the pursuit and arrest of the criminal, secretly hoping for his escape or the interposition of some circumstance to avert his punishment.

A day of sullen expectancy to the old men and squaws in camp, of gloomy anxiety to Elijah alone in his lodge, followed the departure of the braves on the warpath. It was midnight when they returned. Elijah, who from his habitual reserve and the accepted etiquette of his exalted station had remained impassive in his tent, only knew from the guttural rejoicings of the squaws that the expedition had been successful and the captive was in their hands.

At any other time he might have thought it an evidence of some growing skepticism of his infallibility of judgment and a diminution of respect that they did not confront him with their prisoner. But he was too glad to escape from the danger of exposure and possible arraignment of his past life by the desperate captive, even though it might not have been understood by the spectators. He reflected that the omission might have arisen from their recollection of his previous aversion to a retaliation on other prisoners. Enough that they would wait his signal for the torture and execution at sunrise the next day.

The night passed slowly. It is more than probable that the selfish and ignoble torments of the sleepless and vacillating judge were greater than those of the prisoner who dozed at the stake between his curses. Yet it was part of Elijah's fatal weakness that his kinder and more human instincts were dominated even at that moment by his lawless passion for the Indian agent's wife, and his indecision as to the fate of his captive was as much due to this preoccupation as to a selfish consideration of her relations to the result. He hated the prisoner for his infelicitous and untimely crime, yet he could not make up his mind to his death. He paced the ground before his lodge in dishonorable incertitude. The small eyes of the submissive Wachita watched him with vague solicitude.

Toward morning he was struck by a shameful inspiration. He would creep unperceived to the victim's side, unloose his bonds, and bid him fly to the Indian agency. There he was to inform Mrs. Dall that her husband's safety depended upon his absenting himself for a few days, but that she was to remain and communicate with Elijah. She would understand everything, perhaps; at least she would know that the prisoner's release was to please her, but even if she did not, no harm would be done, a white man's life would be saved, and his real motive would not be suspected. He turned with feverish eagerness to the lodge. Wachita had disappeared—probably to join the other women. It was well; she would not suspect him.

The tree to which the doomed man was bound was, by custom, selected nearest the chief's lodge, within its sacred enclosure, with no other protection than that offered by its reserved seclusion and the outer semicircle of warriors' tents before it. To escape, the captive would therefore have to pass beside the chief's lodge to the rear and descend the hill toward the shore. Elijah would show him the way, and make it appear as if he had escaped unaided. As he glided into the shadow of a group of pines, he could dimly discern the outline of the destined victim, secured against one of the larger trees in a sitting posture, with his head fallen forward on his breast as if in sleep. But at the same moment another figure glided out from the shadow and approached the fatal tree. It was Wachita!

He stopped in amazement. But in another instant a flash of intelligence made it clear. He remembered her vague uneasiness and solicitude at his agitation, her sudden disappearance; she had fathomed his perplexity, as she had once before. Of her own accord she was going to release the prisoner! The knife to cut his cords glittered in her hand. Brave and faithful animal!

He held his breath as he drew nearer. But, to his horror, the knife suddenly flashed in the air and darted down, again and again, upon the body of the helpless man. There was a convulsive struggle, but no outcry, and the next moment the body hung limp and inert in its cords. Elijah would himself have fallen, half-fainting, against a tree, but, by a revulsion of feeling, came the quick revelation that the desperate girl had rightly solved the problem! She had done what he ought to have done—and his loyalty and manhood were preserved. That conviction and the courage to act upon it—to have called the sleeping braves to witness his sacrifice—would have saved him, but it was ordered otherwise.

As the girl rapidly passed him he threw out his hand and seized her wrist. "Who did you do this for?" he demanded.

"For you," she said, stupidly.

"And why?"

"Because you no kill him—you love his squaw."

"*His* squaw!" He staggered back. A terrible suspicion flashed upon him. He dashed Wachita aside and ran to the tree. It was the body of the Indian agent! Aboriginal justice had been satisfied. The warriors had not caught the *murderer*, but, true to their idea of vicarious retribution, had determined upon the expiatory sacrifice of a life as valuable and innocent as the one they had lost.

"So the Gov'rment hev at last woke up and wiped out them cussed Digger Minyos," said Snapshot Harry, as he laid down the newspaper, in the brand-new saloon of the brand-new town of Redwood. "I see they've stampeded both banks of the Minyo River, and sent off a lot to the reservation. I reckon the soldiers at Fort Cass got sick o' senti- ment after those hounds killed the Injun agent, and are beginning to agree with us that the only 'good Injun' is a dead one."

"And it turns out that that wonderful chief, that them two packers used to rave about, woz about as big a devil ez any, and tried to run off with the agent's wife, only the warriors killed her. I'd like to know what become of him. Some says he was killed, others allow that he got away. I've heerd tell that he was originally some kind of Methodist preacher!—a kind o' saint that got a sort o' spiritooal holt on the old squaws and children."

"Why don't you ask old Skeesicks? I see he's back here ag'in—and grubbin' along at a dollar a day on tailin's. He's been somewhere up north, they say."

"What, Skeesicks? that shiftless, o'n'ry cuss! You bet he wusn't anywhere where there was danger of fighting. Why, you might as well hev suspected *him* of being the big chief himself! There he comes—ask him."

And the laughter was so general that Elijah Martin—alias Skeesicks—lounging shyly into the barroom, joined in it weakly.

THE STRANGER

---

by
Ambrose Bierce

Ambrose Bierce (1842–1914?) is known today for the cynical, sarcastic The Devil's Dictionary, and his Civil War stories, such as "An Occurrence at Owl Creek Bridge"— many of which were written from personal experience. He fought with the Ninth Indiana Infantry at Shiloh, Picketts's Mill, and Chickamunga, among others. He left the military after being shot in the head by a Confederate sniper at the Battle of Kennesaw Mountain and suffering from dizziness and blackouts. He originally enlisted as a private, but by the time he left held a rank of first lieutenant with an honorary rank of brevet major for distinguish service.

In 1866, Bierce undertook a dangerous expedition from Omaha through Indian Territory to San Francisco inspecting military outposts. Once in San Francisco he took a job as watchman at the U.S. Mint. About a year later he began writing for California newspapers, eventually becoming an editor. In 1880, as the general agent for the Black Hills Placer Mining Company in the Dakota Territory, Bierce fought off stagecoach robbers who attempted to steal a payroll shipment. When the mining company went bankrupt, Bierce returned to California where he continued writing and working as an editor, eventually becoming a regular columnist for William Randolph Hearst's San Francisco Examiner. For twenty-two years he continued to write for Hearst, ultimately resigning—adding the comment, "Nobody but God loves him...."

In 1913, Bierce took off for Mexico to write about Pancho Villa during the Mexican Revolution, but he vanished without a trace not long after. His disappearance remains one of the world's most famous missing persons cases.

During Bierce's life he became friends with Mark Twain, Bret Harte, H. L. Mencken, and had a drinking contest with Jack London at the famed Bohemian Grove. In addition to his war stories, humor, novels, and sarcastic criticism, he also wrote supernatural stories and tales of the West. This one is a bit of both.

A man stepped out of the darkness into the little illuminated circle about our failing campfire and seated himself upon a rock.

"You are not the first to explore this region," he said, gravely.

Nobody controverted his statement; he was himself proof of its truth, for he was not of our party and must have been somewhere near when we camped. Moreover, he must have companions not far away; it was not a place where one would be living or traveling alone. For more than a week we had seen, besides ourselves and our animals, only such living things as rattlesnakes and horned toads. In an Arizona desert one does not long coexist with only such creatures as these: one must have pack animals, supplies, arms—"an outfit." And all these imply comrades. It was perhaps a doubt as to what manner of men this unceremonious stranger's comrades might be, together with something in his words interpretable as a challenge, that caused every man of our half-dozen "gentlemen adventurers" to rise to a sitting posture and lay his hand upon a weapon—an act signifying, in that time and place, a policy of expectation. The stranger gave the matter no attention and began again to speak in the same deliberate, uninflected monotone in which he had delivered his first sentence:

"Thirty years ago Ramon Gallegos, William Shaw, George W. Kent and Berry Davis, all of Tucson, crossed the Santa Catalina mountains and traveled due west, as nearly as the configuration of the country permitted. We were prospecting and it was our intention, if we found nothing, to push through to the Gila river at some point near Big Bend, where we understood there was a settlement. We had a good outfit but no guide—just Ramon Gallegos, William Shaw, George W. Kent and Berry Davis."

The man repeated the names slowly and distinctly, as if to fix them in the memories of his audience, every member of which was now attentively observing him, but with a slackened apprehension regarding his possible companions somewhere in the darkness that seemed to enclose us like a black wall; in the manner of this volunteer historian was no suggestion of an unfriendly purpose. His act was rather that of a harmless lunatic than an enemy. We were not so new to the country as not to know that the solitary life of many a plainsman had a tendency to develop eccentricities of conduct and character not always easily distinguishable from mental aberration. A man is like a tree: in a forest of his fellows he will grow as straight as his generic and individual nature permits; alone in the open, he yields to the deforming stresses and distortions that environ him. Some such thoughts were in my mind as I watched the man from the shadow of my hat, pulled low to shut out the firelight. A witless fellow, no doubt, but what could he be doing there in the heart of a desert?

Having undertaken to tell this story, I wish that I could describe the man's appearance; that would be a natural thing to do. Unfortunately, and somewhat strangely, I find myself unable to do so with any degree of confidence, for afterward no two of us agreed as to what he wore and how he looked; and when I try to set down my own impressions they elude me. Anyone can tell some kind of story; narration is one of the elemental powers of the race. But the talent for description is a gift.

Nobody having broken silence the visitor went on to say:

"This country was not then what it is now. There was not a ranch between the Gila and the Gulf. There was a little game here and there in the mountains, and near the infrequent water-holes grass enough to keep our animals from starvation. If we should be so fortunate as to encounter no Indians we might get through. But within a week the purpose of the expedition had altered from discovery of wealth to preservation of life. We had gone too far to go back, for what was ahead could be no worse than what was behind; so we pushed on, riding by night to avoid Indians and the intolerable heat, and concealing ourselves by day as best we could. Sometimes, having exhausted our supply of wild meat and emptied our casks, we were days without food or drink; then a water-hole or a shallow pool in the bottom of an arroyo so restored our strength and sanity that we were able to shoot some of the wild animals that sought it also. Sometimes it was a bear, sometimes an antelope, a coyote, a cougar—that was as God pleased; all were food.

"One morning as we skirted a mountain range, seeking a practicable pass, we were attacked by a band of Apaches who had followed our trail up a gulch—it is not far from here. Knowing that they outnumbered us ten to one, they took none of their usual cowardly precautions, but dashed upon us at a gallop, firing and yelling. Fighting was out of the question: we urged our feeble animals up the gulch as far as there was footing for a hoof, then threw ourselves out of our saddles and took to the chaparral on one of the slopes, abandoning our entire outfit to the enemy. But we retained our rifles, every man—Ramon Gallegos, William Shaw, George W. Kent and Berry Davis."

"Same old crowd," said the humorist of our party. He was an Eastern man, unfamiliar with the decent observances of social intercourse. A gesture of disapproval from our leader silenced him and the stranger proceeded with his tale:

"The savages dismounted also, and some of them ran up the gulch beyond the point at which we had left it, cutting off further retreat in that direction and forcing us on up the side. Unfortunately the chaparral extended only a short distance up the slope, and as we came into the open ground above we took the fire of a dozen rifles; but Apaches shoot badly when in a hurry, and God so willed it that none of us fell. Twenty yards up the slope, beyond the edge of the brush, were vertical cliffs, in which, directly in front of us, was a narrow opening. Into that we ran, finding ourselves in a cavern about as large as an ordinary room in a house. Here for a time we were safe: a single man with a repeating rifle could defend the entrance against all the Apaches in the land. But against hunger and thirst we had no defense. Courage we still had, but hope was a memory.

"Not one of those Indians did we afterward see, but by the smoke and glare of their fires in the gulch we knew that by day and by night they watched with ready rifles in the edge of the bush—knew that if we made a sortie not a man of us would live to take three steps into the open. For three days, watching in turn, we held out before our suffering became insupportable. Then—it was the morning of the fourth day—Ramon Gallegos said:

" 'Señores, I know not well of the good God and what please him. I have live without religion, and I am not acquaint with that of you. Pardon, señores, if I shock you, but for me the time is come to beat the game of the Apache.'

"He knelt upon the rock floor of the cave and pressed his pistol against his temple. 'Madre de Dios,' he said, 'comes now the soul of Ramon Gallegos.'

"And so he left us—William Shaw, George W. Kent and Berry Davis.

"I was the leader: it was for me to speak.

" 'He was a brave man,' I said—'he knew when to die, and how. It is foolish to go mad from thirst and fall by Apache bullets, or be skinned alive—it is in bad taste. Let us join Ramon Gallegos.'

" 'That is right,' said William Shaw.

" 'That is right,' said George W. Kent.

"I straightened the limbs of Ramon Gallegos and put a handkerchief over his face. Then William Shaw said: 'I should like to look like that—a little while.'

"And George W. Kent said that he felt that way, too.

" 'It shall be so,' I said: 'the red devils will wait a week. William Shaw and George W. Kent, draw and kneel.'

"They did so and I stood before them.

" 'Almighty God, our Father,' said I.

" 'Almighty God, our Father,' said William Shaw.

" 'Almighty God, our Father,' said George W. Kent.

" 'Forgive us our sins,' said I.

" 'Forgive us our sins,' said they.

" 'And receive our souls.'

" 'And receive our souls.'

" 'Amen!'

" 'Amen!'

"I laid them beside Ramon Gallegos and covered their faces."

There was a quick commotion on the opposite side of the campfire: one of our party had sprung to his feet, pistol in hand.

"And you!" he shouted—"*you* dared to escape?—you dare to be alive? You cowardly hound, I'll send you to join them if I hang for it!"

But with the leap of a panther the captain was upon him, grasping his wrist. "Hold it in, Sam Yountsey, hold it in!"

We were now all upon our feet—except the stranger, who sat motionless and apparently inattentive. Someone seized Yountsey's other arm.

"Captain," I said, "there is something wrong here. This fellow is either a lunatic or merely a liar—just a plain, every-day liar whom Yountsey has no call to kill. If this man was of that party it had five members, one of whom—probably himself—he has not named."

⚹ **THE STRANGER** ⚹

"Yes," said the captain, releasing the insurgent, who sat down, "there is some-thing—unusual. Years ago four dead bodies of white men, scalped and shamefully mutilated, were found about the mouth of that cave. They are buried there; I have seen the graves—we shall all see them to-morrow."

The stranger rose, standing tall in the light of the expiring fire, which in our breathless attention to his story we had neglected to keep going.

"There were four," he said—"Ramon Gallegos, William Shaw, George W. Kent and Berry Davis."

With this reiterated roll-call of the dead he walked into the darkness and we saw him no more.

At that moment one of our party, who had been on guard, strode in among us, rifle in hand and somewhat excited.

"Captain," he said, "for the last half-hour three men have been standing out there on the mesa." He pointed in the direction taken by the stranger. "I could see them distinctly, for the moon is up, but as they had no guns and I had them covered with mine I thought it was their move. They have made none, but, damn it! they have got on to my nerves."

"Go back to your post, and stay till you see them again," said the captain. "The rest of you lie down again, or I'll kick you all into the fire."

The sentinel obediently withdrew, swearing, and did not return. As we were arranging our blankets the fiery Yountsey said: "I beg your pardon, Captain, but who the devil do you take them to be?"

"Ramon Gallegos, William Shaw and George W. Kent."

"But how about Berry Davis? I ought to have shot him."

"Quite needless; you couldn't have made him any deader. Go to sleep."

The HORSES

of

BOSTIL'S FORD

by
Zane Grey

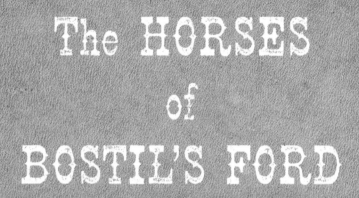

Erle Stanley Gardner, mystery author and creator of Perry Mason, said of Zane Grey, he "had the knack of tying his characters into the land, and the land into the story. There were other Eastern writers who had fast and furious action, but Zane Grey was the one who could make the action not only convincing but inevitable, and somehow you got the impression that the bigness of the country generated a bigness of character."

In this story Grey pits the love two men have for a woman against the love they have for their horses.

Bostil himself was half horse. The half of him that was human he divided between love of his fleet racers and his daughter Lucy.

He had seen ten years of hard riding on that wild Utah border, where a horse meant all the world to a man; and then lucky strikes of water and gold on the vast plateau wilderness north of the Rio Virgin had made him richer than he knew. His ranges beyond Bostil's Ford were practically boundless, his cattle numberless, and, many as were his riders, he always had need of more.

In those border days every rider loved his horse as a part of himself. If there was a difference between any rider of the sage and Bostil, it was that, as Bostil had more horses, so he had more love.

If he had any unhappiness, it was because he could not buy Wildfire and Nagger, thoroughbreds belonging to one Lamar, a poor daredevil rider who would not have parted with them for all the gold in the uplands. And Lamar had dared to cast longing eyes at Lucy. When he clashed with Bostil he avowed his love, and offered to stake his horses and his life against the girl's hand, deciding the wager by a race between Wildfire and the rancher's great gray, Sage King.

Among the riders, when they sat around their campfires, there had been much speculation regarding the outcome of such a race. There never had been a race, and never would be, so the riders gossiped, unless Lamar were to ride off with Lucy. In that case there would be the grandest race ever run on the uplands, with the odds against Wildfire only if he carried double.

If Lamar put Lucy up on Wildfire, and he rode Nagger, there would be another story. Lucy was a slip of a girl, born on a horse, and could ride like a burr sticking in a horse's mane. With Wildfire she would run away from any one on Sage King—which for Bostil would be a double tragedy, equally in the loss of his daughter and the beating of his favorite. Then such a race was likely to end in heart-break for all concerned, because the Sage King would outrun Nagger, and that would bring riders within gunshot.

Bostil swore by all the gods that the King was the swiftest horse in the wild upland of wonderful horses. He swore that the gray could look back over his shoulder and run away from Nagger, and that he could kill Wildfire on his feet. That poor beggar Lamar's opinion of his steeds was as preposterous as his love for Lucy!

Now, Bostil had a great fear which made him ever restless, ever watchful. That fear was of Cordts, the rustler. Cordts hid back in the untrodden ways. He had fast horses, faithful followers, gold for the digging, cattle by the thousand, and women when he chose to ride off with them. He had always had what he wanted—except one thing. That was a horse. That horse was the Sage King.

Cordts was a gunman, outlaw, rustler, a lord over the free ranges; but, more than all else, he was a rider. He knew a horse. He was as much horse as Bostil. He was a prince of rustlers, who thought a horse-thief worse than a dog; but he intended to become a horse-thief. He had openly declared it. The passion he had conceived, for the Sage King was the passion of a man for an unattainable woman. He swore that he would never rest—that he would not die till he owned the King; so Bostil had reason for his great fear.

One morning, as was sometimes the rancher's custom, he ordered the racers to be brought from the corrals and turned loose in the alfalfa fields near the house. Bostil loved to watch them graze; but ever he saw that the riders were close at hand, and that the horses did not graze too close to the sage.

He sat back and gloried in the sight. He owned a thousand horses; near at hand was a field full of them, fine and mettlesome and racy; but Bostil had eyes only for the six blooded favorites. There was Plume, a superb mare that got her name from the way her mane swept in the wind when she was on the run; there were Bullet, huge, rangy, leaden in color, and Two-Face, sleek and glossy and cunning; there was the black stallion Sarchedon, and close to him the bay Dusty Ben; and lastly Sage King, the color of the upland sage, a horse proud and wild and beautiful.

"Where's Lucy?" presently asked Bostil. As he divided his love, so he divided his anxiety.

Some rider had seen Lucy riding off, with her golden hair flying in the breeze.

"She's got to keep out of the sage," growled Bostil. "Where's my glass? I want to take a look out there. Where's my glass?"

The glass could not be found.

"What're those specks in the sage? Antelope?"

"I reckon thet's a bunch of bosses," replied a hawk-eyed rider.

"Huh! I don't like it. Lucy oughtn't to be ridin' round alone. If she meets Lamar again, I'll rope her in a corral!"

Another rider drew Bostil's attention from the gray waste of rolling sage.

"Bostil, look! Look at the King! He smells somethin'—he's lookin' for somethin'! So does Sarch!"

"Yes," replied the rancher. "Better drive them up. They're too close to the sage."

Sage King whistled shrilly and began to prance.

"What in the—" muttered Bostil.

Suddenly up out of the alfalfa sprang a dark form. Like a panther it leaped at the horse and caught his mane. Snorting wildly, Sage King reared aloft and plunged. The dark form swung up. It was a rider, and cruelly he spurred the racer.

Other dark forms rose almost as swiftly, and leaped upon the other plunging horses. There was a violent, pounding shock of frightened horses bunching into action. With a magnificent bound, Sage King got clear of the tangle and led the way.

Like Indians, the riders hung low and spurred. In a single swift moment they had the horses tearing into the sage.

"Rustlers! *Cordts! Cordts!*" screamed Bostil. "He sneaked up in the sage! Quick men—rifles, rifles! No! No! Don't shoot! *You might kill a horse!* Let them go. They'll get the girl, too—there must be more rustlers in the sage—they've got her now! There they go! Gone! Gone! All that I loved!"

At almost the exact hour of the rustling of the racers, Lucy Bostil was with Jim Lamar at their well-hidden rendezvous on a high, cedared slope some eight or ten miles from the ranch. From an opening in the cedars they could see down across the gray sage to the alfalfa fields, the corrals, and the house. In Lucy's lap, with her gauntlets, lay the field-glass that Bostil's riders could not find; and close by, halted under a cedar, Lucy's pinto tossed his spotted head at Lamar's magnificent horses.

"You unhappy boy!" Lucy was saying. "Of course I love you; but, Jim, I can't meet you anymore like this. It's not playing square with dad."

"Lucy, if you give it up, you don't love me," he protested.

"I *do* love you."

"Well, then—"

He leaned over her. Lucy's long lashes drooped and warm color flushed her face as she shyly lifted it to give the proof exacted by her lover.

They were silent a moment, and she lay with her head on his breast. A soft wind moaned through the cedars, and bees hummed in the patches of pale lavender daisies. The still air was heavily laden with the fragrance of the sage.

Lamar gently released her, got up, and seemed to be shaking off a kind of spell.

"Lucy, I know you mustn't meet me anymore. But oh, Lord, Lord, I do love you so! I had nothing in the world but the hope of seeing you, and now that'll be gone. I'll lie such a miserable beggar!"

Lucy demurely eyed him.

"Jim, your clothes are pretty ragged, and you look a little in need of some good food, but it strikes me you're a splendid-looking beggar. You suit me. You oughtn't say you have nothing. Look at your horses!"

Lamar's keen gray eyes softened. Indeed, he was immeasurably rich, and he gazed at his horses as if that were the first moment he had ever laid eyes on them.

Both were of tremendous build. Nagger was dark and shaggy, with arched neck and noble head, that suggested race, loyalty, and speed. Wildfire was so finely pointed, so perfectly balanced, that he appeared smaller than Nagger; but he was as high, as long, and he had the same great breadth of chest; and though not so heavy, he had the same wonderful look of power. As red as fire, with sweeping mane and tail, like dark-tinged flames, and holding himself with a strange alert wildness, he looked his name.

"Jimmy, you have those grand horses," went on Lucy. "And look at *me*!"

Lamar did look at her, yearningly. She was as lithe as a young panther. Her rider's suit, like a boy's, rather emphasized than hid the graceful roundness of her slender form. Lamar thought her hair the gold of the sage at sunset, her eyes the blue of the deep haze in the distance, her mouth the sweet red of the upland rose.

"Jimmy, you've got me corralled," she continued archly, "and I'm dad's only child."

"But, Lucy, I *haven't* got you!" he passionately burst out.

"Yes, you have. All you need is patience. Keep hanging round the Ford till dad gives in. He hasn't one thing against you, except that you wouldn't sell him your horses. Dad's crazy about horses. Jim, he wasn't so angry because you wanted to race Wildfire against the King *for me*; he was furious because you were so sure you'd win. And see here, Jim dear—if ever you and dad race the red and the gray, you let the gray win, if you love me and want me! Else you'll *never* get me in this world."

"Lucy! I wouldn't pull Wildfire—I wouldn't break that horse's heart even to—to get you!"

"That's the rider in you, Jim. I like you better for it; but all the same, I know you would."

"I wouldn't!"

"You don't love me!"

"I do love you."

"Well—then!" she mocked, and lifted her face—

"Oh, child, you could make me do anything," went on Lamar presently. "But, Lucy, you've ridden the King, and you're the only person besides me who was ever up on Wildfire. Tell me, isn't Wildfire the better horse?"

"Jim, you've asked me that a thousand times."

"Have I? Well, tell me."

"Yes, Jim, if you can compare two such horses, Wildfire is the better."

"You darling! Lucy, did Bostil ever ask you that?"

"About seven million times."

"And what did you tell him?" asked Lamar, laughing, yet earnest withal.

"I wouldn't dare tell dad anything but that Sage King could run Wildfire off his legs."

"You—you little hypocrite! Which of us were you really lying to?"

"I reckon it was dad," replied Lucy seriously. "Jim, I can ride, but I haven't much horse sense. So what I think mayn't be right. I love the King and Wildfire—all horses. Really I love Nagger best of all. He's so faithful. Why, it's because he loves you that he nags you. Wildfire's no horse for a woman. He's wild. I don't think he's actually any faster than the King; only he's a desert stallion, and has killed many horses. His spirit would break the King. It's in the King to outrun a horse; it's in Wildfire to kill him. What a shame ever to let those great horses race!"

"They never will, Lucy, dear. And now I'll see if the sage is clear; for you must be going."

Lamar's eye swept the gray expanse. A few miles out he saw a funnel-shaped dust-cloud rising behind a bunch of dark horses, and farther on toward the ranch more puffs of dust and moving black specks.

"Lucy, something's wrong," he said quietly. "Take your glass. Look there!"

"Oh, dear, I'm afraid dad has put the boys on my trail," rejoined Lucy, as she readjusted the glass and leveled it. Instantly she cried, "Three riders and three led horses—unsaddled. I don't know the riders. Jim! I see Sarchedon and Bullet, if ever I saw them in my life!"

"Rustlers! I knew it before you looked," said Jim, with compressed lips. "Give me the glass." He looked, and while he held the glass leveled he spoke, "Yes, Sarch and Bullet—there's Two-Face. The three unsaddled horses I don't know. They're dark bays—rustlers' horses. That second bunch I can't make out so well for dust, but it's the same kind of a bunch—three riders—three led horses. Lucy, there's the King. Cordts has got him!"

"Oh, Jim, it will ruin dad!" cried Lucy, wringing her hands.

Lamar appeared suddenly to become obsessed by a strange excitement.

"Why, Jim, we're safe hidden here," said Lucy, in surprise.

"Girl! Do you think me afraid? It's only that I'm—" His face grew tense, his eyes burned, his hands trembled. "What a chance for me! Lucy, listen. Cordts and his men—picked men, probably—sneaked up in the sage to the ranch, and run off bareback on the racers. They've had their horses hidden, and then changed saddles. They're traveling light. There's not a long gun among them. *I've got my rifle.* I can stop that bunch—kill some of them, or maybe all—get the horses back. If I only had more shells for my rifle! I've only ten in the magazine. I'm so poor I can't buy shells for my rifle."

"Dear Jim, don't risk it, then," said Lucy, trembling.

"I will risk it," he cried. "It's the chance of my life. Dearest, think—think what it'd mean to Bostil if I killed Cordts and got back the King! Think what it'd mean for me! Cordts is the bane of the uplands. He's a murderer, a stealer of women. Bostil can't sleep for fear of him. I will risk it. I can do it. Little girl, watch, and you'll have something to tell your father!"

With his mind made up and action begun, Jim grew cold and deliberate. Freeing Lucy's pinto, he put her saddle on Nagger, muttering, "If we have to run for it, you'll be safe on him."

As he tightened the cinches on Wildfire, he spoke low to the red stallion. A twitching ripple quivered over the horse, and he pounded the ground and champed his bit.

"S-sh! Quiet there!" Jim called, louder, and put a hand on the horse.

Wildfire seemed to turn to stone. Next Lamar drew the long rifle from its sheath and carefully examined it.

"Come," he said to Lucy. "We'll go down and hide in the edge of the cedars. That bunch'll pass on the trail within a hundred paces."

Lamar led the way down the slope, and took up a position in a clump of cedars. The cover was not so dense as he had thought it would be. There was not, however, any time to hunt for better.

"Lucy, hold the horses here. Look at Wildfire's ears! Already he's seen that bunch. Dear, you're not afraid—for once we've got the best of the rustlers. If only Cordts comes up in time!"

As the rustlers approached, Lamar, peering from his covert, felt himself grow colder and grimmer. Presently he knew that the two groups were too far apart for them both to pass near him at the same time. He formed a resolve to let the first party go by. It was Cordts he wanted—and the King.

Lamar lay low while moments passed. The breeze brought the sharp sound of iron- shod hoofs. Lamar heard also a coarse laugh—gruff voices—the jingle of spurs. There came a silence—then the piercing whistle of a frightened horse.

Lamar raised himself to see that the rustlers had halted within pistol-shot. The rider on Two-Face was in the lead, and the cunning mare had given the alarm. Jim thought what a fool he had been to imagine that he could ambush rustlers when they had Two-Face. She had squared away, head high, ears up, and she looked straight at the hiding-place.

It appeared as if all the rustlers pulled guns at the same instant, and a hail of bullets pattered around Lamar. Leaping up, he shot once—twice—three times. Riderless horses leaped, wildly plunged, and sheered off into the sage.

Lamar shifted his gaze to Cordts and his followers. At sound of the shots, the rustlers had halted, now scarcely a quarter of a mile distant.

"Are y-you all right, Jim?" whispered Lucy.

Lamar turned, to see the girl standing with eyes tight shut.

"Yes, I'm all right, but I'm stumped now. Cordts heard the shots from my rifle. He and his men won't ride any closer. There, they've started again—they've left the trail!"

Lucy opened her eyes.

"Jim, they're cutting across to head off Sarch. He's leading. If they ever catch the other racers, it'll be too late for you."

"Too late?"

"They'll be able to change mounts—you can't catch them then."

"Lucy!"

"Get up on Wildfire—go after Cordts!" cried the girl breathlessly.

"Great Scott, I hadn't thought of that! Lucy, it's Wildfire against the King. That race *will* be run! Climb up on Nagger. Girl, you're going with me. You'll be safer trailing after me than hiding here. If they turn on us, I can drop them all."

He had to lift her upon Nagger; but once in the saddle, when the huge black began to show how he wanted to run, her father's blood began to throb and burn in the girl, and she looked down upon her lover with a darkening fire in her eyes.

"Girl, it'll be the race we've dreamed of! It's for your father. It's Wildfire against the King!"

"I'll stay with you—as long as Nagger lasts," she said.

Lamar leaped astride Wildfire, and ducked low under the cedars as the horse bolted. He heard Nagger crash through close behind him. Cordts and his companions were riding off toward the racers. Sarch was leading Bullet and Two-Face around in the direction of the ranch. The three unsaddled mounts were riding off to the left.

One rustler turned to look back, then another. When Cordts turned, he wheeled the King, and stopped as if in surprise. Probably he thought that his men had been ambushed by a company of riders. Not improbably, the idea of actual pursuit had scarcely dawned upon them; and the possibility of anyone running them down, now that they were astride Bostil's swift horses, had never occurred to them at all. Motionless they sat, evidently trying to make out their pursuers.

When Lamar stood up in his stirrups, and waved his long rifle at them, it was probably at that instant they recognized him. The effect was significant. They dropped the halters of the three unsaddled horses, and headed their mounts to the left, toward the trail.

Which way they went was of no moment to Lamar. Wildfire and Nagger could run low, stretched out at length, in brush or in the open. It was evident, however, that Cordts preferred open running, and as he cut across the trail, Lamar gained. This trail was one long used by the rustlers in driving cattle, and it was a wide, hard-packed road. Lamar knew it for ten miles, until it turned into the rugged and broken passes. He believed the race would be ended before Cordts had a chance to take to the canyons.

Nagger had his nose even with Wildfire's flank. Lucy rode with both hands at strong tension on the bridle. Her face was pale, her eyes were gleaming darker, and wisps of her bound hair whipped in the wind. Lamar's one pride, after what he felt for his horses, was in Lucy, and in the fact that she could ride them. She was a sweetheart for a rider!

"Pull him, Lucy, pull him!" he shouted. "Don't let him get going on you. Wait till Plume and Ben are out of it!"

As for himself, he drew an iron arm on Wildfire's bridle. The grimness passed from Lamar's mood, taking with it the cold, sickening sense of death already administered, and of impending fight and blood.

Lucy was close behind on the thundering Nagger, and he had no fear for her, only a wild joy in her, that she was a girl capable of riding this race with him. So, as the sage flashed by, and the wind bit sweet, and the quick, rhythmic music of Wildfire's hoofs rang in his ears, Lamar began to live the sweetest thing in a rider's career—the glory of the one running race wherein he staked pride in his horse, love of a girl, and life.

Wildfire was not really running yet; he had not lengthened out of his gallop. He had himself in control, as if the spirit in him awaited the call of his master. As for the speed of the moment, it was enough for Lamar to see the space between him and Cordts gradually grow less and less. He wanted to revel in that ride while he could. He saw, and was somehow glad, that Cordts was holding in the King.

His sweeping gaze caught a glimpse of Bullet and Two-Face and Sarchedon dotting the blue horizon-line; and he thrilled with the thought of the consternation and joy and excitement there would be at Bostil's ranch when the riderless horses trooped in. He looked back at Lucy to smile into her face, to feel his heart swell at the beauty and wonder of her. With a rider's keen scrutiny, he glanced at her saddle and stirrups, and at the saddle-girths.

He helped Wildfire to choose the going, and at the turns of the trail he guided him across curves that might gain a yard in the race. And this caution seemed ordered in the fringe of Lamar's thought, with most of his mind given to the sheer sensations of the ride—the flashing colored sage, the speeding white trail, the sharp bitter-sweetness of the air, the tang and sting of the wind, the feel of Wildfire under him, a wonderful, quivering, restrained muscular force, ready at a call to launch itself into a thunderbolt. For the moment with Lamar it was the ride—the ride!

As he lived it to the full, the miles sped by. He gained on Dusty Ben and Plume; the King slowly cut out ahead; and the first part of the race neared an end, whatever that was to be.

The two nearer rustlers whirled in their saddles to fire at Lamar. Bullets sped wildly and low, kicking up little puffs of dust. They were harmless, but they quickened Lamar's pulse, and the cold, grim mood returned to him. He loosened the bridle. Wildfire sank a little and lengthened; his speed increased, and his action grew smoother. Lamar turned to the girl and yelled, "Let him go!"

Nagger shot forward, once more with his great black head at Wildfire's flank.

Then Lamar began to return the fire of the rustlers, aiming carefully and high, so as to be sure not to hit one of the racers. As he gained upon them, the bullets from their revolvers skipped uncomfortably close past Wildfire's legs.

Lamar, warming to the fight, shot four times before he remembered how careful he must be of his ammunition. He must get closer!

Soon the rustlers pulled Ben and Plume, half lifting them in the air, and, leaping off the breaking horses, they dashed into the sage, one on each side of the trail. The move startled Lamar; he might have pulled Wildfire in time, but Lucy could never stop Nagger in such short distance. Lamar's quick decision was that it would be better to risk shots as they sped on. He yelled to Lucy to hug the saddle, and watched for the hiding rustlers.

He saw spouts of red—puffs of smoke—then a dark form behind a sage-bush. Firing, he thought he heard a cry. Then, whirling to the other side, he felt the wind of bullets near his face—saw another dark form—and fired as he rode by.

Over his shoulder he saw Lucy hunched low in her saddle, and the big black running as if the peril had spurred him. Lamar sent out a wild and exulting cry. Ben and Plume were now off the trail, speeding in line, and they would not stop soon; and out in front, perhaps a hundred yards, ran the Sage King in beautiful action. Cordts fitted the horse. If the King was greater than Wildfire, Cordts was the rider to bring it out.

"*Jim! Jim!*" suddenly pealed in Lamar's ears. He turned with a tightening round his heart. "*Nagger! He was hit! He was hit!*" screamed Lucy.

The great black was off his stride.

"Pull him! Pull him! Get off! Hide in the sage!" yelled Lamar.

Lucy made no move to comply with his order. Her face was white. Was she weakening? He saw no change of her poise in the saddle; but her right arm hung limp. She had been hit!

Lamar's heart seemed to freeze in the suspension of its beat, and the clogging of icy blood. He saw her sway.

"Lucy, hang on! Hang on!" he cried, and began to pull the red stallion.

To pull him out of that stride took all Lamar's strength, and then he only pulled him enough to let Nagger come up abreast. Lamar circled Lucy with his arm and lifted her out of her saddle.

"Jim, I'm not hurt much. If I hadn't seen Nagger was hit, I'd never squealed."

"Oh, Lucy!" Lamar choked with the release of his fear and the rush of pride and passion.

"Don't pull Wildfire! He'll catch the King yet!"

Lamar swung the girl behind him. The way she wrapped her uninjured arm about him and clung showed the stuff of which Lucy Bostil was made. Wildfire snorted as if in fierce anger that added weight had been given him, as if he knew it was no fault of his that Sage King had increased the lead.

Lamar bent forward and now called to the stallion—called to him with the wild call of the upland rider to his horse. It was the call that let Wildfire know he was free to choose his going and his pace—free to run—free to run down a rival—free to kill.

And the wild stallion responded. He did not break; he wore into a run that had slow increase. The demon's spirit in him seemed to gather mighty forces, so that every magnificent stride was a little lower, a little longer, a little faster, till the horse had attained a terrible celerity. He was almost flying; and the white space narrowed between him and the Sage King.

Lamar vaguely heard the howling of the wind in his ears, the continuous ringing sound of Wildfire's hoofs. He vaguely noticed the blurring of the sage and the swift fleeting of the trail under him. He scarcely saw the rustler Cordts; he forgot Lucy. All his senses that retained keenness were centered in the running of the Sage King. It was so swift, so beautiful, so worthy of the gray's fame and name, that a pang numbed the rider's breast because Bostil's great horse was doomed to lose the race, if not his life.

For long the gray ran even with his red pursuer. Then, by imperceptible degrees, Wildfire began to gain. He was a desert stallion, born with the desert's ferocity of strife, the desert's imperious will; he never had love for any horse; it was in him to rule and to kill. Lamar felt Wildfire grow wet and hot, felt the marvelous ease of the horse's action gradually wearing to strain.

Another mile, and the trail turned among ridges of rock, along deep washes, at length to enter the broken country of crags and canyons. Cordts bent round in the saddle to shoot at Lamar. The bullet whistled perilously close; but Lamar withheld his fire. He had one shell left in his rifle; he would not risk that till he was sure.

He watched for a break in the King's stride, for the plunge that meant that the gray was finished. Still the race went on and on. And in the lather that flew back to wet Lamar's lips he tasted the hot blood of his horse. If it had been his own blood, the last drops spilled from his heart, he could not have felt more agony.

At last Sage King broke strangely, slowed in a few jumps, and, plunging down, threw Cordts over his head. The rustler leaped up and began to run, seeking cover.

Wildfire thundered on beyond the prostrate King. Then, with terrible muscular convulsion, as of internal collapse, he, too, broke and pounded slow, slower—to a stop.

Lamar slipped down and lifted Lucy from the saddle. Wildfire was white except where he was red, and that red was not now his glossy, naming skin. He groaned and began to sag. On one knee and then the other he knelt, gave a long heave, and lay at length!

Lamar darted back in pursuit of Cordts. He descried the rustler running along the edge of a canyon. Lamar realized that he must be quick; but the rifle wavered because of his terrible eagerness. He was shaken by the intensity of the moment. With tragic earnestness he fought for coolness, for control.

Cordts reached a corner of cliff where he had to go slowly, to cling to the rock. It was then that Lamar felt himself again chilled through and through with that strange, grim power. He pulled trigger. Cordts paused as if to rest. He leaned against the face of the cliff, his hands up, and he kept that posture for a long moment. Then his hands began to slip. Slowly he swayed out over the canyon. His dark face flashed. Headlong he fell, to vanish below the rim.

Lamar hurriedly ran back and saw that the King was a beaten, broken horse, but he would live to run another race. Up the trail Lucy was kneeling beside Wildfire, and before Lamar got there he heard her sobbing. As if he were being dragged to execution, the rider went on, and then he was looking down upon his horse and crying, "Wildfire! Wildfire!"

Choked, blinded, killed on his feet, Wildfire heard the voice of his master.

"Jim! Oh, Jim!" moaned Lucy.

"He beat the King! And he carried double!" whispered Lamar.

While they knelt there, the crippled Nagger came limping up the trail, followed by Dusty Ben and Plume.

Again the rider called to his horse, with a cry now piercing, thrilling; but this time Wildfire did not respond.

The westering sun glanced brightly over the rippling sage, which rolled away from the Ford like a gray sea. Bostil sat on his porch, a stricken man. He faced the blue haze of the West, where, some hours before, all that he loved had vanished. His riders were grouped near him, silent, awed by his face, awaiting orders that did not come.

From behind a ridge puffed up a thin cloud of dust. Bostil saw it, and gave a start. Above the sage appeared a bobbing black dot—the head of a horse.

"Sarch!" exclaimed Bostil.

With spurs clinking, his riders ran and trooped behind him.

"There's Bullet!" cried one.

"An' Two-Face!" added another.

"Saddled an' riderless!"

Then all were tensely quiet, watching the racers come trotting in single file down the ridge. Sarchedon's shrill neigh, like a whistle-blast, pealed in from the sage. From fields and corrals clamored the answer, attended by the clattering of hundreds of hoofs.

Sarchedon and his followers broke from trot to canter—canter to gallop—and soon were cracking their iron shoes on the stony road. Then, like a swarm of bees, the riders surrounded the racers and led them up to Bostil.

On Sarchedon's neck showed a dry, dust-caked stain of reddish tinge. Bostil's right- hand man, the hawk-eyed rider, gray as the sage from long service, carefully examined the stain.

"Wall, the rustler thet was up on Sarch got plugged, an' in fallin' forrard he spilled some blood on the hoss's neck."

"Who shot him?" demanded Bostil.

"I reckon there's only one rider on the sage thet could ever hev got close enough to shoot a rustler up on Sarch."

Bostil wheeled to face the West. His brow was lowering; his hands were clenched. Riders led away the tired racers, and returned to engage with the others in whispered speculation.

The afternoon wore on; the sun lost its brightness, and burned low and red. Again dust-clouds, now like reddened smoke, puffed over the ridge. Four horses, two carrying riders, appeared above the sage.

"Is that—a gray horse—or am I blind?" asked Bostil unsteadily.

The old rider shaded the hawk-eyes with his hand.

"Gray he is—gray as the sage, Bostil—an' so help me if he ain't the King!"

Bostil stared, rubbed his eyes as if his sight was dimmed, and stared again. "Do I see Lucy?"

"Shore—shore!" replied the old rider. "I seen her long ago. Why, sir, I can see thet gold hair of hers a mile across the sage. She's up on Ben."

The light of joy on Bostil's face slowly shaded, and the change was one that silenced his riders. Abruptly he left them, to enter the house.

When he came forth again, brought out by the stamp of hoofs on the stones, his riders were escorting Lucy and Lamar into the courtyard. A wan smile flitted across Lucy's haggard face as she saw her father, and she held out one arm to him. The other was bound in a bloody scarf.

Cursing deep, like the muttering of thunder, Bostil ran out.

"Lucy! For Heaven's sake! You're not bad hurt?"

"Only a little, dad," she said, and slipped down into his arms.

He kissed her pale face, and, carrying her to the door, roared for the women of his household.

When he reappeared, the crowd of riders scattered from around Lamar. Bostil looked at the King. The horse was caked with dusty lather, scratched and disheveled, weary and broken, yet somehow he was still beautiful. He raised his drooping head, and reached for his master with a look as soft and dark and eloquent as a woman's.

No rider there but felt Bostil's grief. He loved the King. He believed the King had been beaten; and his rider's glory and pride were battling with love. Mighty as that was in Bostil, it did not at once overcome his hatred of defeat.

Slowly the gaze of the rancher moved from the King to tired Ben and Plurrie, over the bleeding Nagger, at last to rest on the white-faced Lamar. But Bostil was not looking for Lamar. His hard eyes veered to and fro. Among those horses there was not the horse he sought.

"Where's the red stallion?" he asked. Lamar raised eyes dark with pain, yet they flashed as he looked straight into Bostil's face.

"Wildfire's dead."

"Shot?"

"No."

"What killed him?" Bostil's voice had a vibrating ring.

"The King, sir; killed him on his feet." Bostil's lean jaw bulged and quivered. His hand shook a little as he laid it on the King's tangled mane.

"Jim—what the—" he said brokenly, with voice strangely softened.

"Mr. Bostil, we've had some fighting and running. Lucy was hit—so was Nagger. And the King killed Wildfire on his feet. But I got Cordts and three of his men—maybe four. I've no more to say, sir."

Bostil put his arm round the young man's shoulder.

"Lamar, you've said enough. If I don't know how you feel about the loss of that grand horse, no rider on earth knows. But let me say I reckon I never knew your real worth. You can lead my riders. You can have the girl—God bless you both! And you can have anything else on this ranch—except the King!"

The HIDING of BLACK BILL

by
O. Henry

This humorous story by O. Henry features a rancher, a drifter, and lots of sheep. As mentioned previously, because of his tuberculosis, O. Henry moved from North Carolina to Texas in 1882 where he took up work as a ranch hand and shepherd on a sheep ranch, so much of this story was based on personal experience.

A lank, strong, red-faced man with a Wellington beak and small, fiery eyes tempered by flaxen lashes, sat on the station platform at Los Piños swinging his legs to and fro. At his side sat another man, fat, melancholy, and seedy, who seemed to be his friend. They had the appearance of men to whom life had appeared as a reversible coat—seamy on both sides.

"Ain't seen you in about four years, Ham," said the seedy man. "Which way you been travelling?"

"Texas," said the red-faced man. "It was too cold in Alaska for me. And I found it warm in Texas. I'll tell you about one hot spell I went through there.

"One morning I steps off the International at a water-tank and lets it go on without me. 'Twas a ranch country, and fuller of spite-houses than New York City. Only out there they build 'em twenty miles away so you can't smell what they've got for dinner, instead of running 'em up two inches from their neighbors' windows.

"There wasn't any roads in sight, so I footed it 'cross country. The grass was shoe-top deep, and the mesquite timber looked just like a peach orchard. It was so much like a gentleman's private estate that every minute you expected a kennelful of bulldogs to run out and bite you. But I must have walked twenty miles before I came in sight of a ranch-house. It was a little one, about as big as an elevated-railroad station.

"There was a little man in a white shirt and brown overalls and a pink handkerchief around his neck rolling cigarettes under a tree in front of the door.

" 'Greetings,' says I. 'Any refreshment, welcome, emoluments, or even work for a comparative stranger?'

" 'Oh, come in,' says he, in a refined tone. 'Sit down on that stool, please. I didn't hear your horse coming.'

" 'He isn't near enough yet,' says I. 'I walked. I don't want to be a burden, but I wonder if you have three or four gallons of water handy.'

" 'You do look pretty dusty,' says he; 'but our bathing arrangements—'

" 'It's a drink I want,' says I. 'Never mind the dust that's on the outside.'

"He gets me a dipper of water out of a red jar hanging up, and then goes on:

" 'Do you want work?'

" 'For a time,' says I. 'This is a rather quiet section of the country, isn't it?'

" 'It is,' says he. 'Sometimes—so I have been told—one sees no human being pass for weeks at a time. I've been here only a month. I bought the ranch from an old settler who wanted to move farther west.'

" 'It suits me,' says I. 'Quiet and retirement are good for a man sometimes. And I need a job. I can tend bar, salt mines, lecture, float stock, do a little middle-weight slugging, and play the piano.'

" 'Can you herd sheep?' asks the little ranch-man.

" 'Do you mean have I heard sheep?' says I.

" 'Can you herd 'em—take charge of a flock of 'em?' says he.

" 'Oh,' says I, 'now I understand. You mean chase 'em around and bark at 'em like collie dogs. Well, I might,' says I. 'I've never exactly done any sheep-herding, but I've often seen 'em from car windows masticating daisies, and they don't look dangerous.'

" 'I'm short a herder,' says the ranchman. 'You never can depend on the Mexicans. I've only got two flocks. You may take out my bunch of muttons—there are only eight hundred of 'em—in the morning, if you like. The pay is twelve dollars a month and your rations furnished. You camp in a tent on the prairie with your sheep. You do your own cooking, but wood and water are brought to your camp. It's an easy job.'

" 'I'm on,' says I. 'I'll take the job even if I have to garland my brow and hold on to a crook and wear a loose-effect and play on a pipe like the shepherds do in pictures.'

"So the next morning the little ranchman helps me drive the flock of muttons from the corral to about two miles out and let 'em graze on a little hillside on the prairie. He gives me a lot of instructions about not letting bunches of them stray off from the herd, and driving 'em down to a water-hole to drink at noon.

" 'I'll bring out your tent and camping outfit and rations in the buckboard before night,' says he.

" 'Fine,' says I. 'And don't forget the rations. Nor the camping outfit. And be sure to bring the tent. Your name's Zollicoffer, ain't it?"

" 'My name,' says he, 'is Henry Ogden.'

" 'All right, Mr. Ogden,' says I. 'Mine is Mr. Percival Saint Clair.'

"I herded sheep for five days on the Rancho Chiquito; and then the wool entered my soul. That getting next to Nature certainly got next to me. I was lonesomer than Crusoe's goat. I've seen a lot of persons more entertaining as companions than those sheep were. I'd drive 'em to the corral and pen 'em every evening, and then cook my corn-bread and mutton and coffee, and lie down in a tent the size of a table-cloth, and listen to the coyotes and whippoorwills singing around the camp.

"The fifth evening, after I had corralled my costly but uncongenial muttons, I walked over to the ranch-house and stepped in the door.

" 'Mr. Ogden,' says I, 'you and me have got to get sociable. Sheep are all very well to dot the landscape and furnish eight-dollar cotton suitings for man, but for table-talk and fireside companions they rank along with five-o'clock teazers. If you've got a deck of cards, or a parcheesi outfit, or a game of authors, get 'em out, and let's get on a mental basis. I've got to do something in an intellectual line, if it's only to knock somebody's brains out.'

"This Henry Ogden was a peculiar kind of ranchman. He wore finger-rings and a big gold watch and careful neckties. And his face was calm, and his nose-spectacles was kept very shiny. I saw once, in Muscogee, an outlaw hung for murdering six men, who was a dead ringer for him. But I knew a preacher in Arkansas that you would have taken to be his brother. I didn't care much for him either way; what I wanted was some fellowship and communion with holy saints or lost sinners—anything sheepless would do.

" 'Well, Saint Clair,' says he, laying down the book he was reading, 'I guess it must be pretty lonesome for you at first. And I don't deny that it's monotonous for me. Are you sure you corralled your sheep so they won't stray out?

" 'They're shut up as tight as the jury of a millionaire murderer,' says I. 'And I'll be back with them long before they'll need their trained nurse.'

"So Ogden digs up a deck of cards, and we play casino. After five days and nights of my sheep-camp it was like a toot on Broadway. When I caught big casino I felt as excited as if I had made a million in Trinity. And when H. O. loosened up a little and told the story about the lady in the Pullman car I laughed for five minutes.

"That showed what a comparative thing life is. A man may see so much that he'd be bored to turn his head to look at a $3,000,000 fire or Joe Weber or the Adriatic Sea. But let him herd sheep for a spell, and you'll see him splitting his ribs laughing at 'Curfew Shall Not Ring Tonight,' or really enjoying himself playing cards with ladies.

"By-and-by Ogden gets out a decanter of Bourbon, and then there is a total eclipse of sheep.

" 'Do you remember reading in the papers, about a month ago,' says he, 'about a train hold-up on the M. K. & T.? The express agent was shot through the shoulder, and about $15,000 in currency taken. And it's said that only one man did the job.'

" 'Seems to me I do,' says I. 'But such things happen so often they don't linger long in the human Texas mind. Did they overtake, overhaul, seize, or lay hands upon the despoiler?'

" 'He escaped,' says Ogden. 'And I was just reading in a paper today that the officers have tracked him down into this part of the country. It seems the bills the robber got were all the first issue of currency to the Second National Bank of Espinosa City. And so they've followed the trail where they've been spent, and it leads this way.'

"Ogden pours out some more Bourbon, and shoves me the bottle.

" 'I imagine,' says I, after ingurgitating another modicum of the royal boose, 'that it wouldn't be at all a disingenuous idea for a train robber to run down into this part of the country to hide for a spell. A sheep-ranch, now,' says I, 'would be the finest kind of a place. Who'd ever expect to find such a desperate character among these song-birds and muttons and wild flowers? And, by the way,' says I, kind of looking H. Ogden over, 'was there any description mentioned of this single-handed terror? Was his lineaments or height and thickness or teeth fillings or style of habiliments set forth in print?'

" 'Why, no,' says Ogden; 'they say nobody got a good sight of him because he wore a mask. But they know it was a train-robber called Black Bill, because he always works alone and because he dropped a handkerchief in the express-car that had his name on it.'

" 'All right,' says I. 'I approve of Black Bill's retreat to the sheep-ranges. I guess they won't find him.'

" 'There's one thousand dollars reward for his capture,' says Ogden.

" 'I don't need that kind of money,' says I, looking Mr. Sheepman straight in the eye. 'The twelve dollars a month you pay me is enough. I need a rest, and I can save up until I get enough to pay my fare to Texarkana, where my widowed mother lives. If Black Bill,' I goes on, looking significantly at Ogden, was to have come down this way—say, a month ago—and bought a little sheep-ranch and—'

" 'Stop,' says Ogden, getting out of his chair and looking pretty vicious. 'Do you mean to insinuate—'

" 'Nothing,' says I; 'no insinuations. I'm stating a hypodermical case. I say, if Black Bill had come down here and bought a sheep-ranch and hired me to Little-Boy-Blue 'em and treated me square and friendly, as you've done, he'd never have anything to fear from me. A man is a man, regardless of any complications he may have with sheep or railroad trains. Now you know where I stand.'

"Ogden looks black as camp-coffee for nine seconds, and then he laughs, amused.

" 'You'll do, Saint Clair,' says he. 'If I was Black Bill I wouldn't be afraid to trust you. Let's have a game or two of seven-up tonight. That is, if you don't mind playing with a train-robber.'

" 'I've told you,' says I, 'my oral sentiments, and there's no strings to 'em.'

"While I was shuffling after the first hand, I asks Ogden, as if the idea was a kind of a casualty, where he was from.

" 'Oh,' says he, 'from the Mississippi Valley.'

" 'That's a nice little place,' says I. 'I've often stopped over there. But didn't you find the sheets a little damp and the food poor? Now, I hail,' says I, 'from the Pacific Slope. Ever put up there?'

" 'Too draughty,' says Ogden. 'But if you've ever in the Middle West just mention my name, and you'll get foot-warmers and dripped coffee.'

" 'Well,' says I, 'I wasn't exactly fishing for your private telephone number and the middle name of your aunt that carried off the Cumberland Presbyterian minister. It don't matter. I just want you to know you are safe in the hands of your shepherd. Now, don't play hearts on spades, and don't get nervous.'

" 'Still harping,' says Ogden, laughing again. 'Don't you suppose that if I was Black Bill and thought you suspected me, I'd put a Winchester bullet into you and stop my nervousness, if I had any?'

" 'Not any,' says I. 'A man who's got the nerve to hold up a train single-handed wouldn't do a trick like that. I've knocked about enough to know that them are the kind of men who put a value on a friend. Not that I can claim being a friend of yours, Mr. Ogden,' says I, 'being only your sheep-herder; but under more expeditious circumstances we might have been.'

" 'Forget the sheep temporarily, I beg,' says Ogden, 'and cut for deal.'

"About four days afterward, while my muttons was nooning on the water-hole and I deep in the interstices of making a pot of coffee, up rides softly on the grass a mysterious person in the garb of the being he wished to represent. He was dressed somewhere between a Kansas City detective, Buffalo Bill, and the town dog-catcher of Baton Rouge. His chin and eye wasn't molded on fighting lines, so I knew he was only a scout.

" 'Herdin' sheep?' he asks me.

" 'Well,' says I, 'to a man of your evident gumptional endowments, I wouldn't have the nerve to state that I am engaged in decorating old bronzes or oiling bicycle sprockets.'

" 'You don't talk or look like a sheep-herder to me,' says he.

" 'But you talk like what you look like to me,' says I.

"And then he asks me who I was working for, and I shows him Rancho Chiquito, two miles away, in the shadow of a low hill, and he tells me he's a deputy sheriff.

" 'There's a train-robber called Black Bill supposed to be somewhere in these parts,' says the scout. 'He's been traced as far as San Antonio, and maybe farther. Have you seen or heard of any strangers around here during the past month?'

" 'I have not,' says I, 'except a report of one over at the Mexican quarters of Loomis' ranch, on the Frio.'

" 'What do you know about him?' asks the deputy.

" 'He's three days old,' says I.

" 'What kind of a looking man is the man you work for?' he asks. 'Does old George Ramey own this place yet? He's run sheep here for the last ten years, but never had no success.'

" 'The old man has sold out and gone West,' I tells him. 'Another sheep-fancier bought him out about a month ago.'

" 'What kind of a looking man is he?' asks the deputy again.

" 'Oh,' says I, 'a big, fat kind of a Dutchman with long whiskers and blue specs. I don't think he knows a sheep from a ground-squirrel. I guess old George soaked him pretty well on the deal,' says I.

"After indulging himself in a lot more non-communicative information and two-thirds of my dinner, the deputy rides away.

"That night I mentions the matter to Ogden. " 'They're drawing the tendrils of the octopus around Black Bill,' says I. And then I told him about the deputy sheriff, and how I'd described him to the deputy, and what the deputy said about the matter.

" 'Oh, well,' says Ogden, 'let's don't borrow any of Black Bill's troubles. We've a few of our own. Get the Bourbon out of the cupboard and we'll drink to his health—unless,' says he, with his little cackling laugh, 'you're prejudiced against train-robbers.'

" 'I'll drink,' says I, 'to any man who's a friend to a friend. And I believe that Black Bill,' I goes on, 'would be that. So here's to Black Bill, and may he have good luck.'

"And both of us drank.

"About two weeks later comes shearing-time. The sheep had to be driven up to the ranch, and a lot of frowzy-headed Mexicans would snip the fur off of them with back-action scissors. So the afternoon before the barbers were to come I hustled my under-done muttons over the hill, across the dell, down by the winding brook, and up to the ranch-house, where I penned 'em in a corral and bade 'em my nightly adieus.

"I went from there to the ranch-house. I find H. Ogden, Esquire, lying asleep on his little cot bed. I guess he had been overcome by anti-insomnia or diswakefulness or some of the diseases peculiar to the sheep business. His mouth and vest were open, and he breathed like a second-hand bicycle pump. I looked at him and gave vent to just a few musings. 'Imperial Caesar,' says I, 'asleep in such a way, might shut his mouth and keep the wind away.'

A man asleep is certainly a sight to make angels weep. What good is all his brain, muscle, backing, nerve, influence, and family connections? He's at the mercy of his enemies, and more so of his friends. And he's about as beautiful as a cab-horse leaning against the Metropolitan Opera House at 12.30 A.M. dreaming of the plains of Arabia. Now, a woman asleep you regard as different. No matter how she looks, you know it's better for all hands for her to be that way.

"Well, I took a drink of Bourbon and one for Ogden, and started in to be comfortable while he was taking his nap. He had some books on his table on indigenous subjects, such as Japan and drainage and physical culture—and some tobacco, which seemed more to the point.

"After I'd smoked a few, and listened to the sartorial breathing of H. O., I happened to look out the window toward the shearing-pens, where there was a kind of a road coming up from a kind of a road across a kind of a creek farther away.

"I saw five men riding up to the house. All of 'em carried guns across their saddles, and among 'em was the deputy that had talked to me at my camp.

"They rode up careful, in open formation, with their guns ready. I set apart with my eye the one I opinionated to be the boss muck-raker of this law-and-order cavalry.

" 'Good-evening, gents,' says I. 'Won't you 'light, and tie your horses?'

"The boss rides up close, and swings his gun over till the opening in it seems to cover my whole front elevation.

" 'Don't you move your hands none,' says he, 'till you and me indulge in a adequate amount of necessary conversation.'

" 'I will not,' says I. 'I am no deaf-mute, and therefore will not have to disobey your injunctions in replying.'

" 'We are on the lookout,' says he, 'for Black Bill, the man that held up the Katy for $15,000 in May. We are searching the ranches and everybody on 'em. What is your name, and what do you do on this ranch?'

" 'Captain,' says I, 'Percival Saint Clair is my occupation, and my name is sheep-herder. I've got my flock of veals—no, muttons—penned here tonight. The shearers are coming tomorrow to give them a hair-cut—with baa-a-rum, I suppose.'

" 'Where's the boss of this ranch?' the captain of the gang asks me.

" 'Wait just a minute, cap'n,' says I. 'Wasn't there a kind of a reward offered for the capture of this desperate character you have referred to in your preamble?'

" 'There's a thousand dollars reward offered,' says the captain, 'but it's for his capture and conviction. There don't seem to be no provision made for an informer.'

" 'It looks like it might rain in a day or so,' says I, in a tired way, looking up at the cerulean blue sky.

" 'If you know anything about the locality, disposition, or secretiveness of this here Black Bill,' says he, in a severe dialect, 'you are amiable to the law in not reporting it.'

" 'I heard a fence-rider say,' says I, in a desultory kind of voice, 'that a Mexican told a cowboy named Jake over at Pidgin's store on the Nueces that he heard that Black Bill had been seen in Matamoras by a sheepman's cousin two weeks ago.'

" 'Tell you what I'll do, Tight Mouth,' says the captain, after looking me over for bargains. 'If you put us on so we can scoop Black Bill, I'll pay you a hundred dollars out of my own—out of our own—pockets. That's liberal,' says he. 'You ain't entitled to anything. Now, what do you say?'

" 'Cash down now?' I asks.

"The captain has a sort of discussion with his helpmates, and they all produce the contents of their pockets for analysis. Out of the general results they figured up $102.30 in cash and $31 worth of plug tobacco.

" 'Come nearer, capitan meeo,' says I, 'and listen.' He so did.

" 'I am mighty poor and low down in the world,' says I. 'I am working for twelve dollars a month trying to keep a lot of animals together whose only thought seems to be to get asunder. Although,' says I, 'I regard myself as some better than the State of

South Dakota, it's a come-down to a man who has heretofore regarded sheep only in the form of chops. I'm pretty far reduced in the world on account of foiled ambitions and rum and a kind of cocktail they make along the P. R. R. all the way from Scranton to Cincinnati—dry gin, French vermouth, one squeeze of a lime, and a good dash of orange bitters. If you're ever up that way, don't fail to let one try you. And, again,' says I, 'I have never yet went back on a friend. I've stayed by 'em when they had plenty, and when adversity's overtaken me I've never forsook 'em.

" 'But,' I goes on, 'this is not exactly the case of a friend. Twelve dollars a month is only bowing-acquaintance money. And I do not consider brown beans and corn-bread the food of friendship. I am a poor man,' says I, 'and I have a widowed mother in Texarkana. You will find Black Bill,' says I, 'lying asleep in this house on a cot in the room to your right. He's the man you want, as I know from his words and conversation. He was in a way a friend,' I explains, 'and if I was the man I once was the entire product of the mines of Gondola would not have tempted me to betray him. But,' says I, 'every week half of the beans was wormy, and not nigh enough wood in camp.

" 'Better go in careful, gentlemen,' says I. 'He seems impatient at times, and when you think of his late professional pursuits one would look for abrupt actions if he was come upon sudden.'

"So the whole posse unmounts and ties their horses, and unlimbers their ammunition and equipments, and tiptoes into the house. And I follows, like Delilah when she set the Philip Stein on to Samson.

"The leader of the posse shakes Ogden and wakes him up. And then he jumps up, and two more of the reward-hunters grab him. Ogden was mighty tough with all his slimness, and he gives 'em as neat a single-footed tussle against odds as I ever see.

" 'What does this mean?' he says, after they had him down.

" 'You're scooped in, Mr. Black Bill,' says the captain. 'That's all.'

" 'It's an outrage,' says H. Ogden, madder yet.

" 'It was,' says the peace-and-good-will man. 'The Katy wasn't bothering you, and there's a law against monkeying with express packages.'

"And he sits on H. Ogden's stomach and goes through his pockets symptomatically and careful.

" 'I'll make you perspire for this,' says Ogden, perspiring some himself. 'I can prove who I am.'

" 'So can I,' says the captain, as he draws from H. Ogden's inside coat-pocket a handful of new bills of the Second National Bank of Espinosa City. 'Your regular engraved Tuesdays-and-Fridays visiting-card wouldn't have a louder voice in proclaiming your indemnity than this here currency. You can get up now and prepare to go with us and expatriate your sins.

"H. Ogden gets up and fixes his necktie. He says no more after they have taken the money off of him.

" 'A well-greased idea,' says the sheriff captain, admiring, 'to slip off down here and buy a little sheep-ranch where the hand of man is seldom heard. It was the slickest hide-out I ever see,' says the captain.

"So one of the men goes to the shearing-pen and hunts up the other herder, a Mexican they call John Sallies, and he saddles Ogden's horse, and the sheriffs all ride tip close around him with their guns in hand, ready to take their prisoner to town.

"Before starting, Ogden puts the ranch in John Sallies' hands and gives him orders about the shearing and where to graze the sheep, just as if he intended to be back in a few days. And a couple of hours afterward one Percival Saint Clair, an ex-sheep-herder of the Rancho Chiquito, might have been seen, with a hundred and nine dollars—wages and blood-money—in his pocket, riding south on another horse belonging to said ranch."

The red-faced man paused and listened. The whistle of a coming freight-train sounded far away among the low hills.

The fat, seedy man at his side sniffed, and shook his frowzy head slowly and disparagingly.

"What is it, Snipy?" asked the other. "Got the blues again?"

"No, I ain't" said the seedy one, sniffing again. "But I don't like your talk. You and me have been friends, off and on, for fifteen year; and I never yet knew or heard of you giving anybody up to the law—not no one. And here was a man whose saleratus you had et and at whose table you had played games of cards—if casino can be so called. And yet you inform him to the law and take money for it. It never was like you, I say."

"This H. Ogden," resumed the red-faced man, "through a lawyer, proved himself free by alibis and other legal terminalities, as I so heard afterward. He never suffered no harm. He did me favors, and I hated to hand him over."

"How about the bills they found in his pocket?" asked the seedy man.

"I put 'em there," said the red-faced man, "while he was asleep, when I saw the posse riding up. I was Black Bill. Look out, Snipy, here she comes! We'll board her on the bumpers when she takes water at the tank."

PHOTOGRAPHY CREDITS